# The 4th Man

## Doug Booth

# The 4<sup>th</sup> Man

## October 11
## Eighteen Months Later

### 1

"I do."

"And do you, Christine Gabrielle Benton, take Bret Alexandre Wilmington as your lawfully wedded husband, to love him, honour him and be with him until death do you part?"

She kissed him before the minister pronounced the final declaration that would bond them together for better or worse. "I do," she answered simply, flushed with joy. She stood by his side, beautiful and elegant, and to each of the four hundred invited guests she was now one of them. She was a Wilmington. Indeed she was, albeit in name alone.

The huge crowd stood amid their thunderous applause, save one who did not belong. He stood ominously silent between the arched and intricate mahogany doors framing the cavernous vestibule of St. Anthony's, staring intently into the back of the man he had sworn an oath to kill. Angelo Bardollini walked the daytime streets of Montreal unrecognized, especially in the ritzy and naïve suburb of Westmount whose citizens were more interested in the Society and Financial pages than the front page news which increasingly focused on him.

John Gunn's columns were as exaggerated and unsubstantiated as they were colourful, often portraying Bardollini's activities with vague or embellished language to the point of fiction. The mob boss' future was certain, Gunn wrote. The indictment against Bardollini was imminent. The task squad had spent three years coercing dozens of witnesses into betrayal with promises of new names and fresh beginnings, many of whom had gone missing without new names. Despite the setback his indictment would lead to prosecution and subsequent imprisonment for a term likely to exceed the remainder of his natural life. They'd been trying to nail him for thirty years, always one step behind. And that's where he intended they would stay. Much of the evidence against him, compiled from an obscure history, would be difficult to prove or deny, though Gunn wasn't helping matters: a two-bit reporter whose incessant need to survive one sensational column at a time, the stuff of novels, had glorified Bardollini. The reality was that neither man would survive much longer.

Privacy was sacred to Bardollini, a reluctant celebrity in his own right, though no suburban cop would recognize him. He didn't fit in, yet he did, an anomaly dressed in thousand-dollar tailor-made suits, cashmere coats and silk-lined fedoras that were his signature as much as his camouflage, his protective coating. However only when the darkness of night slowly overtook his city, his world, transforming its already sinister corners into places of secrets and favours, debts and death, did he come alive.

He lived in a world within a world, a culture within a culture, inductees selected by virtue of one's birth or the misfortune of one's life, an inescapable and forbidding world whose denizens were his only family. His world was his element. He was known by all, he was the lord, the father and the law.

The 9mm 92FS Berretta pressing into his side was so much a part of him that he no longer felt the weight of the detachable black lethal limb and, he thought, squeezing off two rounds would be a simple matter. No one would see him, or admit they had. People like them never confronted the threat of real danger. They would cower in unison. They would look up from their knees or bellies, too afraid to pray.

He sniggered at the thought. Even the white-haired and Gucci-clad Anglican bishop whom he had earlier seen climbing from a shiny, silver Mercedes would join his scattered and fearful flock on the floor in an effort to avoid premature contact with their once-a-week God. Later the cleric would have nothing more to report to the police than anyone else. And what did the Lord's Prayer sound like in surround sound at zero to sixty in four-point-five seconds, he wondered? In God we trust, especially with real leather seats.

Failing wasn't an option, as foreign to his creed as treachery. His oath was solemn and irrevocable. Bret Wilmington would die by his hand alone and any change to the agenda would be his prerogative. He took a moment to study the bride dispassionately with a quiet chuckle, shrugging before turning to leave, smiling widely at the irony: a rare enough event any time. His gift would necessarily be belated. Best of all, not even the blushing bride would know.

He pushed against the brass bar to open the heavy door, glancing over his shoulder at the very moment the aging mechanism's clang prompted the two ushers to look back. He stared at one, then the other, their brief glimpse into the burning intensity of his half-sheltered eyes freezing them in place. Somehow they knew to stay where they were and not follow after the unannounced and uninvited man.

Each one experienced an immediate shrinking sensation in his scrotum, and Bardollini knew it as he stepped into the bitter and furious maelstrom uncommon for mid-October. He had studied them as well: Chad Rivers, Thurston Williams and the best man, Shane Pendleton. He knew each one intimately, every detail of their recent lives. Although he had never seen them in person, he knew everything about them. He knew about their homes and offices. He knew what they did, when, and with whom. He knew what they ate, what they drank and how much. They could never have suspected that for the past few months, as their separate and final moments drew near, their every movement had been minutely monitored. Patient attention to detail had allowed him to survive thirty years, which was of tertiary importance at the moment. Wilmington was his sole concern, the one whose file was the thickest and who would ultimately have the most to fear. Wilmington would be the fourth man, but not before he understood the expectation of one's death was far worse than the death itself.

The midday sky was dark, jagged bolts of bright light speared the air in concert with deafening explosions as rain-filled, black-grey clouds thundered together in a ponderous battle. The wind slammed hard against him, tugging and tearing at his open coat, forcing the brim of his black fedora over his eyes. He had seen enough to torment him and satiate him.

The rain began to fall, pelting the SUV relentlessly. No one in the vehicle spoke.

# 2

"I love you, my darling. You are my one true love. I will always love you," she whispered shyly.

With all her heart she wanted the tenderness of her words to be heard and felt beyond time and space. Secretly she knew they would be. She had spoken those very words for so many nights as she fell into a restless and fitful sleep to dream alone with tear-filled eyes. She looked up at her husband, smiling, knowing her dream had come true. She was the newest Mrs. Wilmington and wife of the newly appointed junior partner at the internationally respected engineering and architectural firm of The Wilmingtons & Pendleton. She was his and he was hers. She had won.

"I will always love you," she whispered before once more looking into his eyes.

He beamed, seeing her lips form passionate words from behind her veil, muffled by the drone of polite whispers of the women and the deafening reverberation of raucous, good-natured cheers from the men folk. She felt at peace.

# 3

Eighteen months had passed, with much less time left to him. He didn't care. What did matter were the oath, the promise and his unalterable first commandment to kill, if he might not, or be killed. The chain of command followed by the chain of commitment and don't screw up, especially with someone like him. He wasn't anxious in a nervous way, though his every nerve ending tingled nonetheless. He was ready to kill. He never enjoyed ending a life, he simply did what had to be done, a pre-emptive and punitive last resort, though this time he would and Wilmington would be his last.

His vivid memories of those distant twenty-four hours swept away the stinging wetness from his face along with the threatening clouds and the foul-blowing winds swirling around him. He remembered how the rain had fallen perfectly straight that day: a cleansing and revitalizing rain flushing away the lethargy of winter, bringing life to a new season. That same evening the city was cloaked in a light dampness and the freshness of spring that makes everyone want to breathe more deeply and instinctively feel more alive.

For most the hour was late, intimidating in an increasingly dangerous city; for him the dark pre-dawn of another day was freedom. He waited until all the visitors had gone, for all but one light to be extinguished in the building before giving the okay. Then he waited for the signal from the one who was his constant shadow before climbing from the all-black SUV.

The driver remained stern-faced in the car, as a less than light-footed Angie puddle-jumped and cursed his way across the pothole-filled road, splashing up more water than he avoided. Enjoying a good laugh with him was never a problem, laughing at him was a once-in-a-lifetime happening. The funeral home was an old mansion, renovated to maintain a stately façade and not appear as a home for the dead, the dearly departed whose keepers were as cold and unfeeling as the resident guests. He hated the thought of being there. The plate-glass doors were open by the time he climbed the few steps to the landing. He was backlit against a single street light enshrouding him in a grey-white misty halo, though the fedora was always worn down and his hands were always at his side, at the ready. No one had seen his face in years.

The regretful situation had been quickly explained to the satisfaction of the anxious man who answered the door, eagerly making an exception for a dearly departed's out-of-town relatives. The visitors didn't care that undertakers endure a private and revered sense of mortality, disguising fear of death with practiced respect and formal aloofness most times. This wasn't most times. The dark energy surrounding the men standing in front of him was unmistakable and the mortician sensed instinctively that "yes" would mean well-being, and "no" would mean not-so-well-being. He stepped aside as they walked in.

Marcus looked at Angie, then to the formaldehyde-scented stick of a man who stood in front of them with his white sleeves rolled up and his dull grey tie askew. His face was liquor-red and its skin was sallow and hanging from his chin to his gullet. His eyes were yellowed from an abusive life, housed in sunken blue-black pits. Thick blue veins bulged against a transparent onion-like skin and the thin strands of his lacquered hair were stuck together in a comb-over which gave the appearance of a tight-fitting skull cap. He was disintegrating. He was in the right place

Hearing the name of the one they had come to remember, the mortician nodded with professional indifference. His curiosity was overpowered by fear; his fear was overpowered by cowardice. Whatever they wanted was fine with him and he walked ahead of them to the salon. She was twenty-five, 1.72 metres, blonde, perfectly proportioned, perfect skin and perfect teeth. No autopsy had been performed in Mexico where DNA often meant: Do Nothing Amigo. The authorities had done a rape-kit analysis and blood work so that time-sensitive information could be sent to Montreal authorities, and once back in Canada the father disallowed the autopsy based on religious conviction, he insisted. What was the point? Whether the true cause of her death had been suffocation or choking was irrelevant to him. She had died from terror still etched onto her face when they delivered her body to him in a cheap and ordinary pine coffin, "hecho en México" burned carelessly into the side, a terror and net result of callous multiple rapes.

They had trouble keeping up with him. When they arrived at the parlour the thin, tremulous man pushed apart the glazed French doors and stepped inside. Marcus took him by the arm, ushering him back into the hallway, explaining they would need a few moments alone. Then he closed the doors and braced his back against them to give his boss privacy. Angelo Bardollini raised the lid of the casket and leaned forward to rest his open palms on the cherrywood-satin interface, unprepared for such youthful innocence and purity as she lay so still and so near to him. It's not what he expected to see, not what he expected to feel. Death had never bothered him. He had buried so many and had killed so many more, but this was the death of innocence and, strangely, her death was his re-birth.

She was an angel of the highest order, a seraph and the epitome of youthful beauty. She looked so much at peace with her still vibrant blonde hair spread across the cream-coloured silk pillow and her slightly tanned hands folded in contrast against her cream-coloured silk gown.

He recognized the pendant at her neck and wondered whether the sepia-aged photographs of his wife and daughter were still framed inside. He remembered how his wife had cried when he had given it to her on their daughter's first birthday.

He thought to touch the dead girl's cheek, perhaps feeling compassion, perhaps feeling a need for love so long denied, a love he had blindly lost. Instead he flinched. Evil had no place in the presence of such innocence. Touching her would be a sin, an affront against someone precious whom he needed more than a God that for so long had sat in judgment of him and now waited to refuse him. In life he had always been alone, unafraid that in death he would be abandoned. He chortled under his breath. If his life had been such a bitch, what could he expect in death?

Seeing the girl he finally understood, despising himself, wanting desperately to take back the cruel words he had yelled at his daughter, the crude gestures that had cut so deeply into her young heart. He lowered the cover, returning the young body to a darkness that would be eternal from then on. He turned away silently, walking through the opened doors and into the damp darkness of his familiar nether world. Neither man spoke. Neither one had anything to say.

The next day, so long ago, was sunny and warm with no wind amidst the idyllic setting of a green meadow with chirping birds, soft tears and the sensitive, meaningless words of people lost in selfish grief. The scene was a pathetic backdrop to the silent words, he remembered: the social elite gathered to bid farewell, puppets unaware their lives were mundane roles scripted for them to act out, the final scenes predetermined and irrevocable. Perhaps, if they were fortunate, they would be missed by a few, for a while. Then eventually they would be forgotten completely by virtue of time or the continuum of death. He felt a deep, seething disgust towards them. They were shallow and worth nothing, not even to themselves. They were sad fools with no sense of anything beyond another ordinary day that would later be condensed for them into easy-to-understand, second-hand and corrupted news. Save one, and he wondered whether she would miss him, or grieve for him, or love him in death. He thought not.

The catholic priest had dressed in a simple black suit that shone with age and reflected the sun in a way that made him appear unearthly from afar. He spoke authoritatively in sombre monotones about accepting death as part of life, a passage into a better place, as though he knew something everyone else didn't. In fact he was no better and knew no more or no less about dying. No one accepted death unless they controlled it, like surgeons or killers. Most simply waited for the unexpected, never knowing, a few dared to meet fate head-on and still fewer contrived a more convenient time or place. That was the reality he knew.

Such people were expendable to people like Angelo Bardollini, collateral damage. Life was cheap… poof, poof. He remembered spitting small bursts of air past his lips, his forefinger twitching simultaneously at his side: a habit, the way some people whistle so annoyingly. When had killing become so easy, he wondered at the time, not really caring, or when had he begun not thinking of killing as being wrong? If he had ever thought that way it had been too long ago for him to remember.

# 4

Only three people were ever allowed in the vehicle. On October 11, there were two. The black LX 570 was double parked, rivulets of beaded rain disappearing over the hood, splattering across heavily tinted windows making the day all the more oppressive and sullen. Peering through the armoured glass as he waited for the church doors to open he was suddenly morose, unable to dispel the memories of that day in the meadow when he had let himself drift into his past in a rare and dangerous moment of leisure. But Angelo Bardollini had not been alone. He seldom was, unless by design. Neither had his wife been. So why had she died? He hadn't stopped missing her, nor feeling responsible for her death. He had always loved her so deeply and still wondered if she came to realize that in death. However this wasn't about her and he knew she would understand. As much as they were so different, this she would understand and give her blessing.

He remembered every detail of those moments in the meadow when reality had shaken him. When, without warning, his young daughter looked up in the distance, staring straight into his eyes with a precision and penetrating depth that froze his blood, as though she knew where he would be standing, and when, as though she had expected him, hoping he would be there. She had seen him clearly, her desperate eyes fusing with his for an instant.

The reaction to the grip on his arm had come too late to do any good. Angelo stood frozen in the moment, inert, watching warm tears burst from her reddened brown eyes. Her friends had lurched forward, trying to prevent her sudden collapse as the coffin began its slow descent into the ground; them, instead of the dead girl's father who stood by so stoically and unmoved. Angelo had studied the man closely, wondering who the worst father was, wondering whether the man grieved alone in some solitary darkness, a private world that was his confessional.

His own daughter had been overcome with hysterical sorrow and he remembered wanting with every fibre of his soul to run to her, but he couldn't. He dared not, as much for her as for himself. She had found herself once and she would again without any help from him. She didn't need him. She had made that very clear.

Angelo Bardollini had been pulled into the reality of his dark existence, though not before their eyes had locked, not before he had been as suddenly and as deeply gripped by a grief as by the vice-like grip that encircled his arm. He prayed not to have imagined the fleeting message in her eyes, and what he had felt terrified him as much as pleased him. The entire depth of her anguish was so deeply etched into the beautiful olive features of her youthful face, the very features her mother had passed on to her. He would never forget the moment the two men fell back into the relatively protective shadows of the massive oak trees decorating the private cemetery of a family Angelo had never known. He ignored the persistent pressure on his arm, unable to do anything but witness her sorrow, unable to help her, unable to go to her.

He had come to know everything about the man who stood alongside his daughter, the man who hadn't flinched when she fell to her knees. They were from different worlds, although they weren't so different. One father knew who and what he was, the other knew that he didn't want to know. What neither man could know was that very soon the pristine would join with the soiled for whatever sense each one had of what was good and what was decent: a common goal certain to stain one life and cleanse the other for separate eternities that would forever remain conjoined.

Seeing his daughter's young face tremble so

uncontrollably, drenched with copious tears, seeing strangers holding her, giving her false strength, he saw a much younger girl. He saw the girl he had seen when her mother was buried so long ago, when he should have reached out to her to comfort her as a father who loved her, as he wanted to now. Sadly, there was no more time and he hadn't turned away out of pride. He had gone there for her, which would have been enough for him had she never known. He was dead to her. He had been for a very long time. So, shit happens. So what? But she did know.

Neither man spoke as they backed away from the shadows.

# 5

The driver had been instructed to be somewhere else and Marcus didn't need to turn his head to see the pages were folded to the Marriages and Obituaries section when his boss threw the daily over the front seat. Angelo was speaking to himself in non-Catholic prose and Marcus chose not to comment. The irony was blatantly obvious. They turned back to their respective windows, the front page facing upward on the back seat.

"Angie," Marcus called out.

"I know. I see."

The bells began chiming, alerting the crisply uniformed chauffeur who jumped from the first of several white limos idling quietly as the other drivers waited lethargically. He darted up the stairs, the umbrella fighting against the wind. When the doors opened, the bride's midnight blue cape and cowl concealed all but her hands and face and the chauffeur immediately took charge of her safe conduct to the Cadillac. The groom followed behind. She was absolutely gorgeous, beautiful and serene amidst the grey tempest surrounding her. She hurried without rushing, expertly escorted down the granite steps and away from the grimacing throng behind her that now thought of themselves and not the beautiful bride.

Her eyes pierced the armoured tint and Angelo instinctively shrank into his seat as the glistening limo carried away the newest Mrs. Wilmington and the proud groom. One by one the guests began hurried and hectic dashes to the waiting limos as the high speed digital Nikon clicked continuously from behind Marcus' lowered window, completely unnoticed or completely ignored by the self-centred horde.

The lens zoomed in to frame the face of the man who

stood alongside the bishop at the top of the stairs. They were shaking hands, exchanging the time-honoured honorarium: a payoff in any other business, Marcus thought. The exchange was discreet, the two men taking in the chaos in front of them as the camera clicked several times more. The subject was Shane Pendleton, the best man, and his thin smile revealed as much about the man as the information in his file. The best photographs would be printed and affixed to his file, as would the best of the other photos to their respective files.

As the SUV moved forward Angelo reached into an inside pocket of his suit, retrieving the black and gold Mont Blanc. He slumped sideways against the rear seat and pushed the newspaper up against the opposite side, ignoring the headline he chose not to read:

CROWN SEEKS TO INDICT CRIME BOSS ANGELO BARDOLLINI HIGH SECURITY IN PLACE FOR THOSE EXPECTED TO TESTIFY
DATES FOR PRELIMINARY TESTIMONIES NOT YET ANNOUNCED

The storyline continued on page A-2, but the information he needed was on A-1: the name of the contributing freelance journalist, John Gunn, self-appointed nemesis of the mob, his mob, his family. He circled the name and added the folded page to the front seat. No reaction was expected: the result of a finely tuned synergy between uncle and nephew. The time had come for them to go and soon John's time would come. The day had been long and trying and Angelo needed release. He would speak with her in whispers as he had done each night for the past five years. Then he would sleep.

18

# 6

The brightly lighted and ornate ballroom of the Ritz-Carlton slowly swelled to full capacity as the white-gloved staff greeted each guest with fluted glasses of house-brand champagne: The house of Wilmington. When all the invitees were present and accounted for, Shane Pendleton separated himself from Thurston Williams and Chad Rivers.

"Ladies and gentlemen, please raise your glasses" he said confidently into his purple-blinking remote headset through to the discreetly placed speakers, "and may I present to you Mr. and Mrs. Bret Wilmington."

No one saw either of the servers pulling at the oversized doors by the brass handles sparkling under the exaggerated lighting emanating from the hundreds of recessed spotlights encircling the centre-piece chandelier. The bride glowed, gliding forward effortlessly, her arm entwined with his for show. She was in full control, she knew. She hadn't doubted his infatuation with her from day they first met. So much had changed since that initial moment, but not her firm resolve to become the next Mrs. Wilmington.

She had not changed in any way. The bride who glided into the hall in midnight blue satin pumps was still the young, beautiful and determined sophisticate whom Bret Wilmington had met a year earlier and none in the room was prouder. The cape had gone, taken by one of her bride's maids and her simple designer gown came to life even more than when she had stood under the comparatively solemn lighting of the church. She was stunning, making even the best-dressed guest appear plain and ordinary. The satin gown was strapless, draped sensuously over the contours of a well-toned body, a pleated front slit opening discreetly to reveal the inside of both thighs above the knees. The décolleté front was deep-V to below her breasts and the sides were held together with two narrow bands of sapphire-coloured stones. Her perfectly smooth back was entirely bare, the loosely hanging fabric intended to reveal and tantalize, not conceal.

She was a bride, not a nun. She was independent, liberated, and would not be dictated to. Her neck was adorned with a simple deep-blue sapphire that had been her mother's, her earrings specially crafted to match the heirloom. Her lustrous cherry-blonde hair was swept up tightly into a triple French braid which had been her signature style for years, intended to accentuate the jewellery and the exquisitely chiselled lines of her face, neck and bared shoulders. To accent the jewellery she wore blue contacts that gleamed as much as the true green-gold of her hazel eyes.

The crowd applauded, as was expected, the men drowning out the women. The day belonged to her and everyone was expected to play the part. The father of the groom stepped in to take her arm, leading her to the head table. His wife followed on her son's arm, still pooh-poohing the bride's so-called wedding gown she had seen for the first time as Christine began her measured steps through the hushed gauntlet of shocked expressions and approving gazes, completely in command and completely satisfied.

Mother Wilmington had tried so persistently and in vain to instill in her daughter-in-law-to-be an appreciation for tradition and a regard for custom, which, to Christine, meant a proclivity for the prudish and a self-righteous sense of hierarchal propriety and indignation. The older woman was privy to the bride's choice of gown or colour and when she saw it for the first time she lost her balance to where her husband had needed to take her arm.

The guests fell robotically into the congested serpentine queue as Bret and Christine stood to greet them; behind the couple stood his parents and the best man, precisely as Christine had indicated during the rehearsal. Mr. and Mrs. Benton were not in attendance. She had died some five years earlier and he not long after the day of the funeral. In any event, he had always been a devout Catholic who thought purgatory had been created for the afterlife confinement of non-Catholics. He would have wanted no part of the event, she thought, and certainly no part of them.

Her special day was strictly a formality. Those who counted had warmly accepted her months earlier, though she soon discovered how the Wilmingtons lived and breathed formality. The rest of the faceless horde in attendance would likely never see her again. They were either clients of the firm, neighbours of the Wilmingtons or friends. Christine had no friends of her own, neither did Bret. Two of his best friends had moved away after graduation, returning for the wedding to serve as his ushers. The third one, his best friend and best man, was also a junior partner in the fathers' firm and she wanted very little to do with him.

She did know Shane might easily have been the one she married. She leaned slightly outward, beyond the parents, making eye contact with him. He had no idea how close he had actually come, she thought. Luck of the draw. Maybe one day she would tell him how close she had come to being a Pendleton.

The elaborate meal would come first, much needed by everyone after the tedium of protocol that each of them either loved to hate or hated to love and she had become part of who and what they were for better or worse.

# 7

The silver dessert forks clinked repeatedly, reverberating loudly against matching wine and water goblets. Each time the couple kissed perfunctorily. To the younger women the couple was magical and romantic, to the younger men Christine was untouchable and Bret had left their ranks. To older contingent they were just married and the sixth effort was interpreted as excessive by even the most enthusiastic clapper amongst them. Shane Pendleton once again followed Bret's indiscernible cue.

The headwaiter wheeled in a silver cart heading a procession of smaller brass carts, each holding a smaller likeness of the pure white, multi-tiered cake coming to a stop in front of the bride. All eyes were on the happy couple as tradition continued and they moved to pose momentarily by the cart, knife-in-hand, following the firm directions of the photographer for Bret to place his hand steadily over Christine's. He felt not the slightest tremor, squeezing gently as he reached over to pull the two inanimate and miniature ivory look-alikes from the precarious altar atop the unique creation which was mere moments away from being meticulously destroyed. No one noticed, not even the watchful and critical mother Wilmington noticed the figurines were devoid of facial features. They were anonymous and emotionless. Christine handed them to the waiter without instruction. The man knew what was expected of him.

The dull blade sliced easily through several layers as the place erupted into a wild and expected applause.

# 8

The hall cleared to allow the staff to remove the place settings and replace the soiled linen. Space was made for dancing and an impromptu stage magically appeared complete with eighteen chairs and a polished instrument placed in front of each one. The disc jockey's station off to the side, another obvious compromise between mother-in-law and daughter-in-law that would be defined in half-hour increments: something new, something old.

The older men had loosened their belts to offset the immediate consequences of gluttony, the younger women took off their pantyhose and most of the older women wished they had or could, feeling the same effects as their husbands. The bride's waltz with her groom came first, then with her father-in-law...and then came Shane.

"I'm deeply hurt, Chrissie. You said I would be first." He beamed widely, peering into the deep blue of her eyes that were ten centimetres below his.

"Being first isn't always a good thing, Shane," she teased. "Besides, you and Bret are practically brothers. It's impossible not to see how close you are." His smile was too perfect. "He's often told me how you are so much like brothers, how you've always been together, sharing everything, competing, each of you wanting to come first."

"Friendly competition," he countered. "Frederick and my dad were the same way. They competed all through college, and now they co-own the best known firm in the business."

"You must be proud of them, as they are of you and Bret. Imagine, fathers and sons working together."

"I never thought about it. That's why it's The Wilmingtons. Bret joining the firm was always a given. Whether I would was never clear to me. All I cared about was getting through, and before that I was too young to care." He took a deep breath. "We've had a busy five years."

"Getting through what?"

"M. Arch. 1, architecture" he answered. "Keeping up with the best isn't easy. Quite frankly, I'm surprised I got through and I'm glad it's over... or practically over. I still have finals for M. Arch. II hanging over my head."

"You'll do fine. I know you will."

"You blew away a lot of people with this phenomenal gown, Chrissie." He stepped back, taking her all in. "It's fantastic. Bret's a lucky man."

He was leering openly at her breasts, enjoying them. Nothing had changed.

"I'm a lucky woman."

She hated the feel of his hand at the base of her bare back as they moved in slow concentric circles to Beethoven and Bach and she wondered whether her husband was watching. She knew the other Mrs. Wilmington was. Then she saw Chad Rivers coming timidly to her rescue and she moved back, relieved to be free of Shane's grasp that held her so uncomfortably close.

"May I cut in?"

"Thank you, Chad. I believe I've already taken too much of Shane's attention away from the other ladies. I would love to dance with you."

Shane frowned, stepping aside reluctantly to let Chad ease in. Their friendship had waned out of necessity over the past year, both men so preoccupied with new lives and new responsibilities, and simply because of distance. Though they both knew that wasn't the case.

The seniors at The Wilmingtons & Pendleton had offered Chad a job immediately after graduation which he had at first gladly accepted, only to later flatly decline the offer, claiming a better and more challenging opportunity was his for the taking on the West Coast. Of course, no such job existed. Chad knew, so did the other three.

They had drifted apart, which wasn't a big deal. Friends would always come and go, and Chad's trip to Montreal for the wedding was the first time they had seen each other since returning from Ixtapa - Zihuatanejo eighteen months earlier. They both knew the friendship was dead. Shane thought of Chad as a vendu, a sell-out, a quitter and walked away as though he hadn't been with the most beautiful woman in the room.

Chad lacked personality. He couldn't get a date in a ladies' prison, let alone anywhere else, Shane knew, let alone winning a non-entry level position at the premier industrial design firm on the West Coast. He had come to Montreal under duress to serve as usher, Bret's duress, otherwise thought of by most as a compelling personality. Chad had refused several times, claiming his job left him with little or no personal time and a vacation would be viewed badly by senior associates. Though, as expected, eventually he succumbed to his friend's persistence. Bret wanted him there, and Bret normally got what he wanted.

Chad's hands were moist and clammy. Any other man would have pressed his palms against the inside of his pant pockets, but Chad wasn't au courant about women or life. He was a geek, a hanger-on, a follower whose most outstanding achievement was his complete lack of self-esteem which had led to the worst of many bad decisions in his life. He had followed once too often and the fact he very deeply regretted his actions would have no bearing on the death sentence already decided upon.

"You're so lovely and so elegant," he spoke in a whisper, his face turning beet red. "I don't dance very well, Christine, especially to this stuff. Sorry. I've spent most of my life studying. Guess you can call it the geek syndrome."

"You're no geek, Chad. Believe me. I've heard you're

quite the ladies' man." She stepped back. "Look at you, all dressed and dashing in Armani."

She had met him once before, at the rehearsal a few days earlier, yet she felt as though she had known him forever.

"He thinks so, everyone does." He admired the suit, pulling at the lapels. "It's rented."

"What do you care about Shane? You've done just as well as the others. What does it matter what he thinks? Besides, everyone has a time to come first, Chad, the famous fifteen minutes. Be patient. You'll be first one day. Anyway, this is my day, and you're supposed to be happy for me. So let's show these old fogies how happy they used to be."

She widened the distance between them imperceptibly. Chad's inner stature, his sense of self made him seem smaller than he was. The distance reduced the effect of the flaw that was integral to his personality and for a brief time they spoke about him. He was flattered and lost for words, but she was too beautiful to care anything about him. He knew, and he had no illusions. Whatever woman he would end up with would never be like her. The Brets of the world would always end up with women like her, not him. He wanted desperately to leave, to get out of there, to go home and be innocuous. Then:

"Chad, it's time for a real man to cut in, buddy. Someone has to show this heavenly vision that not all life on earth is sad and pitiful."

Thurston Williams stood there, unmoving; Chad looked at Christine with defeat in his eyes as his hands fell away from her as though he'd been touching her inappropriately.

She leaned into him. "We will see each other again very soon, Chad. I promise. Now go party and remember what I've said to you." The transition was as smooth as the handsome Thurston himself. "That was cruel, Thurston."

"Don't worry about him, Christine. He's used to our

joking with him. He's always been a bit shy, a bit different and a bit small-minded about things." He held both her hands at arm's length, admiring her. "That damned Bret, damn his soul. What does he have that could possibly make such a beauty and obviously superior chick want to marry him?"

"Superior?" She frowned, narrowing her eyes. "I don't see myself that way, and certainly not as a chick. I believe different might be a better choice of words."

"You're definitely different. There's nothing like you back home, nothing home-grown anyway. The best we've got are polyester-clad females who look more like men and are more terrified of the bathroom scale than a reptile. Actually, the scales are probably the most afraid. Talk about pressure." He laughed, grimacing. "No one needs to break a mirror for seven years bad luck. Say I do, and you're done. Off comes the gown, on go the weight and the polyester. One afternoon of magic we never stop paying for whether we stay in or get out: the curse of the modern age."

She recoiled, though not entirely seriously.

"Thurston, please try to remember you're at a wedding...mine. That's horrible of you to say such a thing, and very crude. I see cruelty is part of your nature. You certainly aren't given to compassion, which, by the way, is what we women want most in a man. Cruelty is not widely considered an asset in a relationship. How did you ever find your wife, talking like that?"

He kissed her hand. "I apologize. I suppose it's subliminally driven by man's need to be free. What's the expression? First comes love, then comes marriage, then comes..." He paused with a smirk he thought was more debonair than it was. "It's what comes after the last "then comes" that I don't want or need."

"You don't like children? You don't want any?"

"No, I don't, on both counts. Quite frankly, I have no

understanding of those who do…or profess to. The list is endless."

"You have a list."

"Memorized," he answered, "and engrained."

"Perhaps we can go over that list at a later time. What does your wife think about that sentiment, or does she know?"

"She's a Human Resources type, strictly business. She's not the prettiest thing on the block, though, happily, she's not the poorest either. She's got a great job, which sort of makes up for the rest of her."

"And she's not here. Why?"

"Embarrassed," was all he said.

Christine frowned. She hadn't seen Thurston once in the time she had known Bret. He, too, had moved away immediately after the post-graduation vacation in Mexico, accepting a junior position in the Toronto office of a Chicago-based architectural firm, recently marrying a woman who hadn't come with him for reasons that didn't particularly matter to anyone.

"Your wife?" she questioned.

"Not her, me. We had a long weekend in Vegas. Too long," he explained, "with too much booze and powder. What can I say? She was a whole lot prettier at the chapel than Monday morning." He grinned. "Fair trade, I suppose. She's got the good job; I've got the, well, what you see."

She thought she had heard everything about him, except the man was impossibly more arrogant than Shane. He was a womanizer and a shameless pig. He was also a low achiever who had graduated with disappointing grades certain to guarantee him a mediocre career with firms of lesser reputations. Working at The Wilmingtons and Pendleton was never an option. The nicest one was Chad, she thought indifferently, feeling no compassion for him. He didn't fit the Wilmington-Pendleton mould and she forgot him as she stepped away from Thurston.

"Should I take that to mean I am being dismissed?"

He feigned disbelief, when what he actually felt was relief. There was an indefinable aura about her he didn't like. She was a stuck up bitch. She carried herself in a way that was both inviting and detached. Her energy was palpable; he felt an unfamiliar disadvantage being near her and her eyes possessed a disturbing, piercing quality. He was being dismissed, and they both knew.

"No, you shouldn't," she giggled, "not at all. You should take it to mean the bride has to rest for a moment before she drops."

He escorted her to the head table, her arm draped through his as they weaved a path through the colourful fabrics of their guests. He shook Bret's hand, then Shane's as he leaned in to whisper when he was certain no one could overhear. His apologies were profuse. Something had come up, something urgent brought to his attention during the drive from the church to the reception hall. He would be leaving on the last flight out that evening. He had no choice, nor could he be more embarrassed.

He couldn't stay, he wouldn't stay. Every nerve-ending in his body told him he should go. He shouldn't have come, he told himself. Being together again wasn't natural. None of them should have come, particularly Chad. What had he been thinking? He was the dangerous one, he was their liability. Bret's grip was commandingly firm. He regretted his friend's early departure, but first they would meet privately as they would not see one another again for a very long time, for the better.

# 9

The bride excused herself for a brief moment of privacy to prepare for the final and much anticipated wedding tradition. She was alone in the ladies room, except for the nondescript female attendant who stood by mechanically after the door closed, even though the bride obviously had no purse.

Christine had been through too much, constant effort without any release. She had no one to confide in, no friend with whom to share her dreams or fears. She should have been the happiest woman in the world, yet she wasn't. When the flood of emotion erupted she was completely unprepared for the intensity that startled her as much as the young Latina attendant standing behind her, unsure of what she should do.

"Señora, ¿qué le pasa?" she ventured in an inaudible, almost secretive murmur, though with an undertone that was unmistakably confident and self-assured.

Christine wasn't expecting the question and had no immediate answer to offer. She stood facing into the mirror as the two women gazed at each other, reading each other's thoughts, each one instantly and noticeably curious about the other. Christine could see the young Latina was naturally beautiful and shapely, despite her loose-fitting black frock and drab white apron. Each young woman scrutinized the other unabashedly from head to toe, Christine not knowing what to say, the other not knowing what to do. When their eyes locked Christine took an extra moment, inhaling deeply as she leaned on the counter for support. Somehow she felt worse than when she came in. When she finally did speak, after mere seconds, the attendant beamed, the social distance between them instantly narrowing to arm's length.

"He hecho un gran error, señorita," Christine gulped.

"No debería me haber casárselo."

The attendant shook her head, understanding the new bride's fears. She had seen the groom. Who would not want to marry such a man, she thought? "No, señora, es un hombre muy bueno, usted tiene mucha suerte." She smiled warmly. "Lo sé. Not all men are as good and kind as I know your caballero must be señora. Él debería estar muy enamorado de usted."

Beautiful words from a world away, a world of innocence. How was she was so lucky? How much of herself had she lost or given up in order to gain so little? How much had she changed in so little time? She turned to the young Latina who instinctively hugged the beautiful bride to comfort her the way women could without feeling shame, the way men would never understand. Men would slap each other on the back and say something expected, something appropriately macho, suitably deprecating, and then they would go to a bar, get drunk and prove to each other they'd been right all along.

Her name was Selena, she was Venezuelan and she had recently arrived in Montreal. She was going to night school to learn French. English would come later, she insisted adamantly. Then someone would recognize her credentials, she hoped. She had spent her first nights feeling alone and afraid, unsure of the future, but all that was over. She would not spend one moment longer than necessary in a public washroom handing out squares of flimsy two-ply for loose change.

That alone catapulted Christine out of her self-pity. What Selena said to her was true. By the next morning she would see the world differently, she would be alone with her husband and all the fuss would be over with. She looked at the elastic ribbon she had tossed onto the fake granite counter, expressionless. Selena reached for the shapeless midnight blue satin laced with black silk, admiring it against the background of her open hand.

She knelt, pulling away a satin pump, easing Christine's stocking-covered right foot onto her thigh. Christine took the cue, raising her foot enough for Selena to slide the ribbon upward to her knee. Selena was a little unsure, smiling at Christine's carefree shrug. She didn't want to leave, though they both knew she had to go. She had stayed too long, but felt so much better. They kissed each other's cheek tenderly and compassionately. At first sight they appeared socially as far apart as possible. Now they were sisters in sorrow. All women were sisters in times of sadness and the time had come for Christine to once again be the happy bride.

"Nos veremos otra vez, Selena. Créeme, lo sé." She took the attendant's hand, squeezing gently. "Gracias, amiga mía. Muchas gracias por todo." Christine didn't need to hope they would see each other again. They would, as much as Selena knew they would not.

"Buena vida, Señora Cristina, te espero muy buena vida, y te doy gracias igualmente. Muchísimas gracias."

How much Selena wanted to believe, and then maybe she could dream, though she would never allow herself to believe. Those few moments with the beautiful bride were surreal, so unexpected, but life didn't work out that way. She had overheard other hotel staff talking about the wedding and the family. What would such an important woman ever have in common with someone who cleaned toilets and sinks? Why would she even say such a thing? She supposed the bride was caught up in the emotion of the moment, and when the door closed she recognized in the mirror the deep sadness which had become gradually less incongruous to her each day. For one fleeting moment her determination waned and she reached for a tissue to wipe away a tear before returning to her stool in the corner.

When the door closed silently behind Christine she

turned back, unaware she was smiling or that she was happy once again. She had no doubt fate had worked to bring her together with Selena, no doubt they would see each other again. She wondered whether Selena believed her, feeling an overwhelming sadness at leaving the beautiful young girl alone in her cold and sanitized ceramic cell.

She knew her failing nerves had put her on edge. Selena was right. Bret wasn't the problem, though his mother had tried tirelessly to encroach on her sanity, constantly asserting herself as the family matriarch, probing, never satisfied. Christine was tired of all the planning, hers and theirs together: a choreographed joining of man and woman more for the benefit of social obligation than the love of a young couple who had decided to share their lives forever. Love had been left out of the equation by design, she thought, another plan, another Wilmington project.

She was eager to get away from all of them, if only to be alone with him for a few moments, after one more public performance. She played her part well when the time came for her groom to reach under her gown and retrieve the much sought-after prize. He lingered much too long to be fanciful or romantic, encouraging more loud and raucous applause from the men and mixed expressions from the women who, for the most part, mimicked the quiet histrionics of the disgusted mother-in-law.

Bret hadn't known. Strangely enough, he hadn't even thought about it. Discovering in public that his bride's thighs were completely bare between the elastic tops of her nylons and her panties drew his fingers instinctively to the soft, smooth skin, completely oblivious to the crowd.

She tapped his face lightly, feigning exasperation, bringing him back to reality. His face was flushed and he was visibly anxious for more. The garter slid easily past her shoe and he barely took notice when he tossed it blindly over his shoulder, preoccupied with urgent thoughts of her, wanting her.

Neither one saw or cared who caught the highly coveted prize, though judging by the loud scream of delight the fortunate recipient was the most in need. The bride and groom bowed out gracefully, applauded by those who were close enough to see.

# 10

"You could at least have given me some warning," he chortled. "I could have dropped dead. That was so incredibly sexy, Chrissie." He jumped onto the bed like an eager schoolboy who had never seen a naked woman. "Strip for me, Chrissie. Strip. I have to see what's under there."

"We don't have very long. They're expecting us."

"To hell with them. That's what I've got Shane for."

"Okay, but no touching. I don't want anyone thinking we've done something, when we haven't."

He pulled at the bow-tie, then at the hematite studs along the front of his shirt. "Just do it before I lose my frigging mind."

They were so predictable. They lived for it. They would even kill or die for it. They were fools. No woman would pay, kill or conspire for sex. A man would, nature's way of giving all women balance, an equal chance at survival in a man's world. One shoulder dropped, slowly baring a breast that had no other cover. The other shoulder dropped and she stood in front of him, vulnerable and in control. Her breasts were perfectly shaped, crowned with petite, caramel nipples and he should have known by seeing them that she would not be joining him on the bed.

Effortlessly, she pushed the smooth fabric encircling her hips to the floor, giving her the appearance of standing at the centre of a crumpled, fabric pedestal. They had not been together sexually over the year since they had met, and he had never seen her naked. Her virginity was her strictest condition and occasionally fondling a breast or managing to grab at her buttocks from under a dress was the most she had ever let him manage. She was one of those women who were as naked when they were dressed as when they were not. She exuded sexuality and being seen with her was enough for him, most times. And those times together had been functional at best: spur of the moment dinners whenever they could find the time or fleeting moments over lunch. Working for his father while struggling to complete his Master of Architecture was far removed from the easy life he had anticipated. Wilmington senior had achieved his success the hard way, so would his son, or he could work elsewhere. He would work and study as one combined schedule and he would succeed, or he could work for a lesser known firm. The same applied to Shane.

Christine had been one of Bret's first clients. In fact, had she not selected The Wilmingtons and Pendleton to design her business facility and condo of corporate offices, they never would have met. They never would have married. She had insisted she would only work with one of the firm's recent graduates, someone who was young, talented and sufficiently creative to transpose her dream from the imaginary to the real. The project would last two years; one the firm had vigorously debated before agreeing to take on the new client who was independently wealthy and oozed refined sexuality. They had reeled at her candour and acumen, which they found decidedly irritating, Bret finally stopping short of begging the senior partners to accept the contract and appoint him as Account Manager, not Shane.

The dates had been specified, the late penalties had been agreed to, and hers was the one signature on the lengthy contract that was not a Wilmington or a Pendleton. They worked closely together from the beginning and business meetings that began as lunches soon became dinners and the increasingly less business-like dinners eventually gave way to a proposal that intrigued her and disappointed him.

He'd been living in his parents' home. She lived alone in the quiet luxury of her upscale condo, which was also her office, and would continue living alone until the wedding, adamant her condo would not be sold until she found a buyer who could afford the asking price.

Inwardly she was delighted, outwardly she was coolly coquettish and elusively compelling, although she had never invited Bret to her home. Nor had he ever asked why. Possibly, he had known better. She knew being together twenty-four-seven wouldn't be healthy for either of them and wasn't an option, even though Frederick Wilmington had offered her a private office at his corporate headquarters and Mother Wilmington had spent months speaking to the benefits of newlyweds moving into a family home.

As much as her marriage was all-important to her, she would not play the daily role of the perfect daughter-in-law. His maternal domination had to come to an end. They could at last enjoy being a couple, and not in Westmount, which was her single greatest victory over mother Wilmington, Mother Bitch. Their new South Shore home had been completed a few weeks earlier, Christine insisting throughout that Bret work with the contractors to please his father and satisfy the firm's requisite for full partnership. Her home would be beautiful, he promised, insisting she not see it until after the honeymoon.

The hotel room was brightly lit, the full-length mirror directly behind her giving him a view of her body that could not be any more detailed, and she knew it. Watching her intentionally taunt him with slow, precise moves was unbearable. An intense inner pressure was steadily building to a painful crescendo as he tore recklessly at the rest of his clothes, barely blinking, not wanting to miss a moment of what he was seeing. Her skin was perfect. She kicked away the crumpled gown and stood with her feet apart, her long, smooth legs ending at a clean apex of soft folds barely covered by the V and narrow ribbons of her flimsy silk and satin panties.

Her hands cupped her breasts for a brief moment before

tracing an invisible line to her belly, then to her panties, before turning her attention to her dark blue stay-up stockings. He begged her not to, imploring her to stay as she was and to join him. He was so ready for her. She ignored him, pushing each nylon slowly to her ankles before placing the heel of each foot one at a time on the edge of the bed for balance and pulling each stocking provocatively away from its respective leg. He moved closer, his hands reaching out to touch her, to grab at her.

She moved back. Her panties remained in place, such as they were, and he didn't know where to look first. Her ass was gorgeous, he thought, flawless, yet he wanted what was behind the flimsy curtain of see-through silk even more. The cleft in her panties was unmistakable, exciting him, moving in concert with her breathing. He had waited a long time to see her naked, to see it and touch it. He would be her first, and he would know soon enough whether she'd been telling the truth, and soon enough whether she was worth the wait and Shane's ridicule.

"You want me, don't you, Bret? Right now, you want me right now, don't you?"

Her question was as rhetorical as his inevitable response was obvious. She bent completely over, pushing her tiny panties to her ankles, kicking away the twisted silk and satin string as she stood. The folds at the apex of her legs were as smooth as anywhere on her body and his thoughts were anything but a secret to her. She blew him a kiss as she turned towards the bathroom. The bride had first rights to the shower. The groom would have to wait. She was the newest Mrs. Wilmington, in more ways than one, he was about to discover.

# 11

By midnight virtually all the guests had gone home, at least the oldsters. By 3:00 AM those who remained were under thirty, blurred images of groping hands and bare thighs. From time to time anxious couples would hurry from the hall, reappearing moments later, satisfied and flushed with the exertions of impromptu needs. They had no particular schedule to respect, beyond the immediacy of the moment, and Selena had gone home several hours earlier. The groom had also gone hours earlier, promising he would not be long. He and Shane needed to speak with Chad and Thurston before they left for the airport.

Bret spoke first, as usual. Why, none of them really remembered. He just did. "I'm glad the two of you decided to come, though I'm disappointed you left so early last night."

"Disappointed why, Bret? That we weren't there to watch you get it wet? What's for us to celebrate?" Thurston answered. "Your bride's beautiful. No shit. She's makes the thing I can't shake loose a definite double-bagger and the best Rivers will ever snag is sloppy seconds, but all this happy marriage bullshit doesn't change what happened. Shane's up your ass, and that's fine. I'm not. I didn't stay last night because those days are over. They're gone, so deal with it."

"Fuck you, Thurston, and all your fucking rhetoric. We could give a fuck if you and shit-face over there came to the wedding or not. You're here because we had to know. We had to see both of you to be sure. Understand that. We had to know, that's all."

"So now you're sure, Bret. So fuck off." Thurston stood, draining the rest of his Rémy Martin, turning his attention to Chad. "Here's your weak link, right here. Deal with him if you're so worried, but leave me out of it." He was talking to Shane. "But I'm curious as to how you're going to do that. Do you intend to kill him too?"

"I didn't kill anyone," defended Shane.

"No, you didn't. You're right. We all did. And don't you forget it. Let me tell you something. What we shared in the past, what passed as a fucked up fraternity, is gone. What remains is a potentially deadly tontine: the eventual inheritance a guaranteed silence and guaranteed peace of mind, in succession and over time. What's interesting about a tontine is that one member benefits, the others lose, and there's only one way to lose in a tontine." He paused, scanning the room for affect. "One can only be completely safe from the others by winning the tontine, when the other three are dead."

Chad broke in. "What are you talking about, Thurston? And what's all this talk about tontines and dying. We're leaving. We'll be home in a few hours. What happened back then was an accident, a long time ago." He looked over to Bret. "Why are we even bringing this up when we should be getting on with our lives and letting the past be the past?" He turned to Thurston. "You're saying none of us can be trusted."

"Chad, you're an idiot. You've always been an idiot, not to mention excessively gullible, and what you just said is crap. That makes you dangerous to me." He gestured towards Bret and Shane. "Them, I couldn't care less about. Fuck fraternal pride. We're not school kids anymore. You're the one who worries me, Chad. Personally, I'm glad you moved as far away as you did."

Shane stood. "Your analogy of a tontine makes sense, Thurston. I agree with you in principle. However, as you implied, the objective of a tontine is to survive the others, to become the beneficiary, which should be uppermost on our minds. Our common objective should be longevity, survival, not death, and certainly not treachery."

Thurston walked to the door. "My best wishes to you and your bride, Bret. Don't call me again." He stared directly at Shane, Bret, and then Chad. "You must know as much as the four of us want to forget what happened...others won't." He opened the door without bravado. "Don't forget the others, gentlemen, because they won't forget us. None of you call me again. I don't exist."

The door closed with a slight click. Shane broke the deafening silence, speaking to Bret as though they were alone. "Thurston has a dramatic flair I wasn't aware of." He sipped the last of his cognac. "Guess we won't be seeing him again."

"Don't be so sure," answered Bret. "He wasn't wrong about the tontine. We are a liability to each other, as much as we're each other's insurance. I think staying in touch would be a smart thing, from a distance."

"Accomplishing what, exactly? Who would he tell, the Mexicans?" Shane grinned, reaching for the decanter. "He's not about to let himself become some guy's bitch in a Mexican jail."

Bret shrugged. "Anyway, I have to get back to the wife." He stopped himself halfway out of the easy chair, bursting into a laugh. "How strange is that to say?"

"I don't know, and I don't care to know." Shane glanced indifferently at Chad who either couldn't bring himself to stand or sensed he needed permission. "I suppose you're leaving."

"My flight's at 6:00 AM. Yeah, I'm leaving."

He was calm, as though he recognizing and accepting his fate. He felt a dark and ominous sensation, a frightening feeling he couldn't explain to himself, let alone anyone else. He thought he was smiling, when he wasn't. He was grimacing, trapped in a troubled world as the two sat staring at him. What he felt invade his body was instantly visible to them, as though witnessing an out-of-body experience. Even his voice altered noticeably.

"I suppose I came here for the same reason you wanted me here. I had to see what had changed, if anything." He shrugged. "But nothing's changed, status quo."

"So, tell us. What's got Thurston so jumpy?"

"Bret, Shane, you can trust me. Believe me when I say I would never give you up." He stood, checking his watch. He wanted to leave, to get away from them. At the door he turned back, watching Bret fill Shane's half-full glass. "Bret, the others Thurston was talking about," he paused, though not for affect. "A man was at the church, a man who shouldn't have been there. I think he was standing behind us for a long time, watching. I'm sure he was watching us. He stared straight at me, through me, then at Thurston. He scared me, Bret. He knows. I'm sure he knows. That's what Thurston was talking about."

Bret laughed derisively. Thurston hadn't been wrong about Rivers. He was the weak link, their Achilles heel. Unfortunately, he and Shane were much more adept at architecture than killing and neither one commented when Rivers closed the door behind him. When he and Shane returned to the reception hall everyone had gone. The place was deserted and Shane had no advice to offer his friend that was worth listening to. Bret was on his own, a schoolboy, a spoiled son who had somehow instantly transformed into the husband of the quintessential woman.

She hadn't waited for him. She had enjoyed her time alone, away from people she cared little about. She showered again and changed into ivory pinstripe silk pyjamas before climbing under the heavy duvet and losing herself in thoughts of her past and her future, too excited to sleep.

He crept into the room cravenly, making no noise whatsoever. She did have complete control, she knew.

Some things never do change. When he crawled into her bed he smelled of expensive liquor and she winced quietly when he grabbed at her breasts through the smoothness of Italy's finest silk with uncaring and immature hands. Soon, hearing his tell-tale troubled breathing, she reached slowly and indifferently, blindly searching for any indication she should force herself to stay awake and be a wife to her husband on their wedding night, a vital woman for both of them. There was none and she pushed him away easily. Boys would be boys, men would be men and that would never change either. What more could she ask, other than completing her dream project on time, their dream which had had taken awhile and worth every moment?

She rolled over, feeling content. By the time she fell asleep her flushed cheeks were stained blackish-blue with mascara and her closed eyes had squeezed out tiny droplets of warm and salted tears.

# 12

Maria would never forget July 18, one week after her 21ˢᵗ birthday. She had been free for seven days to go wherever she wanted and do whatever as she wished, free to be alone. She had never been alone that she could remember, certainly not since her mother's murder two years earlier.

The day she met Addison in Almería the midday sun was brilliant, the sky Mediterranean blue and everyone strolling along the Avenida Federico García Lorca was beautiful. A light wind whistled unheard through the swaying leaves of tall and magnificent palm trees lining the avenue like silent sentinels, the warm breeze playing teasingly with the silk and satin skirts of young señoritas who wanted to be seen, much to the delight of young caballeros who wanted to see.

She felt pleasantly lethargic from the seafood tapas and her second glass of vino blanco at El Quinto Toro, one of the most frequented tapa bars on La Rambla. The world was passing her by in slow motion, allowing her to capture each unhurried movement as she slouched slightly on her private park bench. Nothing could penetrate her dream-like state. She was alone and at peace. No one knew her and for once she felt no guilt or humiliation. If only for a short time, she was free. She knew the freedom would end, that she would have to go back, but until the very last moment that seemed so far away she could be who she wanted to be and not who she was.

Her eyes closed, letting her other senses enhance the moment, tilting her head back and letting her luscious, deep-coloured chestnut red hair cascade over the smooth upper edge of the wrought iron frame. She inhaled the warm scented air as deeply as she could. She felt so much a part of what was happening around her, a part of each person's day, knowing as many men were eyeing her as they were the other young and beautiful passers-by.

They would talk amongst themselves after each glance, as though mesmerized by the sheen of her black patent leather pumps sparkling hypnotically in the sunlight. The winter-white miniskirt of her bouclé suit rode nicely over her crossed legs, showing off her tanned thighs and her black lace décolleté blouse revealed enough of her accentuated breasts to ensure appreciation. The matching lab coat was lined with silk, sculpted with three-quarter sleeves and the slim faux-pockets were trimmed in black. She was elegant in every way: a lady refined, a lady reborn. She had dressed for the day, for the mood, so engrossed in the ambiance she was taken by surprise when the soft voice broke into her silent world.

"Perdóneme, señorita, pero, con permiso, ¿puedo sentarme?"

She turned, half-blinded by the sun which had eased unnoticed to the west, taking what she thought was a brief moment to answer, though she took much longer. Regardless, the response was instinctive. "Sí, claro, siéntese, por favor."

The compelling stranger sat, accepting the invitation. "Dígàme, señorita ¿no es usted de aquí? Usted es española, yo creo."

The accent was good, the pronunciation excellent. Maria spoke four languages with inherent fluency and detected a formal linguistic training more than natural ease. "No lo soy," she answered, almost certain, "I'm American."

"From your accent I'd say somewhere in the Southeast, possibly Miami?"

A perfect day had become spectacular. "Sorry, I should have said Canadian. Most people here relate more to America."

"I didn't mean to interrupt you. I just had to come over

and tell you how gorgeous you are. You're an absolute vision. I hope you don't mind me saying so, but I couldn't stay away." The hesitation was brief, to savour the moment. "Are you waiting for someone? Please tell me you're not."

"No, I'm not."

"Then may I invite you to lunch? By the way, I'm Addison from Montreal. And you are?"

"Maria, from Canada," she wanted immediately to step back in time, but what was done was done, "and, no thank you. I've already eaten, though perhaps a bit too early and perhaps a bit too much. Sorry."

"Then dinner, and I won't take no for an answer." Addison peered straight into her eyes, pensively, unabashedly hopeful.

They had both sensed a single energy drawing them inexorably together, each one unsure, eager as their moist lips pressed together in response to a surge of inner warmth penetrating them beyond the physical. They each knew instinctively they had been brought together and words had no place. They stood, drawn up by a palpable energy, oblivious to the surroundings as they strolled hand in hand to the end of La Rambla as comfortably as any of the other lovers. When they parted, each stood for a moment, studying the other before reluctantly turning away.

# 13

Addison left Maria off at the hotel and would be back to escort her to dinner at 8:30. They would dine with the moonlit Gulf of Almería as their backdrop and Maria spent the remainder of the afternoon in a blur of flushed excitement. She actually had a date, not a web-site pick-up, not a cross-your-fingers blind date, a real date and she laid out as many clothes on the bed as were in the closet. The evening was going to be special, and so would she.

She had no idea whether to wait for the concierge to call up to her room, or wait in the lobby for Addison to arrive, deciding on the lobby despite the early hour. She was excited and hadn't thought for a moment Addison would be there to watch her every step as she floated down the winding stairs. She glowed, barely able to contain her girlish eagerness, much less subdue her uncertainty about what was about to happen between them.

Addison wasn't disappointed. She was an angel descending from heaven. Maria had chosen a navy blue ruched corset blouse with a tie-top which she left untied. Her skirt was deep-red, full to the knees with ribbon trim and cinched at her waist with a wide belt. Her bare legs completed the look, bringing an unmistakable gleam to the most brilliantly blue eyes Maria had ever seen.

"You are beautiful, Maria, absolutely beautiful. The stars and the moon won't shine as bright with you by my side tonight."

"I'm starved," she giggled, not knowing what else to say "And you're gorgeous too, Addison. We'll be the most attractive couple at the marina. Is that still where we're going?" She had hoped so. "I love boats."

They were expected at the Marina. Addison wanted the evening to exceed perfection and had spent the afternoon seeing to every minute detail. Motor and sailing yachts, from the grandest to the most modest, floated securely in blackened and rippling waters; smaller craft squeaked noisily against their fenders, the larger ones did not.

The faint breeze made the warm evening more pleasant. The spacious open-air terrace was decorated with twisted narrow rolls of red and white crêpe, lighted in a muted amber glow. The tables were private, covered with red and white chequered table cloths. The waiters were dressed in loose-fitting white cotton shirts with wide sleeves, red and white chequered bandanas at their open-necks and form-fitting black pants better suited to the corrida. They were discreet. Their guests had come to escape, together or alone, and the couple wanted to be alone, though the evening came to an end too quickly for both of them. They barely touched their food or wine. They had so much to say to one another, constantly cutting one another off in mid-sentence, neither one caring, neither one speaking the words which would have come so easily, victims of the human condition: fear of love trumps love.

"Maria, I have something to confess." Addison reached for her open hand. "I hope I haven't gone and spoiled our evening."

"Sounds serious," Maria replied. "What is it?"

"This afternoon, after we left each other… I changed hotels. I wanted to be near you." Addison reached for what remained of the classic Rojo wine, deciding against raising the glass with trembling hands. "Please tell you're not angry."

Maria couldn't have been more shocked, or more ecstatic. Being closer to Addison was all she could have hoped for. "We're in the same hotel?"

Addison nodded, searching Maria's eyes. "Same hotel, same floor, same adjoining door…for a few extra Euros. Please tell me you don't mind. I was terrified of telling you all evening, and I'm not much better now. It's your call, Maria... I want so much to spend more time with you."

"And I want more time with you. I've wanted you all evening, so let's get out of here before I go crazy."

"I think we're both going crazy." Addison smiled suggestively, dropping more bills than needed onto the table to save precious minutes. "I can't wait to see all of you, to feel all of you. God, you're so gorgeous."

The fashionable bistro tables and straight-back chairs had long since been pushed to the wall by weary waiters anxious to enjoy what remained of the late evening. To the young Spaniards, 1:00 AM meant Pernod with as little water as possible and breath-robbing pitillos in a dance club where music was anything but traditional and the night was as young as they were. Los gaiteros who had strolled to and fro in front of the quaint terraza playing traditional love ballads had gone, happy with their tips and anxious to join with family and friends, their music drifting out across the moonlit and darkened waters of the gulf as they disappeared up the winding road leading beyond the yacht club.

Everyone had gone home, which they didn't realize until the rising sun began casting its early morning warmth, set in a golden ridge as perfectly as any diamond on a band of glittering gold. Maria appeared as an angel to Addison, framed in the near-blinding glow of a celestial halo, a captivating and beautiful fairy-tale princess who had escaped from the prison of her pages so they might be together forever, her jewelled tiara exploding with a radiant and blinding yellow light.

They kissed with a passion they had earlier held back, their heated lips coming together, joining them tightly as one, a prelude to a day of intimate and passionate love-making that would dissolve into evening and a prelude to a life together as best friends and lovers.

# 14

Maria felt like a despondent prisoner of Spain after Addison returned home a week earlier, not a happy tourist. They had tried to change their flights, even the airline in desperation, with absolutely no success: sad victims of peak season inflexibility. Everything was booked solid.

At the security gate they were the hour's pro tem distraction for curious and admiring eyes as much as for the cynicism and disapproval of hurried and harried travellers in the tightly woven throng. No one noticed their anguish or the welling tears seeping from reddened and tired eyes to streak and stain youthful faces which hours earlier had been so carefree and vibrant. Maria felt utterly alone and abandoned throughout most of the week that followed, knowing in her heart that wasn't true. They had been inseparable the better part of two weeks, spending their time exploring each other, loving, kissing and being alone, turning heads in public and seeing nothing beyond the intimate borders of their brave new world. Addison hadn't pressed. There would be time to discover and love everything about Maria, and Maria would come to know and love everything about the one she would spend the rest of her life with: Addison Larivière, the next in line to take over the Larivière Empire.

# 15

The week alone was long and difficult, without purpose for either one. They spoke by phone each afternoon and evening, saying everything, saying nothing, dreaming aloud or simply letting the sound of long, deep breaths fill rare voids. They had discovered so much about each other in Spain, including a dream they could share and the violent deaths of their mothers. Still, each one had so much to say, to learn about the other, so much to enjoy in young lives that would soon unfold together.

The day she thought would never come did come. The flight was long and monotonous, not the adventurous eastward journey of a few weeks earlier. She tried sleeping and couldn't. She crossed and uncrossed her legs repeatedly, before standing and sitting repeatedly, all to the annoyance of her immediate fellow passengers whom she classified by weight, dress code, body language and odour. No one matched up to Addison. She couldn't imagine anyone ever would.

When Maria finally exited the crowded Jetway in Montreal, Addison was waiting, barely visible behind a wall of fragrant flowers and holding a small card handwritten in script and scented with her favourite perfume. The sentiment was real: Que je t'aime, Maria; que je t'aime. Each wiped away the other's tears, squeezing each other tightly, kissing cheeks that were wet and flushed. They were together, and would always be together. Nothing would tear them apart and the next thirty-six hours were an endless continuum of baths, showers, oils, pampering, and love-making. They talked incessantly, mostly about Addison and not Maria who was still reticent, afraid of what Addison might think if she said too much, hoping that very soon the truth wouldn't matter. She'd been very wrong and would soon discover her past would never matter.

Addison had always been expected to one day take over from the family patriarch as president and CEO of La Corporation Larivière, a Montreal-based holding company controlling most of the exclusive retail clothing in North America and a large part of the manufacturing side of the industry. Were you to speak the words rag, rag trade or rag district when talking with him, he would likely walk away. If you worked for him, the sad day would likely be your last on the job. Jean-Émile Larivière had always strived to be the best, and keeping up with him was an impossible quest for most. Those were the ones who would never succeed in climbing to the top of the industry, meaning to the top of LCL, whereas those who could and did, often wished they hadn't. Success had come at a very high cost to each one of them, and none cared that Jean-Émile constantly paid a higher price.

The inner conflict had once rested heavily on Addison's mind, consumed by the weight of family pressures, the need to continue the family name and the family mission which was once an all-consuming passion. Now no such mission existed, the passion supplanted by obsession, transformed instantly by harsh reality into sad desperation the day of her mother's funeral when the expectation immediately ceased being a concern.

The long-awaited graduation with honours from McGill's School of Business had been yet another day unnoticed by one who should have cared. The following day his secretary had delivered the hand-written note indicating a proposed time to discuss Addison's recent acceptance into the MBA programme and the entry-level position with the firm.

If Jean-Émile was anything other than successful, he was blind to most non-business related issues. He saw nothing beyond the bottom line of each corporate division.

When issues had nothing to do with profit and loss, investments with the expectation of substantial and immediate returns on investment, he wasn't interested. He had no social life which didn't include closing a deal and had as many Canadian and Mexican politicians in his pockets as he had employees at his downtown corporate headquarters. He spoke fluent Spanish, though communicated entirely through intermediaries; he was prematurely grey at fifty-four and had survived two heart attacks. He worked eighteen-hour days, seven days a week and whatever time off he did allow himself was in the company of business associates.

His wife had died tragically five years earlier. She'd been a passenger in the car he was driving, arguing with him about Addison's future. Her final image of him was the raw rage painted on his face; his was the absolute terror on hers. Her last words were a wild and terrified scream and he buried her three days later. Addison moved out from the family home the same day following a short and inevitable confrontation during which the senior Larivière had been particularly cruel in his rebukes. Any plan Addison might have had to earn an MBA was long forgotten by the time the 747 landed in Madrid that weekend. There would be no senior managerial position, no junior vice-presidency and no future devoid of passion. Neither would there be a father who, in a constant struggle to assuage his deep guilt and dissipate his grief, worked increasingly longer hours and became generally less of a human being.

# 16

By April 07th those twenty-one months seemed more like weeks since Addison had taken her directly from the airport to the home they would share. Within a week Maria had moved all her worldly belongings from her father's home. When his door had closed behind her with a force of uncontrolled savage violence, slammed by a man who would kill on a whim, the other men in the house at the time had found something else to do or somewhere else to be. No one doubted the door would remain closed to her forever.

He would never have dared to strike her, not on her mother's grave. She knew his weakness, and that alone gave her the fleeting confidence and courage she had needed. As vulnerable as she may have seemed, she was determined. She had never loved anyone as much as Addison, including the one who had once been her father. Her life was hers to live, the beginning of their new life together and she didn't care what he or anyone thought. She never went back, never wrote to him and never sent him a gift on father's day or on any other special day. She was her father's daughter and had been taught well. Those were the times she had needed Addison the most, when lovers transformed into friends to listen without judging, to hold one another close without expectation.

Two weeks later Addison became Addison M. Larivière, MBA, and was as unemployed as Jean-Émile was furious when they met after a difficult two-year rift. No door had slammed. Such indignities were not permitted at any time at LCL, and he was no exception, though the door had slammed all the same, with equal emotion, albeit soundlessly. He would never again see the child who would have listened to him, who would have forgiven him, had he ever made the effort. Pride comes before the fall, and he would never pick himself up.

They had become self-proclaimed orphans, though they had one another and that's what mattered. They hadn't had much time for friends or evenings out. Addison made a commitment to Maria to complete the Masters within two-years and Maria immersed herself in the final two years of a Bachelor of Arts with a major in Art and a minor in Interior Design.

She had planned the special evening to perfection, for Addison, their night to celebrate, their time to be proud of one another, to kiss, hug and be lovers. The evening would be special in every way from the lingerie she had laid out to the two bottles of requisite white wine, with one held in reserve. She had spent all day preparing while in a world of her own, not to mention the tickets Addison had discovered absolutely nothing about.

# 17

The meal was fantastic, prepared and served to perfection: one of the personal gifts Maria's mother had left her in life. Addison was allowed nowhere near the kitchen and spent the day reading over the fine print of several unsolicited job offers sent by special delivery, which she would politely decline. They had spent the last two years developing a unique business plan, something they believed in and would do together. They would be unique, the best, and they were about to transition into the final phase that would make the dream come true.

The bank had eagerly agreed with them, willing to offer the most competitive terms and charge reasonable fees for all their services. Best of all, their personal funds would be safely locked up, frozen for their security, all the while earning interest that, while not exactly preferential, was practically guaranteed not to change negatively for an unknown period. The bank would also be able to audit them twice yearly, making certain the business was healthy and flourishing, at a minimal charge, naturally, which could be added to the initial loan at the outset and certainly nothing they would have to worry about later.

They had listened graciously to the Account Manager, leaving him to wonder as they stood whether they would both cancel their accounts. They decided they would, when convenient. While not wealthy, they were far from poor thanks to each of the mothers who had made substantial posthumous provisions for their children. They didn't need the bank. Soon the banks would need them.

Maria decided they should dress for dinner, very much to Addison's disappointment who was instructed in the same breath to run a deep bath and be in it by the time the oven's buzzer sounded: five minutes and counting. Addison argued uselessly that, since they would already be naked, they should stay that way for dinner: much more relaxed and cosier. That was until the buzzer broke the silence and within moments Maria came into the bathroom with sky-blue silk panties and a matching chemise draped over one hanger, white silk boxers and a matching smoking jacket with satin lapels hanging from another. Case closed.

When they climbed from the still warm water, glowing pink and tingling from the effect of the scented salts, they spread the thick fleecy towel under their feet to soak up what they let drip to the floor. They dried each other briskly and completely as though it was a cold winter's day and not the warmest April 08<sup>th</sup> on record. Then they lingered as each one watched the other dress for dinner in accordance with the preferences of the hostess. They had no reason to hurry, the evening was young and so were they.

Maria went to open the wine, an unmistakeable glow emanating from within. Her mother had taught her well. The salade Niçoisse was incomparable, complemented perfectly with her choice of a delicate dry Riesling which also accompanied the ginger broth with lemongrass that followed. The main course was baked salmon, accented with the special flavour of fresh Italian parsley and thyme to bring out the flavour of the salsa verde, slivers of golden-brown baked potatoes and a sprinkling of ground peppers. The Sauternes was more complicated in its aromas, more imposing. The pale amber liquid had been decanted, poured into fine crystal and savoured with lingering sips before Maria began clearing the table as quickly as she could.

She had instructed Addison to open the bottle of sparkling wine, change the CDs, lay out the napkins and cutlery on the area rug in the living room, and she would be there in a minute. She was nervous and excited, anxious to serve her homemade peach ice cream with homemade wafer–like white rose petals she had laboured over much of the day and the ensuing crash should have rung out loudly on the tiled floor, piercing the quiet ambiance. Instead the plate inverted, landing between her feet with a dull thud, a dull, ice cream-coated thud splashing up to her ankles. Shit and double shit. She needed to breathe, to relax, she told herself. The big moment had come and sticky ankles weren't going to spoil her surprise. They would share. What the hell.

Whereas, from Addison's perspective, sitting cross-legged on the floor and smiling up at Maria standing in her silk tap pants with high-vented sides and open chemise, she was the dessert.

"Are you going to take this, or do I stand here all night?"

"You stand there all night."

"That's not funny."

"You're beautiful, and I love you. I love seeing you this way."

"Okay, it was funny. Now take this so I can sit with you."

Addison considered the ankles for a moment, then the plate. "Where's yours?"

"Now that isn't funny. This one's mine, I dropped yours, but I'll share with you." She smirked, giving over the plate. "Sorry. I got flustered. I wanted our evening to be special."

"Every night is special with you, mi amor. Why would tonight be any different?"

"I love you. Do you believe it's been almost two years, and I feel no different than I did our first afternoon in Almería? I love you so much." She hesitated. "I have a present for you, actually, for us," the pent-up tension draining away. She lifted the edge of the carpet, feeling under the roughly woven underside for the large, glossy envelope.

"It's for both of us, Addie. We deserve. I hope you like

it."

Addison opened the envelope, slowly pulling out the brochures, round trip tickets, vouchers, and Customs papers for the two-week trip in Ixtapa - Zihuatanejo Maria had planned.

# 18

Two empty bottles lay on their sides in the sink, wedged tightly between thinly crusted plates and smudged glasses that weren't as elegant as the night before. The sparkling wine was half full, standing upright on the plush living room carpet as though guarding the crumpled pile of delicate white and blue silk topping the scattered array of travel information. They had read the brochures a dozen times, as many times as Addison had kissed happy tears from Maria's glistening brown eyes. The evening could not have been more successful, and as often as they read the tempting and exotic blurbs as though the information would change, nothing had.

The long awaited vacation would be the first in two long years of studying and not doing many of the things they wanted to do together, the honeymoon they had spent so many nights talking about in bed. They flipped through the glossy brochures, first wanting to go here, before wanting to go there. They hadn't stopped planning or talking about it ad infinitum, each time adding a new element and forgetting what they had said moments before in favour of something else, like a shopping spree before they left.

Sneaking away without anyone knowing would be their elopement, their honeymoon, so why not a new wardrobe? Mexicana Airlines flight MX 881 would leave Saturday, the fourteenth, at 8:05 AM, and, with one brief equipment change at Juarez International in Mexico City, flight 1353 would arrive at 3:25 PM local time, for two beautiful and lazy sun drenched weeks no matter how often they flipped the pages.

Addison enjoyed taking the lead most times and Maria never argued. She enjoyed every moment of their lovemaking, every sensation of tenderness and intensity, her time for her to luxuriate in every embrace, every movement, every lingering touch and kiss, to delight in being a young, vital woman. She had made the day and the evening special for them, and the moment had come for Addison to reciprocate. Her chemise fell open as she rolled onto her back, her arms outstretched and her hips raised, waiting for the first touch, the first whisper. What had begun on the living room floor had carried over to the chic and very modern bedroom they had designed together with love and total relaxation being the sole criterion. The silk chemise and smoking jacket hadn't casually fallen to the floor; they'd landed there, blindly cast off with flailing arms and legs in a struggle for the cover of satin sheets and the warmth of each other's bare skin.

Addison had become an expert lover who was never eager, never anxious, whose fingertips glided over Maria's soft and supple skin which was always smooth and flushed with anticipation. Maria lay back, sensitive to each stroke, mentally tracing the probing fingers she knew were searching out specific nerve endings to titillate and arouse her, making her yield to the warmth of each fingertip exploring the epicentres of each erogenous zone that would both weaken and strengthen her.

# 19

As Maria and Addison reluctantly fell into a peaceful sleep wrapped in the warmth of each other's arms, the sensation of whispered kisses giving way to the sweetness of each other's imperceptible breathing, the sun began setting in Ixtapa - Zihuatanejo.

Ixtapa was modern, more American than Mexican, created by Mexicans to meet the growing needs of the jet set of the seventies and eighties and the increasing numbers of international travellers needing change from the overcrowded beaches of Europe. The town had also quickly become a premier destination for Spring Breakers and by early April the party was far from over.

A short taxi ride across the mountain was Zihuatanejo, a step back into history: a quaint and relaxed fishing village thriving on tourism while preserving a culture. The red brick streets were narrow, lined with low-rise buildings painted white with stucco and decorated with brightly coloured doors and windows, and the streets would soon be lighted as much by the muted brilliance of a silvery moon as by the weak amber glow of sporadically placed lampposts.

Most people learned about the village while en route to Ixtapa, a place for a day at a different beach, a departure point for deep-sea fishing, or for the more sedate who wanted quiet evenings alone to sit and watch the locals come and go along the plaza. Zihuatanejo was not a place for four bachelors who had paid the single's supplement for privacy. That was Ixtapa's internationally accepted rasion d'être, and that's where they were going. They arrived moments before what they thought should be the dinner hour, to discover dinner wouldn't be for another two hours that would better spent at the pool checking out female arrivals who would be as tell-tale pale as they were. By the time the pool closed, dinner had been reduced to sloppy burritos filled with beans and meat which they gorged on at the patio while still wearing flip-flops, metre-long cargo trunks dripping through the iron-mesh chairs and wet hotel towels draped over their fronts from around their necks. They were on schedule, estimating they had ninety minutes before long lines would begin to form at the club that opened at ten every night to those eager to dance, drink, get raunchy and meet someone to spend the week with on a first-come, first-serve basis.

Saturday was the first night in Ixtapa, the busiest night at La Chica Descarada where the poolside bartender had insisted they go first, assuring them they would not be disappointed and drinks began flowing as soon as the wrought iron latch flipped upwards and the single door opened to an eager crowd, starting with an endless row of complimentary tequila shooters. The nightlong process had begun, and to the victor would go the spoils. Strategic offences would be formulated by the strong and defences would be dropped by the weak. Ladies' night, two-for-one, have another, although ladies' night wasn't actually for the ladies. Men's night was more apropos and the price was right. They fit in perfectly. Have another, my treat. Why not?

La Chica Descarada was the place to be, as all arrivals to the resort area quickly discovered, and she was living up to her reputation of being naughty to the point of lewdness and open sensuality. The club also advertised a menu of not-too-spicy American-flavoured Mexican food prepared in a way that no one's Mexican mamá used to make it. Eating food at La Chica was a declaration of defeat ordered by would-be-lovers-of-a-Latina who had come too late or should not have come at all, believing that eating disguised the fact he was alone. The plan had failed. He had failed, and would wake up alone, again, so most did their best not to order.

The three girls came in at 10:30, raising the hopes of every man who hadn't yet connected, who didn't want to order from the menu. Some tried in vain to make eye contact, while three others succeeded. The girls were young, and if they made it past the door they were either legal or convincing. They wore identical tight-fitting white cami tops with micro-fibre skirts that held absolutely no secrets, each one with a differently coloured silk string they allowed to ride over exposed hips, guiding the eyes of prospective champions for the evening to bare midriffs and heightened expectation. By the time the waiter returned with the drinks they had been introduced and Bret had reached into his pockets for thickest wad of bills he could fit into his silver clip before leaving the hotel. The girls hit pay dirt. They would enjoy another free night, maybe another free week.

At first the girls danced together as the men drew lots by colour, a single sacrifice agreed to for the greater good. By midnight they had danced together as couples, according to the draw, each time becoming bolder in how they held the women and how the women reciprocated. By 1:00 AM occasional lingering kisses on the neck became occasional gropes under their skirts as they danced. By 2:00 AM the dancing stopped and the girls didn't mind their skirts were being pushed up past their hips as they sat on low-back bar stools, letting their new acquaintances get to know them better. The waiters had seen everything before. Everyone was at La Chica for the same reason and by 3:00 the girls made a final unsteady trip to the ladies' room, hardly bothering to adjust their skirts. They had come prepared to party and wanted to make sure they hadn't left anything in their room that might spoil the evening.

The men had one-for-the-road waiting for them when they got back and wasted no time repositioning a free hand under the skirt of their assigned colour, not needing to probe, exchanging approving nods. They would leave in thirty minutes. If the girls were ready to party then, within an hour they'd be begging for it.

Chad had long since gone. By midnight he had drunk one tequila sunrise too many and had managed a tasteless burrito he didn't want. He managed to stumble his way to his room where he sat alone on the balcony to temporarily enjoy more tequilas.

# 20

They had gone through the four years together, Bret and Shane more so because their futures had been secured. Thurston and Chad weren't part of the total picture. They weren't family, as much as they were good to have around, especially Chad. He needed friends and didn't mind being a chump or go-boy as long as he was part of it.

All those late study nights had come to an end, deprived of their rights as young virile men, watched over by parents, graded by professors and judged by both as to where they would fit into the final scheme of things. They were no longer boys. They were men living the good and exotic life in Mexico, sent by their parents as a token of appreciation for grades well-earned, all expenses paid. They were men, and men they would be. Chad poured himself another tequila.

At graduation Bret had received W & P shares valued at fifty thousand dollars and a gold Rolex. Shane received a pink gold Cartier timepiece and a share in the fathers' business equal to Bret's. And both graduates were given keys to new BMW convertibles. Thurston's parents had managed to scrape together the money for a well-deserved vacation for their only son, even though they would stay home another year and not travel. There was no watch. All they had to share was each other. Though Chad had been the most creative, knowing his parents wouldn't help him. Four years earlier he had refused an offer to join the family home building business, eventually to take over and keep it in the family. His father had taken the answer as a personal affront and from that point Chad was on his own, barely scraped through with various evening and weekend jobs and never anything left for a frivolous vacation with the guys. He had never joined them for Spring Break, work had always come first. This year was different. He would be with them and not have to settle for viewing digital photos of naked girls at the beach or their nightly conquests stretched out naked and drunk on their beds.

He had managed somehow to take out a bank loan based on the job offer from The Wilmingtons and Pendleton. He had asked Frederick Wilmington not to mention the bank's verification of his credit information to Bret or Shane, and he hadn't. Chad didn't care about watches; he didn't care about company shares. He did care about being accepted and being as good as those who didn't care about him.

# 21

Sunday afternoon the girls awoke one by one. Samantha was the first to open her eyes and lay quietly for a moment, gradually aware of all the sensations assailing her. She was alone on her bed while her two friends shared the other double. She turned her head towards them, her aching body resisting the need to move. They were both lying naked on their backs, over the covers, one with her legs together, the other with hers wide open and Samantha felt an urge to throw up. She wanted to stand, to go to them, barely able to ease her legs over the side of the bed before her entire body went rigid, crying out with from the sudden and unfamiliar searing pain. She keeled over, violently, gasping for breath, with hardly enough time to twist her limp body around before vomiting noisily, clutching uselessly at her constricted stomach and squeezing her eyes closed. When they opened they were wide with disbelief. She hadn't seen the patch of dark red until then. She covered it over with more sudden vomit and fell to her knees where she stayed.

The other two girls hadn't budged and Samantha had no idea how much time had elapsed. She stripped the bed, trading what was left of her dignity for the cost of a sheet. She didn't think to dress, easing herself slowly onto the other bed, gently straddling one of Cindy's legs and one of Pam's. They had seen each other naked before, pulling at each other's towels for fun and giggling, but seeing her friends so horribly degraded defied all her sensibilities. The sheet was stained, the dampness emitting a pungent odour that made her clutch her throat. The girls' labia were as red and swollen as hers and she could see blood where Cindy's bruised thighs came together. She leaned forward, stroking their faces, wanting to wake them as gently as she could, and burst into tears.

Pam opened her eyes first, groggily, unaware of her pain though instinctively terrified at seeing Samantha's bruised and discoloured face so close to her, her naked body convulsing to a spastic rhythm. Pam raised her arms, wrapping them around Samantha, pulling her friend between her and Cindy, hugging her closely. She didn't have to be told. The pain began its travels and they lay quietly, wiping coloured tears from each other's face, kissing each other tenderly. When they noticed Cindy, her eyes were narrow slits, the pillow under her head stained deep blue with mascara, her lips quivering uncontrollably, her body trembling from the cruel assault of overpowering sensations. She rolled onto her side, reaching out to them. The men had done the worst to Cindy, the girl in green. Her panties were missing, nowhere to be seen. So were Samantha's red thongs and Pam's black: trophies of victory. All that remained was carnage.

As Pam lay on her side, holding Cindy in her arms, softly stroking her hair and the length of her back to comfort her, Samantha explored between her bruised buttocks as gently as she could, barely able to contain herself when she saw the coagulated blood. Next she examined Pam before reclining for her own intimate audit and none of the three could remember a single moment.

They knew where they had gone the night before, with no memory of leaving, or with whom. Worst of all: someone knew them, where they were staying and what they had done. They had gone into the bar as girls, barely nineteen, naively catapulted to an age beyond their comprehension. They bathed and cared for each other in a way they hadn't thought possible, huddling together to cry and comfort each other. Spring Break was over, so was their time of innocence.

## 22

They had been at the resort for one blurred week of separate and unconscious twenty-four hour increments and didn't know or care the girls had cut short their vacation to return home, though the panties hadn't been discarded. They remained as precious silk trophies of the week's conquests and would be tallied and boasted about at the end of another week.

The mornings were miserable experiences which included crushing head pain accompanied by nausea to the exclusion of breakfast. Afternoons were spent slouching over the pool bar and sitting at the beach with phone cameras aimed at the closest and barest of the female tourists. Volleyball was out of the question, so was water polo. They hadn't thought it wise to go back to La Chica the next night or Monday, and by Tuesday all the worthwhile hook-ups had been made at the different hotels. What were left were the ugly daughters and sisters who couldn't be drunk pretty by 6:00 AM and the four decided unanimously that deficiency didn't matter. No problema. Everyone needed love, even the ugly sisters, they had laughingly agreed, subject to a case by case evaluation. Best of all, there would be no need to deplete the sacrosanct supply of Rohypnol required for another entertaining Saturday night.

They hadn't seen the three girls again, which was both fine and desirable. Each one had made a deliberate point to stay far away from their small part of the three-kilometre beach. They couldn't remember whether they had known the girls' names, not that they dwelled on the issue, referring to them by colour, leaving out none of the many details when bragging about the three-in-one conquests to Chad. Bret had been the first to finish with Green, lying by her side to watch Shane on Red and Thurston on Black.

Green was very good, he recounted, thinking she must be twenty-one until he checked her purse to discover she was nineteen. So were Red and Black.

Then he lay beside Red. She was curled onto her side, tempting, naked and vulnerable. He began fondling her breasts, first one, then the other, before pinching her nipples hard in search of a reaction. He smiled to himself. The timing was perfect. He rolled her slowly onto her front, pushing apart her legs to position himself strategically behind her. Pulling her up like a feather he was fascinated and instantly aroused at seeing the perfect curves of her fully tanned buttocks opening naturally to the glistening wetness he would use to make the first thrust easier and less painful for him. The sensation was better than he remembered, and when he finished with her, thrusting hard one last time before easing backward, he noticed Shane and Thurston had turned over Green and Black.

For each of them the night was young, and so was the week.

# 23

April 14<sup>th</sup>, Saturday, was changeover day. Friday's Fiesta Night had come and gone and the tanned and tired were ready to go home, leaving behind new or dark secrets, or carrying with them inflated stories of male prowess or feminine guile. All this as yet another throng of pasty-white and beleaguered travellers arrived to struggle with confused heaps of luggage, misunderstood questions, unintelligible answers, passports, room changes, obligatory tips and a severely diluted tequila punch. It was also a safe time to be seen at La Chica Descarada, to pick and choose the best of a new crop.

Chad returned to the club Tuesday and Wednesday, though, despite being full both nights, the club wasn't as active as the weekend. He met during his late meal on Wednesday, when the waiter thought to put their plates together, discreetly encouraging him to move over, hombre a hombre. By the time they had left together he believed the evening was going his way. She was paying attention to him and let him pay for the dinner and drinks. However the hour was late. She thanked him with a hug and said she would love to join him for cocktails the next evening. And she did.

They dined together on the popular Paseo de Ixtapa with its endless selection of fine restaurants, and more importantly, away from Bret, Shane and Thurston. They talked and danced all evening and into the morning. She let him fondle her discreetly. She was a tease. He didn't care. Things were going his way. He could do it. He could do her. She would spend the evening with him, and the next. She would have sooner, she admitted, were she not been leaving on Saturday and afraid to reconcile herself to any degree of physical intimacy for such a short term. She was in her final year of a B. Ed, she wanted to teach primary in a town somewhere near Seattle and she wasn't accustomed to attractive men pursuing her.

His time had come. His night had come. Yes! Go Chad, go! You the man, you the hombre! But when he came come back to her from the men's room, she was gone. At first he naturally thought to wait, assuming she had gone to do what women do before giving themselves over to the male need, but his thinking began to change with the waiter's increasingly sympathetic expression and finally with his last drink that was on the house.

By the time Chad managed his way back to his room he could barely read 3:00 AM on the clock and the full glass of tequila practically cleared the vast courtyard-shaped compound. There was no way he would endure another day of taunting from the three of them, the three pricks. No way, no more, not ever again. He poured one drink, downing it, then a second in a fresh glass before throwing the covers to the floor and jumping several times on the bed to ruffle the sheets as convincingly as possible. Then he kneeled unsteadily, awkwardly positioning himself over the pillows with one hand on the mattress for balance as he made himself as erect as he could. She was right there in front of him, stretched out and naked, ready to take him in with her legs open and her hips rotating in the pungent air between them as inaccurate thick spurts of his ejaculate shot out into the centre of the bed.

Before having a few more serious drinks and passing out naked, he washed away the spermicidal powder from two new condoms, filling them with more of his sticky white fluid. He threw one onto the floor, the other dead-centre of his first splatter that had begun to dry. Then he did her again and would still be dead to the world by the time they came knocking on his door, as unconcerned as they would be curious. The four rooms adjoined and convincing one of the timid señoritas in housekeeping to open the door would be an easy matter. Then they'd see for themselves that he was as good as any one of them.

## 24

The woman had actually left early Friday morning, he'd discovered later, and had probably gone straight from the bar to pack and leave for the airport. By Saturday morning he had relegated her to the foggy background of his memory. More to the point, he continued wallowing in the praise and macho recognition of his penis-guided peers who had charged expectantly into his room early that afternoon. They had witnessed firsthand the aftermath of his heated and sex-filled evening as he had meticulously planned despite his drunken stupor, and the most violent hangover he had ever experienced. Yes, he told them, she was insatiable and, yes, she had let him do things to her that he had never done before. Yes, they would keep in touch. Yes, she was everything he had hoped for. And yes, he was up for it again.

He had discarded the condoms along with her fake phone number. Saturday night was always a good time to start over and the guys were waiting. He was set to go again and this time he was confident he wouldn't leave alone.

# 25

The fifty-five minute flight from Mexico City seemed like as many hours before the M87 landed at precisely 3:25 local time. The cabin doors remained closed for long moments while the anonymous uniforms behind the steel-reinforced cockpit door completed and signed off on their final cross check, immune to the familiar urgency mounting in the cabin behind them,

When the cabin doors finally did open, the cool air onboard was expelled by the incoming surge of heavier humidity. Each passenger instantly tore away even the lightest sweater or reached for zippers that would convert out-dated cargo pants into equally unfashionable makeshift shorts, each person blinded as they filed out onto the first of several steep steps leading to the black heat of the reflective tarmac. The yellow and white lines apparently intended by the FAA to confuse and intimidate the novice traveller who invariably followed the first courageous passenger who demonstrated sufficient confidence to distance him or herself from the horde.

Addison followed the white line, Maria trailing behind, giggling as she jogged to catch up until they both slowed for the obligatory photo shoot as one faceless brown hand turned upward telling them to stop and the other thumbed the cable release. Then their smiling faces were greeted with an expressionless authority framed by a Plexiglas shield as their passports were taken, pulled into the cubicle, verified, stamped and pushed out with an indifference that comes with routine boredom.

Addison's light flashed green, Maria's red flashing light signalled her to the smiling Mexican Customs agent who was surprised she could actually speak his language. The inspection was cursory: a few friendly words of welcome and wishes for an enjoyable vacation. He'd seen enough tourists pass through his inspection station to distinguish the good from the bad, the ones who had come to party and those who had come to enjoy.

The bus ride was uneventful, especially for those who had chosen to wait or hadn't worked effectively during the flight to secure a worthwhile female for the duration. The same held true from a fundamentally different perspective: a good-looking, dependable source of a week-long ladies' night, a benefactor, a sucker or any man who gave his penis precedence over his wallet.

Their stop was the last and the bus had emptied completely by the time they arrived at the third hotel. Spring Break was in full swing, though Maria had worked with her travel agent to find a five-star property which was a step above the others. The resort was beyond the reach of average students or their making-do parents, boasting individual attention and a private, luxurious full-service spa.

# 26

The fourth-floor room at El Presidente was spacious, with a wide semi-private balcony affording a spectacular view of the sparkling Ixtapa bay. There would be time to enjoy the view. First on the agenda were the pool, a few exotic drinks and the beginning of a great tan.

Clothes so neatly placed into the suitcases were thrown onto the spare bed. Separate piles of bikinis were located, grabbed in a single small hand and spread across the other bed for final selection, deciding they would wait to see how many other women were topless before becoming anyone's centre of attention. They knew the European flavour was acceptable, but Spring Break ruled and they didn't want to be mistaken for something or someone they were not. Also, it would be a reminder they weren't alone. Addison had a habit of occasionally forgetting and being beside Maria sans top would be agonizingly tempting.

At the pool Addison's bright yellow body-hugging micro-fibre import was the attention-getter for men and women alike, until Maria dropped her cover-up by the chaise-longue and stood like a Romanesque statuette with her arms outstretched, waiting for Addison to do her back. Her one-piece slingshot bikini scarcely covered the bare essentials in the front and nothing at all in the back, the metallic-gold fabric radiating light from the two narrow and strategic strips of skin it did cover.

She had been right in what to expect. Addison immediately pulled out the digital and began composing the first of several hundred shots they were certain would not be enough. She liked the way Addison gazed at her. Naked or dressed, the fascination never waned. She dropped into the pool, disappearing feet-first, and when she reappeared Addison was by her side with arms wrapping around her and carrying her back down. The kiss was ruined with laughter and water rushing up into their noses.

"I love it, mi amor. It's so tiny. You're naked!" she whispered more loudly than she had intended.

"I'm glad, Addie, because yours are metallic red and white and I have another, a blue one. I can't wait to see you in them."

"You're evil." They kissed, quickly, "and I love it. You've brought me to heaven, mi amor, my darling. Those guys at the bar will think they've died and gone to heaven, too."

"You're a tease, Addie. I don't care about them." She paused. "And neither do you."

"No, darling, not a tease… pragmatic." She closed her hands around Maria's strategic straps "Two beautiful women together, in these. Are you kidding? That's not teasing, mi armor, that's death-by-wife. Now you know what's meant by "to die for."

"You're incorrigible."

"Hey, you're the one who brought them, and we're going to wear them." A bright row of white teeth shone through Addison's deep red lip gloss. "It must be the drinks. I'm sorry. You're right. I am incorrigible. Let's go to the pool bar for another."

She still had her hands around Maria's straps at the waterline, her temptation to push them away inscribed across her face.

"Not a chance, no way, pretty girl, and if you haven't realized, the sun's almost gone. So, let's get out of here."

She turned, raising an arm to the stainless steel ladder, pulling one foot slowly past the other. Addison was mesmerised, and when she glanced toward the bar she realized she wasn't the only one: pigs. They'd been lost in the moment. Shadows were long, the sun resting over the hills of Isla Ixtapa. Most of the men who had spent the day at the bar pool had lingered for one, two or three more, avoiding the status quo waiting for each of them under hotel towels and baseball caps, and they were glad they had. They had maintained their dumbstruck and dedicated poolside scans, zeroing in through duty-free dark or silver-coated glasses and thinking the scantily clad women in their field of vision believed otherwise.

The German and French women were topless, the Spanish-speaking were backless in thongs or t-back strings, the rest were easily identified as American or Canadian. The heavier fabrics of drab or faded suits offered the more conservative women built-in belly-reducing panels or modesty skirts that could never conceal the ravages of time or an excessive proclivity for junk food. European women wore simple or elaborate sheer cover-ups of silk or satin, the others wore damp, rough towels used throughout the day to cover hot vinyl cushions. Europeans wore chic turbans decorated with silver or gold broaches, some inlaid with colourful stones, some not. The others wore inexpensive baseball caps facing backwards, decorated with meaningless slogans translating figuratively into "it's not my fault", or, "close your eyes and try me."

Later, at dinner, the Europeans would be perfectly tanned, quintessentially European in long silk skirts and silk blouses, short cotton skirts with form-fitting bra top camis, heeled sandals or stilettos. The others would arrive for dinner in flip flops, their only make-up the narrow white scars crossing blister-red foreheads. Wider white scars would travel over thick and rounded shoulders, made purple and blotchy by the sun and their private white abysses beyond would be too loosely cloaked by white cotton moo-moos printed with circa '70s starbursts. The ones from small towns would opt for drab-coloured, multi-wash tee-shirts that might as well read: Fat Fish Are Juicier, or Seeking Single White Blind Man.

Addison and Maria chose the Spanish quarter to the delight of the barstool adjudicators who all belonged to the other camp, and who, for some reason, weren't facing in the direction of their own women. The girls were in plain view, yeah, baby, without the need for anyone to leave a sacred barstool for a gratuitous trip to the john. Life was good.

# 27

Pilar and Ercilia had been at the resort for a fantastic week alone and weren't eager for the second week that would go by as quickly. They had stayed to themselves because they spoke only Spanish and didn't want to spend time with people they had gone on vacation to get away from. But they hadn't come not to meet other people. After all, Pilar had explained to exhaustion, Ercilia's: Wasn't Heraclites the one who taught us that change is the fundamental nature of reality? And didn't that mean meeting other women who weren't like them? As often as possible, Ercilia tried to ignore the philosophical side of her lover, especially now.

The cute redhead certainly could not be American. She couldn't be Ercilia thought. No one seeing her in that bikini would believe she was anything but Latina, though her blonde friend might be and neither woman saw the need to peer through the dark glasses each wore as a headband. Subterfuge was a man thing. Women had an inherent right to stare openly and talk with their lips visibly moving. Any real woman would know and accept that, and they listened intently as the two came closer.

"They're watching us, mi amor. What language do you want to speak?"

"Italian," Maria answered.

Addison smacked her bare buttocks. "Bitch."

"Cow," was the reply to another, louder smack as they passed the two tanned Latinas, smiling and waving discreetly, Addison speaking Spanish, Maria speaking French.

Pilar reclined after the girls passed them by. The one who acknowledged Ercilia spoke gibberish. The other was absolutely gorgeous in yellow and had looked straight at her while wishing her a fun evening. Maybe the evening would be fun. She loved being with Ercilia, but why wouldn't they meet someone new? The four women were the same age, give or take a year or two and, waiting as long as she thought proper, without being overly suggestive or dissuasive, Pilar turned to Ercilia who was eyeing Maria and took her hand.

"She's stunning, Pi. I have to ask her where she bought her outstanding bikini." She took her friend's hand. "Let's try to meet them. They seem very nice."

"Sí, cariño, quizá sí. Tienes razón," she paused, "y, de veras, quisiera verte en este clase de biquini." They held hands. "Quizá esta noche, veremos. Hay una razón para todo, ¿no es verdad?"

Pilar gazed across to Addison who had settled herself into a chaise-longue, exchanging a casual glance before Addison lay back easily and took Maria's hand in her own, setting the tone. All four women closed their eyes, moving their lips and toes to the up-beat salsa rhythm of La Camisa Negra.

# 28

Pilar thought before dinner, Ercilia said most likely after. Maria and Addison agreed most likely for dessert on the terrace, though what Addison really wanted to know was where Maria had hidden her slingshots. Not thinking she would have to wrestle her for them.

Saturday dinner was buffet-style with open seating due the hectic ebb and flow of weekend human tsunamis, complete with Mariachis and vendors selling the best and most uniquely crafted bracelet, necklace, ring or blanket at the best possible price. No kidding, lady. There were also quintessential twenty-centimetre cigars for any man who could claim title as el cacique de su casa, most of whom would turn green at night and wake up the following morning to brush their teeth and spit out a foul-tasting brownish-yellow dentifrice foam.

The Europeans weren't the best behaved, although better behaved than the North Americans who always chose the earlier sitting. Europeans preferred the second, as did the Latinos who were the most reserved, the most polite, the least demanding. A question of lifestyle: the Europeans and Latinos had one. For them, eating was a pleasant event, a time for meeting and talking, while for the non-linguist others eating was a question of being first in line and assuming the louder they spoke the more all the foreigners would understand English.

By the time Addison and Maria arrived for the second sitting, fewer people meant less talk, a corresponding reduction of shuffling feet and the subliminal noise of empty plates being filled beyond maximum capacities. The Mariachis were more inclined towards romantic ballads by then, which suited Addison's dreamy mood. When she reached to cover Maria's hand, the Euros ignored her and the few Americans who arrived too late for the first sitting couldn't stop staring or gossiping about them as the two lovers relished the moment.

The two Mexicans had also gone to the second sitting, although earlier. Pilar had approached the archipelago of tropical delicacies from one side, Ercilia with plate in-hand from the other, each one adept at avoiding the starving masses whose sole objective was to eat as much of the limitless food supply as possible. As for the Germans, the girls had concluded the first night; they must never have tasted bread. What else could explain the unabashed single-mindedness to devour so much of it, besides fearing they might never taste any again?

Much to the discreet amusement of the staff, the Germans saw nothing wrong in creating personalized and unstable mountains of delectable baked goods on precariously small plates, leaving behind unfinished puzzles of half-pulled, half-chewed crusty remains strewn across beds of crumbs on white linen.

# 29

Ercilia had been right, though Maria half expected to see them when Addison followed her onto the canopy-covered terrace. The scoop of Häagen Dazs she had put on her dessert plate had become a succulent rich sauce spreading around the single sweet tart and Addison's double scoop was much worse.

The Mariachis had moved outside to the poolside which had been commandeered by local craftsmen and vendors, their bright tables and backdrops. There was something for everybody. The more expensive and intricate pieces of jewellery were more expensive than in town, though no one cared, the less expensive pieces of costume jewellery made perfect gifts destined to one day find their way to church rummage sales.

To Maria the pleasant chaos was surreal with millions of bright flickering stars lighting a pure black sky and the pool's iridescent lighting reflecting upward to splash the animated human canvas encircling it with warm hues of green and blue. Unknowing heads turned towards uncertain heads, while heads tilting one way were answered with shrugging shoulders and heads shaking the other way with beaming faces, a flurry of movement and a friendly handshake sealing the deal. Buy from the first table or the last table. No importa, no problema. Try it, you'll like it. I made it for you, lady.

"Buenas noches, señoritas, y bienvenida," he beamed, the gold rims of his upper and lower front teeth sparkling against a double ridge of pearly white that was all the whiter against his sun-baked skin, giving him the appearance of years he didn't need and probably didn't want.

Follow the code, Addison had prompted: walk slowly, appear disinterested and when in Rome don't do as the

Romans do, or in this case, cual es el rey, tal la grey, o no. Above all, don't get into a conversation. And soon Addison joined the ranks of shaking heads, shaking hers at Maria and wondering why she was fully immersed in conversation with her next best friend who had much of Moctezuma's past wealth wedged between most of his teeth. He was the father and the owner of the atelier who had learned his trade of carving intricate features into figurines from his father, using mostly bone and stone he would first shape and polish. His father had adopted carving as a hobby, his single escape from a Mexican jail where he'd been sent for doing something not so bad, señorita. He was a bandito, lady, but nothing so bad.

Maria's hand touched the Five Senses, Los Cinco Sentidos, his creation from the heart, which had taken him weeks to complete, and Addison thought he would take as long to explain the intricate details. She leaned forward, whispering as she moved a hand across the small of Maria's back. She smiled at the man, paid him, and left to put the artwork in their room.

Addison went to the bar that was full to capacity, a constant low drone emanating from the crowd of patrons made weary by sun or travel, yet unwilling to surrender precious vacation time to meaningless sleep. They could sleep at home for free and, though Addison wasn't the first at the stand-up bar, she was the next one served. Men were such obvious sluts, she thought. What they mistook for modern-day gentility, she understood as expectation. Sorry guys, and she walked away after pushing a few pesos to the inside edge of the counter where they were quickly retrieved.

They turned in unison. Not a man was left facing the bar, leaving the barman trying to see past an uneven wall of backs and pates. Tall, short, thick or thin, bald, thinning or thankful, the thought process was singular and historically unique to the male of the specie, common to the herd of male sluts. Addison was wearing a ruffled off-the-shoulder baby doll dress, flaring out from the cinched waist in narrow pleats that danced mischievously and teasingly around her bare thighs. She was spectacular, every man in the bar activating his hormone-driven imagination in response to the male need to visualize the unknown. Maria would never find her, Addison first thinking to catch up to her with the Chardonnays.

"Me llamo Pilar, señorita," the gentle hand warmed Addison's shoulder until she turned, and then a while longer. "¿Dónde está tu amiga? ¿Ella no está contigo esta noche?"

"Sí, claro, está aquí Pilar." Addison smiled to herself, "y me llamo Addison."

"Adishone," Pilar tried, seeing Addison's real smile. "No, importa," she laughed, "siempre podré practicar, ¿no es verdad?"

"Maybe a little, but it's a very easy name, if not as pretty as Pilar." She paused. "And where is your friend?"

"Ercilia is over in the corner, waiting for us, if you want to join us."

"I would love to, Pilar. So would Maria."

"And Maria is Spanish, no?"

"No, she's Italian-Canadian."

"No importa, Adishone," and she took Addison by the hand.

# 30

By the time Maria arrived at the bar the three girls were talking as though they had been fast friends for years. Pilar and Ercilia lived in Mexico City where they shared a small apartment. They were both twenty-five and had been a couple for seven years. Their mothers couldn't understand the relationship, the fathers wouldn't understand, their brothers were embarrassed and their brothers' friends thought they were a turn-on. When one of them once asked Pilar what it was like to sleep with a woman, Pilar had answered by asking why he didn't know.

They had moved in together when they had both turned twenty-one, working at various part-time jobs until they completed their schooling. They worked as full-time physiotherapists in sports medicine and their next trip would be to Spain. And where did Maria get that gorgeous bikini?

By 11:30 most guests had left the hotel bar and the long queue at La Chica Descarada had disappeared. Pilar and Ercilia hadn't wanted to go alone, admitting to a certain curiosity. All four women were accustomed to turning heads, instantly becoming the centre of attention when they walked arm in arm into La Chica. Latinos and Euros were accustomed to women openly showing each other affection, not so the Americans who were intrigued, not to mention intimidated by a quartet of beautiful women, and none but the most self-assured or self-infatuated tried their best, failing miserably. After the third disappointment, the other would-be contenders, who had been rating the competition as well as the women, understood the message.

Maria got up first, pulling Ercilia with her, leaving the other two behind to discuss life. Ercilia was in a satin crop top and matching mini. Her T-strap pumps were part of her and Maria wore a short flyaway Marrakech dress with sling back stilettos. They might have been sisters. Even the other women in the bar found it hard not to watch them flirt with each other and tease everyone else. Addison didn't care. She enjoyed seeing Maria having a good time. Neither did Pilar, who knew what Ercilia was going to do before she knew herself.

When Addison did get up, Pilar joined her, after which no one could tell who was dancing with whom in a flurry of young bare legs and arms, the fortunate few catching occasional glimpses of something more. One amongst them deciding he must have the girl he'd been waiting for. Then suddenly Saturday night was Sunday morning, the dance floor a stage for a few real couples or those who had hooked-up, dancing to entertain the losers.

Slowly, the bar began to empty. The sad and lonely leaving first, tired couples trickling out behind them, the most energetic staying as long as they could before surrendering to the end of a long day, or to the beginning of another. Finally one man was left sitting at the bar and the staff paid him no attention. He was different from the other men who had spent the evening alone, staring at the four girls, or the friends who had been with him earlier. On the outside he was nondescript at best: ordinary and unremarkable. On the inside he was frustrated, envious and needing desperately to prove himself.

He hoped as he watched them leave that they wouldn't take a taxi to wherever they were going next, which he hoped was another bar, and staying well behind them required concentrated effort. With each step towards the hotel his disappointment grew as he imagined himself with the blonde. He fantasized ripping away her panties, seeing her naked, probing every centimetre of her body, lying on top of her, seeing her squirm beneath him with passion as she strained not to scream with pleasure. He could hear her.

She was whispering his name, demanding more of him.

He had been there an entire week and the second Saturday had passed him by as quickly as the first. His so-called friends had ignored him all evening, which would change. He was as good as they were any day, and he'd show them. He had graduated with the best grades, he'd written the most creative papers and the senior partners of The Wilmingtons & Pendleton had invited him to join the firm. Not because he was family, because he was good, at the top of his class. That's why they mocked and teased him. They knew how good he was and they resented the daddies thinking more of his talent than they ever would of their sons'.

Before leaving the bar they had laughed at the girls, calling them dykes, lesbian bitches. He let them talk, knowing better. They weren't lesbians. They were having fun together without men who would use them for a night and forget them. And he knew where they were staying.

# 31

That second Saturday was as productive as the first for Bret, Shane and Thurston. The three girls who had left the bar with them were the embodiment of what any young and eager male animal would envision as the perfect female. They were young, attractive with critical body parts well-proportioned, and they were drunk.

They were women. They had talked so often about being real women with real men, and like, it was finally happening. The men were so totally charming and had paid for all the drinks, and were like really interested in them, listening to like absolutely everything they had said. They didn't even talk like the boys at home, either. They were totally mature, and like they never used the F word, and they didn't touch them the same way, either. They were like so totally different, so totally tingly everywhere, especially there.

They didn't mind that the three older men spent the entire evening slowly becoming more familiar with their most intimate parts, fondling them under loose blouses and easing unrelenting hands between their legs they parted exactly the way older women would. They were like really super guys and the evening proved a good investment in time for the three partners in the architectural firm, or whatever.

Laurie was the oldest by a matter of days or weeks, and had spent the evening completely in awe of what the senior partner in the firm had accomplished in his short career, letting no one get in his way, and all he planned to accomplish. She had jerked and spilled her Bud Light across the bar, gasping for breath as Bret had brought his hand from under her skirt, pleased with the response he'd been slowly working towards for several minutes. He wasn't at all like the boys she had known in the past. He was a real man. And what they were sharing wasn't just flirting, she knew. He like really wanted her, the way a man wants a woman, as much as she wanted him, she guessed.

But all that changed by late Sunday morning when the three girls who had hours earlier fallen into the well-being of mindless stupors as women began groggily awakening to a new reality. They had regressed to once again being young and vulnerable girls who wanted their mommies and daddies.

Laurie took a while to understand she was in the same bed as Erin, that both girls were naked and lying on their backs on top of the dishevelled sheets. Erin had bruises on her breasts and hips, and bright red smudges across her mouth and nipples. Her hair was matted, still damp with sweat, her face a horrible mask of dark colours. She touched her face, bringing her hand away smudged with the same black and green smearing Erin's face. She shook her friend by the shoulder, with none of the care or warmth Samantha had taken a week earlier with Pam and Cindy. She was enveloped in numbness, not the euphoria allowing Erin to wake as slowly as she did. When Erin did finally open her eyes to the frightened face beside her, she jerked sideways so abruptly she fell from the bed, crashing her head into the side table and squealing noisily.

She lay there, not moving, not aware at first Laurie was open-mouthed with shock and staring between her legs that were wide apart. At first hesitant, Laurie searched hesitantly between her own legs. Erin did the same, both girls flinching disbelievingly from their delicate touches. They burst into noisy sobbing, each one recoiling instantly into the solace of a private world for long moments, curled into a tight ball and sobbing, dwelling on secret fears and the selfishness of their predicament. Deidre was far from their thoughts, neither girl showing tenderness or concern for one another, only a self-centred fear of the unknown and the uncertainty of the very immediate future.

Erin pulled herself from the floor onto the other bed, shivering and aching as much from her fall and the cold, unforgiving floor tiles as from whatever had happened to her. Her body ached everywhere and she put her quivering hands between her thighs for the softness and warmth. The affect was soothing and she felt no shame that Laurie, who was still huddled into herself, was looking across to her with expressionless and red-stained eyes.

Why did she hurt so much, everywhere? She had never felt that way before. She saw the bruises around Laurie's lips that were smeared with her own deeper shade of cherry blossom gloss. She touched her lips, wincing. God, what had they done? The burning pain was getting worse, but she was afraid to touch herself there. She never had before, not even out of curiosity, no one had. What was his name? She forced herself to remember, her head reverberating from the after-effects of too many straight tequilas and beer chasers. There were three of them, she remembered that much, and Laurie had been with the most outgoing. They were businessmen, engineers or something, and successful, the best at whatever they did. But what were their names?

Then she heard strained and muffled sobbing coming from the outside, through open doors. Erin eased herself to her feet slowly, using her mattress for support, each movement increasingly agonizing. Laurie raised herself painfully onto an elbow, her ribs screaming out to be careful, each girl moving awkwardly and unabashedly to the outside balcony, sinking clumsily around the friend they had forgotten with no sense they were still exposed and vulnerable.

Deidre had opened her eyes to blinding daylight seeing the blurred upper floors of the complex across a bright blue midday sky. Her skin felt super-heated and her front had begun colouring to a deep red that would later blossom to dark crimson. Her mouth had never been so dry and her pursed lips had begun to crack and blister. She looked up at one girl, puzzled, then the other without moving her head. When she went to speak, she couldn't; neither could she cry because she didn't know why she should. They were naked and so was she. But why, and why were they crying?

They didn't understand how to touch her, how to talk to her. They were too young. Whatever maturity they had thought they possessed had dissolved and no trendy piece of fashion or capricious celebrity magazine would bring it back. Becoming the women they had once hoped to be would forever be lost to them and neither Laurie nor Erin possessed the strength to bring Deidre to her feet. Instead they rolled her over and guided her onto her knees so she could crawl into the room, closing their eyes to the still sticky blood.

Once in the room Erin turned to close the door, taking a moment to scan the courtyard to see if anyone had noticed them. So what? Nothing mattered now. Maybe someone had seen them through a window. Anyway, no one would care about three naked girls, except that they were naked. No one would complain or report them. No. They would wait and watch in the hope of seeing more. Besides, everyone would be at the beach or the pool and she made a mental note to remove the tiny cluster of red specks from the balcony before housekeeping came in.

The clock showed 2:00 PM, later than they thought, and, by the time Laurie and Erin finished showering, Deidre was still as they had put her on the bed, sobbing quietly. She was the youngest. Now they were of an equal age that was neither young nor old, identified by the shared date of a horrific rebirth they would never expunge. The party had gone horribly wrong. What was to have been a sexy and innocent safe-sex night with some older guys had turned into a vulgar, punishing rape, leaving what innocence remained in shreds. Anyone seeing them would not wonder what happened. Nothing like this had ever happened to them before, and no deep tan or expensive make-up would cover the bruises. Neither would any amount of talking ever remedy the scars and, perhaps worse, no amount of thinking would bring back the memories of what had been done to them or what they had done with each other and they stayed silent.

At first the steamy and harsh assault of the shower was unbearable, accentuating the sensation of the sticky film coating their bodies from the night before. The incongruity of the vile sensation against what had become a feigned youthfulness instantly made each one convulse and vomit violently, eventually retching empty gasps of foul air. They each had their turn, and with each turn came the realization they were alone. They had thought the worst was not being able to remember, not so. The newest secret they shared was the worst. In the blur of one short night they had gone from being close friends to being three self-centred girls who had begun to grow apart.

Deidre was the only one to bathe after her shower, but Laurie poured the bath and Erin helped her in without the love or compassion she needed so badly to feel. She sank back slowly, raising her feet and parting them as widely as possible to let the soothing hot water find and infuse her most intimate recesses with its curative properties. The other two girls looked on in a daze, neither one understanding her tearful murmurs, neither one able to comfort her.

They left her alone, and when she finished, before the water cooled, she climbed out cautiously, wrapping her flushed and tingling body in a fleecy towel. She padded past them silently, curling into the chaise-longue on the balcony, and when the sun touched the horizon she let the towel fall open, studying the full length of her body. She stayed as she was, gazing out to nowhere, transfixed, the others not knowing what to say or do. She had recently turned eighteen and wondered if her breasts would ever be bigger than they were. Strange, she thought, that she would think such a thing at such a time. And what did her breasts matter? Who else would ever want her body now?

It hadn't been her first experience with a guy, a man. But those other times were always at parties, after school or playing around with the coolest guys, and always quick, like the way all the in-girls did it. Everyone was doing it, so what was the big deal? She didn't know. This was different, or hadn't the guys at home learned enough? She reached for the body cream and began spreading it leisurely and liberally across her front in long, easy strokes from her head to her toes and then she stood to do her back. The gaze in her clearing eyes was distant, her movements mechanical. When she finished she loosely layered one side of the towel over the other, holding each one in place with her folded arms as she reclined with her eyes closed, comforted by the heat escaping from her sunburned skin.

Laurie and Erin decided to stay in until the second sitting for dinner, mutely stripping the beds and stacking the empty glasses and beer bottles into a corner. It's when they saw the sickening, pungent contents of the wastepaper basket: a mélange of twisted Latex sheaths over a bed of foil wrappers. The glistening opaqueness tinted with pinkish-red hues made Erin fold over and throw up gastric water into the pail, transforming the slippery condoms into slithering reptilian-life forms. Laurie slumped onto the bed and cried with her face buried in her lap as Erin threw up again. Of the dozen, at least one was torn

Deidre hadn't moved from the comfort and warmth emanating from the tingling heat under her fleecy white shroud. She didn't care that what she felt was lifelessness, or that they shared her secret. She had failed her daddy with a guilt she could never share with him, her daddy who had always loved her so much and who would always be with her.

She stood listlessly and went to the door, leaning against the jamb before shaking Laurie and Erin from their misery with whispered words they barely heard from a world far away: her private world so horribly shattered.

"They took our panties."

# 32

Deidre was resolute. She would not change her mind. While her roommates were at dinner without her, she went to make the necessary changes without feeling the need to explain why, and the tour representative accommodated her without feeling the need to question her reason. She had aged. She had become a woman in a girl's body, so why not act the part? She would never again be her daddy's little girl, even though daddies were always supposed to understand? She took a deep breath. She would know soon enough.

By the time Laurie and Erin finished the elaborate meals they hadn't tasted or enjoyed, and had gone back to their empty room, housekeeping had been in and Deidre had left for the airport. She didn't leave a note. She had gone, which was note enough. She would be home in a few hours to begin her new life. Eventually new friends would help her forget the old, praying as the 737 vibrated and roared to altitude for happy memories to one day replace everything that was now so terrible to her, above all for her daddy to love her. She leaned into the starboard porthole, drifting into a peaceful and dreamless sleep, not seeing the bright turquoise waters below transform to white before crashing onto glistening golden sands.

## 33

Bret, Shane, and Thurston got back to their hotel at the other end of el Paseo at four-thirty, and a pale amber glow that proceeded each new day was barely beginning to brighten the horizon.

Girl-chasers were on him, Bret insisted, in his room, and Shane went directly to the in-room bar to open a Corona as soon as Bret stepped aside with the room key still in the door. Thurston was right behind him and filled his glass with a double shot of cheap Mexican brandy before filling Bret's with an equal measure of his Special Reserve whisky he picked up each day at the beach market, which wasn't special at all.

Bret spoke first. "Here's to Laurie." They raised their glasses. "Damn, did you see how fast she took to the other one once they stripped?"

"Erin," Shane helped. "Shit, I've never stripped off that fast."

"Yeah, her," Bret smirked. "They were on each other like glue. I almost hated pulling them apart."

"It took you long enough. They just didn't want to let go. Wonder if they'll remember how much fun they had with each other before we cut in?"

"Like you care," Bret answered. "Thurston here had the best of both worlds. He was doing the little one at the same time as he was watching the lesbo show."

Thurston defended himself, laughing. "If you think that's so easy, try it sometime. Shit, I started passing out from dehydration. Thought I was going to drown her and kill myself doing it."

Bret raised his glass, the others followed. "Here's to the weak and the willing. God love them," the two glasses clinked against the clear bottle, "and keep them weak, willing and coming."

The Bret and Shane roared laughter and the three panties were tossed onto the moulded PVC chair beside the one Thurston had dropped into. "My knees hurt like a bitch," he complained, waiting for Shane to wipe away the white speckled froth bursting from his nostrils. "No shit, like a bitch." Thurston put his drink aside, pressing hard on each kneecap. "Went for a leak after doing her a few times and when I got back she was outside curled up on the balcony like a frigging baby. Took a shitload of time to straighten her out and flip her over. It was like kneeling on frigging stones for Christ sake."

"But in this case the end justifies the means," Bret laughed, "so to speak."

"Damn right," he boasted to a chorus of "you the man." He grimaced. "Feels like I need a frigging skin graft."

The laughing was too loud for the hour. "Anywhere in particular?"

"Yeah, there too, damn right, and on my frigging back." He stood. "But not because of her, because of the one you took first," he turned to Bret, "the one with the big tits her friend couldn't get enough of. Shit, I thought at first I was the only one who was going to get laid while you guys were just sitting around watching. It's like she had frigging teeth in there."

They were bent over laughing so hard Bret threw his glass over his shoulder to avoid dropping it. The second round was also on him, breakfast to go, and moments later three solid oak doors slammed closed sequentially with a thunderous resonance alerting dozens of other guests to the end of another victorious evening.

They had agreed on the time to meet, as well as the need not to phone each other to confirm. Shane volunteered to phone Chad, if he happened to remember Mr. Jerkoff. Lunch was at 3:30 at the pool bar, at least for the three of them.

Chad chose to eat elsewhere closer to noon, telling Shane on the cell he might see them later for dinner. What he didn't say was that he'd been on his balcony as the sun had begun to rise, fantasizing over a girl he had seen the night before, a girl he hoped to soon meet and spend time with. He had heard every word the trio had spoken about the teenage whores and Mr.Jerkoff. He had seen Bret's glass fly away into the darkness, though they hadn't heard his door close. Dick-guided assholes, he mumbled. He'd show them, and he'd do it with a real woman.

## 34

First on the menu for the weary threesome were matching Coronas followed by three more. Then they stopped, agreeing the games to come were more important than the fleeting moment at hand. They would rest and regroup for dinner to anticipate the evening ahead. Not so for Chad. He'd do his own thing, which didn't include being seen by the girls. His night would be one on the town, albeit alone.

## 35

Sunday morning came early for Chad. He arrived at the girls' hotel as quickly as he could manage after racing against himself to finish breakfast. He couldn't get the blonde out of his mind and he couldn't get there fast enough to see her.

When she finally exited elevator into the lobby his heart all but pounded to a complete stop. Love was blind, and Chad was in love. His experience with women to-date had been primarily with staple-perforated centrefolds, not real women who came equipped with pulses.

The two had gone to the travel desk by themselves and when Pilar and Ercilia joined them they hugged and exchanged kisses. Back home in Montreal he saw women kiss all the time at school, on the street, in restaurants, absolutely everywhere: the French culture, a culture that wasn't his. Who cared? Seeing women kiss was hot, a turn-on. And when French mixed with Spanish, holy shit it was sexy, he thought, fixated on the blonde as the girls flipped excitedly through the pages.

The smiling rep sat patiently, enjoying the good beginning to his day as the four girls made up their minds about what they wanted to do first. Finally the credit cards were swiped and the girls were gone in a flurry of short swirling cotton dresses, causing heads to turn, tongues to drop and Chad to stand and walk over to make his own arrangements.

# 36

The Muchacha Libre sailed from Puerto Mío three hours later with all four girls onboard. The season was at its peak, making the price prohibitive to those vacationing on their parents' already stressed budgets. When the bow thruster of the fifteen-metre Grand Banks churned and gurgled, pushing the motor yacht from the dock, eleven passengers, three crew members and the captain were onboard.

Chad boarded last, making sure to separate himself from the older couples who were obvious in their search for someone to adopt for the six-hour cruise. He stood alone, breathing deeply, staring at her from behind newly purchased dark glasses. What he saw next made him blind to everything around him. At that moment in time the sea did not exist, neither did the sun or the sky. She alone existed: the blonde Goddess who had so completely captivated him and captured his heart, the one he knew would love him forever. Twin and barely visible metallic red threads stretched from her bare buttocks to her bare shoulders. The girl she'd been dancing with the night before took her by the hands and swung her around, giggling something that made the blonde beam.

He forced the red away, imagining her completely naked, ignoring Maria who pushed down her sundress to show Pilar and Ercilia the gold bikini she'd been wearing at the pool. The other two examined their own thongs, feeling overdressed as Maria and Addison appreciated each other, nodding and smiling with a smug superiority.

Taking as much time as she could, Maria reached into her beach bag, retrieving two little packages, giving one to Addison. Both girls peered into the tiny bags, beaming as Pilar and Ercilia pouted. Until Maria and Addison stretched out their arms, giving Pilar and Ercilia the unexpected gifts each girl instantly ripped at, smiling widely, taking no time at all before hurrying back from the privacy of the captain's state room.

The three older women were openly disgusted, particularly with their husbands. The girls were hugging, kissing each other, shamelessly pirouetting, hopping around like giddy school girls. Pilar wore white that glared against her dark skin, Ercilia's was blue and the old ladies aghast as the girls bent over to retrieve beach towels from their bags. They stopped at the open bar en route to the bow in single file, the captain declaring over the loud hailer on behalf of his smiling crew that he was declaring the cruise the best of the year.

Chad stood immobilized as they passed by, straightening his stance and doing his best to flatten his stomach without being obvious. He had taken his first tequila sunrise from one of the deckhands and had swallowed half the chilled contents without taking his eyes away from her. Each man onboard had the same goal: Take one perfect photo of four naked and non-pacemaker-approved girls lying on beach towels, without having to crop out the wives at a later date. The crew weren't concerned with any such complication. They had the perfect motive: photographs for their souvenir scrapbook of Special Guests. Only one had no reason, no excuse, the one who wanted it the most.

Thirty minutes later Chad made his way to the bow with another tequila sunrise in one hand, the yacht's railing in the other, feeling as though he had crossed over into heaven. Two of the four girls had pulled away the strings from their shoulders, laying on their fronts so the other two could lotion their backs. He didn't know Pilar was the one smoothing cream over Ercilia, or that Maria was massaging Addison's back. They were virtually naked; that's what he knew.

They ignored him, which was worse than not noticing him. Seeing Maria touch Addison so seductively, with long tender strokes leaving her body glistening in the sun was too much for him. Maria's hand came to rest where the small of Addison's back transitioned to the roundness of her smooth bare buttocks, completely covering the miniscule red fabric. But, to Chad, his hand was feeling her smooth skin, her warmth. When Maria saw him next the man was lurching away, his internal metronome defying the rhythm of the waves, his legs oblivious to the blaring Latin beat.

# 37

They sailed around Punta Ixtapa and along the coast to Playa Las Gatas where the older men couldn't decide whether they should float on their backs in the water drinking beer, or onboard watching the girls put on PFDs. Pilar leaped from the deck, Maria followed Ercilia along the gangplank. Addison stayed onboard clicking shots of them splashing and waving at her as she tracked them from amidships to where they disappeared under the prow. The old men moved as slowly as they could, but with three girls in the water and the fourth disappearing from view, they had no reason not to jump in as well, leaving their wives behind to carry on about stupid men and cheap hussies.

Addison was on her tiptoes, leaning over the forward railing. Her legs were taut; her arms stretched out and locked at the elbows when he came up behind her. He couldn't remember ever seeing anything so exotic, with no idea what he would say to her, unaware the girls expected him to come by at some point. What normal male wouldn't? The camera's soft click made her turn.

"Don't you like the water?"

"I love the water. I don't like the salt," she answered. "I'm more of a pool person. And you?"

"I can't swim very well, and I hate wearing those jackets." He leaned halfway over the railing. "It sounds like they're having fun."

"They are. They're crazy."

"Your English is perfect." He hesitated, not to stumble on his words. "I heard you all speaking Spanish."

"I'm neither. I'm from Quebec. I studied Spanish and my mother is French." She leaned forward to put down the camera. "And you?"

"I'm an architect," he lied.

"An architect, that's interesting. With any firm I know?"

Oh, shit. Where was this going? Suddenly he felt stupid. "Probably not, though it's one of the biggest firms around: The Wilmingtons & Pendleton. I've been with them for a while." Addison shook her head; he nodded dumbly, searching an empty mind for something more to say. "So far I've taken on some pretty impressive projects. They're pretty old school, but some day they'll read well on the résumé."

"I suppose, but I meant to ask where you're from."

"From Montreal, my name's Chad."

"Hi, Chad. I'm Addison."

"Small world... you being from Montreal, I mean." He'd committed his first blunder, and he knew before finishing the words.

"I didn't say I'm from Montreal. I said I'm from Quebec."

He tried not to appear as nervous as he was. He wanted desperately to wet his lips that felt as though they were about to blister and crack right there in front of her. He had already finished his second tequila sunrise, yet his mouth was bone dry with no liquid resource of its own to spare. He should have left, but he couldn't take his eyes from her.

"That's a unique name for a woman, Addison," he said, as though she didn't know. "Did your parents want a boy?" You frigging idiot, he thought simultaneously, counting number two.

"No, they wanted a girl," she answered simply, hearing Maria shout up for her to take more pictures. "Like I said, they're crazy."

She leaned over the railing, composing a better shot, knowing full-well his eyes were all over her. Her legs were together, taut, smooth and glistening, the thinnest and perfectly straight line separating the two sides of her body to the pushed out curve of her bare buttocks and the small of her back that was perfection. Her stomach was flat without being chiselled, her breasts perfectly shaped, the perfect size, and the tiny strip of sparkling red decorating them mesmerized him. Her hair was lustrous, pulled into a braided style he knew nothing about. He was transported back in time to his teens, when his mother had caught him doing that disgusting thing in his room, with the magazine opened across the top of the bureau. He turned beet red, as he had then, convulsing involuntarily.

You poor man, she thought. "Guess I'll get more sun while it's still quiet around here."

He nodded stupidly, lost for words. "And time for another tequila sunrise," he managed. "I can bring you one if you'd like. One of the guys was telling me it's the best, something called ciento por ciento from the province of Tequila somewhere near here. He even said it's too good for the lime and salt thing." He gestured, making his bad day worse. "You know, with the salt, then licking it off this way," strike three, as though counting his losses mattered.

She suppressed the giggle she thought he might misinterpret. "Yes, I know. The sun will be fine for now, thank you. And ciento por ciento means a hundred percent, so be careful with those things. They have a way of coming back on you."

He raised the empty glass. "Here's to come backs. Enjoy your tanning, Addison."

"Thanks, Chad, and you enjoy your tequila."

By the time he'd enjoyed that and another tequila, he'd thought a hundred times of going back to see her, though as he was about to give into temptation the captain's brass bell clanged loudly, signalling that lunch was being served on deck. Maria was first, Ercilia second with Pilar following close behind. The old men still floated on their backs with empty cans and dumb smiles, unanimously agreeing they would linger a while to enjoy the remedial qualities of the cool water.

Lunch was a seafood buffet. The girls pulled cover-ups from their bags, much to everyone's disappointment, save the old women who had earlier decided they were flaunting exhibitionists. Besides, weren't they so rude speaking that Spanish in front of everyone, and who did they think they were prancing around naked, talking about everyone? On her way to the bow Pilar hissed something they didn't understand, smiling as she stooped for a fallen napkin in front of the husbands who had climbed onboard once the memories of bare bums had given way to thoughts of food.

# 38

Chad waited as long as he could. He couldn't resist any longer, convinced he couldn't care less what others onboard might think, including her friends. Everyone would know he was going to the bow to watch them sunning with their bodies glowing under the sun. He knew, so why wouldn't everyone else? No one had talked to him beyond a few brief words from the captain, the older couples were happily talking amongst themselves and the crew knew which people wanted their space and who would be interesting. They all agreed he wouldn't be.

The very moment he pushed himself from the portside gunwale, the twin Volvo engines groaned alive, urging the trawler through turquoise waters, keeping time with the anchor chain retreating into its fibreglass locker at the feet of four beautiful women. They had spent the afternoon laughing, reading, dozing off and enjoying special service from a crew who realized sympathetically the bar was located inconveniently far from the women. And Chad discovered the answer to his dilemma, a God-sent answer he hadn't prayed for. He would take pictures of the crew hauling the anchor, until he discovered too late the winch was electric. There was no forward crew, and finally he had no choice but to take pictures of a barren blue sea.

"¿Que hace? Pi." Ercilia wanted to know. "No hay nada allí, mi amor."

"Es un hombre, cariño, ¿qué piensas?"

Maria offered, "Maybe we should all spank each other for him. What do you think, Addie?"

"I think you're absolutely horrible," she responded, squeezing Maria's waist that was slippery with lotion, "beautiful, but horrible." She knew Maria enjoyed being squeezed. She would often feign pouting during their frequent girl-talks knowing Addison would squeeze and hug her. "His name is Chad. He's from Montreal. He's an architect."

He grimaced, grinding his teeth tightly together when his name unexpectedly stood out in a blur of meaningless prattle, not even thinking of the possible context. He swivelled from the waist as slowly as he could manage.

"Hi again, Chad. I was telling my friends you're an architect."

Seeing them was like stepping into a living, breathing South Beach postcard. They glowed. They were gorgeous; they were eyeing him and were actually talking to him, at least Addison was.

"Hola, ladies." Fool, he thought. Idiot!

Addison pointed to the deck. "Would you like to join us?"

"No, thank you. I think I would spoil a perfect picture."

"¿Qué dijo, Adishone?" Pilar wanted to know.

"Él quiere sacar una foto de nosotros, pero es muy tímido, yo creo."

"Another guy with a camera," responded Pilar. "They're all the same."

"I'm sorry, what did she say?" Chad asked.

"She said we should move so you can get a better picture of the bow. We've kind of taken over this part of the boat all day."

"I don't think anybody minds."

"Would you like one of us to take a picture of you before we dock? It's hard to take one of yourself."

He beamed, passing her the camera. "I would like that. Thanks"

Chad had never claimed religion as a virtue, though he believed some god was by his side that very moment. As Addison stood he committed each of her movements to memory, each beautiful angle, each beautiful body part, causing the other girls to look at each other nonplussed.

"He couldn't be more obvious," Pilar muttered to herself. "Why doesn't he stand there with a video camera and ask us to fondle each other and play with our pussies while he plays with his little thing, the way he will later? And what is with those stupid sunglasses?"

Addison ignored her, taking aim with the SLR. "Don't be so serious, Chad." Then she clicked several frames before returning it to him.

"Thanks." He knew exactly how it would feel to kiss her breasts, run his hands up between her legs and to squeeze her ass. "Guess I should go get my stuff together."

He wanted her to turn so he could see her that way again, but she wasn't going to. He had at least one picture of her, and he could always take more of her around the pool with a different lens. He would take more of her around the pool, the next day.

# 39

The crew threw off pure white braided bow and stern lines, jumping to the floating dock as the thrusters worked effortlessly to nestle the white fibreglass motor yacht against its private slip. The tip jar was passed around and filled, the captain thanked everyone and the old women had dressed for the trip back. The men stayed in their cargo trunks, allowing the world to marvel at their red, distended bellies as though two-tone spindly arms were not fashion statement enough.

Those couples exchanged phone numbers and addresses they would never use, the men shook hands and the women simply said goodbye, still shaking their heads at the horrible girls who had seemed so nice at first, then to become so vulgar. Flaunting themselves that way was deplorable and indecent. Whatever would their parents possibly think of such behaviour?

The vulgar girls were first to disembark, Pilar locating her pink SUV, wasting no time leaving the parking lot, passing Chad who was first at the queue of taxis. Neither man spoke the other's language and Chad had no idea how to say follow or catch up, or anything else, so he settled for the next best thing: He spent the twenty-minute drive staring at the image on the back of his camera. He was leaving on Saturday and somehow he would be with her before that. He would, no matter what.

# 40

Addison and Maria had done exactly what they had promised themselves they wouldn't do: They had spent the entire week with Pilar and Ercilia. The four had instantly become inseparable friends and had changed rooms which would give them an adjoining door and shared balconies. By the end of the week there wasn't much they didn't know about each other.

They became expected visitors to the Representative's desk each morning, the days too short for everything they wanted to do. The only time spent at the beach was for parasailing or jet skiing, and the pool was a place to relax at the end of each gruelling day of touring and shopping. Night time became girl time after dinner each evening, with endless talking about everything as they modelled new dresses, lingerie and bikinis for each other. They had thought to go dancing one night, but Addison and Maria had so fascinated Pilar and Ercilia with the business venture they were about to embark upon that dancing was completely forgotten.

Though Friday night would be their last night together and the Fiesta was a must do, even though saying goodbye seemed so far away. Then the biggest question was what to wear.

# 41

They didn't believe Chad about the four girls on the boat, or the slingshot bikinis, not until he showed them the photo of the blonde girl leaning over the railing of the Grand Banks. His subsequent nights started out with them and he'd even lucked out on Tuesday with a woman from Kansas who had enjoyed more than one too many that he had paid for and who had been conveniently staying at the same hotel.

He poured her a double brandy from the bar in her room and all that remained for him to do was choose a few charming words and bring her in closer. Long before she woke he had gone and was nowhere to be seen throughout the day. Wednesday evening was another matter. Chad found no escape and he was the one needing double brandies, and few more before indulging her need for love. He managed to convince himself she was the best thing around, though not before the amber liquid took effect, beginning a delicate process of balancing his adequately blurred vision with the male need to perform even under the worst conditions. He never returned to eat at the hotel, nor did he ever return to La Chica.

As the week went on the availability of women who fit their criterion for a perfect evening dwindled to near zero, being much more difficult to hit on three or four women when only one or two of them were worth the effort. Wednesday night Shane flipped the coin before tossing it to Thurston for the second flip who then tossed to Bret in a best two out of three which would decide the winner, the runner-up, and the loser. Shane won the best of the three, Bret came in second and Thurston took his defeat in stride, leaving the bar to check out a few hotel lobbies after a few lonesome vodkas while Bret took the one on the left and Shane the one on the right.

Thursday morning, Chad woke from the glare of the sun, taking a few moments to collect his thoughts and quickly dispel any that lingered from the night before. Though not until he rolled over to stand did he see the naked girls lying on top of the bed that had been empty when he had returned from his mission of mercy. One girl was lying on her back, the other was on her front with a piece of hotel note paper sticking out from between the tops of her thighs: a note from Bret wishing him bon appetite, hoping he enjoyed his room-service breakfast, and explaining why one girl was on the left and the other on the right. Both girls were either dead asleep or unconscious. Either way, he had no need to hurry.

He kicked aside the small pile of crumpled clothing, not bothering to close the bathroom door behind him. Then he went to the main door to hang the No Moleste card and to the other bedside table for the eight-by-ten glossy which he placed on the left-side pillow so he could see Addison perfectly from his side. Then he pushed away his boxers and positioned himself over Miss Right.

# 42

The housekeeping staff had seen everything, but never young women passed out and huddled together completely naked in one of the stairwells with their shoes, skirts and tops neatly placed at their feet; not even during Spring Break. At first they were shocked, until checking to see that the girls' breathing was stable and anxiety gave way to giggles. They covered the girls with towels, deciding to leave them as they were and periodically check on them. By nine the girls had changed positions once, by ten they had gone with the towels and Chad had finished his breakfast at El Presidente. He had seen Addison and the other girls from a safe distance each afternoon at the pool, with no qualms about what he was becoming or what he was doing because stalking had never crossed his mind. Being close to her was a means to an end.

The girls spent all their time together, so did the guys. So what? They did nothing after dinner each evening except go to their rooms. He made sure of that before leaving her, and each day was a different set of activities that excluded him as much as he had wanted to take part in her day. Thursday night would be the night, at dinner. He would ask her to go dancing, somewhere he wasn't known, and the rest would fall into place. He knew where they sat each night and the number of the neighbouring table. When he left the restaurant after breakfast he went to the front desk to book the reservation before going into town to make certain her evening would be one to remember.

She was with him every step of the way from the upscale unisex hair salon to the haberdasher to the shoe store to the jeweller where he bought a gold chain, a gold signet ring and a bracelet he later attempted to age by rubbing them with a handful of fine sand: his second trip into town. Tuesday he had gone in to find a copy service where he could convert her digital body into something tangible, something smooth he could hold in his hands that would keep her close to him. He hadn't told the other three more than he felt he had to, however this was different, this he couldn't hide. The new shoes were deep blue tasselled loafers, the perfect accessory to his Mediterranean-blue tropical suit.

He called housekeeping for an iron to press out the tell-tale folds which would scream out "new" about his shirt instead of crisp and white. The blue of his belt matched his shoes and the sales clerk hadn't let him leave the store without a white silk pocket hanky and instructions on how to wear his shirt without a tie. He hadn't let the girl at the salon put lacquer on his nails, although she had filed them to perfectly even lengths while his hair was being styled and blow-dried. His shave had been the final luxury and the final touch. Though his day had been longer than hers and he had missed her at the pool. He had tried to rest a little at the pool of his hotel complex, but the others wouldn't let him.

He tried not talking about his day by thanking them for his double-girl breakfast and giving them the details they wanted to hear. He couldn't have been happier with the reaction, especially when he got to the part where he had managed to walk the girls separately down the flight of stairs to the next floor and leave them. When he told them how the clothes had required a third trip, and how he had folded each item, they each blew beer foam from their noses. He was one of them, not Mr. Jerkoff, and he couldn't wait to show them the pictures he had taken of the girls.

They had no choice but to concede his victory and when they noticed the jewellery, he failed miserably at explaining the cluster of boxes and suit bag. Chad was a bad liar, particularly in front of Bret, and no one was about to leave until he told all. They migrated to the balcony while he showered, succeeding in getting nothing wet above his neck. Earlier at the pool he'd spent his time in the shade to avoid dampening his hair wet with sweat. When he stepped from the shower he was in bright red silk shorts and endured the mocking like the man he was.

They promised not to look, once he promised to go out for ice in his new red silk shorts and serve them each another drink on the balcony. He did, and when he stepped onto the balcony to a chorus of profane praises, cheering, and howling, he was the man of the moment. Not even Bret said anything that would spoil his time in the spotlight. He even agreed she probably wasn't a dyke, besides, even if she were, Chad would be the one to turn her around, or turn her over. One thing was certain: Once she saw him like that, and with a few drinks in her, there was no way he wouldn't bag her.

# 43

He hadn't let himself sit, timing his departure from the room so he wouldn't have to, so he could go directly from his hotel to hers. He would make himself as perfect as he could for her and unsightly creases across his perfectly pressed pants weren't an option. Bret had put the silk hanky properly in the jacket pocket, but Chad wouldn't wear it until he arrived at her hotel and the guys had been told not to expect him anytime soon, as though they cared.

The lights were bright in the restaurant and he asked the maître d' to seat him facing the gorgeous girl with the blond hair. When the chair was pulled out for him he sat as casually as he possibly could, wondering whether the four women could hear the heated blood pounding through his pulsating veins. The one with the big mouth and attitude spoke first and he wasn't surprised. He forced himself to ignore them. He had earlier slipped the maître d' an American ten, asking that he have a bottle of their best white wine delivered to his table immediately.

He disregarded the cork. He knew they were studying him, talking about him as he first approved the nose of the wine, the colour, then the texture and flavour as it travelled through his inexperienced mouth that was moist at last. He knew the waiter wasn't impressed, though the nod was expected as he placed the glass the on the table.

"Chad?"

His head pivoted, exactly as he had practiced over and over again. "Addison? How nice to see you again. How's the vacation going?"

"It's going great," she answered, "couldn't be better. How about yours? I didn't think you were staying here."

"I'm not. I needed a different place for dinner. I've been with my friends for the past couple of weeks, except for

Sunday." he shrugged. "It doesn't hurt to have a bit of breathing space once in a while."

¿Qué dicen, Maria, y qué hace aquí este chico?" Ercilia wanted to know, leaning over to Maria who tried to answer her with a straight face.

"She's being polite, Ercilia. The poor guy's all by himself."

"No importa," replied Pilar, "no es nada más que un tonto. There's always a reason when a man is by himself. He must feel stupid."

He tried shutting them out. "Sure is a beautiful language, and fast. I suppose the learning curve is pretty steep."

"I suppose so," replied Addison, happy Pilar stopped talking long enough to take a sip of wine, "unless you're into French or some other Latin language."

"That leaves me out. I never got past voulez-vous in school. I'm much better at designing and creating things."

He raised his wine glass in a silent toast to her, not at all disappointed the other girls had decided to ignore him, including Maria who didn't see the need for him to know she spoke English or anything else about her. What mattered was that Addison was talking with him.

The girls opted for the buffet dinner, leaving to his à la carte meal twice to go in search of another mélange of tasty morsels. The third time Addison stayed while the others went to select a perfect dessert.

"May I ask you something?"

"Yes, as long as we're not getting personal."

"Earlier I noticed sort of a nice dance club in this hotel, and I was wondering." He stopped short, thinking that was the thing to do. "I'd really enjoy your company for a cocktail after dinner, and perhaps, if you don't find me too clumsy, a dance or two. I can't think of a better way to end my trip."

The man had to be blind not to have noticed.

"That's a hard invitation to refuse, Chad. Unfortunately I've made plans. I promised my friends I'd spend the evening with them, talking girl talk. Pilar and Ercilia," she pointed to the empty chairs, "are driving home to Mexico City very early the day after tomorrow and we get along so well we want to spend as much time with them as possible before they go."

"Well, there's no way I'm good enough to entertain four women, or to compete with three. Anyway, I'm glad I asked."

What he wasn't glad about was not getting the hell away from them. The waiter was being discreet for no good reason, thinking he was doing him a favour by staying away. Just bring the frigging check!

"I'm sure you wouldn't have any trouble at all keeping four women entertained, Chad. Actually, I'm not all interesting and I dance horribly."

Now there was the lie. He'd seen her dance at La Chica. It had been all he could do not to grab himself. Bitch, he thought. That's what she was alright. He hadn't spent as much on clothes over the past five years. The meal alone would set him back a hundred plus and he barely ate, not to mention the ten he'd given the Mexican penguin. The guys were right, they were always right. She was a lesbian bitch, a dirty, frigging dyke.

He called out for the waiter, tossing his card to the edge of the other place setting on his table, steeling himself against the next four or five minutes which would be an interminable lifetime spent in hell.

"Are you going to the Fiesta evening tomorrow?" he asked.

"Yes, I am. The girls love shopping and picking up knick-knacks. Perhaps if we see each other I'll take you up on that drink."

"I'll probably be with my friends. I'll leave mine if you

124

leave yours."

She smiled, thinking probably not a fair trade as the girls came back. "They're really hard to get rid of," she replied, thinly, wanting him to go because he was becoming bothersome and she had nothing more to say.

The waiter stood over Chad who was mentally costing the meal that was excessively extravagant for a man alone, ostensibly demonstrating good service. At any other time he would have argued the price of the wine, no way in front of her and he had said he wanted the best of the wines. If no one else was noticing his hesitation, the waiter was, saying something Chad had no clue about. He didn't bother acknowledging the comment. When he glanced at Addison she simply conveyed the message.

"He said his name is Jaime. He hopes you enjoyed the meal and the service."

Chad eyed the man indignantly. "Thanks, Herman. You made the evening perfect." Now piss off, he thought, adding a firmly written twenty-five to the bill that was in US dollars and seemed to make Jaime happy.

"I hope you and your friends enjoy your evening, Addison. Perhaps we'll bump into each other tomorrow." Of course we will, you lying bitch, "and I will buy you a drink."

"That would be nice, Chad. Enjoy your evening as well."

"Please say good night to the other ladies for me. You're all absolutely gorgeous."

"I will, and they'll love hearing they're gorgeous." She watched him stand, they all did. "And by the way, you're pretty impressive yourself. I wonder why more men don't dress as well. Good night, Chad."

"Good night, Addison." He acknowledged the others with a nod that was too abrupt, then he walked away as evenly as he could.

## 44

He made it to his room well before the other three even thought to end the evening, not turning on the lights to shower for fear they might come in early and discover him alone. He stayed dripping wet, enjoying the sensation of the cool draft from the ceiling fan against his skin as he gathered together what he needed for the rest of the evening.

The lights stayed off as he sat stretched out and naked, indifferent to the quiet heaviness filling the balcony and the cloak of total darkness. He fell asleep with an empty glass in his hands, one empty bottle by his feet. By the time he woke the sun was completing its full accent atop the horizon, a second bottle which might have been half-full had toppled over and rolled away. The glass lay shattered between his feet. He would never know or care how long he had stayed there, bent over with his throbbing head sagging in too close proximity to a shrunken and purple-coloured fleshy thimble staring into eyes that were blurred slits stuck together with the early morning crust of sweat and salted tears. The lonely abuse which hours before had consoled him had transformed his body into a bloated mass of foul-smelling gasses which he felt no need to retain. He recoiled from one expulsion at the very moment gastric acids burned his throat, irrigating his mouth with a cocktail of rancid juices as he belched with sufficient force to draw attention from anyone who was only half asleep in the complex.

Her photograph was still on the table beside him, ruined and curled with a sticky wetness which had leeched through the paper to distort the fine lines of the true-to-life image. He reached for her, crumpling her with one hand into an unusable ball of papier-mâché. He would have time to think of her later, to remember their evening together. First things were first, as he struggled to understand what actually had to come first.

He would need the day alone to repair the damage she had done to him, and would avoid them at all cost until he had a believable story to tell them. The first step was a revitalizing cold shower, then a humanizing shave, neither of which came anywhere close to expectation. His face was pale and bloated with puffy darkness around his red-streaked eyes transforming a youthful face into an older and miserable facsimile. She had caused him to do that.

The air in the bathroom remained putrid with a pungent mix of lingering odours refusing to dissipate, made worse when he thought to swallow the foamy toothpaste in his mouth rather than spit it out. The resulting gastric load shot up his throat like a barbed rocket that left him on his knees, grasping the splattered and slippery porcelain edge of the bowl tightly with both hands.

He stayed as he was for what seemed forever, shivering and sweating away flashes of hot and cold emanating from his body. Perhaps he could die. That would be good, he thought. Then he reached for the unfinished beer.

He left the room as silently as he could manage, meandering his way without hurrying to the familiar backstairs with his third beer in-hand. He rubbed his way along the handrail, supporting himself as much as guiding himself, instinctively knowing not to trust his eye-to-foot coordination. When he did reach the bottom he braced himself against the stuccoed wall, his bare feet wide apart. He downed half the beer in one gulp, waving away the ensuing stale air with his free hand and looking halfway up the stairs to study a fixed point for as long as he took to swallow the second mouthful. He tossed the empty bottle onto the lawn, walking out from the narrow arched entrance into full daylight and feeling worse. He would never again think of the two girls he'd put there. More importantly, he needed another beer from the bar which was on the way to the beach, then the ocean and at some point he would eat. He'd done enough thinking.

# 45

They had planned the day the previous night, the final day the girls would spend together before Pilar and Ercilia began the demanding 430 kilometres of hairpin curves and steep climbs along route 130 which would bring them to Mexico City seven hours later. So they would make the day a lazy one of full-service, applying a final layer of sun, neither couple eager to part from the other. They had become as close as sisters during the week, and sisters could always visit each other. They promised they would before winter, when they could still be sexy without their ears turning white and falling off from the cold, as Pilar was certain they would. No. They would visit during late summer or early fall, no later she insisted.

By mid-week Pilar and Ercilia had agreed on the need to buy a third suitcase and spent Friday evening before dinner packing for the trip home: a reluctant task. Neither woman wanted to leave. Unfortunately the hotel was fully booked for the coming week, which Pilar had much to say about. As much as she loved Ercilia, she adored Adishone and would miss her greatly over the summer. The others put the suitcases out of sight and out of mind, letting let her rant on about stupid Mexicanos and their stupid macho airs. What did they know anyway? And what a stupid hotel, she would never stay there again. ¡Nunca! She declared.

Ercilia burst out laughing, then Addison and Maria. Maria picked up a pillow in an effort to stop the tirade and the soft blow struck Pilar moments before Ercilia's. Addison had no choice but to join ranks with Pilar, and the war was on until a truce was declared on equal terms and both sides surrendered to the day. When Pilar woke Addison was lying beside her, curled into her down-filled weapon. She took a moment to absorb the image before stirring her with a soundless whisper and a lingering kiss as light and as soft as two feathers coming together; one she could not resist and one Addison had barely felt.

They smiled together, stretching out their sleepiness before Pilar leaned over her to explain a new strategy requiring absolute stealth, precise timing, utmost courage and lots of ice cubes. As quietly as she could, Pilar picked up the clothing she had laid out for the evening, leaving Addison to ease open the door so they could sneak out to dress for dinner in lingerie and dresses they had picked out earlier by majority rule and for maximum affect. The war could wait.   Addison always enjoyed watching Maria undress, sometimes titillating, at times mischievous, though watching another woman was intriguing. Pilar wasn't merely taking off her clothes, she was stripping. She was natural, lost in the moment, relishing each sensual stroke, tug and pull as though choreographed. And so was Addison. Pilar was a photographer's dream.

Addison wasn't seeing anything she hadn't seen all week, yet she was seeing something which excited her and made her feel guilty at once. She enjoyed being alone with Pilar for the first time, and entirely naked. They set their dresses and panties aside, and before stepping into the shower Pilar simply asked which towel she could use. When she finished, Addison stepped in and, as much as the cool water felt so good, she hurried out to see more of Pilar standing naked and unaffected, bent over on the balcony combing out her long black hair with one hand over the other.

"Can I get you a glass of wine, Pi?" Addison asked, wrapped in a towel.

"Blanco, no tinto, gracias, Adishone."

"Coming up."

Pilar threw back her perfectly straight hair as Addison stepped onto the balcony, holding two inexpensive wine goblets. She took the glass. Then she took the towel and beamed. "You're on vacation, Adishone, and who will mind? You're beautiful. I wanted to tell you before I go home. I will miss you and Maria very much until we meet again." She took Addison by the hand, leading her inside. "No need to wake the losers." She paused "We will see you and Maria again, won't we?"

"Yes, Pi. Though maybe they shouldn't catch us like this. You know what jealous dykes are like."

Pilar rested her glass, covering her mouth to muffle her laughter and when that didn't work she went to Addison who willingly opened her arms and they both laughed. Addison put her seven-centimetre stiletto sandals on first, then her backless silk thongs with a white satin front. Pilar did the opposite with a red satin V-string. Her ten-centimetre stiletto sandals followed.

"Should we go outside and stand for a while with our wine"

She was incorrigible.

"No, we shouldn't. I never realized you were such a tease. What a man killer you are."

"What is your point, Adishone? ¡No importa!"

"Put on your dress while I close the doors. We have a war to finish, or have you forgotten."

"No, Adishone, I have not. You know, I wish I had a special name for you, like," she hesitated, pensively, "like I don't know what … something special."

"Pi, believe me, Adishone is special enough…you know I love you."

The words had come out unexpectedly, robbing Addison of breath and words.

"I love you the same way, Adishone, the way Ercilia loves Maria. Now let's go find our girls, the loser girls."

"Think maybe we should put our dresses on before we do that?"

"Must we?"

"Yes, we must, unless you want to go to the restaurant like that."

Pilar seductively palmed her silky skin, which had likely caused at least a few marital discussions during her stay. "You don't like what you see."

"I love what I see, you saucy bitch. But they'll be serving Mexican tonight, Fiesta Night, remember, and you'll spoil their appetites. Y ahora, chica, vístete y ¡date prisa¡"

Pilar wore a red tiered and slim-fitting satin dress which was décolleté with a plunging back, three of Ercilia's hand widths above the knee, and bought to please her lover. Addison slipped into an emerald green faux-wrap mini-skirt, meant to mesmerize Maria as much as any man, as her friend sat on the bed.

"I can't call you Adishone. Doing so makes me feel stupid, as though people are laughing at me. Will you teach me to say your name properly, and can I call you something special like cariño or Adisita?"

"What a horrible thing to say, Pi! Cariño! What do you mean by wanting to call me such a name?" She thought she was going to burst out laughing before teasing Pilar more. "How can you hurt me so by calling me such a common name?" That's what you call Ercilia, and now me."

Pilar froze, stunned, her open mouth a pale-pink cavern of brilliant white stalagmites and stalactites. Her eyes actually glazed over, causing Addison's to do the same.

She and Addison were two of a kind. Addison realized she had gone too far and pulled Pilar into her. "I'm so sorry, Pi, I was joking. I would love you to call me Adisita. I can't think of a cuter name for you and me. I was trying to be funny, instead I was stupid."

"Maria won't mind?"

"No. Maria knows we've become close the way she and

132

Ercilia have. I can't believe how the four of us have come together." She drew back a little. "Now, if you don't mind, I'm half-naked and we do have a war to wage."

The contoured and bowed halter top was deep yellow, swept up quickly by Adisita before Pi could even think of lunging, though the efforts of both women were needed to pull it on and push it down before realizing they had stayed much too long. The sun had set and the other two were still fast asleep.

"Adisita, you're beautiful, and I will hate leaving you and Maria. But before we go can we talk as serious and intelligent women?"

"Yes, Pi, but you're scaring me a little. What is it you want to say?"

Pilar closed the patio door, gently pulling Adisita from a wicker chair to sit side-by-side on the bed. "You must be careful when this dog comes around, chasing after you as though you are some cheap bitch for him to sniff, Adisita. You must be careful when he comes around wagging his tail like a puppy with big eyes, when all he wants is to put his bone in any little bitch like the dog that he is."

"He's a young boy on vacation, Pi. You mustn't worry about me. I'm sure he's forgotten me, especially after last night. Besides, we don't even know if he'll show. If he does, I'll get rid of him, nicely…nicely, Pi."

"That's a good thing, Adisita. The guy wants to see you through only one eye, the one which sees only ceramic and pussies," she paused, peering straight into Addison's eyes, hers black and unblinking. "This is not a time to joke or be casual, ¿comprendes, chica?"

"Sí, lo comprendo, Pi, y te doy gracias."

"No importa. I don't need your thanks, Adisita. I want you to be safe. We all do. You are too special, ¿tú comprendes?"

Pilar's hand against her cheek was tender, yet strangely

admonishing. "Sí, mi amor, comprendo. De veras, comprendo, Pi. Can we go now?" Addison was feeling uneasy, wanting to end the conversation. "And can you do something for me?"

"Yes, of course. What is it you want?"

"Kiss me once more, the way you did when you thought you were waking me."

Pilar showed no surprise. She brought up her other hand, kissing Adisita, though she didn't understand the English words she muffled. No importa.

# 46

They stood over the girls lying spooned in separate worlds. Maria and Ercilia hadn't budged a centimetre.

"They seem so cozy, so peaceful, Pi. Are you sure we should do this?"

"Of course I am, Adisita. Go. Take your side. This will be very funny."

"Funny for us," Addison replied, suddenly not so sure.

Pilar didn't answer, pinching a corner of the sheet Ercilia had thrown back earlier. Addison took the other corner, pulling up and over the girls in sync with Pilar who had the bowl of ice cubes in the other hand. The cubes barely touched the soft warm targets when Pilar yanked her side of the sheet, falling quickly and exactly the way Addison did, pinning the victims tightly together in a wet, cold shroud.

Maria screeched in English mixed with Italian. Ercilia made shrill, squeaky noises which could have been in any language. To Pilar it all sounded the same except for one word she had sublimely learned around the pool, hearing men say what a beach, as though they didn't like the beach, which was probably why they were always at the pool. The war was easily won, the writhing and whimpering enemy unwillingly conceding defeat, the victors wisely seeking the security of neutral ground, running for the balcony, closing the door behind them and giggling at the losers hugging each other, trying to rub each other warm. The single click coming from the door lock turned Pi's and Adisita's laughing to pouting, from pouting to desperation: They had forgotten their drinks and would neither beg nor negotiate.

Ercilia left to prepare for the evening and Maria disappeared into her bathroom. Not long after Ercilia was back wearing platform shoes, beige linen pants that showed no lines and a pale bronze bra top corset. She poured a drink for herself and Maria before sitting side saddle on the small table she had converted into a vanity complete with mirror and two weeks' worth of make-up. Maria was sitting in a black bustier trimmed with pink silk, decorated with a silk bow, which she left untied, meant to see under the tan-coloured linen shirt she hadn't yet decided to wear. Her string panties matched her bustier, the matching side bow intended to hang over the band of her black hip-hugger skirt, which would be hidden if she wore the shirt. Ercilia agreed. She wouldn't wear the shirt, but time wasn't standing still and they agreed with exaggerated nods they should get going.

They exchanged curious expressions, puzzled by the tapping sound at the patio doors, the glass doors muting their devious whispers as they peered into the darkness and then at each other before shrugging and peering out once more.

"Son locas, Adisita, son muy, muy locas."

"No cabe duda, Pi. They're nuts. Por cierto."

"¿Cuál es nuts?" she wanted to know.

"No importa."

They both buckled over, not hearing the door open.

# 47

Pilar held Adisita's hand, Maria held Ercilia's, confusing the other guests who had seen them all week.

"Pi's right, Addie. The guy's spooky. He's got a real thing for you. He couldn't be more obvious if he had "hard-on" stamped on his forehead."

"You're right, mi amor, and if he does come by I'll get rid of him, like I did last night." She nodded with pursed lips as confirmation. "I promise. Besides, the complex is huge and all the hotels are into this Fiesta Night thing, even the street vendors and he's probably found some girl from his hotel."

"He couldn't pick himself up, Adisita. Did you see his face when his bill came last night? I thought he was going to die from fright."

Ercilia broke in. "Anyway, he's probably in town trying to get a refund for that suit. What was he thinking? Stupid man. Guys like him don't wear suits like that. The clerk must have been very good."

"Who would want such a boorish clown? Did you hear him with the waiter last night, calling him such a stupid name?"

Addison giggled. "He must have been nervous. He did seem a little anxious to leave."

"No importa." And there wasn't much more to say, except for Pilar to call over Jaime to order a bottle of wine and tell the girls their last dinner together would be from the menu, her treat.

# 48

Jaime was the envy of every man in the restaurant when the four girls gave him a hug, even Pilar had to admit he was charming, justifying that at least he was Mexican. The hotel grounds were crowded with as many performers and vendors as with guests from the hotel and local Mexican couples who had paid to join in on the special night. Everyone was dressed except for several North American men who saw nothing wrong with showing how far their sunburned chests had fallen, prompting Pilar to ask how they could possibly find it, let alone hold it.

"They don't hold it," Ercilia answered, "they sit like we do and let it dangle."

"Then they must wipe it, or shake it, or something," Maria added, not to be outdone, "But what about those things on the wall?"

Pilar answered. "I saw a movie once. They just put it back in without wiping and walk out without washing their dirty hands. Some even put their coffee cups on the wall things."

"Pi, you're terrible."

"No, I'm not. I wash after I wipe."

"Then let's go see, Pi, I have to go to the bathroom," Ercilia urged, and Maria leaned into Pilar, laughing, explaining that, in English, Pi would be going for a pee."

Pilar looked at Addison. "Es loca, esta amiga tuya. Adisita. Te dije" and she went with Ercilia.

"Mi amor, I have to tell you something that's bothering me." Maria lost her smile, not certain what was coming next. "When Pi woke me earlier, she kissed me. Then, when we sneaked out to get ready, I asked her to kiss me again. I'm Sorry."

Maria started to laugh. "Addie, you scared me. I thought

you were going to say something serious. Is she a good kisser?"

"Yes, mi amor, she's a very good kisser."

"Good. So is Ercilia, which doesn't mean I don't love you. I had a chance to kiss her, and I did…three times. We were lying there talking, and then kissing seemed so natural, Addie. We were having fun, and I'm sorry too. We had more time than you guys, but you did startle us when you opened the door. I hardly had enough time to roll over"

"You weren't sleeping!"

"No, we were talking."

"And kissing," Addison added, smiling.

She nodded, reaching for Addison's hand. "Yes, kissing…just a little. Addie, I love you. We're both bad."

"We're not bad. We're fun, and so are they, mi amor. I don't mind you feeling the way you do about Ercilia. Pi and I were speaking about how much we've come to feel so close to each other so quickly.

"When she wasn't kissing her little A-d-i-s-i-t-a?" Maria teased.

When Pilar and Ercilia came from behind, Addison and Maria were quietly holding hands. Pilar was first to break the silence. "Adisita, our girls played together when we were gone. What should we do?"

"Spank them, Pi. We should definitely spank them."

More than one man stopped talking to his wife to watch the errant girls' bums being patted, making them long for the same punishment, and not by the wives. Ercilia pulled Maria away after the patting, pouting and consoling her friend in a tight embrace both could have held until morning. When they did pull away, a little, seeing each other's glistening eyes, they hugged again. Ten PM had come and Pilar exchanged glances with Addison saying she never thought she would have a child, let alone two.

Walking away slowly enough for the Maria and Ercilia

to catch up, the power of women to the fourth power was intimidating even to the most machísmo Latino, and to a man they stepped aside as the foursome passed. The patio bar was once again the focal point of the evening's festivities beyond the pool, filled to capacity, no one noticing the brightly coloured lights and kilometres of colourful crêpe ribbons lining the entire area from the hotel to the very edge of the beach. The waiters were handsome in white-on-black in a way unique to Latinos, the waitresses uniquely Latina with bright, shy smiles against the soft hue of lightly-coloured skin. Gaily decorated peasants skirts were traditional, coloured with bright reds, greens and yellows which should have made the men appear dull, but didn't. Headdresses were hand- stitched with long silk ribbons trailing against crisp white blouses as the women weaved their way through precariously narrow and meandering paths between the tables with unwavering trays balanced deftly on small open palms. The sound system blared out salsa, leaving the Mariachi to stroll and strum between hotels serenading couples who felt the need for quiet or sought distance from the noise of everyone else's gaiety. White men were doing their best at proving they can't dance and their women were no better, dancing various interpretations of rock 'n roll to whatever song was being played, many of them sitting when Pi and Adisita walked to the centre of the floor while Maria went for drinks. When she and Ercilia joined them on the floor the remaining white-footed partiers understood they had been subtly made to relinquish their space to those who would make better use of it. And from a conveniently dark corner four men watched the girls glide sensually against each other in perfect time to the rapid Latin rhythm.

# 49

Ercilia wanted to know why North American women never seemed happy and why they wore such ugly clothes with no shape. She asked why the one over there was wearing flip-flops and why the fat one over there was wearing a shapeless dress that showed each fatty bump on her legs and her buttocks that would never be a cute bum or a sexy ass. Pilar answered because they were with fat and ugly men who wore ugly clothes, who couldn't shake it and wouldn't wash their hands even if they could shake it. What did they have to be happy about? Then they noticed their own stern-faced norteamericanas.

That was at eleven, when they had laughed and giggled. Now midnight was minutes away and the laughing stopped. If parting was so difficult for them, Ercilia asked, why had they been brought to together to become as close as sisters?

# 50

"You were right, Rivers. She's hot. They all are and I've got first dibs on the redhead."

"There's one for each of us, if we work smart." Chad answered, ignoring him. "They've each had three drinks I've counted so far. Who knows how many they sucked back before?"

Thurston moved his chair to see around the man who blocked his view. "I'll take the one in the pants. I saw her coming out of the can. You can see her thong right through them. She's got an ass to die for, nice tits too."

Shane said nothing. He'd spent the past hour talking with them without seeing them. He was studying Pilar, imagining what she was wearing under her dress and how easily he could get them off.

Bret chose Maria without any toss of a coin or the draw of a swizzle stick. He had to have her. There was something about her. Chad could have his blonde and the other two could share the salsa girls. He wanted the redhead. At least he wanted her first, and definitely both ways. Then maybe Chad's blonde before the Mexicans. The last night promised to be a busy one. They hadn't done four girls together once during the two weeks and probably just as well. The supply was running low with a precious six left between them, six they had crushed and re-crushed into a fine powder and put into a single envelope. So the time had come to start thinking by weight and height.

# 51

"Adisita, if you come with us our children will not sleep," Pilar chuckled, "unless to touch their little noses together once more. We will leave you here, to enjoy the music and dance a while longer."

Maria and Ercilia were already hugging when Pi wrapped her arms around Adisita. "We will phone each other often, Pi, and you will come to Montreal this summer. After that Maria and I will come to Mexico again."

"Sí, Adisita. We will see each other very soon." They eased away from the warm embrace. "Ven aquí, pequeña," she said to Maria, "you who have made my Ercilia so unhappy to leave you. Come. Hug me and make me just as sad, you little vixen."

"Addie and I won't forget our promises, Pi. We will call, and you'll call us. The rest of our vacation will seem so empty now. We'll just stay around the pool and crying all week."

"Good, pequeña, and I hope you annoy Adisita with your noisy tears as much as Ercilia will annoy me on our way home." She squeezed harder. "I love you, we love you both. Adios."

The four huddled and hugged together, kissing streaked cheeks and wiping away each other's warm tears.

# 52

"I don't believe it! They're taking off," said Shane, drowned out by the music. "What the fuck! I told you they'd leave early to go home."

Bret was laughing. "Take it easy, Shane. There's enough to go around. Don't sweat the small stuff. The code still applies: All on one, one on all."

"But, holy shit, the one in the red dress. Did you see her dancing? Did you see those legs, and shit, her ass and her tits?"

"Yeah, and the redhead has tits too, which I get to first. You get seconds unless I get busy with her. Comprendo?"

Thurston asked the key question: "How do we get the drinks to them? Doesn't the blonde think Chad's a dickhead?"

"Fuck you, Williams."

"Rivers, it'll be easier for you to fuck me if we don't think of something real fast. And, fuck you."

"Check it out, the redhead's leaving."

"Maybe she needs to take a leak."

"No. They don't do that huggy stuff when they go for a piss. She's taking off."

Bret shoved Chad violently. "Chad, get the fuck over there, now. We are not going home dry. Understand? Now get over there and tell her drinks are on the way because you saw her sitting alone and this time don't act like a fucking asshole."

"What if she wants to leave?"

Bret answered as he stood. "Don't let her, unless you don't want to get into her. Then I'll go."

Shane and Thurston followed Bret to the bar.

# 53

"Hello, Addison."

She turned. "Hi, Chad. Going to do some dancing?"

"No, the heat would kill me. I was walking around and stopped for a drink at the bar before heading to my room to pack. I'm leaving around eight." He hesitated for affect, his eyes searching past her. "I saw your friends leave and took the liberty to order you a glass of white wine. Let's call it an apology for acting so geeky on the boat and last night."

"You're not at all geeky, Chad." What else could she say?

"I try not to be most times, but I am around you."

"Are you going to stand there until your bus leaves tomorrow, or are you going to sit and relax?"

Yes! He sat, pulling out the chair closest to her as the drinks arrived. "Thank you." He worried more than pensive. "I didn't think to order three drinks. Is Maria coming back?"

"Maybe a little later, if she doesn't fall asleep. She's gone to freshen up. She had a lot of sun today, and a few drinks. She's also sad about Pilar and Ercilia leaving."

"I hope I didn't make you feel crowded last night. I really enjoyed talking with you, and on the boat. If I'd seen you first I probably would have asked for a different table so you wouldn't think I planned to meet you."

"Not at all, Chad, I enjoyed talking with you, and I didn't think any such thing," she lied. "Sometimes girl talk can be so one-sided, a little slanted."

"You mean you were talking about how bad we guys are."

"No, we were talking about everything, including guys, or whatever happened to come up next. You know, vacation talk."

His shirt was sticking to him. Good planning, Chad, geek, he thought, wearing a silk shirt in thirty-plus Celsius heat. His heart was pounding and he could feel his temples pulsating erratically. He wanted to reach over and peel apart the layers of her skirt to see her panties, to squeeze her bare thighs, pull her onto his lap and push his mouth hard against her beautiful, round breasts as he pushed his hardening member as deep as he possibly could inside her.

# 54

The guys told the bartender what they wanted delivered to their friend with the sexy blonde, and as the wine and tequila were placed on the tray they ordered three more for themselves. When the young man went to fill those glasses Bret Wilmington did in a calculated instant what would alter Maria's life forever. And, not long after, when Chad casually signalled for another round, he had no way of knowing he and his three fraternity brothers had sealed the fate of innocent young women who loved each other deeply. Nor could he have known that when Bret had settled the tab, he had thoughtlessly signed certificates for each of their subsequent deaths.

Bret threw the empty plastic envelope into an ashtray on his way to join his buddies at a table where they could see Addison and judge Chad. Then they forgot him and gave Addison their full attention, though none could remember her name. She was the blonde, the lesbian dyke, the real question being: Was Chad the one who deserved her panties? Shane dug into his pockets for the quarter: one out of three, then one out of two, and they deferred to Bret once again.

## 55

"Okay, Chad, but don't feel badly if I don't finish it. I'm starting to feel a bit of a buzz."

"I promise I'll get you home safe and sound, without a headache. If you prefer, I'll get one of the ladies here to take you back."

"I'm not that bad. Now, tell me more about your fascinating career." He did, and Addison had no difficulty listening as she thought about Maria and the friends she would miss so much until the next time. "That's so interesting, Cha…"

"Are you okay, Addison? It's pretty hot. Would you like some water or something?"

"No, I don't think so. But, you're right, the air is very warm."

"Let me get you some water, and ice cubes for your wrists."

Then, moments later, "here's your water, Addison, and your ice cubes."

"Who are you?" she asked the man.

"I'm a friend of Chad. He asked me to bring the water for you." Bret put the glass in front of her. He needn't have bothered. The drug had begun taking affect whether she took the tequila-spiked water or not. "Chad will join us in a few moments. He's gone to the men's room. We told him we'd stay with you until he comes back."

Addison nodded knowingly. "Hope he wipes," she said weakly. "We know about that, we all know."

Shane shrugged his shoulders. "What does that mean, some kind of dyke talk?"

"What else? And where's Mr. Jerkoff?"

Thurston couldn't resist. "He's still in the can getting the tool ready."

"What tool?" Addison wanted to know, wondering where all the voices were coming from. She could only see one man, certain he wasn't the one from before.

"Addison, let me walk you to your room. It's very late. You must be tired."

She looked up without seeing him. "Thanks," she thought she wanted to say more, but she couldn't remember his name. What she did want was her little Maria, her warm and soft Maria. She had to leave and held out her hand to Chad.

The couples dancing ignored them. To those seated around the bar she was another tipsy girl who hadn't known when to stop, one of a dozen others that and every other night. Most were indifferent. Those who weren't didn't know what to do, so they did nothing. Bret had selected the perfect spot, not even the security guards would hear or see them. The entire complex was noisy with the surround sound of the loud Latin beat and the ceaseless thunder of the ocean was metres away. Better yet, the guards were focused on the event, not the sea.

"Get her in. Hurry, for fuck sake." Bret ordered. "And Thurston, you get more beers and tequila. Be cool about it and make sure no one fucking sees you coming back."

Thurston left, not even thinking of himself as Bret's replacement go-boy, and Addison wondered why the stairway to her room was so dark and why she couldn't stand on her own.

"Shane, I need you to hold her steady. When I say so, throw her over my shoulder." Bret retreated a few steps, taking her full weight as Shane let her fall forward onto his shoulders.

Shane followed behind. "Damn, that's frigging sexy, Bret."

"What is?"

"I can see her entire bare ass. Her skirt's hanging over

her back. This one's going to be fun. Shit ...talk about nice and tight."

Chad asked if she was alright, Bret answering that she was about to get a whole lot better and Shane reached up, gripping her bare buttocks.

"Shane, get off. We've got all night."

"Sorry Bret. Couldn't help myself. Shit she's nice."

"And don't forget she's mine," Chad whispered forcefully. "So get your filthy hands off her."

"Whatever, Chad, but can we all just frigging shut up?"

The top floor of the open-air massage station was an ideal venue made that much better by three vinyl beds specially constructed with various body positions in mind, the same body positions Bret, Shane and Thurston had in mind. Perfect, but a deal was a deal and Chad got to go first. She lay in front of him with her legs together and her arms by her side: absolutely the most beautiful thing he had ever seen and he eased both hands under her half opened skirt as his friends stood scanning the black sea. Chad's time had come.

Her skin was warm and soft. He tugged at the snaps, letting her skirt fall away, draping over the sides of the narrow table. Her belly was bare, her pale tan deeper in the moonlight and against the pure white of her panties. He reached forward grabbing at the silky white bands, pulling back, not thinking he might have hurt her. The panties came away easily for him, mindless he had put each of her knees over his shoulders. He had never seen anything like it. He'd seen labia before, but Addison's were soft pink and smooth, with none of the coarseness or harsher colouring he found so unfeminine on other women. She was a goddess; he loved her, and would have to share her later. But for the moment she was his alone. He would tell her later they had been alone, when they would wake up in his bed together. She would never discover the truth, she would never

150

remember. She was his, and she felt the same way. He pushed the halter top to her neck, unable to reach farther or kiss the warmth of her perfectly rounded breasts with the perfectly round little buds which were finally his to press his hands into and pinch and kiss. He gently dropped her legs, letting them hang over the end of the table as he moved to the other end without once taking his hands from her. Her arms came up easily and gently over her head, and her halter slid between her shoulders and the vinyl table without resistance. He pulled her forward so he could mount the table with less difficulty, but first he went to each side of the table and sucked intently on each breast as the closest hand pressed firmly against the moist, bare folds of her labia. Bret glance over his shoulder, shaking his head, then seeing the panties on the floor he went to pick them up without paying much attention to Chad whose head disappeared between slightly-tanned thighs, sounding as though he was slurping milk from a bowl.

He tripped when kicking his pants away, so what? They hadn't seen. He hadn't thought of how he would feel making love to his girl in front of three other guys. He left his underwear on, pushing them under his genitals, ready to love her hard enough to take her away from her lesbian whore friend. Addison wasn't like that, she was different, she simply didn't know better.

He had never been in a woman so tight, so hot, or so in love with him. He wiped away her tears, telling her how much he loved her as his hot breath became one with her own, blocking her muffled words. He hadn't been wrong. She was begging for his forgiveness, telling him with each urgent thrust how she had been so wrong, how she loved him so much.

# 56

Maria, my heart, my love, te quiero mi amor, te amo. Je t'aime, je t'aimerai toujours my precious little girl. I will always love you. I know who is doing this to me. I know I should be with you now, I know, and please don't ever hate me for what is happening to me. I am so sorry. Please forgive me little girl, mi amor. I was wrong not to stay with you. I love you. I will always love you very much. I never thought I could be so stupid, I never thought I could be so naïve. What he is doing hurts so much, mi amor. I cannot tell you how much.

She screamed out the very moment Chad ground himself into her with a final thrust, pulling out reluctantly. He was jubilant, not because he'd done her, not because he'd been with her, because they knew she'd be better than any of the others and she was his.

# 57

Bret was the first to react to her scream, slapping his hand tightly over her open her mouth. He tried hard to focus on the outer folds of her lips and not Chad's hardened member retreating slowly from them as though he was the one being tortured by inexperience.

He was up next and rinsed away Chad with what was left of his beer. He could see her pinkness even in the muted darkness and hoped she was as smooth as he'd imagined. She wouldn't be as good as the redhead, but what the hell. She was pre-lubed, ready and glistening, and girls loved getting laid. They all did, so here it comes, and get ready. If this doesn't turn you around nothing will. I'm Bret Wilmington, he told himself. I'm the man, the best. I have to be, I will be, and don't you ever forget it bitch. So lay back and enjoy, and she was as good for Bret as he had hoped. For Addison, what he did was excruciatingly and inexplicably painful, and although she had no sense of time, she did sense it wasn't over.

Shane was third, doing exactly what Chad had done, if not for the same reason. When her knees were over his shoulders he raised her off the table to wipe away Bret and the beer from the table, then he wiped her buttocks with her halter top before dropping her legs and telling Thurston and Bret to take each of her hands at the other end as he pulled her by her thighs into a comfortable position. Her thighs were tight against his hips for the best results and he was too preoccupied to notice his assistants enjoying the use of their free hands or that his pants and boxers had fallen to his ankles.

## 58

Pi, es Adisita, your friend and Ercilia's friend. I am glad we kissed, Pi. I am glad my little Maria kissed Ercilia. I am trying very hard to remember that right now Pi. Your soft lips pressing against mine and our gentleness was nice, not like this. We had fun together, sensuous and innocent, not like this. How we both came to adore you and Ercilia, how I love you both. Did I ever tell you how much I love my little Maria? Can I tell you now? Can I tell you how much I will miss her? Be her friend for me, Pi. I will hold you to your promise and Ercilia to hers. Tell her how much I love her and that I am with her. I will always be with her. Tell her how sorry I am that I will never see her again.

# 59

"Do all your women mutter and moan this much, Pendleton?"

"It's like doing a frigging virgin, if I ever knew what that was like. Shit, I couldn't grab myself this hard."

"She's a lesbian. How many times do you think she's got it this way? She probably is a virgin. And do you think you could finish up and get out of her to make room for someone else? It's not like we've got all night."

Shane looked over to Chad who was facing away. "Guess Chad over there knows how to pick them after all." He took a deep breath before lunging, squeezing his eyes closed, exhaling deeply. "Done. God that's hard on the back. I'm sweating like a pig."

Thurston passed him his beer as he lingered a few extra moments to enjoy the view as her full length was pulled onto the table. Thurston came in last, luck of the draw, but they were guys and he didn't mind. He'd probably be first next time. Anyway, what mattered was that she was warm, wet and tight. That's what Spring Break was for. The supply was endless and who came first seldom mattered.

"Shane, Bret, help me flip her over and hold her like that for me till I get going." He saw Chad spin around, answering him even before he spoke. "You know I like them sunny side up. Tits don't do it for me and ass like this doesn't come along every day."

"No!" Chad's whisper was violent, not the Chad they knew. "Not that way."

"I didn't mean doing her that way, I meant I like playing with their asses more than their tits when I'm getting into it, so to speak. Now, do you mind?"

He barely moved. Addison came to him, slowly, the perfect cleft of her smooth buttocks lining him up until he felt her engulf him. He pushed her tight into the edge of the table so she wouldn't slide back to interfere with him, each thrust pushing precious air from her lungs. Her face was flat against the heated vinyl and the motion of Thurston pushing so hard made her face and breasts push and pull reluctantly against the table top, causing her head to take on a comical jerking attitude that was disruptive to him, preventing a fluid motion and making a good rhythm impossible. He told them to get a pillow and put it under her head, not waiting for them to react before using her pungent moisture to help with his probing that became progressively eager and aggressive as soon as Chad turned away.

# 60

Mi amor, my little girl, my heart, my love and my life, how can I tell you what I feel, and how I love you so? I have spoken with Pi, Maria. She knows how much I love you and she understands it's alright for all of us to love each other the way we do, with our hearts. She will always be there for you, mi amor, and you for them. All of you being together will make all of us whole again in our hearts, but you must feel what I am telling you right now, though I know you will need time. Do not hate me, mi amor. What he is doing to me hurts so much, though I cannot scream, and I do not understand why not, and yet I do. It hurts so much Maria. You could never hate me more than I do myself right now, and I could not bear that you do.

# 61

"Four for four, gents, and I think this lady needs a rest. Bret, you pull, I'll push. Chad, pass me the rest of my beer."

Thurston went for his own beer. Chad went to Addison, placing his hands over her buttocks, kneading them with his eyes closed as though praying before telling them to help turn her onto her back.

When they were done Shane and Bret sat on one outer table, Chad and Thurston on the other. Addison lay in the centre, her glazed eyes staring at Chad for help or compassion. There was still time. Her body glistened as though covered with millions of minute sequins. She was completely motionless, her arms by her side, her eyes unblinking, and Thurston jumped down to check, clasping her wrist between his thumb and forefinger. He let her wrist drop limply by her side, smiling. Yes, gentlemen, he assured them, she was up for round two. She was up for one more, though she needed something to keep her in the mood and Bret brought over the full glass of tequila as Thurston raised the dead weight of her head and shoulders from the pillow. When they were done they took their seats beside Shane and Chad to watch her.

"No!" Chad was adamant, "she's had enough. You guys have to help me get her to my room. That was the deal."

"Chad, get real." Thurston answered. "We do that and we'll be as fucked as she is. Besides, she knew what she was doing or she would've gone with the other dykes. Right, gentlemen?"

They agreed. The time was 2:00 AM. They could be gone before three if Chad got back with the beers and her tequila without screwing up. He'd be at least twenty minutes, giving each of them more than enough time once they repositioned her.

# 62

Pi; tell my little girl she must find another Addie, another girl who will fill her heart with the love and joy and tenderness she will want to feel once again. Tell her I love her because she will not understand at first what has happened. The pain is unbearable. There is no warm feeling, no tenderness or love, yet I feel strangely warm inside, even though the warm night air is cool. I feel at peace, Pi, and I am so in love with my little girl. I feel so strange. I wish I could explain. Can I tell you what I know Pi? I know I will be with you once again, with you and Ercilia forever, and we will be with Maria who will always need us.

Maria, my baby girl, it's me, Addie, and I need you not to be afraid for me. It's over, mi amor, it's over, and how I hate that I will never again feel your smooth warmth and hear your endless chatter I always loved so much. But you will never be alone. I have taken care of you one last time and I will wait for you here, where time does not exist, for as long as you take to be with me. But you must also live, mi amor, for me as much as for yourself. You must live and be happy. I know you will feel what I am saying, that soon you will believe what I say and understand. Pi will help you, and Ercilia. Mi amor, what I am feeling is as euphoric as it is inconsolable to me. How I want to absorb all the pain I know you will soon feel, into the sense well-being which is beginning to infuse me. My body is leaving you now, Maria, not me, not the Addie you know, not the Addie who will be with you forever, until we can once again be together. Please believe me, my precious girl, and forgive me. I was always your protector, and you were mine, and who will protect you now?

Maria, how wonderful, how happy I am. I can see you perfectly. I feel you as I never have before and I hear your breath, a secret whisper between us, as though I am one with you, mi amor. I am beside you, Maria. Do you feel me? Please show me that you feel me this one last time, my little girl. How I want to feel your arms around me one more time. Yes, a bit more, Maria, a little bit more. Can you feel my kiss, mi amor, can you feel by breath? Can you hear me Maria?

# 63

From the courtyard entrance, both rooms were dark. Maria told herself she would touch up her make-up, pee, and hurry back to Addison. Though when she walked through the door to their room darkness prevailed and she succumbed to her day, leaving a scattered trail of shoes, her bustier and skirt before falling atop the ruffled bed and slipping reluctantly into a dreamy and blissful sleep.

Curled into her pillow, the warm breeze blowing across the bed from the balcony was as soothing as a tender caress she might have dreamt was real. She inhaled deeply, luxuriating in the blissful moment, easing her pillow to one side and laying on her back. She brought her arms across her front against a wisp of cooler air, pressing her fingertips unconsciously against her lips, unaware she had whispered, unaware Addison's response was as real, that she would love Maria forever and forever remain by her lover's side.

## 64

Addison lay perfectly still as Chad leaned against the door frame at the top of the stairs, four opened beers wedged between his fingers. His three buds waited quietly, the beach becoming increasingly dark as threatening clouds came noisily together to eradicate the soft light of the moon. Addison was as he had left her, though one of her legs had fallen over the side of the table. He should have been angry with them; instead he was mesmerized by her smooth moist lips and her openness.

Bret snapped his fingers for his beer, startling Chad before speaking to Shane, though he was speaking to all of them. "Let's get our asses the fuck out of here. It's going to piss rain any minute, and the last thing we need is someone seeing us leave this shit place."

"What about Addison?" asked Chad, not very certain of himself.

"What about her? The party's over."

"You promised." He stood by her side, not thinking to bring up her leg, unconsciously massaging her in small tight circles, feeling her softness and her lingering moist warmth, not realizing his fingers had worked their way into the tight curvatures of her buttocks. Her skin had dried and her body had cooled, he thought, enough for her to be more comfortable and he brought his fingers to his face to inhale her essence one last time before dressing her. He wouldn't do to her what they wanted. He felt a special closeness to her, something they had shared, and he pressed himself against the edge to make himself feel good until he saw the blood.

"It's going to start pissing any minute, Rivers. We've got to get out of here. You've had your shot. If you need one more, that's fine. We're gone."

"She can't stay here. She's starting to get cold."

The three exchanged glances, forgetting their beers.

"Then stop playing with it and cover it with a towel so we can get out of here." Bret's voice was commanding without its usual arrogance. "She'll be fine, Rivers. This place is perfectly protected. She'll wake up in the morning feeling great. They all do, so what if she's a little embarrassed. So let's just get the frig out of here."

They didn't wait for him to decide. Thurston took Chad by one arm, Shane the other, and Bret checked the floor. Chad wanted her once more, he needed more of her, but the time was closing in on three and Bret was always right. He strained over his shoulder to see her one last time. He didn't expect her arms to fall from her sides, swaying imperceptibly, or her other leg falling to balance her, leaving Chad with a memory which would titillate and haunt him for the rest of his life. He made a mental note to secretly check on her in the morning, knowing they wouldn't let him. He had seen the blood on his fingertips as they pulled him away, but, of course, she was a virgin. She would have bled, and he had no need to go back.

They had waited for him because they couldn't trust him. They could accept him being a geek and a jerk, that was one thing, but they weren't about to jeopardize prosperous futures because he wanted to get laid. Everyone got what they wanted or needed, including the blonde, and it was time for them to go. They agreed three-to-one and pulled him down the stairs.

# 65

Maria woke near seven Saturday morning. She ran to the balcony, leaning as far as she could into Pilar's and Ercilia's darkened room before hurrying into the corridor to knock as loudly as she dared on their door. No answer came, the cold sweeping through Maria's body paralyzing her. Addison would have phoned her on her cell, or called the room, or something. She would never have stayed out all night by herself.

They didn't know anyone and the rain falling since the dark dawn was torrential and relentless. In her heart she knew and she ran barefooted without thinking to the front desk where the hotel manager immediately escorted her into his private office. She was a sight: completely drenched with her tee-shirt and shorts clinging to her glistening skin, dishevelled red hair hanging in thick chestnut strands, greenish make-up streaking her face from eyes reddened with imploring tears.

The informal search began without hesitation, with exact instructions directly from the manager that all parts of the complex and surrounding areas were to be searched by security, housekeeping and the activities committee. Then he contacted his counterparts in the adjacent properties before ordering a warm breakfast to his office for Maria and instructing Housekeeping to bring dry clothing from her room.

Once she had eaten what little she could, and changed, he stayed with her until his phone rang at 10:00 AM, when he left to attend to hotel business, explaining he would not be long. And he hadn't been long at all. The security staff had found Addison and was waiting for his direction before calling the police.

# 66

The guards hadn't run into the open-air massage station to search for Addison, rather to escape the ceaseless deluge and only by chance did one of them notice the stairway, the narrow trickle of rose-coloured rainwater prompting him to climb the stairs, thinking he would close the shutters someone had left open. What erupted from his mouth was a shriek, obviating the need to yell to his partners. Within seconds the three men stood in shock, kissing their clenched fists and crossing themselves in murmured prayers.

The young girl's body was naked, lying face-up with her bruised legs and arms dangling over the sides of the narrow table. Her hair draped over the top edge, matted with the same rain water trickling from her discoloured face in large droplets. The concave of her abdomen was a shallow reservoir draining from her sides in thin rivulets and the wide V of her open legs channelled a diluted red water to the inside of her bare calves. They couldn't take their eyes from her, but what they felt was far from sexual. All three were fathers, and devout. What they saw was a little girl, not a young woman, who died violently at the malicious hands of someone evil who hadn't cared enough to cover her before abandoning her.

Each one sensed that to speak between themselves would break the sanctity of the young girl's ascent, each one wondering about the evil that had preceded them. Finally, long seconds later, one reached for his walkie-talkie as the others went to where dry towels had been folded for the coming day. Señor Rayo arrived moments later and what he saw was incongruous to him: three visibly distraught men standing by the side of a young female corpse whose body was strangely covered by towels fluttering in the harsh wind as the men tried to keep the towels from falling away. Then the orders came and all three responded without hesitation, thankful the big boss had come to take over, though Rayo didn't stay long and before returning to his villa and Maria he instructed a barman to pour three fingers of tequila that he emptied in as many gulps. The liquid warmed and relaxed him, doing nothing to prepare him. It was one of those times when it's best to dull the mind. Then he reached for the phone to first call the police before calling the assistant manager to have Maria brought to his private villa where her reaction would not disturb the other guests, and where his wife could help him the way no man could.

# 67

He'd been gone thirty minutes, which to him seemed like seconds and to Maria, hours. His wife had left the door unlocked and when he walked through into the wide expanse of the foyer his entire body shivered at what he saw. His wife was grasping Maria's hands in hers, trying her best to console the young girl, probably telling her everything would work out, he thought. ¡Mierda! Nothing would work out, and the women knew as much as soon as they saw his eyes glazed over, his body enshrouded in defeat and trying desperately not to appear useless. None but a few gardeners would have heard Maria's scream; anyone watching would wonder whether los Rayo were keeping Maria from collapsing or hugging her.

# 68

His grip was firm, his embrace tender, and his wife cried, feeling completely useless. Addison was dead and he wouldn't talk about specifics, though the police would arrive within moments and would talk with her honestly and openly, on his word as a gentleman, and Maria believed him.

Numbness took over from reality. Addison wasn't dead. They were all wrong. She was sleeping, or playing games, or something. She wasn't dead, not Addie. However police mentality has a way of changing such comforting thoughts. Familiarity with death makes them vulgar in the face of misery, immune and insensitive, and Sr. Rayo intervened making certain the questions were brief and routine. When the police returned to the body, he escorted them to ensure the dead girl would be treated with due respect.

Señora Rayo didn't stop cradling Maria throughout the interview, holding her close until their family doctor arrived to sedate her. She wasn't allowed to see Addison and the manner in which Sr. Rayo spoke was gentle yet firm as he told Maria everything while saying nothing. Precisely at 11:45 Addison was carried away as a precious cargo under Sr. Rayo's supervision, no one arguing at his insistence that his men be responsible for carrying the young woman to the ambulance. The three guards volunteered and Addison was transported to La Clínica Regional for processing restricted to a rape kit, blood work and an external examination until her family could be contacted.

# 69

Flight 7230 departed for Mexico City on time with four, visibly uneasy passengers. Drinking more than they had was impossible, not drinking more was the difficult part, but being refused boarding privileges would have meant being somewhere they no longer found entertaining.

# 70

On any other day of the week the LCL corporate jet would have taken off within minutes of the matter-of-fact phone call from the Mexican authorities, however Saturday the pilot wasn't scheduled to fly. The instruction was clear: Leave what you're doing and get here now. When he hurried through the doors of the private lounge reserved for a privileged few, dressed in paint-stained Dockers and tee-shirt, all heads pivoted, some frowning at the affront while others smirked at the quizzical lack of decorum.

Larivière and his personal assistant were by the pilot's side immediately, without disrupting their cellular conversations and the Challenger 604 was airborne en route to Zihuantanejo at 6:00 PM eastern. None but those in the flight decks of the lined-up commercial jets were privy to the reason for the priority take-off which would arrive before nine, local time.

Most high-ranking politicians preferred hiding behind voice-mails and Larivière managed to speak to only one of his several contacts in the State department. He would need each minute of the four-hour flight time to locate the others and for those persons to contact their Mexican counterparts, many of whom he knew, some of whom were very close to Los Pinos.

The Challenger's wheels touched down at five-past-nine, two hours after coming within mere kilometres of Mexicana flight 880 over Nashville. All had been taken care of according to his wishes, notwithstanding certain formalities he could not circumvent, irrespective of favours owed, and the Montreal Police would meet him with the Medical Examiner at the airport upon his return. In Mexico, senior officers met him in the company of grim-faced senior state officials without the glitter of flashing Nikons, smiling señoritas in vibrant red costumes and the usual Customs agents.

# 71

MX 880 took off on time and moments later three hands raised prohibited mickies in a toast of relief. Their earlier bravado, which had soon changed to fear and a festering paranoia, slowly returned, immune from Chad's haunting realization that Addison might not have awakened, that he was possibly an accomplice to murder. Eventually his sullenness lightened with the departure of their connecting flight, his bravado returning under the influence and exhilaration of booze. By the time they arrived in Montreal he knew the girl hadn't been raped and killed. She had been done by the best. The worst for Chad being that he had shared the girl he loved with his friends, though he had been the first.

# 72

Larivière wasn't prepared. Despite having been told in discreet terms what to expect, they had said nothing remotely close to what he was seeing. Her face was uncovered for identification with clinical indifference by a novice technician, Addison's mask of torment as gruesome as hours earlier, despite the female medical examiner thought to clean her face and comb her hair. When he asked to see everything his daughter had suffered, the ME lightly touched his arm compassionately and shook her head.

She had been raped by four different men within a very short time frame, and sodomized by three. They hadn't worn protection. Either they had known she was a virgin or hadn't anticipated the opportunity. Her blood-alcohol levels were high, most likely induced by them, and she had ingested an extremely dangerous amount of the date-rape roofies, the reason she hadn't struggled, though the cause of death was suffocation due to her face down position during the final moments of her assault. The internal and external bruising was extreme, particularly across her hips and her breasts, likely caused by contact with the edge of the table which was consistent with aggressive, non-consensual sexual activity as well as her contact with the surface of the table. Her death would have taken a few hours and would have been very cruel.

The body would be prepared for transport and the official medical report would be forwarded Canadian authorities. He had no need to see more. Seeing her face and what they told him was sufficient. She had died very badly and no one could do anything about it. There was DNA, which was overrated by all but those who knew its limitations. They had found her in an open area between expansive hotel properties at the peak of a torrential rain storm, where hundreds of people had come together the previous night to party, and since her discovery at least a dozen flights would have departed from Zihuantanejo. So where would one search for four men in the company of thousands?

# 73

The procession of blue flashing lights stopped behind the barrier at the entrance to the hotel complex where guards instructed the police to follow them to the manager's private villa. Larivière didn't want to be there, driven by an uncharacteristic sense of decency. He had never met her, he had never seen her. She was young, cute he thought, and obviously devastated in spite of the sedative holding her emotions in check. She was smaller than Addison, shorter by a centimetre and slimmer, yet her small frame stood before him with a defiance he wouldn't recall until weeks later.

"Elle vous a aimé profondément, M. Larivière. Your daughter loved you as much as I loved her, but now you will never hear her speak the words."

She spoke matter-of-factly, apologizing to Señora Rayo for her use of French before switching to Spanish which she knew everyone understood. The exchange was uncomfortable and functional, excluding Maria for the most part as she came and went according to her level of concentration. She would spend the night with Sr. and Sra. Rayo, Larivière and his assistant would be given complimentary accommodations at the hotel and everyone else would leave. There was nothing more to say. Social graces and niceties would have been shallow, out of place. The officials would return at 8:00 AM, the jet would be ready at nine and Addison would be onboard.

# 74

Señora Rayo insisted with Latina obstinacy that she stay with Maria until the girl was buckled into her seat on the plane. They had become close for all the wrong reasons, which Maria would always remember.

The silver LCL Challenger took off at 9:00 AM. The pilot had spent the night onboard with airport privileges and three pre-flight hours were spent securing Addison's coffin to the interior of the Challenger intended for pampered executives, not the dead daughters of those executives.

Seconds after the wheels left the ground the jet disappeared from sight and Señora Rayo lapsed into tears, the events of the past twenty-four hours reaching a pressurized crescendo. She had listened to Maria's softly spoken words, quietly aware the distraught young woman meant to be sincere. She understood, and said goodbye to Maria in her thoughts.

Larivière chose to sit by the pilot, leaving his assistant in the cabin with his daughter and her friend. There was no need to hurry. The flight time was five hours and Maria's hand wouldn't move a millimetre on the rough coffin throughout the flight. The normally impervious assistant knew not to speak, not wanting to invade Maria's final moments alone with Addison who had become her whole life. She understood the young women were sharing their final hours together and peered into the porthole to allow them privacy while hiding her own compassionate tears, musing how she would ever again admire the cold-hearted man hiding in the flight deck.

# 75

Señor Rayo kept his promise to Maria. He didn't stop calling and leaving messages for Pilar or Ercilia. They were to call him no matter what the hour, and when he was called away on hotel business his wife took over the duty until noon on Sunday when the phone rang and he explained to an excitable Pilar why they had wanted so desperately to speak with her.

Her scream was piercing, long moments passing before the phone was answered by a voice that was both afraid and aggressive. Ercilia tried to listen intently, but she was shaking and crying, stamping her feet, barely able to hear his horrible words beyond her loud denials. When he finished she glanced at her watch, shaking her head in agreement before disconnecting and sinking to the floor to cradle a convulsing Pilar in her trembling arms.

## 76

Maria stepped from the jet at 4:00 PM eastern, immune to the red–blue flashes of police cruisers and the yellow-orange of airport escort vehicles. She had grown up not being impressed or intimidated by the police. More likely was the reverse. They were there to meet the daughter of mob boss Angie Bardollini, whose dyke girlfriend had been murdered, and the camera clicked repeated frames as though they had never before taken her photograph.

She refused to travel in a police car. She would accompany her girlfriend in the ambulance. She mocked them when admonished not to interfere with a police investigation, responding that the crime was committed in Mexico and they all knew any investigation would be a joke at best. And if they wanted any information at all from her they would get out of her way and let her be with Addison. Larivière was equally accommodating, for different reasons: he knew how to talk to those whom he considered less than his equal, which certainly included the Montreal police and when the convoy of flashing lights pulled away, his black limo trailed behind. He would meet with them the next day at his office. His assistant would arrange the time, and if she, the friend, wanted to handle the arrangements he had no objection. The sooner he could get away from her, the better.

# 77

The examination was a formality, a formal waste of time. An autopsy was refused and the Medical Examiner found nothing he could add to the Mexican report, noting he had no reason to desecrate her body any more than she had been and Maria travelled with Addison one last time to the funeral home.

They understood completely, they told her. Mademoiselle Larivière would be treated with the utmost delicacy and respect, without the usual invasive procedures, though that would certainly necessitate expediency. The funeral directors drove her home as a courtesy. She had no friends, no family, though they knew that wasn't quite true. The hour was also late and she was beyond tired, fighting against the effects of the sedatives, unable to focus on one thought before another took over. She had no sense of the sombre limousine moving. She had forgotten her luggage on the plane, Larivière could go to hell, her father could kill him, Pi hadn't called her, Addison should be with her, she left Addison alone that night, what happened was her fault, Ercilia should have called her, she hated her father, she would never see Addie again, Pi loved Adisita so why hadn't she called, Señora Rayo was so nice, she loved Addison, she would always love Addison.

When the limo pulled in front of the carriage-style condo the driver climbed out first to open her door as Maria looked over, thinking Addison had climbed out from the other side. She must have, she wasn't there. Then she remembered and cried. She would always be alone, Addison would never come back. She took the driver's hand without noticing the car across the street running with its lights on. He helped her to the door, opening his hand for the key and waited until the door closed behind her and he saw a second light go on.

She fell onto the sofa, exhausted as much from the medication as from crying and cried again for the first time since hearing the door of her father's house slam shut behind her. She tried hard not to let her mind race, with so much to do in so little time. She had already made certain decisions at the funeral home, and Pi should have called her by now. There was no red light, no message. She would have to buy Addie a new dress and she'd been gone thirty-six hours. Why hadn't Pilar called? If anyone should have worried for her, she should have. She and Addison had acted like sisters all week, mother hens making fun of her and Ercilia who was no better. She wasn't calling either.

Something very wrong must have happened. She had to stop thinking of herself. They must have been killed in the mountains, on their way home, or maybe something worse had happened to them, something horrible, like what happened to Addie. She reached for her purse, emptying the contents onto the sofa, and ran to the phone to dial the number pencilled in by Ercilia's name.

"Ercilia, Pilar, please answer me. It's Maria. Please tell me nothing bad has happened to you. Addie is dead, Pilar. It happened after you left us on Friday. I left her too, that's why she's dead. It wouldn't have happened if I had been with her to protect her. She was raped and murdered and wasn't found by the hotel guards until late in the morning. She stayed for the fiesta so I fell asleep and forgot her. I forgot Addie. We searched for her everywhere. They left her body uncovered in the pouring rain on one of the tables at the beach. They didn't let me see her, Ercilia. I can't see Addie again until tomorrow morning. What they did to her was horrible. She's never been with a man, Pi, and I cry each time I think of her terror and her pain. They told me there were four of them. They hurt her everywhere, Pi…"

# 78

The tiny red dot began flashing as Ercilia pressed her thumb onto the send button. They had seen her arrive in the limo, when Pilar stopped Ercilia with a firm pressure on her hand.

"Es ella, Pi, es Maria. She's calling us."

"Don't waste time with her message, chica. Call her. Tell her to open the door. Tell her we are here. We…"

The door slammed hard, cutting off the words, and Pilar moved quickly to catch up with Ercilia before her hands began pounding against the steel-reinforced door. Pilar let her be, pressing the doorbell and calling out a loud "chica" seconds before the door flew open.

"No importa nada, mi amor," using Addie's endearment, "estamos aquí para ti, estamos aquí."

Maria pulled them into the entrance where they cried together in a huddle of kisses. Once inside they listened to her, curled onto the sofa, Pilar on one side, Ercilia on the other. She left nothing out, and when she finished Pilar went to the kitchen to make soup and sandwiches before Maria spent the rest of the night showing and telling them everything she could about Addie. She repeated herself often, and they let her. She was talking about Adisita, and then she asked them to forgive her for what she had done and she buckled over in tears.

"Forgive you for what, chica? What do you think you have done?"

Pilar and Ercilia stroked her back and her hair, waiting.

"It was my fault. I never left her before. I left her alone. I should have stayed with her. Then this wouldn't have happened." She wrapped her arms around Ercilia. "I can't remember if I told her how much I love her. I always told her how much, now I can't remember."

"I do remember mi amor. You told her all the time. We

heard you."

"But I really loved her, Pi" Maria sniffled.

"Mi amor, she knows. She always has, and she always will. She is with us. Don't you feel her? I feel her, Maria. I feel her with us now, and I know she will always be with you." Pilar stood. "Now tell me where your laundry room is so we will be ready for tomorrow." She turned to Ercilia. "Put her in a hot shower, and then to bed. You both look horrible. Adisita would not want to see either of you this way."

They had left home so quickly after Señor Rayo insisted they accept his offer on behalf of the hotel to pay their airfare to Montreal that they hadn't washed their clothes. Pilar watched them leave and waited to hear the water before she went to find the laundry room Maria had forgotten to tell her about. When the clothes were laundered and pressed she went into the bedroom where Maria was sleeping inside Ercilia's arms, their faces touching, still damp with tears. She smiled, shaking her head as she whispered quietly to Adisita. Some things never change, and now she was alone to care for her girls. She had seen the wine cellar and the little bar recessed into the dining room wall and who cared sunrise was moments away. The first brandy burned, the second didn't, and the third was mellow. Adisita's murder was her fault as much as Maria's. She was the one who insisted they not go back to their rooms. They would have if she had let them, and now she knew they should have.

"Lo arrepiento, Adisita, muchísimo. Te amo, lo arrepiento, y te echaré de menos para siempre."

She did feel Addison beside her. She knew Addison felt her love and that she would always be missed. Her lips curled in a soft smile as she felt Adisita's lips press gently against her cheek, opening her eyes to bright sunlight as Ercilia took the empty snifter from her laced fingers.

# 79

The day would be long day and began with Pilar complaining about the lack of Spanish television. When Maria told her Latino programming was limited to certain times on the shared ethic station she was unstoppable, bringing a smile to Maria's lips for the first time in two days and Pilar instantly forgot about listening to the news in Spanish or any other language. ¡Étnico!

Shopping was the first priority, for Addison, and for the three of them before the hairdresser. They would beautiful for Addison and she would be beautiful for them. Then they would be unable to avoid Larivière because Addison would be buried beside her mother at the family estate and Maria wanted to know everything was being done according to her wishes despite Larivière refusing her call. Instead his assistant spoke with Maria who thought at the time she sensed a difference in the older woman, a measured humanity she hadn't noticed when they first met.

Maria needed the influence of the Larivière family, and cost wasn't an issue. She needed the work done, and in time for Addie's goodbye. The assistant noted the details precisely without asking Maria to repeat a single word, assuring her one woman to another that all would be done according to her wishes. Then it was time for them to see Addie, to make sure she was perfect in every way and that she would have something with which she would always remember Maria: a simple gold pendant her mother had been wearing at the time of her death. Miniature photos of mother and daughter were clasped inside and her mother had once told Maria that, with the pendant, they would always be together. The necklace was Maria's most important possession. Her mother had always been with her, and now Addison would forever be with them.

Even the most sorrowful visitor to the funeral home stopped to acknowledge the three young women who had agreed not to spoil their make-up with tears as they walked into the salon. Maria had told Pilar and Ercilia not to expect visitors, something she and Addison once discussed as they thought of the future which was supposed to have endured decades longer.

However one visitor did arrive and did so in a limousine. She had instructed the LCL chauffeur to arrive at her home promptly at four, and had taken a rare afternoon off work to answer the striking epiphany which had come to her during the flight from Mexico with Maria.

There was much to say and hear and much to Pilar's delight the woman was fluent in Spanish, even if her accent was Castilian, so everyone could share her memories of Addison. She had known Addison from the day she was born and didn't wait long before giving Maria the neatly wrapped gift she'd been holding in her lap: several dozen photographs of Addison growing up, each one with a story and time became lost to all of them.

He came in at eight, seeing his daughter who seemed as though she would soon awaken, as though she would speak with him and tell him how much she loved him. He knew she had loved him, once, the same way he never stopped loving her. But her ridiculous idea, her stupid dream; what had she been thinking to give up a wonderful career, and for what, a silly dream? And her female friend; with all the successful men she could have had she wanted another woman without once thinking of the embarrassment she caused him. It had all been too much and now he felt their eyes drilling into his back. Not even his assistant greeted him, preferring to stay with the three of them. He would give anything to leave, to walk out, and he would have, were image not all-important, irrespective of Madame Harnais already being intimately familiar with every minute detail of his life. He was the father of the dead girl and the boss of a woman who was publicly snubbing him. They could all go to hell.

"Ms. Bardollini, I will exchange sympathies with you, not extend them, as we share a common grief and mourn a mutual loss. I loved my daughter, mademoiselle. I simply did not realize she loved me. Madame Harnais, I will not expect you at the office tomorrow and my chauffeur will be at your service once again, as well as for these young ladies. I have made separate arrangements for my transportation to the farm." He bowed ever so slightly, addressing Maria and surprising them all. "Buenas noches, señoras. Nos veremos por la mañana al mediodía. Hasta entonces."

He went to Addison one last time, lingering, his hand resting gently against her cheek before walking out, leaving the four women confused. The lights dimmed and the director came into the salon to ask the ladies if it might not be time for them to rest for the difficult day ahead.

Madame Harnais didn't think it proper to kiss Addie, yet she understood when the others did, finally responding to Maria's encouraging nod. Addie needed as much real love as they could give her and Maria made very sure before leaving that the director knew not to erase the different coloured kisses.

He would have preferred them to leave first, however Maria insisted he lower the cherrywood cover while she could see Addie encased gently into darkness. He understood her wanting to do as much as she could for Addie in the little time left to them, though he'd been right. She cried copious tears throughout most of the night thinking of Addison alone in the dark, held closely between caring friends who cried with her and made her believe Addison wasn't alone. And neither were they. And Addison wasn't entirely alone. One more visitor came to see her later that evening, someone well-acquainted with violent death, someone Maria despised with a passion.

# 80

In the Estrie region east of Montreal no one paid attention to fences defining property lines crisscrossing a panorama of rolling hills, where the deep greens of spring and summer eventually burst into the bright yellows and reds of autumn before beginning once again after slowly shedding the thick coats of winter white. Trust was a common quality and everyone loved tourists as long as they didn't overstay their welcome, and as long as they didn't buy out properties on any of those rolling hills, irrespective of the colours on the pastoral palette.

Those who did buy preferred articulating their affluence in the easily understood and relevant terms of excess. They were unlikely to give much thought to what simple country folk might think about thorough bred horses, always-polished and high-end imports or elaborate swimming pools which were the sparkling aqua jewels of perfectly manicured lawns inside the pretty white fences.

Jean-Émile Larivière was one of them, and his white fence delineated the most expansive property in the county. Whether he saw the black Navigator with dark-tinted windows or not, the imposing vehicle was appropriate amongst the procession of the favoured few and the obligated following behind the few who did want to be there with nothing to gain beyond being close to Addison. They had come to bid farewell to her and they knew she was proud of them.

When Maria climbed from the limo without taking the driver's hand, immediately seeing the empty grave, tears pouring from her eyes as she tried to focus on Madame Harnais who stood strong and unwavering. She had promised, and had done nothing. She had been so adamant at the time and Maria believed her. Even Ercilia turned to

187

Pilar, asking why the stern old woman had disappointed them, why she was so unmoved. They all wondered. Perhaps she'd been too long with Larivière, Maria thought, perhaps time had not allowed.

The few dozen obligés were dressed in sombre blacks and greys, most of the women had masked their faces in dark mesh and no one was surprised when Pilar thought openly in Spanish that it wasn't a bad thing. They had asked Madame Harnais to dress for Addison in a way that would celebrate her, not bore her, or make her laugh, and she had done so with the complete approval of Pilar and her two charges. The three young ladies had spent hours that morning getting ready as they cried and laughed, remembering all they could about Addison and pushing away anything bad or that made them feel sad. The day was Addie's with them, and they would all be happy before they would all be sad.

Larivière expected no less, the rest were shocked, and the shadowed man by the old oak tree regretted he had once thought to hate her. He'd been terribly wrong. Maria was the image of her mother, his wife who had always been so beautiful, and how much he wanted his daughter back for the short time left to him. They wore brightly coloured silk party dresses, Pilar insisting the dresses not be above the knee and that they wear hats, gloves and, of course, silk shawls. Maria wore bright yellow, Ercilia, pink, and Pilar a shade of white no one else could wear against such dark skin in April. The dresses were décolleté: Maria's and Ercilia's were flared, circa fifties; Pilar wore a form-fitting wrap-around.

They knew the other women were chattering about them behind mesh-facials, that the men had forgotten Addison, if they had ever thought about her. No importa. They were young women in control and everyone followed with their eyes as Madame Harnais led the way to Larivière's side.

Pilar followed behind, everyone's world standing still when she removed her dark glasses to stare at each one with the blackest eyes any of them had ever seen.

# 81

The meadow had always been Addison's private playground for as long as he could remember. He had never forgotten how many times he had needed to order her from the pond after her lips turned blue and her little body refused to stop shivering as her skin came alive with tiny little bumps that he had always told her would not go away until she listened to him. How many summer days did he sit watching his wife rub his daughter briskly with a thick fleecy towel before hugging her closely to make the cool, late afternoon air go away, the same way he now wanted all of them to go away. He shook limp hands and kissed the loose cheeks of women whose names he couldn't remember or had never known. They were all so sorry, so sad, and he wondered why it had taken her death to make him hate them all so much. How much longer would they take to bury her, how much longer would he have to endure them? He was fifty-four and half-dead himself. Why could he not have died instead?

He wondered whether his wife was looking at him from her own grave, or whether there was something else and they were seeing him together from a place more celestial, forgiving him. Or waiting for him. Perhaps it wasn't too late for each to forgive him and love him again. Maria followed Madame Harnais who stopped beside Larivière after everyone had paid their respects to the grieving father, knowing no one would quite know how to console the grieving child who was the dead girl's special friend. Nothing was said. He had known his assistant long enough to know what was in her mind, not caring in the least what was in her heart.

Madame Harnais stayed as she was, with Maria and her friends on her right, as the single rear door of the hearse swung open slowly and the cherry wood coffin was eased out to glisten under the bright sun. Pilar and Ercilia gently took Maria by the arms. They were supposed to be playing in the ocean, teasing each other in the hotel pool and having Margaritas. She wasn't supposed to be burying Addie. It wasn't real, it wasn't fair, and why were they lowering her into the ground?

The coffin was gently placed on the lateral bands with professional empathy, and lowered enough to define the grieving spectators by strength and weakness. No one cried. They stared, mostly at the ground, as the priest began speaking words which had lost their relevance decades earlier, if not centuries past. Pilar despised them all for their shallowness. There could be no God. There could be no better place. And why did Adishone have to die to find happiness and peace when she already had both?

The funeral director knew he should wait for Maria's nod, acknowledging the father instead, and Addison began her descent to her mother's side. That was when Maria saw him for the first time in nearly two years: her father, the personification of evil on earth, and why wasn't he coming to her when she needed him the most, as she had needed him once before? He was her father, her papa. He had always been her papa. So why was he letting himself be so easily pulled away by her cousin Marcus?

Seeing the men standing alone in the distance was too much for her to think about and Pilar moved quickly with Ercilia, seconds too late to prevent her from falling.

## 82

There was no reason for any of them to stay longer, and all but four tear-streaked women trailed Larivière to the grand house to eat catered food and drink liquor better suited to a gourmet meal in an overpriced Montreal restaurant. Maria sank to her knees again, staring at the coffin and the silk-lined walls of the deep grave. The private work crew had been instructed to stand off to the side and wait, though Pilar and Ercilia were prepared to move quickly. They knew Maria well, and at the moment, as much as they loved her, they didn't trust her in the slightest.

"Madame Harnais, vous m'avez promis, vous m'avez promis," though she hadn't stopped gazing at Addison.

"Yes, child, I did promise you. I promised your wishes would be carried out properly, for my Addison as much as for Addie. I would not disappoint Addison, whom I have always loved as a daughter, and I would not disappoint you, Maria. What would he or anyone gain by seeing your final gift to Addie? We have no reason to share something so special with those who don't care." She tilted her head. "Raise your head child, and see your gift."

Maria hadn't noticed Mme. Harnais discreetly raising an arm. The gleaming Ford Bronco came from behind as though travelling on air and stopped before reversing into a half circle. The custom-paint work perfectly matched the cream colour of Addison's gown, etched with dozens of miniature stencilled yellow bows matching the bright yellow of Maria's dress which made distinguishing the cream-coloured granite stone resting in the open cargo area of the truck difficult.

The workmen moved in and the driver climbed out, all dressed in fresh cream-coloured coveralls and yellow shirts, unaccustomed to working with an audience and trying hard not to appear clumsy or silly in front of the four women. They had been watching from afar, aware of how important their task was. They wanted to do it right for Maria and as they worked at setting the heavy stone, the driver laid out a blanket for the women as the softening Madame Harnais filled four glasses with the finest champagne.

When the men finished they might have simply walked away, though they didn't. They had heard about Addison and wanted to show Maria they were good men, not like the others who had hurt Addison. They formed a small line, bowing their heads, facing the four women fitted snugly between the corners of the woollen blanket. They felt good for having done their job well. They had worked quickly and the twelve yellow carnations were the unspoken words they knew would be inadequate.

Maria took the flowers, holding the man's hand against her face. When she let him go the man withdrew his dampened hand, his eyes watering the very moment he turned away, thankful she hadn't seen. Madame Harnais answered Maria's question, embracing the girl: She didn't think any man would want to drive it, and she didn't think any woman would need it. The truck had served one purpose and would remain on the farm.

She would leave the young women alone to say goodbye. But first she would see Maria glow for the first time since they had met. Madame Harnais stood, easing away the square of yellow silk from the granite stone.

ADDISON
Will Always Be Loved By Us
And Never Forgotten
We Will Be Together Again Addie
We Love You

# 83

The girls stayed with Maria for two weeks following the funeral, helping her cope with the overwhelming and lingering formalities of death, neither did Madame Harnais abandon her. However, the time had come to leave and for Maria to find herself. They weren't leaving Maria, they were leaving Montreal. They promised to call her every week and Maria would call them at least as often. The schedule seemed to work well for all three, especially Ercilia who didn't want to leave her friend a second time.

Before they left, and when Ercilia wasn't with them, Maria took Pilar aside. They had spoken together for hours, yet so much remained unspoken and Pilar sat quietly intrigued, listening to a Maria she hadn't yet come to know as well as she eventually would. She had always seen Maria as an enigma, though as cute and flighty as she was, or once was, she realized Maria possessed inherent qualities that commanded one's attention. Despite the girlish fun and frolicking in the waves, despite cute pillow fights each night and the teasing, something about Maria was serious and dark. She kissed Maria hard on the cheek, warning her against becoming cold and unloving. She and Adisita would always be part of one another.

When they finally did part, Pilar harboured no doubt they would see Maria again, a day she hoped Maria would be at peace with herself.

## 84

At first Father's Day had seemed far enough away for her to be comfortable with her plan, now the long-awaited day had come and she was afraid. She hadn't been his daughter for over two years and she wanted him back.

The Thursday morning was bright and a sunny twenty-two degrees that was warm for Montreal in June. She drove her MX-5 to a downtown hotel where she changed over to a taxi whose driver understood the significance of the address once he saw the three-metre high double rows of thick, black wrought-iron fencing. He had no intention of getting out. She had barely opened the rear passenger door before two very serious men appeared behind the second iron barrier.

She hadn't called him to say she was coming. She was too afraid of what he might say to her, yet she remembered clearly what she recognized in his solemn expression the day of the funeral. Perhaps there was still a chance for each of them to forget the hurtful words once exchanged in the heat of fleeting emotional moments so far in the past and unimportant. If not, so what? The plan would be a business arrangement. Money was money, and that he would understand.

The police had done nothing in seven weeks. They had called once after the funeral to keep her updated that nothing had happened, claiming they were actively working the case when she knew otherwise. The crime had happened in Mexico, they explained, and the Mexicans weren't being very helpful. They asked if she had a name, anything she could add which would help the investigation. She said no. She had heard for so many years how the system worked, or didn't.

She did have a name, his first name, and knew how she

could get his last name, as well as the names of the other three without the police finding out. She would bring the fathers together. They were her one hope, and she was scared. If she failed, if they let her down, she'd have to give the police the name and watch four violent murderers and rapists go unpunished with slaps on the wrist for what they had done. She wouldn't let that happen. She would put aside her pride and go to him for help. She had spent the past five weeks meticulously formulating, developing each of the five steps to her plan and if he refused to help her with the initial step she would have no hope at all.

They were very large men, not given to smiling, though they did when she straightened and they saw her through double rows of wrought iron bars, Maria struggling not to appear as vulnerable as she felt. She knew them both. She had grown up with them, and the biggest one raised a forefinger to his lips when she went to speak. Breaking the house rule when outside was never forgiven: Silence was golden. The first gate opened and closed quickly as Marcus pushed the button cutting the current to the second gate that swung inwardly and closed as quickly.

She hardly had time to pass through before Marcus reached for her with his huge arms opened wide to squeeze his cousin, lifting her feet from the ground, and when she tried to hug him in return her arms barely reached around his shoulders. When he set her down he was smiling, rubbing his thumbs gently across her eyes to wipe away the tears. He hadn't changed one bit. He was big, he was handsome and still the quintessential gentleman. He was ten years older and had always been her big brother, never a cousin, and she was crying for having forgotten how much she missed him.

She was full of questions, mostly about him, yet he knew one was coming which wouldn't be. No. He still hadn't found the perfect girl. Yes. He had lost a few pounds,

The 4th Man

mostly because her father had told him to. Yes. He still lived next door and, yes, he came to Sunday dinner. Yes. He still preferred Italian silk and, no, he never would like Italian wine. Yes. Her father missed her, which didn't mean whatever would soon follow would be easy. He wasn't an easy man, which didn't mean he didn't love her. He did. No. He never talked about her, which didn't mean he didn't think about her every moment.

The Bardollini residence was centred inside a two-acre property forty-five minutes north of the city. Besides being encircled with twin electrified fencing, the chateau-styled home was guarded twenty-four-seven and had a surveillance system to monitor the entire area as well as the main gates and five adjoining homes. The numerous stone gardens and various manicured trees and hedges strategically spaced along the inside fence brought a sense of serenity and quiet to the private compound, as much as protecting his men from accidental contact with it.

Marcus lived on one side, Angelo's senior lieutenant lived on the other, and both men had private access from their own fenced-in properties any time they wanted or needed it. Three other luxury homes were situated at the rear, its wide perimeter scrutinized tirelessly by concealed cameras intended to warn of any attempt to breach the fence, particularly via the home centred directly behind Angelo Bardollini's. They didn't care about the owner who, on several occasions, had rejected excessively generous offers by interested parties who were always represented by agents who were never inclined to identify their clients. Angelo knew of the interest the police had in the Franklin home, and that they were still interested in the property.

Franklin never troubled the Bardollini family, and in return he was never troubled by them, other than the occasional fly-over by police helicopters. In fact, Angelo Bardollini had specifically instructed his men to ignore him completely. In essence, he was a good neighbour and convenient buffer, which was good for all of them. And, he was seldom there. John Franklin was president and CEO of IED Services, an import-export distribution service headquartered in Montreal with affiliate offices in Newark and Miami. He kept to himself, he lived alone, his housekeeper came in every other day and he kept his nose clean. The last thing he wanted was to get involved with the mob or Angie Bardollini.

# 85

Marcus forewent the requisite formality of contacting the house by scrambled radio, though he did explain to Maria they couldn't simply walk in unannounced. He wouldn't be more than a few minutes. Everything would be fine, he promised very unconvincingly.

He left her and she faced away, waiting until she heard the door close behind her before raising her wrist to keep time with the black second hand circling the mother of pearl face on the Marc Jacobs that Addison had given her for their last Christmas together: an eternity she both hated and needed.

She examined her clothes, not lowering her wrist. She had made a special effort to dress conservatively for him, wearing fitted slacks with a matching jacket and low-heeled pumps instead of her usual stilettos. Marcus wasn't coming out. She had put her hair into a ponytail thinking she would appear less frivolous, more serious, even though she was dead serious. He wasn't coming out and her heart began pounding, thinking of the long walk to the gate, knowing they'd be watching her walk away. The minute hand had moved from the two to the quarter-past position. She had put on very little make-up because he had always told her perfection should never be covered. She had brought him a present, monogrammed silver cufflinks, and now she had nowhere to put them. She would leave them at the gate. She had to get away as quickly as possible and not having a waiting taxi was the least of her problems.

Had she first glanced over her shoulder she would have seen the open door. She would have seen him and she had only taken a few halting steps with her head held high before her name thundered across the short distance, paralyzing her. She jerked around, unable to control the trembling coursing through her body and the deep flush washing across her face. He didn't seem real to her standing there larger than life, as though held in place by the wide, steel-reinforced doorframe.

His quiet reaction terrified her and for the first time in her adult life she saw what she had always failed to see, or had refused to accept. She saw what everyone feared about the man who stood in front of her, so ominous and imposing with huge hands at his side, at the ready, his feet wide apart. His signature stance and she understood in an instant why her mother had been killed: because he couldn't be and she felt smaller than ever seeing him study her.

"Meme," was all he said, calling her with open arms.

She had been right to come. She was still his little girl. He hadn't called her Meme in so many years and she knew she could run to him and all would be well again. When she was a little girl she could never stay quiet and could never understand why he would call her motor mouth as he tickled her. As hard as she would try to mimic him, she could only ever manage me-me and then he'd laugh at her and she quickly became his Meme. He was her papa. She was still his little girl, she always had been, briefly torn apart by stupid family pride, a pride he had instilled in her. She had been wrong. She'd never be wrong again.

"Papa, I'm sorry."

His arms were warm, and very strong. "We both are, Meme."

"I saw you, papa. I saw you watching." A pent up torrent of emotion erupted from deep inside her so unexpectedly that she gulped air to catch her breath. The tears she cried each night had slowly begun to change from hysterical tears to endless quiet sobbing into an empty bed, not like this, not since Pilar had taken Ercilia home. "I loved her so much, papa. I miss her."

"I know you do, Meme. Addison was a very special

person. Anyone who saw her would know that. I wish I hadn't waited until it was too late to know for myself. Now, come inside. I don't like breaking my own rules."

## 86

"How did you see her, papa? How do you know her name?"

"You've never been far from me, Maria, and since I heard about you on the news that night Marcus has been assigned to watch after you. I should say he assigned himself and, to answer your question, I saw Addison the night before the funeral, after you and your friends left the funeral home. We paid our respects." Marcus brought in wine and poured them each a glass before tugging at her ponytail and leaving them alone to talk. "I promised your dead mother I would always care for you, be there for you. Apparently I haven't been very good at keeping my promises and once again I have disappointed her."

"No papa. I did. What happened was my fault. Pilar told me no. She said if I was to blame, then she was also guilty because she told us to stay at the fiesta and have fun instead of going with them. But what happened was my fault. I bought the tickets and planned the trip. Then I left her alone. I helped them kill Addie, papa."

He understood the emotion. He wanted to wrap his arms tightly around her and comfort her, and later he would. In the meantime nothing would help until she understood.

"Start at the beginning, Meme, if you want me to follow what you're saying, and don't leave out a single word. Do you understand me?"

By the time she finished Marcus had come in to turn on the lights. He told Angelo another place was set for dinner, reminding Maria with a nod and raised eyebrows. Angelo made a showy appearance moments later, adjusting the French cuffs of his starched black shirt neatly clasped between brushed Florentine silver, tolerating the unfamiliar and effusive attention throughout dinner. The meal finished, Marcus stood to leave, telling Maria that her father would only then be the best dressed man in the house. When he hugged her she immediately felt protected, frail, and needed. He left feeling good.

"Your friend Pilar was right, Maria. Your reason in life was Addison, yet being with her every moment would have been wrong. Neither of you would have grown. That's life, Meme. There are times when we must be apart so that we can share when we're together. As much as we want to, we can't always protect the ones we love, Meme. I'm my worst example. With all my resources, still I was unable to protect her. She was your mother and you still grieve for her, but Carmella was my life. So believe me when I say I understand and share your new grief." He clasped his hands solemnly. "I promise you will feel this way about your next partner, Meme. That's love, as much as you might not believe me at this time of deep hurt and confusion. You must not stop loving, or feeling loved Meme. Family, real family, is all we have when all is said and done."

"That won't be for a very long time, papa, but I love you for saying so." She let him take her hands, seeing them disappear between his.

"The love we feel turns to sorrow, Maria, when we let ourselves forget. You have much to remember, even though you were together for such a short time, you have much to remember. When the time is right for you, you'll understand what I'm saying is true." He paused, unsure of the unfamiliar ground, "And when you feel the time is right, I would like very much if you were to share part of your life with Addison with me…when the time is right."

Those words were too much for Maria. She fell onto his chest, sobbing. "She was so tender, so loving and kind, papa. She was so beautiful inside and out."

Even though his compassion was real, he realized he had said too much. He could only nod, not quite knowing how to respond, more disturbed than he would ever admit by the memory of what he had so cruelly yelled at her the day she stormed from the house.

"And you're beautiful inside and out, Meme: a gift from your mother I could never equal. We become who and what we are meant to be and, unfortunately for you, you were raised as a beautiful flower in a compost heap. Despite that, you survived as you were meant to, and I'm proud of you. Your mother's proud of you." He paused, shrugging. "I should have known Addison, and will always regret I did not. I should have let myself know that part of you. I won't let that happen again, Maria. I promise you on my life."

"Thank you, papa." She fell silent, not knowing where to begin. "Papa, I need your help. I know who one of them is. I know his first name."

He leaned back easing her to arm's length. "You know who killed Addison…and you haven't told the cops."

"No, I never told them. They have to pay for what they did papa, and I can find out the names of the other three. But I need your help."

"And when you do, what then? What will you do with the names, Meme?"

"I'll find them, and I'll kill them. I'm dead, papa. I never thought I could feel like this. You have no idea how I want to be with Addie."

His response compassionate, not condescending. "As much as Addison loved you, Meme, she doesn't want you with her anytime soon, not if she loved you as much as you love her. When we leave this earth we have no timeframe, Meme. When you are together again, for her, your separation will have been a fleeting moment in time."

She ignored him. "They have to pay, papa. I have a plan and I know you can help me. The question is: Will you help me?"

"Killing for hate and killing for need are completely different aspects of ending someone's life, Maria, and mutually exclusive. Prisons are filled with those who killed for hate or passion. Those who have a reason and a need to kill, the smart ones, will plan for a very long time and pay attention to minute details you would never consider, details that would keep you out of prison. And I can't believe I'm talking to my daughter about killing." He paused, studying her intently. "How do you intend to get the other names, Maria?"

"Jean-Émile Larivière, Addison's father can help me, if he'd listen, but he won't. He refused to talk to me after Addie's funeral."

He let her talk late into the night about Addison and Larivière, and when he lay alone in bed he spoke with his wife as he did every night, and thanked her. Then he stayed awake until dawn thinking of his daughter. He had known the answer the previous evening and smirked to himself in the semi-darkness. The immediate and horrible death of the man who killed Maria's mother hadn't ingratiated Maria to him and he hadn't expected it would. He hadn't killed the man to satisfy Maria, though he would do whatever was necessary to keep her. He would listen to his daughter, his one link with his past of tender moments which were now intangible tender memories.

Her last question to him before going to bed in her old room was very simple: Yes or no? Maria had said more than any father would ever want to hear, but she had no one else and he listened to every word. The next morning Maria had been up for an hour cooking breakfast for him and when Angelo came into the kitchen she giggled for the first time in seven weeks at the unshaven and dishevelled mob boss-father with his robe tied tightly in the middle.

"Papa, I'm glad I stayed. All we're missing is mom. We're like we used to be…right?"

He stayed quiet, hugging her tightly and mussed her hair. She had prepared a feast and he told her with a laugh that she was a day late, and then he sat to be served by the lady of the house.

# 87

"Meme, the man who killed your mother died badly. His end could not have been worse for him. Enough said, though I promise you the four men you wish to hunt and kill will feel the same horror your Addison felt. They will die like the cowards they are, but not by your hand. I opened the coffin, Meme, and as much as I couldn't accept your lifestyle I'm beginning to understand. It's your life, as I told you the day you stopped listening to what I and your beloved dead mother would tell you. But," he hesitated, "I understand. Addison was beautiful and I could tell by seeing her how you must have loved one another. That said, she was your family, which makes her my family, and I wish by all that's holy I could have known her. I didn't, and I have to live with that part of myself. They'll pay, Maria. I swear on your mother's grave and Addison's that each one will pay for what they did."

She burst into tears. "That's what I want, papa. I need you to teach me," she trembled, "to show me how. I need to be the one who kills them…me."

"You're not listening, Meme. You know who and what I am. The four who did this terrible thing will pay…by my hand, not yours. It's done."

"Yes, papa, I believe you. But I have to make them pay, not you." She collapsed onto her knees. "Papa, I loved her. I hurt so much. I cry every night. I miss her papa."

"Yes, as much as I miss your mother, and as much as I never want to miss you again. That's why I will do what you cannot. This isn't you. What you're thinking isn't inherent in you." He paused, stroking her hair. "I'm your father, Meme, and I love you. I am also Angelo Bardollini and in this you will do as I tell you."

"No! No! You don't understand!"

Few people would dare to raise their voices to him; those who did often discovered the end of the day was also the end of their lives. Though Maria had immediate-family dispensation and he simply put his face into his hands and rubbed hard, thinking for a moment before standing.

"Okay, listen…I'll buy you a puppy, Meme. I'll have Marcus bring you a puppy first thing tomorrow."

"What are you talking about, papa? The last thing I need is a puppy."

He chortled. "I'm not talking about a puppy you'll keep, Meme." He paused. "I'm talking about a puppy you can kill, with this." He pulled out the Beretta. "If you can kill a puppy, you can kill the four gutless pricks who killed your girlfriend. No puppy, no deal."

Her mouth curved into a sneer, her answer sending a streak of cold along his spine as her eyes pierced the air between them. "I already have my puppy picked out, papa. Its name is Chad."

# 88

Saturday, June 24, was the Fête Nationale du Québec, the first real weekend of any summer in Montreal. To Angelo Bardollini the day was Johnnie the Baptist and business as usual, while Jean-Émile Larivière considered the day one of the year's most productive, able to work unimpeded by underlings who were enjoying another statutory three-day weekend at his expense.

The chauffeur of the black Cadillac limo had become blasé over time, driving the same mundane route six days a week. As well-trained as he had once been, he'd lost the edge and had become complaisant, barely taking note of street signs let alone cars that might be following him.

Larivière refused to outfit the executive vehicle with armoured windows and tires, arguing he had already paid an exorbitant premium to send his driver for specialized training so that he might perform his job beyond expectation. Conversely, the driver long ago rationalized that if his boss was unconcerned about possible attacks or kidnapping attempts, neither was he. Neither one ever noticed the other: Larivière always engrossed in paperwork or the financial sections of several international newspapers, never thinking to pay attention or speak to the chauffeur, the chauffeur no longer thinking to pay attention to the environment outside the limo. And that unfortunate status quo prevailed as the Navigator passed them by and the black LX570 pulled in behind them in full view and perfectly obscure as the three vehicles travelled the Bonaventure Expressway en route to the Anglophone stronghold of Hampstead.

The trip was their sixth together that week, though when they veered onto the deserted chemin Côte-St-Luc the timing would never be better. Marcus slowed for the yellow light, reversing to within centimetres of the limo as the unsuspecting chauffeur slowed to a stop at the red and Angelo's driver closed the rear gap.

Angelo climbed out. The cell number Maria had given him was on speed dial. The message was succinct, delivered in full by the time he reached the rear door of the limo.

"I'm the father of your daughter's partner, Angelo Bardollini. Open the door, M. Larivière, so we can all go home tonight." When no response came, "open the door for your daughter, monsieur, so I won't have to send you to her on my count of three."

The click came on the second count and Angelo pulled at the chromed handle in the time the light had taken to turn green. He had gathered detailed information about Larivière and he didn't like the man. When Marcus pulled away the chauffeur followed the black Navigator instinctively. Losing his job would be bad enough; losing his life was beyond the pale and he knew who had climbed in with Larivière. He hadn't seen the man, though he knew of the daughter's lesbian friend, which was all he needed to know. In the back, Larivière was unmoved, confident he wasn't going to die. His death would be impossible to explain. The police would know immediately and Bardollini couldn't risk the attention. He also knew such was his rationale, not Bardollini's.

"It's time we met, time we spoke."

"We have met, seven weeks ago at the farm, and quite frankly I preferred that distance between us, if not the intrusion."

"Very good, Larivière, good bravado, but this isn't about you. This is about our daughters."

"My daughter is dead. So I must assume this is about your daughter. What is it? Does she need an honest job?"

He couldn't have imagined a man of Angelo's size moving so quickly, the shock of the blow to his face completely eradicating the stunning sensation of the gloved impact.

Angelo sat patiently, tugging at the edges of his kid leather gloves, letting Larivière recover. "Do you believe in God, Monsieur Larivière?"

"I do."

"Would you like to meet him, right now? I can do that for you…and I will."

Larivière paused, trying to swallow. "Perhaps not at this particular moment. I had a later date in mind."

Angelo chortled. "Good. I also have a later date in mind, for myself…not necessarily you."

"What does your daughter need? And what makes either of you think I can help her?"

"You have contacts, monsieur, as do I. However, in this case yours are the initial imperative. Mine will come later."

"I don't understand your implication, Monsieur Bardollini. I don't see how I might possibly be of help to you or your daughter. I'm a business man with no resources that would be of any assistance to a man with your professional interests."

"Fuck you. Your daughter was raped and murdered by four men and they could just as well have raped my daughter. You're involved. Get used to it and you will help because the option is unenviable and time is of the essence, monsieur."

"My daughter had choices, as did yours. They have each paid a price for those choices. We both understand what goes on at those places during this so-called Spring Break: lewd behaviour to say the least and that is what got her killed. They should have known better. If she hadn't acted like a…" He stopped, searching for the proper word, not finding one before the Beretta crashed into his open mouth.

"No more fucking bullshit. I promised Maria I'd be civil with you, but that stops right here, right now. This is when you listen. You listen, you shut the fuck up and you do what you're told or the first bullet will take half your head out through the side window and the second will go through the windshield with part of your driver's head. Got the picture? You even think of implying that shit about either girl and you'll be explaining in person to your dead wife why you're with her again. You'll keep your mouth shut, monsieur, and you'll listen. Understand?" He fanned the air with the gun, helping Larivière communicate the appropriate muted answer as the car slowed to a stop. "Tell your man to get out, and not to worry. He'll be in good company."

The partition lowered. "Jackson, leave us and enjoy the other gentleman's company. This won't take long." Jackson heard nothing Larivière said. Marcus had already opened the door, which was all he needed to know. The rest was obvious. "Please put that thing away. I am well aware of your skills, M. Bardollini. You have my full attention."

Angelo removed his hat, placing it between them.

"I know everything about you, Monsieur Larivière, from your excellent grades at school to your bank statements to the reasons your wife died and your daughter left home. I also know why she wouldn't work with you and I understand completely how you would hate her. My daughter left me for the same reasons, so, you see, we have a lot in common. Unfortunately, your daughter had to die for me to get my daughter back and I intend not to lose her again. We've lost one girl and I wish now I could have known your daughter. I've taken an oath, Monsieur Larivière, and that's not an implication. In my business it's a matter of living or not living. Are you following me?" Larivière said nothing, his mind was elsewhere and Angelo knew exactly where. "She was family. She loved my daughter, which was no reason to act as badly towards the girls as we did and we both have to live with the truth. My daughter blames herself. Funny thing is, you and I are to blame for thinking what people might say was more important than our daughters. This horrible thing shouldn't have happened, but shit does happen and now we're going to pool our resources and take care of family business."

Larivière faced straight ahead, seeing nothing. "I do love my daughter. I always have and there's nothing either one of us can do bring her back. What is done is done. Even the police have done nothing." He paused, turning to assess his uninvited guest. "What could you possibly have in mind beyond futile wishes?"

"You have contacts in Mexico. I understand they're very good contacts who can be helpful in getting information, informally."

"What information?"

"I have the first name of one man, but there were four of them. We know they probably live in Montreal, they're white Anglophones and they travelled together between April 07<sup>th</sup> and the twenty-second. They were staying in one of hotels close to where the girls stayed."

"We need the names." Larivière stared between his knees, unafraid of the man whose gun was resting on his knee. "And then what?"

"Use your imagination, monsieur. Like I said, we'll pool our resources. There's no need for you to know anything else. You do your thing, I'll do mine."

"What is the name we have?"

"Chad."

"Do we know what airline they flew in on?"

"No, we don't, but we're not talking Atlanta or New York." Angelo admired his Beretta, turning the weapon absently to show both sides before sliding it under his coat. "It's like a third hand. Sometimes I forget I'm holding it. How long will you take? The information," he repeated, "how long before you get back?"

"I don't know. All things in Mexico are relative to the

peso. I don't imagine I should take very long at all. I used up a few favours to bring her home as quickly as I did. However, as I have said, all things are relative and money is one resource I do have."

"It would be best if you were to…"

"I need no further instruction, monsieur. I will be in Mexico by noon tomorrow."

"Good. I look forward to our next meeting."

Angelo pulled at the door handle, pushing the door open with a foot as he reached for his fedora. Their eyes locked, silent messages conveyed. One knowing he was amongst the few who had ever seen the face of mob boss Angie Bardollini, the other realizing a grieving father was coming to terms with himself and would spend the evening fighting his emotions.

They weren't so different.

# 89

The pilot of the silver LCL completed the paperwork for the flight by the time Larivière arrived at 6:00 AM. The plane landed in Zihuantanejo at nine, local time. That evening he dined with the presidents of two affiliate companies and their wives. Monday night he dined with the same men, and one other who took precise notes as Larivière responded to his several questions. The one he didn't ask was obvious by its omission. They knew why Larivière was there and why he called them. They had no desire to know more than they already suspected. What he would do with the information was no concern of theirs. They were all fathers and none would shed a single tear.

Within a few hours of beginning his inquiry the man obtained copies of the passenger rosters from the two airlines flying into Zihuantanejo from Montreal that Saturday in April. On the list was one Chad Rivers. By Wednesday at noon he had compared the roster against all the check-ins at the third of several possible hotels. The four men who had occupied seats 12-C and D across from 12-A and B were also the occupants of rooms 218, 219, 220 and 221. When questioned, several of the women in housekeeping who remembered the four men crossed themselves. They were bad men, the women insisted, and when he asked them why they answered that so many bad things had stopped happening once they left.

He had listened to each of them intently, noting similarities without the slightest discrepancy. When he had reported information to an anxious Larivière he was sombre, knowing full-well he was handing over the names and the lives of the four men. He put a hand compassionately to Larivière's shoulder, saying "buena suerte, amigo, y vaya con dios" before walking away.

Within moments the pilot was instructed to prepare the jet for immediate departure.

# 90

Larivière spent the entire day Thursday pacing the floor of his office, not even Madame Harnais was allowed in. She had been instructed to block all his calls, cancel all appointments and to allow the man in as soon as he arrived. When the private detective had gone, Addison's father sank into the soft leather of his chair. He broke his trance to call Madame Harnais and, moments later, when she returned with his drink, he sent her home. The research had been an easy matter, more complete than Jean-Émile had expected, particularly with the passport numbers he'd been given by his Mexican contact. Bardollini would not be disappointed. The information included social security numbers, addresses, phone numbers, e-mail and cell phone numbers, banking information, educational history and by the next day he would know everything about the men's families.

Chad Rivers was twenty-six. He had been an excellent student, he had never been of interest to the police; he had no medical file to talk about and no credit history other than a small loan taken out prior to his Mexican vacation. He lived with his parents until a month earlier when he moved to Vancouver to work at an entry level position in an industrial design firm. Thurston Williams was twenty-seven, an academic under achiever suspended during his sophomore year at McGill for behaviour deemed inappropriate by the Dean, the same behaviour which caused him to lose his licence the same day for driving his parents' car while under the influence. He had a heavy debt load, mostly school loans, several unpaid tickets and he moved to Toronto within a week of Rivers' departure.

Shane Pendleton was twenty-seven, an average student who still lived with his parents and worked in a junior position at The Wilmingtons and Pendleton. He had heavy credit card debt, nothing in the bank and a new BMW that was a company perk with a collection of paid parking and speeding tickets. Prior to graduation he applied to McGill for post-graduate studies and hadn't yet been accepted. Bret Wilmington was also twenty-seven, a few days apart from Pendleton with grades that were marginally superior. He lived at home, drove the same model BMW and had the same credit card debt with the same number of paid tickets. He also worked with his father in a junior position and was recently accepted into a post-graduate programme at McGill.

When he finished reading the files he poured and drained a single shot of Johnnie Walker Then he reached for the phone.

# 91

Friday evening was long in coming for Maria, not so for Larivière who controlled the timing. For Angelo the meeting was part of a blueprint requiring a good deal of patience and planning, which was potentially problematic.

Jackson's replacement, hired during Larivière's Mexican trip was younger, athletic and well-trained in evasive tactics. His name was Jeff and had been instructed to drive Madame Harnais to her home. When he returned to drive Larivière home he was told where and when to park the vehicle. Larivière's appointment was waiting for him when he arrived.

In a peculiar way he was anxious to once again meet the notorious mob boss. When they spoke on the phone Bardollini sounded like anyone else, except he wasn't anyone else. He was the man preparing to hunt his daughter's killers, and knowing he was helping that happen gradually brought Larivière a feeling of pride. When the rear door closed the front door opened and Jeff stood easily beside Marcus, wondering what to say. Larivière passed Bardollini the thick envelope. Angelo opened the package, first seeing the folder for Rivers, Chad, then randomly at the others. Maria had been right about Larivière.

"Thank you, for Maria," was all he said when he finished.

"Thank you, for Addison." Both men nodded. "Will you let me know?"

"You'll know. On your daughter's grave, I swear each of these four will see me."

"Will you have time?" Angelo's expression spoke for him. He didn't understand the question. "The indictment, will you have time before the indictment?"

The man was nothing like the sinister black and white

images Larivière had seen so many times on the front pages of newspapers or occasionally on the glossy covers of magazines. The gleam in his eyes was warm. When he chuckled at the question he sounded amiable, like the typical big guy next door who flipped hamburgers on the grill and bounced children on his knee. He didn't seem like a mob boss, he seemed very normal.

"I don't believe the indictment will interfere with the agenda. In fact, you have my word." He extended an open hand. "Goodbye. This is our last meeting."

Jeff slid in behind the wheel as Angelo stepped out. He was about to slam the door when Larivière leaned over, putting his hand against the velvet-covered panel. "Monsieur Bardollini, may I have another moment? Briefly, please."

Angelo leaned in after first searching the space behind him. "What?"

"Your daughter, Maria; I would like very much to meet her, to sit and talk with her. I have much to make up for and my apologies are too many to enumerate. Too much, too late, I'm afraid."

"Your time won't be wasted. I'll tell her to expect your call. She likes Italian. Go figure."

"Thank you."

Larivière lowered the privacy screen, watching the man walk away and disappear into his own chauffeured vehicle, once again becoming the mob boss, complete with black trench coat and fedora, a man to respect and fear. Yet Larivière would always picture the man flipping burgers.

# 92

The phone call was made early the next evening, after Larivière fortified himself with a double shot of Johnnie Walker Blue. He had no idea what he would say to her and even less what she would say to him. He had treated her disrespectfully and deserved whatever hateful words she would speak to him. Though, much to his delight, after the first few clumsy minutes of what they both knew had to be said, they were talking as though they had always known each other, as though Addison would be home any minute.

Neither one wanted to say goodbye, each with so much to say. However he did know she liked Italian and, coincidently, she knew the best place in town where reservations would not be an issue. Dinner was Thursday night, and each suspected the other's attire would be semi-formal. He dressed in dark blue Armani with a silk tie and pocket hanky matching the deep silver of his shirt. During the meal she made a mental note that, if the evening went as well as she hoped, she would get him a pair of cuff links. Maria's tiered chiffon dress was black and came to above the knee. The neckline was a shallow V-cut that wasn't provocative, which she complemented with a long chiffon scarf trailing behind her when she walked. Her delicate diamond studs and matching pendant were gifts from Addison on her twenty-second birthday. Her pumps were patent leather.

The limo picked her up at eight, dinner was at eight-thirty and they closed the restaurant after midnight. Everyone in the restaurant knew Maria. He was a stranger and he didn't mind that the evening's events would later be reported in the fullest detail to Angelo Bardollini. He liked her very much, which made being with her that much harder. He had thought hating her, despising her, would be easy. He was wrong. She was intelligent, beautiful and accepting of someone she had every right to despise. They did their best not to cry, though at times the constraint was too overpowering and they cried together.

One rule applied, dictated by Bardollini: Neither one would speak about the files, which wasn't an issue. They had so much to say to each other they forgot the files. She had so many questions about Addie and her mother, and she answered all his questions about Addison's final years. He liked her, very much, and the more they spoke the more she liked him. Maria would never replace Addison, but for as long as he lived she would be a vital connection to his daughter and suddenly she became very special to him. When the limo pulled up in front of her condo he stepped out first, instructing the recently hired chauffeur to remain seated. He hadn't hugged a woman in years and felt good wrapping his arms around her, losing track of time, and Jeff drove away only when her lights went on and she had signalled from the window.

He had invited her to the farm for the next weekend. Of course, Madame Harnais would be with them and Jeff would be at Maria's disposal whenever she would want or need to visit with Addison. She had so much to do before the next weekend, sorting out photographs and choosing a memento for Jean-Émile that would remind him of Addison. She couldn't have asked for a better way to celebrate her twenty-third birthday and she decided silver and sapphire links would go best with his suit.

# 93

By the end of the second week of August the four preliminary files had grown appreciably with current photographs of each man, video tapes and extensive reports detailing their comings and goings over a seven-day period. Although documented separately, the Wilmington and Pendleton files contained much of the same visual and textual information, which might have been superfluous, but who knew what the future held? Death was the one certainty. The one question was: who would be first, and who would be fourth? They were the first of several future reports compiled over time and Angelo assigned the only man he trusted to gather the information. Of secondary importance was the collection of information on the parents, which had taken Marcus much less time and effort.

Maria wasn't given copies of the reports until the information in them was complete and when Angelo handed them over to her he did so against his better judgement, after she swore not do anything rash or stupid. In return, she made him promise not to exclude her from any action, and not to act until she studied the files which she did meticulously over the coming months. She became familiar with every aspect of the men's habits and idiosyncrasies, not certain what the outcome would be other than their deaths. She resolved before beginning that she'd study them dispassionately, yet there was something incomplete about how she was processing the information and she struggled over the coming weeks to understand.

She had listened intently to her father when he told her that remaining single-minded was one thing, becoming obsessed was another. She wanted all four of them dead, not one or two. She wanted them to suffer and she would do nothing to jeopardize the certainty. She wanted them to suffer. She wanted them to feel the fear of death over time as much as the death itself. But how would that happen? And when it did, how would she know?

The one man she recognized from the tapes and photos was the one she had seen on the boat and in the restaurant, wearing a new suit that gave him the unmistakable appearance of a seventies disco geek: Rivers, Chad. As much as she tried she couldn't place the other three, which was moot. Hating them gave her an inner strength she never before understood, the strength to know she had complete control over their lives and their deaths.

# 94

She thought of Addison every day and dreamt of her every night. Five months had gone by since the funeral and over two months since her weekend with Jean-Émile. He spoke with her as often as she spoke with Angelo. She now had two fathers and Madame Harnais was fast becoming a fussing stepmother.

Jean-Émile understood her need to spend Thanksgiving with her father, though he asked whether she might spend a few days with him and Madame Harnais on the farm at Christmas. He promised the day would be special and, of course, her father was invited. She accepted without hesitation and Madame Harnais was immediately instructed to make Christmas the most special ever.

# 95

But Christmas was months away and Maria had to admit she had lost sight of her ambition, the goal she once shared with Addison, and Angelo jolted her abruptly into the present and cruel reality that the time had passed for her to begin the healing process. She would lose part of herself by not going forward, he told her, not the least of which would be the sacred memory of Addison. As difficult as the months ahead might be, she must continue for Addison and for what it would mean to both of them.

Maria and Addison had done in-depth research. They had spoken with arrogant bank managers, they had selected and investigated an enthusiastic and forward-thinking architectural and design firm, and the last step remaining before success or failure had been a much deserved and life-altering two-week vacation in Ixtapa. There had been a time when both fathers mocked the girls, berating them and driving them away: a mindset which had changed drastically and now the men enlisted themselves whole heartedly.

She didn't need financial backing. She needed emotional support. With the generous inheritances and insurance policies left to her by her mother and Addison, which included what Addison's mother had left to her, plus the LCL stocks, Maria was independently wealthy and the business plan was considered as a good risk by both fathers.

Despite the advice, having Jean-Émile in the background was a great help and she suspected he was more involved than he led her to believe. He had committed to supplying all the linens and garments, Angelo matching the amount in third-party labour costs and equipment for the dining areas and kitchens. Though success was a crap shoot, he told her, proud she was to become president and CEO of

Le Ciel sur Terre, a heaven on earth painstakingly designed by both girls, with one change: The new name would be Addisons: Heaven on Earth.

She spent the last few days of September not examining the files, focusing her full attention on the project that was so much a part of her life with Addison, preparing for her initial meeting with Michele Baroque of the young and ambitious architectural firm Les Designs Supérieurs. The meeting lasted all day and into the evening, and Maria knew instinctively she and Addison had made the right choice. Ms. Baroque was a graduate of the finest design school in Europe, she was young, the owner of a successful business and felt none of the tradition-oriented or peer-pressure restraints other firms considered non-negotiable. She had vision, not hindsight, and her vision included knowing Maria would soon be with her once again to fulfil a dream.

She was five years older than Maria. When they first met she had been as intrigued by the girls as by their concept, working hard to make her bid irresistible, delighted when the multi-million dollar contract was awarded right away, contingent on the business plan being approved.

In the few short days that followed, hearing the horrific news about Addison, she felt a deep sadness for Maria, not selfish disappointment for herself, though she hadn't stopped working on the project. When Maria met with her for the first day of work together Michele had much to present, Maria much to absorb. Her father had been right, and she called to thank him. The project would be completed within eighteen months, six months behind the original schedule, Addison's birthday, May 03.

Whenever possible the contractors would be women with zero tolerance of derision by men or women toward the other, and Maria would have the final say in all matters other than technical, when she would rely on Michele's counsel. The parametres were very specific and clear. The spa would be exclusively for women between the ages of twenty-five and fifty-five who could afford the ten-thousand dollar annual membership fee plus the monthly add-on costs for optional meal and bar services, plus gratuities.

When completed the two-floor, full service facility would cover three thousand square metres environmentally controlled by an integrated system of lighting, temperature and theme-based aroma therapy to ensure year-round serenity, peace of mind and pampered luxury in an intimate setting for women, by women. Breakfast, lunch and dinner menus would be served in Mediterranean and Asian settings and silk and satin lounge wear would be as appropriate in the bar as street wear. The inside pool and stand-up whirlpool would be constantly fed by heated waterfalls falls on three sides and have quarterly themes ranging from Grecian to Romanesque to more modern tastes. The rooftop garden and pool would be four-season with themes ranging from northern European in the winter to Caribbean in the summer and clothing in the pool areas would be discouraged. The spa would not encourage out-of-shape women wanting to change their lifestyles. Being in shape would be a premier prerequisite, each member required to sign a covenant of peace and tranquility: an absolute, each guest's commitment to the others. Addisons would be a retreat from private worlds. First names would be used, and client files would be treated with the utmost discretion and with an absolute non-disclosure policy. The facility would be open twenty-four-seven with exterior camera surveillance and a central security system that would communicate instantly with police, fire, and medical response units.

Private rooms would be available with queen-size beds for extended stays or planned weekends for couples or singles. Absolutely no men would be permitted beyond the first set of three doors, which would each require either visual verification by the receptionist or an iris scan of each woman coming in. Clients would be married, single or divorcées with one commonality: they would prefer or need the company of other women in an environment of complete peace of mind and luxury. They would be pampered in massage rooms or unwind in physiotherapy rooms for prescribed treatments before indulging in a full-service beauty salon. Two lounges called Friendly Rooms would be specifically designed for like-minded women to meet or for the curious to experiment without the need to explain or feel the pressures of guilt and limousine service would be available to clients who preferred not spoiling a unique experience by first enduring the annoyances of traffic and parking. Addisons would be the crème de la crème.

## 96

Maria was entirely sleepless when she arrived home late after her working dinner with Michele. She wanted to cry, to remember Addison and miss her, but driving home from the restaurant she had an epiphany she wouldn't ignore and by early morning the epiphany became her plan. She would need his help and understanding, without which she would lose any hope of ever having the one thing she needed most, the one thing that would give her closure.

## 97

The calmness in her voice and how her tone had changed since her last visit with him instantly triggered his inherent sense of self-preservation. She wasn't sorrowful, neither was she sombre. Her voice was dark, strangely self-assured and he didn't know where the change would lead. But his daughter was her mother in every way and he knew it wouldn't be good.

What she was proposing was ridiculous, transcending blind faith which had never been his forte. Worse, she was asking for time which wasn't his to give. It wasn't good at all. What she was suggesting wasn't a game, he admonished. People were going to die, which was secondary to the objective of those doing the killing not to get caught. The process of identifying, locating, establishing a routine, establishing a time and finally the termination, was critical. More critical were the escape and the alibi.

"A successful execution isn't an emotional act, Meme, and must never be dramatic." He shrugged. "You know what I mean? A hit must never be theatrical. That's the difference between a needed execution and a killing, or murder, which will always end badly for the person doing the killing. The process must always be thought out impassively, planned matter-of-factly, and driven by a need. In your case it's strictly revenge, emotional, and that's not good. Other times it's for self-preservation or honour. The need for revenge you feel for Addison is a matter of honour for me, for family. Do you understand?"

"I do have a need, papa. That's not emotional, not revenge."

"And what's that?"

"To know, papa," she gazed up at him, confident yet imploring. "How will I know?"

"Know what, Meme? Their fates are sealed, a fait accompli. What's to know?"

"You told me something once about the fear of death being worse than death itself. Is that true? Do you believe what you said?"

"It's a reality, not a myth. The fear that comes from the expectation of one's death is always greater than the fear of death itself."

"That's what I want to know, papa. That's my need. I need to know and to see the fear they will feel. Killing them is the smallest part. I want them to feel fear, to feel what Addie felt. I want them to feel the same terror."

"They will, I promise."

"That's not good enough, papa. I have to see it, I have to feel it. I have to be there."

He paced silently for long moments before answering, and when he did respond his voice was a level monotone. "Fine, I'll do what you ask, as long as you understand these things take time." He sat beside her. "This changes everything, Maria. Understand one thing: I'm in control, not you. I'm in control of time and place. I will not tolerate any intrusion, not even from you, Maria. Do you understand me?"

"Yes, papa, I understand."

"I believe what you're doing is wrong, Maria." He took the thin envelope from her and slid it into his shirt pocket without inspecting the contents. "Come to me in ten days. I'll have them both by then. Now go home."

He took in his arms like a rag doll, hugged her tightly and walked away without saying anything further. She was twenty-three. He had very little control over her and very little choice in the matter. He'd lost her once, he wouldn't lose her again, which didn't mean he had to like it.

When she left he summoned Marcus.

# 98

The frumpy middle-aged receptionist raised her head slowly and deliberately from her inessential work, examining and instantly assessing the young woman who came through the brass-trimmed glass doors with a poise she found intimidating.

"Good morning."

The woman standing in front of her recognized the smile as false, though requisite for the job.

"Do you have an appointment?"

"No, I don't."

"I'm afraid you must have an appointment, madame. I can arrange one right now for a more convenient time, if that's alright with you."

"Thank you, you're very kind. However right now is convenient to me as my agenda is fully booked. I will see an Account Manager now, if that's alright with you." She didn't pause. "And I will work strictly with someone who is dynamic and young enough to present new ideas. I've researched the firm and know the work they do, much of which is traditional. I don't need traditional. I need modern and fresh and the person who meets me must create an appropriate first impression or I'll be giving preference to one of the other firms who are currently anxious for my business. Did I mention I'm pressed for time?"

The receptionist had been right in her assessment. The woman was a bitch. "I will see if someone is available to meet with you, madame. However I cannot promise, you understand. May I have your name?"

"Christine Benton."

The frumpy and frazzled woman flipped through the in-house directory, stopping at P. She scrolled to Pendleton, Shane before dialling the two-digit extension she already knew.

# 99

Christine pivoted on a heel and strode to the farthest corner, keeping her back to the receptionist as she unbuttoned and threw her black suede coat casually onto one of the matching leather sofas. They didn't seem comfortable, and when she eased herself onto the other she felt as though she'd slide off the moment she relaxed the muscles in her legs.

She was always amused by the way other women would give her the once-over whenever she dressed for business, women who thought elastic waistbands and polyester were fashion statements that didn't say sloppy or lazy. There was a reason for everything, and why wouldn't a woman dress for effect in business, particularly when that business would be with a man. She was turning twenty-seven, she was successful in business with an MBA, and she had a body men enjoyed appreciating. So why not use her visible attributes to her advantage while she could? She had chosen a long-sleeve, black V-neck sweater dress she knew would creep nicely up to show most of her thighs when she crossed her legs. Her every curve was highlighted and when she moved the sensation against her skin was sensual.

She knew what she was showing, when she chose to, delighting in the attention and the envy. If other women didn't like it, too bad; she did, and she smiled at the receptionist as she crossed her legs. Her one flaw was the glasses she had worn since childhood, without which she could barely read a word or see a face.

"Mr. Pendleton will not be able to meet with you, Ms. Benton. I'll speak with Mr. Wilmington to see if he'll make himself available, though I doubt he will. They're very busy." Christine ignored the woman, making tight circles with her foot hovering over the carpeted floor in a black suede knee-high boot and listened to the murmurs from across the room. Then: "Mr. Wilmington has asked for your patience. He will be with you as soon as possible. As I said, he's very busy. You should have called for an appointment."

Christine tilted her head, showing smug satisfaction. Of course he would see her, Miss Plain Jane, and you might as well cancel the rest of his appointments for the day. He won't be seeing anyone else.

# 100

When she saw him coming through the corner of her eye she switched legs without touching her dress. He was certainly handsome, though not gorgeous, and she judged him to be about 1.8 metres. Even with the heels on her boots she would have to look up.

He walked with a confidence borne of wealth, not the self-assurance of authority. He was slim, and quite pale, with perfectly coiffed dark hair. He was well-dressed in teal slacks, a blue blazer and the bright gold of his silk tie highlighted the brass buttons on the jacket. His tie touched the top edge of his belt and his loafers reflected light which told her he came from money that allowed him a privileged life. He had been groomed, was probably still being groomed, or dictated to. He had the appearance of being fit, though not physically strong. She believed clothes made the man and she was about to find out whether he was equal to his expensive wardrobe.

# 101

She was a vision, and he fell in love with her body that very moment. He could barely take his eyes from her legs, hoping she wouldn't look his way so he wouldn't have to. Her dress showed every curve of her body and her breasts were exquisite, perfectly shaped, and he didn't have to imagine exactly how they would look under her dress. If anything, she'd be wearing a thong and a bra would be for the sole purpose of showing her tits more, he thought, not to cover them. The brim of her felt hat was narrow, and what he could see of her hair wasn't quite blonde. He couldn't figure out what the colour was, braided in some sort of complicated style and he wondered if she was the same colour everywhere. The green-gold of her hazel eyes sparkled from behind shiny black thick-rimmed glasses: an indispensable part of her total persona. She was a beautiful package and he wondered who got to open her, and how often.

She obviously had money and lived a pampered life. No average working girl could ever be as stunning, or afford the Dior watch and Vuitton purse. If she did have a husband or a lover he was digging deep to keep her happy. She definitely wouldn't come cheap, an involuntary grin spreading across his face as he wondered whether she screamed when she did.

"Mrs. Benton, I'm Bret Wilmington. I'm sorry to have kept you waiting." Only the coffee table kept him from standing in front of her. "I understand you'd like to meet with an Account Manager as soon as possible."

"Ms. Benton," she corrected, "and, yes, I would appreciate your accommodating me."

He extended his open hand. "My pleasure, Ms. Benton. Please join me in my office. May I take your coat?"

"Thank you. I appreciate your flexibility."

As she stood she made a point to avoid his eyes. He watched her uncross her legs and turn slightly sideways to face him, taking advantage of the moment, gawking like a teenager for as long as he dared. What he saw was very nice.

## 102

The first meeting had gone well, eliminating the need for her to go through the process of a closed bid. The fees were reasonable and the personal tour he had given her of the showrooms and offices demonstrated that W & P would do the best work for her.

He was flirting. As she signed the retainer cheque she could feel his stare crisscrossing her body. He would need a couple of weeks to come up with a preliminary design for her approval, and full design work for the project would probably be completed within six months, with her involvement and sufficient time to select a suitable property. He estimated construction of the facility would take another six to eight months and barring any unforeseen delays the upscale, high-tech business complex would be ready in twelve to fourteen months.

She was currently negotiating a suitable property separately, though she agreed his firm would be responsible for the balance of the turnkey project. She was not at all interested in dealing with contractors. Thus far, she had every reason to believe they would work well together and that W & P would transform her concept of a modern office setting into a reality. They shook hands, not signing the contract she insisted would be contingent on her approval of those preliminary drawings. In the meantime, the retainer would suffice as proof of her good will. He agreed, once his father had. He would call her the moment he finished and then he noted her cell number before helping her on with her coat for reasons exclusive of courtesy.

# 103

The same night Maria sat at home wrapped in Addison's favourite warm woollen blanket. She had spent hours studying the digital images of the other three men, trying to remember, trying to place them in Ixtapa, and suddenly she did. He was Bret Wilmington, and she pressed on the remote to expand the image, filling the plasma screen with the face of a murderer, a face smiling with eyes that were not, and she tried to imagine what lay behind the mask. She had no idea how the saga would end, though she knew how she would begin. She was studying a man whose death was uppermost on her mind, a man Phallicia Hunter would soon kill.

Thanksgiving was quiet. She hadn't cooked for anyone in a very long time and both Angelo and Marcus made a big deal over the turkey. After dinner Marcus excused himself to give them some one-on-one time, though she insisted on doing the dishes first while her father relaxed with one of his dirty cigars, if he had to, she added, and a cognac.

She had always thought of him as a bad man, in her long-ago past along with so many other ideologies and concepts. Now he was just her father, not the notorious mob boss sitting in the living room with his feet up, wrapped in cozy fleece-lined huggy bear slippers. Marcus had laughed to the point of tears when Angelo was left with no choice but to put them on, until he opened his Thanksgiving gift and Angelo was the one doubled over. They were family, and laughter once again resounded throughout the entire house. To Maria nothing else mattered…at the moment.

Angelo waited until Marcus had gone home, not wanting to get into a conversation that might spoil the moment, and when Maria came into the room he hadn't budged. The turkey was excellent and not much was left over. She poured him another Courvoisier and sat across from him before taking a sip from her snifter and telling him the documents seemed so official, like the real ones. The photograph, the data, the feel, everything seemed perfect. Angelo answered that they were perfect, except for the person inside. Phallicia Hunter was a Canadian citizen, twenty-seven, English-speaking, born on July 18, a date she could easily remember, 1.67 metres tall with long blonde hair, blue eyes and didn't wear glasses. She had travelled to the States eight times, to France once and her passport was valid for three more years.

Her current address was a downtown Montreal high-rise, she had never had a moving violation, she had an unrestricted licence, and both her licence and provincial health card were valid for another four years. Her credit rating was triple A, she had five thousand dollars in the bank and her credit card limit was eight thousand, even though she always paid cash.

Post 9-11 laws forbade smiling on government issued photo IDs, yet the unsmiling image on the three photo documents didn't detract from the delicate features of the pretty and youthful face. No one would ever imagine her sole purpose in life was to kill Chad Rivers and his three friends. Angelo sat watching her, wondering what was going through her mind. There was no point in asking her. She'd simply say something to placate him. He'd known for a while he had wasted his time over the years regretting never having a son who would take over control of the family. He was very glad she was family, not the enemy, and Phallicia Hunter was only half of what and who she had become.

# 104

Bret Wilmington completed the preliminary drawings on the Friday of the second week, and the second appointment was set for the following Tuesday. He suggested they meet Saturday or Sunday, to help him with his overburdened agenda, but Christine declined without offering an explanation. The receptionist was wearing the same frumpy two-piece suit, and probably laced, thick-heeled orthopaedic footwear with thick opaque hose, Christine thought. And what was with the coarse, ash-coloured hair, she wondered?

The reception was slightly warmer and cordial than the bitter plus one Celsius temperature and the swirling rain that fell most of the last day of October. The contrasting brilliant colours of early fall had long since disappeared from a city devoid of colour most of the year and known by locals and tourists alike as being one step ruder than Paris.

Montreal was a decaying infrastructure of ruined asphalt, collapsing overpasses, pollution-stained steel and glass, where graffiti was art, litter was more of an accent than trash, and where October's dismal grey cloak would soon turn into a blanket of dirty white lasting into the spring.

Christine's coat and hat were blood-red suede. Her low-heeled boots were tan-coloured suede, matching her straight-fit suede pants sitting low on her waist. Her mohair sweater had a cowl neck and bell sleeves which made her feel warm and look hot. Her jewellery was a deep ruby pendant on a silver chain and perfectly matching stud earrings. She was completely unapproachable to all but the most deserving and threw the coat carelessly on the sofa to annoy the old lady behind her. He could pick it up for her later.

Bret Wilmington had dressed for the day. His slacks were teal blue, his blazer was navy blue, his turtleneck was burgundy and Gus the shoe shine guy on the main floor had expertly polished his oxblood loafers. Not bad, she thought. She had been in his office less than two hours before the general office began clearing out for the evening, only the insecure or success-driven upwardly mobile aspirants to any one of the ten executive offices remaining.

He paused, seeming uncertain as to what he wanted to say next. "Perhaps we could finish discussing this over dinner, Ms. Benton."

"Thank you, Mr. Wilmington, that's very kind, unfortunately I have a busy day tomorrow."

He nodded. "Actually, I have tickets for a show as well, a gift from a satisfied client," he lied, "and no one to go with. I'm afraid my schedule's been too busy to have much of a social life. You can't blame a man for trying."

"I'm honoured, Mr. Wilmington. It's been a while for me, too."

"Then dinner perhaps? No show."

"Perhaps dinner wouldn't be such a bad idea. Dinner, no show, and my friends call me Chrissie."

"Dinner it is, Chrissie. I'll give the tickets to anyone who's in the office when we leave. And my friends call me a lot of things…including Bret."

"Strictly business though, Bret," she added, "and I have to be home early."

"Strictly business, and a taxi whenever you want one. Promise."

# 105

She was well-educated, so was he, though she had an inherent element he lacked which he couldn't identify. She was the kind of beautiful that makes the most erudite and worldly men feel inadequate and unsure. She could be funny and could probably enjoy laughing if she ever relaxed. She was strictly business, all work and no play and he wondered if that would ever reverse. Then he wondered when he would find out, how excited he would be to finally see her naked beside him, how she would feel under him. Her skin was entirely flawless and smooth with a natural glow. She wore no make-up because none was needed and he couldn't let her go. He couldn't let this one get away.

# 106

She accepted his invitation to dinner solely to discover more about the man she'd be working with so closely. The evening would be strictly hands-off business and not go anywhere. He dressed well, spoke well, focused on her, not himself and he knew his wines. He'd obviously been raised to be a gentleman. He had an easy way about him, though slightly arrogant and self-satisfied with those around him. There was also something uncertain and unresolved about him.

He wanted her, she knew. Every woman knew when they were being undressed in public by male companions, new or old, or by the men they aroused, known or unknown, and she wondered how she would feel being undressed by him in private. She imagined what kind of lover he would be, more importantly wondering what kind of lover she would be. She was good at everything she did, so why not sex, and by the end of the evening they had hit it off and she let him know he possibly had half a chance.

# 107

November flew by unseen: a monochromatic and monotonous filler month between October and December, a time to stay at home and dread the coming winter. There was nothing inviting about November in the north: thirty drab days of colourless cold. Strangely, February was known as suicide month in Quebec, though at least in February the days were longer and brighter, with deep snow to shovel or play in. November had no such redeeming qualities: a boring month and all anyone could do was shop early for Christmas or wait for February.

Christmas would be Maria's first alone, despite being with Jean-Émile and Madeleine. Her father understood, happy she'd be spending Christmas with Larivière. And she understood Angelo. Christmas since her mother's death had become a special time alone for him. She had spoken with Ercilia and Pilar every week, as though they lived nearby, but they weren't nearby and she missed them terribly. She had bought them gifts, exceeding her budget with gifts for Angelo, Marcus, Jean-Émile and Madeleine, convincing herself she was enjoying the season when the one gift she had really wanted to buy, she couldn't.

Pilar told her differently. Adisita not being with them was no reason not to give her a gift. She and Ercilia would be thinking of her and Addison every moment over La Navidad. She would be with Señor El Rio, Pilar's name for Larivière, and la señora. They were happy knowing she'd be with those who loved her and Addison. They would speak with her many times before Christmas, especially Christmas morning when she would need them the most.

# 108

The marriage proposal had come as a complete surprise to Christine. The project was halfway through the design stage, she had purchased the property and the construction was slated to begin in April or May. They had spent several evenings together over the past two months dining and dancing, and had gone to the theatre on one occasion. Still, the proposal took her breath away. They had never been romantic and he knew not to be forward. She wasn't the girl next door. He had never experienced a woman like her. She was always graceful, firm when need be, and could let her feminine side acquiesce when she deemed the timing appropriate. She was single-minded, a determined businesswoman and a great dancer. She was private and rarely spoke about her personal life beyond saying her parents were dead, she was single, unattached, liked fast cars, particularly her blue Porsche Cayman, and had few friends.

Occasionally she had let him kiss her platonically at the taxis, though he had never seen her home which was also her office. Something was obviously growing between them. If not dynamic energy, at least a growing feeling that something was happening between them and he knew she felt the same way.

The platinum ring was unique with exquisitely cut sapphires on either side of a solitary one-carat diamond. The jeweller had taken the better part of a month to complete the creation, and when she closed the box she said she would accept his proposal after the New Year, if she felt she could, adding that she wouldn't be with him at New Years. Nor would she join him at Christmas. Mother Wilmington hadn't thought it proper to have a client as a sleep-over guest, especially at Christmas, a time for family, and Christine had previously made plans for New Years. She had made reservations months earlier at a spa in the Estrie region for a week of pampering, being alone, and now to think about their future. Being away from him would be good. She wasn't sure about her feelings. Anyway, he was a man, and even if she answered right away, he would think of his own male prowess, not her. Waiting a week or so wouldn't kill him. If anything, he'd learn not to take her for granted.

She kissed him lightly as he pulled her in close. He would wait. In fact, he needed the time to work on his thesis, so being far away from her wasn't a bad thing. She had met Frederick Wilmington at the W & P offices and he wasn't particularly anxious to introduce her to his mother, not after the family debacle over his wanting to invite Christine for Christmas with the family. He could wait to introduce her to his mother. He knew how she was, how they both were. Together they'd be fire with fire, especially once he made the announcement of their engagement, when he would be in the middle.

# 109

The fact was she had no friends she could tell or who would understand. She felt as though she had beautiful new party dress and no party. He was handsome, and charming, though she wasn't certain she could be his wife. Everyone had a dark side and she hadn't yet seen his. She was aware her dark side existed, a part of her she kept hidden. Hell hath no fury like a woman scorned. What man hadn't been warned at least once of that truth? And more than simple prayers would be needed to protect a simple man from her feminine wrath.

The voice-mail message hadn't changed, the phone simply wouldn't be answered between the twentieth and January 03. She needed time alone. She'd worry about Mother Bitch another time and flatly refused his offer to drive her, preferring to hire a limo instead. Her time would be special and she was worth every penny. She patted his cheek. If he didn't already know, he soon would.
*

Angelo Bardollini wasn't one to get overly excited about much, but he did get excited when the time came for his annual ski trip. Where, no one ever knew. He never told them. His time away was sacrosanct, the one time he could be himself. The special time had once been shared, a time alone with his wife without guns or the threat of guns, his solemn commitment to her: no guns, no family. By which she meant his family, not theirs, and he doubted Maria would remember the secluded getaway. In her teens she had been a teenager like any other: her skirts were short, make-up always a point of contention and her parents continuously embarrassed her. Being with her friends was way cooler, which had been fine with the horrible parents as long as Marcus was never far behind.

The morning of the twenty-first the sky was clear, the snow in the country was crisp, and when Marcus called the phone kept ringing. The boss was gone and no one knew where, not Marcus, and not the task force. Of course he was reachable, with the understanding that if someone wasn't dying, someone would.

*

Marcus had a big heart, a big gun he didn't mind using and a big problem where Maria was concerned. In his heart she was his little sister and he didn't like being told by Angelo to leave her alone, to let her enjoy her time with Larivière on the farm. He didn't like the old Larivière and had tried to convince Angelo he should be at the farm with her, to protect her. Angelo refused, promising Marcus that if anything did happen to Maria, he would have carte blanche. He would have first watch over the Bardollini home, then he'd be free to enjoy the season. The lieutenant would take the second watch and all three would meet on the fourth to review.

*

John Franklin departed on the twenty-second. He'd return home January 05<sup>th</sup> and wouldn't think once about his staff whose time had come to stand alone and if that meant failing this was the time to find out. For thirty years he'd been the owner and Operations Manager of EID Services, though a month earlier his office staff had become the beneficiaries of their hard work when he agreed to sell them equal shares at fair market value. He also agreed to stay on as advisor until spring, when he would leave them without regret.

Very few had ever seen him over the years. He despised being in one place too long, sharing his time between the three locations, delegating authority during his frequent time away. He had looked forward to these particular weeks away for several years. He realized he was taking a gamble when so much was happening around him, but this winter escape was also the final step towards early retirement and he had complete confidence in those reporting to him.

The sixteen-metre San Juan wouldn't be ready for its maiden cruise until sometime in June, and this wouldn't be his last opportunity to make changes to the luxurious onboard amenities. Meanwhile, he would cruise one last time onboard the Hiding Out to his retreat across aqua-blue waters. He'd return at least once more before June to see the vessel officially documented with a name appropriate for his retirement, though he would never again step onboard the slightly longer Bertram. His Miami broker had found a serious buyer and the name was part of the deal. There would be no Hiding Out II and ownership would be transferred on the 31st as a condition of sale. The buyers wanted to spend New Year's Eve onboard and he agreed they would.

At one time he thought he'd enjoy running fishing charters, which didn't last very long. As much as he thought he might enjoy being around people, he never had. He preferred company who knew when to leave and drunken fishermen didn't fit the profile. He didn't look young for his age. He looked precisely his age when other men artificially accelerated the process either by neglect or abuse, his lustrous silver-streaked hair giving him an air of sophistication, not unwanted years. He worked out regularly. He was healthy and strong and in better shape than men twenty years his junior, all part of his retirement plan for better living alone.

His manner should have attracted hordes of hopeful women, had he ever allowed anyone else to be close. He had remained single after the death of his one love, a reconfirmed bachelor who believed any woman interested in him would come with more baggage than he wanted to carry. He preferred being private, which was far less

252

complicated, even though she would have understood.

As much as he loved women, he had only ever loved her, and now he loved his privacy. Perhaps later he would discover another, but for the moment he was content being alone. At home he didn't know whether or not he was liked by his neighbours who rarely saw him. He was a frequent traveller and a recluse, and as long as he didn't bother their children they had no reason to bother with him. The neighbours in back were a different matter and the farther away from them he could be, the better. His personal home-maintenance staff enjoyed working for him, mostly because they never saw him. Though they knew he could always see them.

Over the years he had nurtured an intense apathy towards Christmas, which, for him, had become the easier pretence: though he secretly enjoyed the colours and the carols. He hated snow, and those who didn't. He hated shopping and insincere best wishes. He hated each New Year and those who always thought the coming months would be better when they never did anything to make them better. His year had turned out well; the coming year would be better yet, the best.

What he had wanted and needed most in life had come to him, as did most things he wanted, and what remained for him to accomplish didn't matter at the moment. This was his time to be himself, alone with his memories on Perfect Retreat, his private Bahamian island. At one time, so long ago, they had escaped to their getaway as a family, their perfect retreat where he would soon dock his sixteen-metre Perfect Escape.

He arrived at the marina as the low winter sun was backlighting Miami and immediately felt free of everything he left behind. The sun and the salt air were invigorating and he inhaled deeply as he stood on the wharf inspecting the smooth contours of the Bertram swaying and squeaking against the bright white of the over-sized fenders. The marina dock crew had serviced and cleaned her and she was ready for cruising, though Franklin would wait for first dawn to judge the water and the yellow or red sun before setting his auto-pilot that would guide him to 26°19' 54" N by 76°51'46"W. He felt absolute freedom. He was John Franklin, unknown, obscure, and he alone knew how truly special that was.

*

The pilot of the LCL corporate jet was given the gift of a lifetime by the new and improved Larivière who was doing his best with the help of Mme. Harnais to avoid being visited by the ghosts of Christmas past and present. Many a night since Addison's death he secretly cried over lost years. Now he wanted to change the present, to become a different and better person and perhaps the ghost of Christmas future would come to him as an angel whose name he would know.

The pilot could enjoy personal use of the corporate jet to vacation with his family anywhere in the world he wished, with two stipulations, one of which was being in Montreal the morning of the twenty-fourth.

*

Even though Maria was anxious to spend Christmas and New Years on the farm, she wanted badly to see Pi and Ercilia. Eight months had passed and she missed them as much as she wanted to be with Addison's father who needed her. He had come a long way since they first met, he just couldn't find the words and she didn't want to disappoint him.

Angelo declined as much for Larivière as for himself and Jean-Émile understood why. A member of the men's club doing Christmas with a renowned mob boss simply wouldn't do, though Maria couldn't imagine her father on the ski slopes. She had never seen him ski, and didn't necessarily want to. What was up with that, she wondered, smiling inwardly, attributing his enthusiasm to middle-age male syndrome? Pilar and Ercilia had called her at least once a week, and Maria called them as often. At times Ercilia would sneak in a third call, especially when she had something important to say that couldn't wait, like what new dress she had bought, or how gorgeous she was in her new boots, or how much she missed Maria. Pilar would simply sit and listen, knowing her girls were making each other happy.

They had kept their promise to Adisita. Maria would never be alone, though she hadn't spoken with them for more than a week. They hadn't answered her messages. Christmas had come and they had told her they would have much to prepare, so they must be very busy. She would try calling them Christmas Eve and, if they were out, Christmas morning, or maybe Christmas afternoon.

The limo arrived at the farm early on the morning of December 24<sup>th</sup>. Jeff had been as taken aback by his Christmas bonus as the corporate pilot. His services would be required until mid-afternoon, after which he could enjoy full use of the limo with his family over the festive week, instructed not to peek in the glove box until he arrived home, and a Merry Christmas to you and yours.

The snow was pure white and blinding for as far as the eye could see and Maria went straight from the limo to visit with Addison, stomping along the partially shovelled path and leaving tiny prints in the crisp and pristine snow, each footstep resounding around her in a way particular to winter and she wondered when Ercilia and Pi would ever hear the snow. She had selected the brightest yellow and red long-stem carnations she could find. They were Addison's favourite flowers, her favourite colours and Maria sank to her knees not feeling or hearing the crispy cold. Jean-Émile saw her arrive, and watched the limo leave the property as soon as the chauffeur brought Maria's suitcase and packages to the main entrance of the house. He felt badly for her, and tried to dislike Mme. Harnais for being beside him at the very moment he needed seclusion. The last thing he wanted was for her to see him as she stood watching Maria through her own window. So he did what any man would do. He left. He went upstairs to his study knowing she would call as soon as the doorbell rang which he hoped would not be too soon.

Madeleine saw him leave, shaking her head, saying something in French about stupid men which she knew he heard perfectly, the stupid old fool, and she was equally as happy he hadn't seen her wiping her own glassy eyes.
*

Jean-Émile had done his best to ensure Christmas would be memorable. What more could he do, and when called to greet his young guest he made invisible and feeble excuses through his open office door that a teary-eyed Madeleine explained away to Maria: He was a man, child, and sometimes men needed an extra few moments to prepare. They weren't as strong as women.

He was as anxious as a schoolboy giving his first gift, and the diamond charm bracelet he had bought for Maria would pale by comparison, though the bracelet was far from ordinary. Madame Harnais had commissioned twelve charms that were a history of Addison's life through to the time the girls had met, each one documented on parchment and encased in mahogany and gold fabric.

The final approach of the LCL jet was on-time, the wheels touching down at 10:20 on the twenty-fourth as promised, five hours and twenty minutes after take-off from Juarez International. The passengers had been treated like princesses in-flight, along with the pilot's family, wide-eyed and open-mouthed from the ice-covered Great Lakes eastward; staring at the biggest white blanket they had ever seen.

Above the clouds they had expected to see fleecy white beneath them, but when the pilot requested permission from air traffic control for a slow decent to give them a treat. They had already touched snow once. The pilot thought to take them some from his family vacation in Vale, though neither imagined the sensations of walking and playing in it, even though he made a snowball for Pilar who stared at the fast-melting ball on the tarmac, then to Ercilia, shrugging her shoulders completely convinced she didn't like snow. What she did like were the clothes Jean-Émile sent them weeks earlier from the frozen north, accompanied with a handwritten note to each of them in which he explained the need for secrecy.

He sent a full wardrobe of winter outerwear selected by Madeleine who had done a perfect job with style, size and colours that would suit each one. She once again liked and admired the man, yet for as good a man and father he wanted to be, he was still just a man.
*

When they stepped from the jet the Celsius temperature was minus eighteen, made worse by Montreal's humid island status between two rivers and the jet stream carried even more moist air across Quebec from the Great Lakes. The air was freezing cold and the girls didn't like it. What they liked even less was the pilot's insistence that they have a snowball fight before going through Customs. What was it with men having to throw things, Pilar asked? Sure he was cute, they agreed in woman-code, in kind of a man way, accepting his defeat in a flurry of tarmac-snow and flailing Latina arms propelling the two women around him in a maelstrom.

Worse: the ground crew did nothing to help him and his family stood by witnessing the sad surrender of their father and husband as the pilot failed to scurry away from pathetic

defeat.
*

Maria understood why Jean-Émile wasn't joining her. She understood the emotions he was going through. She was experiencing her own. Her only friends in life weren't returning her calls and she didn't know why. She knew they loved her, which made their forgetfulness much harder to understand and all the more important to understand him.

People who didn't live in the north would never understand the postcard-perfect hell. Skin would freeze below zero in under three minutes, ears would turn white and never return to normal dimensions, noses would turn white and crack, eventually turning red and staying that way, and AutoRoute 10 was one of the worst in the entire country: a driver's nightmare only the best could travel on the worst days. Those who merely imagined they were the best would spend the day waiting for a tow truck or ambulance, if they were fortunate.

The pilot went home sulking with defeat after the chauffeur arrived to take charge of the giggling victors before challenging the unconquerable A-10. The bar was full, the seats were plush, the music was soothing and all the girls could do was stare out from the windows, amazed. Pilar told Ercilia they had come to the North Pole and would never see the sun again. Through the rear view mirror Jeff saw the wide-expressions and smiled, raising the screen as a safety procedure. Ercilia responded that she had read about places in the north that were always frozen and Pilar shook her head and sank back as Ercilia activated the intercom to ask Jeff how long the drive would be. He said sixty minutes more.

She stared at her phone, tempted, struggling with her promise to Jean-Émile when he had spoken with her the previous week.
*

Jean-Émile didn't leave his office until he heard the limo crunching snow under its wheels. Madeleine had served Maria a light lunch and the two spent the early afternoon talking. They spoke about Addison, trading stories and special moments that made them both cry. Maria spoke endlessly about Ercilia and Pi and how she missed them. She would call them later in the day, she said, or in the evening, or the next day. She needed to speak with them and Madeleine empathized. She was certain Maria would soon be speaking with the girls.

The weather had worsened. Furious winds howled from every direction as the temperature plummeted to minus twenty-five. Not a time to frolic outside, not even for the most ardent skier, and the fire inside was roaring hot comfort. Being with Madeleine was like being with her mom. What was missing, Madeleine knew, were flannel jammies and hot coco and she said to hell with it, to hell with him. Let's do it. And they did. They changed into flannel pyjamas, poured each other a mug of hot coco, and sat by the fire.

« Madeleine, il y a quelqu'un, je crois.»

«Oui, ma petite, il y a quelqu'un...pour toi. Vas-y. Vas-y, chérie.»

«Comment?»

"Go, child, so Jean-Émile can finally join us. This is what he's been waiting for, the silly old man. Don't disappoint him. Go quickly."

She had no idea why she was running to open the door and waiting. The black limo was white against bright snow and the man who clambered from his front seat to the open trunk was dressed in blue that quickly became as white. Jeff was very big, she thought, and before completing his first trip to the front door he had spoken into one of the rear windows of the limo. He bowed to Maria from the waist, shrugging and smiling before hurrying away. Maria thought she heard him laughing and moments later he was back with more. He took Maria's hand, kissing it, telling her she had made his Christmas the most special and she had no idea what he was talking about. Then he walked away feeling good, knowing something she didn't.

A deal was a deal, even with a man, he had told them, and when he slid into the front seat and said "go" they went quickly, from both doors, without any help from him. He sat where he was, content as he watched, not taking his eyes from the girls as he reached for the phone. The boss was calling, suggesting that he stay and not defy the murderous weather. No, thank you, Jeff answered. Merry Christmas to all; however in the limo he had full control over current road conditions. He wished he could stay. Who wouldn't want to spend Christmas with four such lovely women?

At that Jean-Émile insisted Jeff stay, if he was so certain about the four women, and that he would drive the limo to Montreal. All he heard was a chuckle and a click as he watched the car drive away.

*

They were a flurry of bright reds, yellows, greens and blues on swirling white that Ercilia was throwing at an unimpressed Pilar and Madeleine wouldn't take no for an answer: Jean-Émile would be there, she insisted, to see every moment with her by his side. Maria saw them through frosted panes, running toward the house, not knowing who they were. Then she saw their gleeful dark faces and couldn't believe her eyes, running towards them all the same, crying out their names and not feeling the cold through her jammies and soft huggy bears.

*

Truth be told, Angelo wasn't sad. He had no doubt Larivière would take care of the girls, though he did have Marcus personally deliver a case of Larivière's favoured scotch to the LCL offices, with his regrets. Marcus had been the real Christmas message and Jean-Émile smiled at the implication. Bardollini was taking care of his girl the way Jean-Émile should have taken care of his. What was wrong with that, apart from guilt?

Jean-Émile insisted on dual Christmases: the midnight French Réveillon and the English Santa Claus morning surprise. For the French who would attend midnight mass, Père Noël, Father Christmas, would conveniently invade their homes during mass to meticulously place all the goodies around silver or green artificial trees or pine-smelling real trees. Jean-Émile's tree was real and everyone returned home to open gifts while gorging themselves on cognac-spiked eggnog and Madeleine's delicious homemade traditional tortières.

Jean-Émile and Madeleine retired early to separate beds, a particularly English Christmas trait and an ironic French extreme for one of the most important French Catholic festive days of the year. They left the girls to talk girl-talk and have time together and later they would all wake to an English-style Christmas in front of a roaring fire and more gifts, though the girls didn't know.

He gave three of the four ladies memberships to Addisons, monogrammed silk robes and matching satin slippers. Maria's gift was a cheque for thirty thousand dollars, five matching gold-embossed binders each containing one hundred membership agreements and covenants of peace and tranquility she hadn't believed he had listened to as she explained the concept to him, along with a guarantee of three satisfied customers.

They encircled him with hugs and kisses, even Madeleine got caught up in the moment and gave him a slight hug and a kiss on the cheek, and Christmas wasn't over. Maria had asked him for a favour weeks earlier, which she could never repay, and assumed he'd been too busy to remember. She couldn't bring herself to ask him again, and she was happy she hadn't. He had done so much for her. She would find a way of getting things done.

She hadn't asked Pilar and Ercilia if they would even consider leaving their home in Mexico to become physiotherapists at Addisons, and not because she thought they'd refuse. She hadn't been sure of time frames and bureaucratic procedures and thought he might help her over the hurdles.

He passed Maria separate envelopes, one for Pilar, the other for Ercilia. The paperwork had begun and the immigration process would be fast-tracked, though the final decision would be up to Pilar and Ercilia once Maria presented them with her complete business plan and proposal that they join her in business as an independent service at the spa. Although, at the moment they could only stare at each other as Maria sat crying and talking gibberish to Señor El Rio before he and Madeleine left them alone once again.

\*

Four thousand kilometres to the south, Selena de Ortega hadn't stooped quickly enough to pick up the broken pieces of the glass she had dropped before her husband's fist crashed viciously into the side of her young face. The second blow was no less furious, losing consciousness the third time her head slammed hard against dining room wall of her middle-class Valencia home in northern Venezuela. There had been no Christmas for her, and a small one for him she could barely afford. He had been terminated from the automobile plant several months earlier and Christmas was the final insult from an insensitive woman who still left home every day to work as an administrative assistant at the same plant.

They had agreed not to exchange gifts, but Selena wanted him to have even a small a gift to open, to make him feel better about himself. It hadn't. The kindness infuriated him and he began drinking the evening before to eradicate the affront and he hadn't stopped. The drinking went on throughout the night and into the morning, and when she dropped his glass after being told to refill it, she knew instantly she had nowhere to run. His reaction was swift and brutal, though she wouldn't realize how brutal for several hours when she'd awaken to a new life, which at first would be difficult and demeaning.

That evening, when Ortega returned home from the bar, Selena Consuelo de la Vega, formerly of Madrid, Spain, was not there to greet or serve him. He would never see her again.

*

Maria had gone over Michele's most recent drawings days before Christmas, noting minor modifications which would take very little time to incorporate into the final drawings she hoped to have approved by the end of January. She eagerly spread the several layers of blueprints across Jean-Émile's living room floor and went over every minute detail. The girls would work independently, they would pay rent to the spa that would do the client billing, Addisons would take a nominal ten percent of that billing and no upfront investment would be required.

Michele Baroque had included several artist renditions of Maria's dream spa and Ercilia wanted immediately to be part of it, though Pilar was more pragmatic. They had a language barrier, not to mention the question of applying for landed status, and that's when Maria gave them each an envelope. They would be taking a risk, she told them, but she had received the best advice and everyone believed she would succeed. So what was so wrong with a few months of winter each year?

By noon Pilar hadn't said much as Ercilia listened to Maria explain the details once more. They didn't have to decide right away. Maria was still months away from interviewing prospective therapists, if they decided not to come.

*

Madeleine insisted Maria and Ercilia eat a hot lunch before running out into the cold to visit Addison, and before climbing onto the horse-drawn sleigh Jean-Émile had arranged. Pilar swept aside the sun curtain covering the plate-glass windows, shaking her head at the antics of the girls who appeared like overstuffed dolls bundled up in thermal snowsuits, hoods, scarves and gloves. They were shrieking loudly, running at each other with flailing arms before awkwardly turning and scrambling to recover as soft balls of snow burst off each of their backs.

Maria enjoyed obvious home team advantage, taking time to form perfect balls and she knew when best to throw them for optimum results. Ercilia was simply throwing handfuls of snow, not properly packed and not properly aimed, though suddenly a defensive technique came to her and she acted immediately, not expecting Maria to react so quickly and she jumped into the air with nothing but cold snow beneath her. When she turned over her face was frosty-white and she ran her tongue over her lips to remove the icy moustache. She had never tasted snow, which just tasted cold. Then Maria was on top of her, pushing her and sweeping her arms in semi-circles before rolling off and doing the same.

*

"Son locas, lo juro," Pilar whispered, shaking her head, "son muy nuts."

She hadn't expected the chortle from behind.

"Se divierten, pero es posible que tienes razón. We must enjoy our youth, for what follows is not always as good or as pleasant as we would wish."

She turned, seeing Jean-Émile. "Señor El Río, gracias, gracias para todo."

He stepped in to stand by her side, pulling the other side of the curtain. She had no reason to thank him, he thought, with no doubt in his mind the inverse was more the case. "Gracias por venir," he responded simply. "I am very glad you and Ercilia came to join us. They're making snow angels, Pilar."

¿Cómo?" Pilar crinkled her nose, not understanding.

"Los ángeles de nieve, snow angels. I haven't done so for years. I used to watch Addison making them. It's a lot of fun. You should join them."

"Señor El Río, ¿podemos hablar en secreto y en serio?"

"Por supuesto, señorita Pi. What would you like to discuss?" He faced her. "May I assume you are not quite certain what to do with regard to Maria's proposal?"

She nodded. "Amo muchísima a Maria y a Adisita, pero yo no conozco su país, sólo mi México. Tengo miedo porque no sé que hacer."

"You have nothing to fear, Pilar. Mexico will always be there for you, as will Maria should you choose not to join her. Perhaps you are thinking too much into the future, Pilar. I can tell you the world becomes smaller as we grow older. There is so much for all of us to see, more than most of us will ever see. Each one of us must decide for ourselves what the balance is to be."

"Una aventura?" she questioned.

"Yes, an adventure, querida…one neither you nor Maria will travel alone. Te lo juro, now why don't you go outside and be with your friends. I see the horses coming. I suppose I should call la Señora Madeleine."
*

When Pilar stepped out, all they could see of her was her face and all she could feel was the warm sun. She wanted to spend time with Adisita, to speak with her and tell her what she thought she had decided. Maybe then she'd be certain. Eight months had passed, almost to the day, and the pain

265

she felt for Addison had not diminished.

The stone glittered in the sunlight and she couldn't imagine the friend she had barely come to know lay in the frozen earth beneath her feet. She remembered her promise to Adisita the day they had all said goodbye to her, and to Ercilia, that they would never let Maria be alone. It would be an adventure and she was certain she could learn to speak enough gibberish to get by, at least at first, and Mexico City's air was so bad in the summer. Moving to Montreal would be a good thing, better for her and Ercilia. They would be businesswomen and the spa would be luxurious. She let her mind go blank, slowly twisting from her hips to her boots to see the huge farm horses standing patiently. Ercilia and Maria were behind the driver and Madeleine was sitting in the rear seat with Jean-Émile, all of them tucked in under thick, woollen throws as though enjoying a summer day.

When the driver saw her coming he patted the seat beside him as he leaned over and reached out his hand to help her up beside him. Much to her surprise she took his hand, justifying she had no choice unless she wanted to sit between an old couple who seemed comfortable together or between excited and incorrigible schoolgirls. Once settled, she twisted in her seat to see them all eyeing at her, pretending to be put out at having to sit up front, behind the smelly beasts. When she spoke a wide smile spread across her face, theirs completely disappeared in unison.

"It is to be so much good. No it is true?"
*

The day was a success and so was the rest of the week, during which Jean-Émile left them alone to work privately in his study, leaving Madeleine to play mother hen. Pilar had decided she liked snowshoeing, not cross-country skiing. She liked snowmobiling and after Jean-Émile had taken her out on her first run he'd found himself committed to at least one hour each afternoon with Madeleine fussing after both of them to dress properly and not forget the hot chocolate and cell phone. He enjoyed every moment with Pilar, as he did with Maria and Ercilia, and Pilar had let him know privately that he wasn't so bad for a man. She liked him.

The time went by quickly. New Years was quiet, no one staying up past the first glass of Champagne. Tears had been expected, though not because their time together had come to an end. Pilar and Ercilia had listened to what Jean-Émile, each one spending time alone in his office before speaking with her parents in Mexico for the first time in years. At first they were hesitant and afraid and he told them not to be, assuring each girl that her parents would be the ones uncertain and afraid. He was right and after the long telephone reunions they broke into tearful smiles and hugs when Jean-Émile asked Madeleine to check with accounting to make certain LCL had sufficient funds to pay for the calls.

The first of the year had been a blur of successive hours, with so much to say and do all week.

The limo came by at 10:00 on the second and the LCL flight was scheduled to leave at 1:00 PM. Pilar and Ercilia each went to Jean-Émile and Madeleine to thank them for everything they'd done with tight hugs and an especially tight hug for making them phone home. They had no way to repay him, but they knew he liked hugs, and them.

Jean-Émile and Madeleine said goodbye to the three girls from inside, giving them time alone to say goodbye to Addison before leaving for the airport. By the time the jet landed at Bonito Juarez, Maria had been at home for three hours and had written personal notes to Jean-Émile and Madeleine. She would call the girls later in the week.

Wednesday would come soon enough. She went to bed and cried.

## 110

She hadn't called him once over the holidays, Bret waiting two tormented weeks for Christine's return from the spa with her answer uppermost on his mind. She knew calling him would encourage persistent questions or a conversation that would be exclusively about him or them, not her. That's why she went away, enjoying every moment as much as she enjoyed making him wait.

She felt no particular joy, sensing that his main objective was to carry on the family name. She realized, however, that continuing to see him outside their mutual business interests he would eventually expect her to take the relationship to another level that would give her control over him, the basis for Mother Bitch not liking her and not inviting her to join the family for Christmas. But the more he tried seducing her, the more she demurred and the more he appeared uncharacteristically willing to wait and she wondered whether or not his acceptance was a ploy.

Though she was also a client of his father's firm and that was something he wouldn't jeopardize. She was getting to know him the way she wanted, in her own time and at her own speed. Although he would soon be able to offer her what every woman dreamed of, she already had that and more. All he had to offer was who and what he was. So the question wasn't whether she needed him, rather did she want him for who and what he was?

She had done a lot of thinking, viewing her wedding the very way his parents would, if Mother Bitch could survive the shock. The wedding would be the parents' as much as hers and his, a business transaction with exhaustive prenuptials to protect the Wilmington family from her marital incursion and provincial law which would automatically award her fifty percent of their combined wealth from the time of marriage, should the marriage be dissolved. That would be the single condition she would agree to. She didn't need his money, and in return she would protect her own present and future wealth from them. She would also insist that he sign one other waiver, one she knew he would loathe.

# 111

Christmas for Bret had been a predictable function, and neither parent had said much when he opened the monogrammed Mont Blanc pen set. New Years was no better, an absolute bore. Shane had gone skiing after giving up trying to convince his friend to go with him. Mother Wilmington had agreed with Shane, disappointed by her son's refusal, and she continued unsuccessfully throughout the week to draw his attention away from her. He had no idea how he would react were Christine to say no. He had always got what he wanted and this couldn't be any different and the closer he came to speaking with her, the more nervous he became. He had known Chrissie was different from the first instant he'd set eyes on her, the moment he knew he had to have her. Not having her was impossible to contemplate.

He had agonized through three long months with no more than a kiss, and a month since he had stopped clubbing with Shane who tried in vain to talk him out of self-ruin. He argued they were too young to give up the weekly hunt, not to mention the trophy collection, and what was likely their last Spring Break together was only a few short months away. He pleaded with Bret not to do anything that would screw up their last chance at a good time.

# 112

The red light of her business cell phone flashed in the dark. She hadn't bothered monitoring the callers because she was still on her special time alone and wanted nothing to break the magic spell.

The first order of business was unpacking and changing into something cosier than the fur-lined suede boots, leather pants and sweater coat she had worn home; the second was pouring a cognac and another before falling asleep on the sofa curled into a ball. The next morning the phone woke her, not the sun or the alarm clock, and she let the system take over without hearing the message. She needed to clear her head before speaking with him.

She hadn't opened the gold and silver gift box before leaving home, and was where she had left it on the sofa table when she returned late that morning from the grocery store. When she did open it, she did so without ceremony, no teasing hesitation, and no eggnog with brandy or brandy without eggnog. He wasn't with her, captivated as she pulled at the ribbons, or to see her anticipation, or her grimace as her brow furrowed into tight lines and she gaped.

Had anyone seen her, they might have thought she had found a dead mouse in the box, not perfectly matched diamond and sapphire earrings. They were perfect, and perfectly boring. The earrings meant as part of a set that should have included her engagement ring. Before opening the gift she had thought to phone him right away, as soon as she opened the box, so that her excitement would sound sincere and unaffected. Now he could wait. He had shown himself as unimaginative and coercive, intending her to see the ring during her time away, reminding her of him, or of them as a couple, and she didn't like the obvious tactic after telling him that she wanted time alone to think.

When she finally did return his calls, she did so to his cell at a time she knew he wouldn't answer. The senior Wilmington and Pendleton prohibited the use of cell phones in the offices or showrooms and future junior partners were no exception to the rule. First she thanked him for the gift as reservedly as she could. Then she told him he could call her Friday evening, and that he could take her to dinner Saturday.

# 113

Angelo's tan hadn't begun to fade and although he should have been relaxed, he wasn't. That part of him had faded as Marcus up-dated him on everything that had happened from the curious task force to a certain family member who had concerned them for some time. He didn't ask about Maria right away. If something noteworthy had happened to her he would already know. Maria had his private number, which changed frequently. Anyone close to him did the same and calling one another from any non-disposable phone was forbidden. They were a minor cost of doing business and completely untraceable.

His phone chimed Sunday morning. She wanted to come by to cook him Sunday dinner and to tell him about her time at the farm. She also wanted to tell him in person what she had finally decided to do regarding what he called family honour, which she couldn't mention on the phone.

# 114

Bret dressed for the answer. She had given him no indication whatsoever, though he did sense the earrings hadn't gone over as well as expected. He justified that they would be together for years and there would likely be many occasions when he would do something to annoy her. Besides, they cost five grand, so what was her problem?

She told him the rooftop restaurant of the Delta Centre-Ville for its dimly lit and elegant ambiance, where reservations were required for any Saturday night not so much to ensure seating but rather to advise the uninitiated that jeans, shorts and tee shirts were not appropriate attire.

Christine glanced at her Dior at 08:07, handing her coat to the cloakroom attendant. That he might be late had never entered her mind. He wouldn't be, or she'd kill him right there, right then, and she stood a while longer by the coat check.

Tourists, bored with each other after one or two weeks together in a colourless city which was excessively expensive and ill-mannered, found solace and escape from each other while peering out over the panoramic view revolving at a monotonous 6° per minute. Many, fearful of intimidating leather-bound menus and Cartes des Vins listing the finest wines, quietly relied on each other's unsure opinion as to how little they could spend on wine without making themselves appear inept, whether the tip was included, or how little they could leave without being accosted by the waiter before reaching the elevator. Locals engaged in animated conversations or danced to the soft and romantic music that made the out-of-towners appear all the more out of place.

The atmosphere was subdued. The Satins and the Silks were the dancers and hand-holders; the Non-wrinkle

Polyesters in bright four-season colours were silent observers. When she walked by, all eyes were on her. Who might have seen who first, was moot. He had missed his chance to walk in with her on his arm, and he wasn't the only one staring at the body housed in a pant suit of deep-blue shimmering satin with a one-button jacket and sequined three-quarter push-up bra she intended to be seen and admired by men and women. Her bare neck was adorned with a simple diamond choker; her ears sparkled with her diamond and sapphire earrings. Her shoes were low-heeled slippers. She was perfection, in keeping with her primary business philosophy: dress to impress, which really meant dress to intimidate. She was a woman men often thought of as a dare, the supreme male challenge which determines who succeeds and who fails, who gets the coveted female prize and who doesn't.

She found him, not the inverse she'd been expecting and he was in deep. He wondered as she came toward him if he would ever have found her on his own, and what he'd be doing at the moment if Shane hadn't been so busy that first morning. Shane might well have been sitting in his place, waiting for the verdict as she sat in front of him glaring. He hadn't thought to stand and she put up a hand as he began swinging his legs from under the private booth.

He had never seen the outfit and if she bought it to make him crazy, she succeeded. No one would mistake them for lovers, not the way she came up to him so nonchalantly. Christine was never demonstrative in public, never showing emotion or tenderness. He thought many of the men might think she was an escort, and with her body she certainly could be. She was sexy and her jacket might have been slung over her arm for the little it covered. Though neither was she the reserved businesswoman and he had no idea at all where he stood with her, or what to say. At the moment he was content to sit mesmerized at her.

She harboured no such reservations about where they stood. "I have a face too, Bret. It's meant to wear this way." She wasn't greatly impressed, managing a generic, "You look very nice."

"You're beautiful, more beautiful each time I see you."

"You will never do this to me again. Do you understand?"

His brow creased. "Do what, Chrissie?"

"Leave me standing outside waiting for you like a hooker needing a meal ticket."

"I'm sorry. I was thinking I would order drinks for us. That's all."

"Not good enough. Don't ever embarrass me again."

"You're still more beautiful each time I see you," he tried.

"I'll settle for that. There's no need to overdo it."

"I'm not, and you are." The remark was shallow and obvious. "You're wearing my earrings."

She didn't touch them. "No. I'm wearing my earrings."

"May I assume…?"

"Yes, I would like some wine. Thank you."

She wasn't letting him off easily, but her answer would be worth every moment.

"I was a jerk, Chrissie. I'm sorry."

She enjoyed a long moment studying the tiny deep-blue velveteen box. "You are a jerk and that's alright. It's who you are."

Her heartbeat was steady, his was racing. She didn't wonder what he saw in her when he was so often so obvious. She knew exactly what he was thinking, what woman wouldn't? She was more curious about the thought process and how long he'd be willing to wait.

"What's in the box?" she teased, raising a forefinger to signal the waiter silently away.

He chortled, grasping the box. "Something beautiful that

will be even more beautiful on your finger, forever." He opened the box slowly with both hands; the diamond and deep blue sapphires instantly refracting light from hundreds of miniature overhead halogen pencil beams. "May I put it on your finger? Will you marry me, Chrissie? I want you so much and I need you that much and more."

Puke. She put out her hand with her fingers spread wide, wondering how often he'd practiced the sad line in front of his bathroom mirror. He certainly wouldn't have recited the verse for his mommy.

"First things first. Yes, Bret, I will marry you, once we talk and settle a few things, not the least of which is your family."

"You'll be my family. Let me worry about my mother and father."

"Not good enough, I'm afraid. Your mother snubbed me at Christmas, and before Christmas. She has to understand that won't happen again and, if you can't convey the point, I will. She also has to understand I don't need the Wilmingtons, Mr. or Mrs." He sat listening. She had come in as a businesswoman after all, and he was as intrigued as he was dumbfounded. "This ring is gorgeous, and essentially an agreement in principle. It's the marriage that's the binding signature on the contract. Do you follow me?"

He was trying. "I'll follow you anywhere and, no, I don't."

"Perhaps we should order, and I would like another bottle of wine. A French Pinot Noir will be fine."

He was happy with the short-lived reprieve, and for all he knew he was having grilled or fried chicken with the Château La Fleur-Pétrus, not Medallions de boeuf garnished with mushrooms sautéed in cognac and a melody of exotic vegetables steamed and glazed with butter. Wine was the last thing on his mind. He raised his glass.

"May I know what exactly we're talking about?"

"We're talking about contracts, verbal and written, and the mistakes people make. The ring is exquisite, though no guarantee I'll say yes." She grinned. "You'll get it back if I don't, though not the earrings." She leaned to one side, reaching into her purse to retrieve twin documents jacketed in familiar legal blue. "The first document is signed by me as an acceptance that I will agree to a prenuptial which protects your family's assets from me, other than what is accorded to me as your wife by law. The document also protects my assets from your family, other than what is accorded to you as my husband by law. That, of course, is fifty-cent of our combined personal assets accumulated from the time of our marriage, excluding my business and yours. The sole exception is death, yours or mine, at which time we each become the other's sole beneficiary." She sipped her wine, staring directly at him, her eyes unblinking. "Those are inflexible conditions, Bret, conditions which I believe your family will understand and accept. Your mother might be interested in knowing that, at this point, my personal assets far outweigh yours."

The air he expelled was loud. "Are you a lawyer or a business woman, or both? Christ, all I want is to marry you. Isn't this a little extreme, not to mention overly cautious and paranoid?"

"Ask your parents, after you tell them the news. After you get your M. Arch II you'll be a partner with the firm. They'll want to protect your interests, the same way I want to protect my business."

"Shit."

"Conditional shit. That's the basis of a contract: a declaration of mutual distrust and nothing to do with love."

He stared at the other unfolded document, "And that one?"

She slid the parchment across the white linen. "In case I

have to return the ring before October 13."

"What's October thirteenth?"

"It's my wedding day, which will be this year, maybe. I hate summer weddings and we both have a lot to get done in the meantime."

He read the text as she spoke.

"You can't be serious. We're talking over nine months."

"Nine months and one week. You don't have to sign right now, Bret. You can think about it." She paused, waiting for the server to place the shallow soup bowls. "It's not open to discussion, Bret. When I get to the church altar, you get to mine. No wedding, no me."

"I'll be a laughing stock," he responded.

"More importantly, I won't be. I would be if you don't sign this and something happens between us, like possible family persuasion. Remember, you haven't told your mother yet."

He agreed, nodding blankly. He would never be able to explain his forced celibacy to Shane. He'd be ridiculed.

"This is pretty heavy stuff. Christ, we've known each other four months and I've hardly touched you, Chrissie. I haven't touched you. What you're asking is unreasonable. Shit, we're not in the nineteenth century."

"It's not compulsory that you sign, Bret. Not signing won't affect my decision to do business with your firm. Something is undeniably happening between us, which I wasn't expecting. This will give us time to know each other better, our habits as well as our faults or weaknesses, maybe even a few secrets."

"You don't have any of those. You're perfect."

"And beautiful, don't forget beautiful."

"You are beautiful. But Chrissie, this is asking a lot."

"And the reverse is asking a lot of me. So who concedes?"

"You won't."

"No, I won't. Nor will I blame you if you'd prefer continuing as a flirtatious bachelor. Otherwise, sign both documents and take the copies. I don't see the need for a witness." Her smile was wide. "Anyway, with these papers all over the table no one will suspect you were proposing."

"What if I suggest a weekend…one weekend to keep me going?"

She shook her head. "Not even a whiff. I have no intention of you leaving me at the altar with my legs open and nothing but bad memories between them. On the other hand, I do have something to keep you going, after you sign. Don't sign and what I have doesn't matter one way or the other."

She undid the single button as a second waiter approached with the second course, first placing her salad, then Bret's, hurrying away to leave them alone. When he was gone Christine raised her glass, letting the lapels of her jacket pull apart and waited for him to raise his glass.

"To our…"

"What is it?" he interrupted.

"What is what?"

"What you have that will keep me going."

She kept her glass raised. "No previous occupants."

# 115

Maria hadn't slept all night, thinking out and rethinking her plan, searching for flaws, for any possible improvement. As hard as she tried she couldn't. She was halfway there and would rely on her father to point out and prove any shortcoming. He looked great. She saw the difference immediately and felt the vitality as soon as she hugged him, though she hadn't gone with the intention of being the loving daughter, certain that within seconds his smile would evaporate and her papa would become Angie Bardollini, crime boss.

She patted the cushion beside her. "Sit, papa. I have something to tell you."

He did sit, expecting the worst, and didn't need to wait long. He was furious, on the border of losing control when Marcus came running into the room.

"You," he screamed, "you get the fuck in here and speak to this goddamn stupid cousin of yours before I fucking go out and kill someone!" He glared at Maria, his face discoloured with rage. "On your mother's grave...we went over this!"

Marcus put an arm around her. "What's up? I haven't seen him this happy since he found out you like girls." He laughed. "He hasn't watched a porno flick since."

"We don't need stupid talk!" Angelo cut in. "We need to put some sense into her stupid head and I'll watch what the fuck I want."

"What set him off, Meme?"

"Nothing, Markie," she began. "When he chills a bit, maybe I can explain. It's a good plan. That's what Phallicia Hunter is all about and that's what the passport and all that other stuff's about." She paused. "I want a gun so I can practice before I kill them. You practice don't you?"

"What I do isn't your business and thank you for not mentioning the subject again."

"Get real, Markie. You're in the goddamn mob for Christ's sake."

"I'm a businessman like any other businessman. Mob's nothing but a word used to sell newspapers and books. We're in business like everyone else…with fundamental differences. End of story."

"So what about the gun? You don't expect me to kill them with my hands do you?"

"You're not killing anyone, Meme. Angie's right. We've gone over this. They'll be taken care of in good time. And you also know it's a long-term thing. It's all about not being reckless."

"I don't want to kill them, Markie. I want to destroy them entirely, and I can. Killing them will be too fast, and then it'll be over. What then? Nothing. I need more. I won't ever have my Addison back. I'll be without her for the rest of my life and I want their pain to last as long as mine."

His confusion showed, Angelo fuming silently with his hands in his pockets, his shoulders hunched over, glowering as though his head might explode.

"So, you want them dead… and you don't want them dead. So why the gun?"

"I do want to see them dead, Markie. They have to pay. It's my plan he doesn't like."

"Angie, why don't you get a drink and take a breath? Let me talk with her."

"I don't need a drink. I need a daughter who has a brain in her head. I don't know this stupid girl."

"Angie, leave us to talk before you say something you'll regret. This time she might not come back to us. And don't forget she can buy her own gun. She's a woman, not a girl. So leave us, because I'll go with her. I swear… I'll go with her."

"No one's going anywhere." He inhaled deeply, noisily, expelling his exasperation "And you're staying to cook dinner for us, if you think you can cook without a brain in your head." He whirled on Marcus, pointing. "If you have any plans for tonight you can cancel them. And do not fucking let me down with your glassy-eyed cousin here who, by the way, plays you like a fucking piano."

When he stormed from the room they smiled at each other, even though Maria's lips still quivered. Her papa loved her and, not for the first time, Marcus wiped away her glistening tear drops.

# 116

Angelo insisted on one absolute before agreeing to the plan, and after she gave her solemn oath to abide by the proviso she told them the rest, much to Marcus' amusement and Angelo's frustration. He had loved his wife deeply when she was alive to be loved, and he missed her deeply in death. But she had left him alone with a daughter who was more trouble than any of the cops who either worked for him or tried in vain to take close-up photos of him from any of a thousand different vantage points. She was a handful and he loved her more than life. He wouldn't lose her again, though he wanted at the moment to give her a good spanking and not like the good old days when she would giggle and wriggle in an attempt to get away from her papa, always ending upside down with a rosy-pink bottom.

By the end of the evening Maria Bardollini understood no good would come from owning a registered gun so she could join a gun club and learn to kill pieces of paper and possibly jeopardize Phallicia Hunter's sole purpose in life. Each woman had much to learn and accomplish over the coming year. What had become one's premier objective in life was the other's unique purpose in life and each would have to understand and respect their specific roles, listening as one, being patient, realizing carelessness and lack of attention to detail was all that separated certain success from certain failure.

Angelo and Marcus assured her they would not fail. Nor would Phallicia Hunter once Maria Bardollini came to terms with whom and what Phallicia was. She was a facilitator, a contrivance that was, more importantly, a means of escape. She was not Maria and Maria was not her. Maria would have to understand the distinction or Phallicia would take her over and Maria would become the victim with unfortunate consequences for the family. That would not be allowed, daughter or no daughter.

## 117

Maria returned home alone that night feeling strangely elated and inexplicably saddened. A year earlier she had been planning her special trip to Mexico with Addison, now she was embarking on an adventure that would end the lives of four men who didn't deserve to live a moment longer than she needed to plan and carry out the executions. She had learned that much. She would execute four mindless rapists who had brutally tortured and killed Addie, and she felt no less a woman for thinking what she did. She didn't know what she felt. She was numb. She had made a solemn promise to her father and Marcus after easily extorting a promise from them: Each of the four would know the fear of death and suffer horrible pain. The question was: how?

When she woke on the Monday she felt as though she had lived in a dream, beginning her day by remembering who and what she was.

# 118

Monday morning Christine lay in bed, wondering if she had done the right thing Saturday night. The tiny box was on her night table, the diamond ring laying atop the blue velveteen lid. The band had felt unfamiliar to her and she removed it from her finger, not ready to be paraded as his prize, his possession or his conquest.

He had signed both contracts with his Mont Blanc, first making a grand show of retrieving the fountain pen from inside his jacket. She would have to meet his parents very soon, the sooner the better and he insisted that he would handle them. They were very nice. She would like them a lot, and Christine had refused. She would give them time to adjust to her, to the situation, to adjust to them as a couple. Besides, she had already met his father and had no doubt that one day his mother would conveniently happen by the office at the same time as one of her meetings, which would become closed-door. She had no intention of taking second seat to mommy dearest. They would meet her on her terms and on neutral territory. She had no intention of asking his mommy where the powder room was, or whether she could help in the kitchen, if his mother even knew where the kitchen was.

Originally his portion of the project was to be completed by late March with construction beginning soon after according to her agreement with her independent contractors, then days before Christmas she gave him news he didn't like: She had decided to change from a new construction to a remodelling project. He was livid, after she left, that she hadn't considered the implications from his perspective as a design architect. In fact, she had, she simply didn't hurry to tell him until she was very certain about which of her several location options would best suit her needs.

He didn't like the change one bit, already far exceeding the time available to him for the project. He had based his designs on a new site, not an existing location that would be stripped to the beams and re-built from the ground up. He didn't like the choice, and she didn't care whether he did or not. The fact he would require several more weeks to modify his designs with absolutely no time for himself was of no consequence to her. She was the client, and the time had come for him to begin thinking of her as more than an account.

And now she was the one wondering who Christine Benton really was, and who she would become. She would have to meet the parents sooner or later, and Bret's best friend Shane whose name was never excluded from a conversation. She wondered what he was all about, whether she would measure up to his expectations. He knew about the wedding proposal and probably more about her than she would want, suspecting they had always swapped secrets about women the way they swapped baseball cards as boys and she wondered what else they had ever swapped.

She wasn't nervous. She was uneasy. She also knew the feeling would pass and rolled over, hugging her favourite pillow, beginning a new day, a new era, wondering who Christine Benton-Wilmington would be. She'd be anyone and anything Christine Benton wanted her to be, and he would soon have to learn that mommy had been usurped.

# 119

The day had come too soon for Christine, though it had come all the same and she was as prepared as she could be to meet the Family Wilmington. The men didn't count, not the father, nor the son. Mother Bitch was the one Christine had meticulously prepared for. Her hair was perfect, so were her make-up, her clothes and perfume. She had done everything possible to defiantly meet the family head on, woman to woman, mother to wife.

The day was neither hers, nor special. Her day was months away. He owned the day, his show and tell day, and she made certain he'd have enough to show and nothing to tell. The already pristine Porsche Cayman sparkled like a blue jewel under the narrow beams of halogen lights bordering the private driveway of the Wilmington's elaborate and expansive Hampstead home. He hadn't been there to greet her and she waited in the car a few moments longer as she pressed her palms against the dealer-installed air horn. Moments later she pressed her gloved finger to the doorbell, alerting the mansion to the arrival of the lowly that had come for a meal. Bret swung open the door, pulling her in and hugging her, when he should have hurried from his parents' home to help her from the car. Instead she had been made to ring the bell like some pathetic door-to-door cosmetic vendor and she whispered in his ear that she wouldn't tolerate a third affront. She was a woman and he would either begin treating her like one or all bets were off.

They were in the parlour. No shit, she thought, the parlour, how quaint, and her husband-to-be suddenly knew not to caution her as to what or what not to do or say. Mother Bitch was trim, though hardly petite. Nor was she tall. She would have been about eye-to-eye with Christine, if Christine hadn't slipped into ten-centimetre stilettos after removing her low-heeled winter boots. The father wore black cuffed pants and a black silk smoking jacket over a loose-fitting black silk shirt in an effort to appear relaxed and debonair, which he did. Bret wore a blue two-piece suit, probably selected by his mommy, and a white shirt open at the collar. She wore a gold-on-silver brocade dress that must have weighed a tonne, Christine thought, and chunky-heeled shoes emphasising her heavy calves. Truth be told, thought Christine, spending a week at a spa wouldn't hurt the old broad.

Christine had prepared for her visit with the family layer by layer. The first layer consisted of a balconet three-quarter bra with scrolled detail, matching V-string thong panties and matching narrow garters with butterfly straps attached to the delicate laced tops of midnight blue stockings and when Bret helped her off with her faux-fur coat and scarf he involuntarily sputtered. She had left her midnight blue silk blouse strategically unbuttoned for the advantage of feminine allure, showing the jewelled balconet bra and what it pushed up.

Her A-line skirt was winter white, five centimetres above her knee with a discreet slit that would become a full fifteen centimetres above the knee and a focal point anytime she sat. Her tapered jacket was also winter white, which she slid from her shoulders and tossed to Bret. Her hair was lustrous cherry-blonde, clipped into a flighty French updo with her favourite obsidian clasp that had deep blue and red inlays, a departure from her usual business braid. She wore the sapphire and diamond trio with her favourite diamond choker, and not because she didn't have others. She liked what she liked. When she didn't like something or someone she never had to say so. She was the epitome of exotic and compelling womanhood, what all women aspired to. She knew and so did Bret who retreated a few steps as soon as he introduced Christine to Mother.

# 120

Father Wilmington had an apparent affinity for young breasts as much as he loved bare thighs and Mother Bitch took note of everything he seemed to love more than her, though he hadn't loved her for years, in or out of bed.

Suzanne Wilmington had heard that her daughter-in-law-to-be was an astute business woman, beautiful, well-spoken, a visionary and financially solvent. Bret had done a verification of her financial standing that was triple A and father Wilmington went one step further, verifying her education and family history. Clearly she had found success on her own. Her parents were dead, she had no living relatives, she was an honour student in Business and she spoke Suzanne's language fluently. She enjoyed excellent credit, drove a Porsche she'd paid for in cash and lived in a privileged downtown high-rise which she paid for in full at the beginning of each year. She was not currently employed, although sufficiently secure financially to satisfy the bank and the CFO of The Wilmingtons and Pendleton who naturally assumed her parents had been well insured: wealthy in death if not in life.

She brought a gift-wrapped forty-year cognac for Frederick and a string of pearls for Suzanne, who suggested immediately that Christine should call her mother. Christine thanked her for the honour; however she was certain they would soon be more like sisters, so she would call her Suzanne.

Frederick was the one to compliment her outfit. He pulled out her seat at the table; he toasted the couple and began the conversation so the evening would at least start out being generic and safe. They spoke about her project, without which she would never have met Bret, though no one was interested and mother asked about her family without the slightest preamble. Christine's response was brief, worded to curtail the intrusion, and began talking about vacation destinations, boating, politics and religion. The one subject they didn't discuss, which Christine had expected, was babies.

The conversation was as safe and predictable as the seven-course meal and the inexcusably expensive and ostentatious wine. She would have been content to wear tights with a skirt and sweater, and sit on the floor with a pizza, but Bret had told her to expect a family show. All through dinner Christine knew what was coming, so did Bret, sitting through each of the courses with visible traces of sweat on his brow. She also knew father and son would soon excuse themselves while the women retired to the parlour and, as though on cue, Frederick asked if he might open his particularly fine cognac as the evening's digestive. Christine tilted her head with a smirk to show approval and the conversation excluded male participation from then on.

Suzanne was Francophone, Christine scarcely blinking when the mid-fifties brocade- enshrouded socialite changed to her mother tongue. Bret was their only son, a man any woman would be proud to marry. Everything was happening so quickly and October might be out of the question, she inferred, what with the many formalities to consider: invitations, at least three or four hundred, the church, the reception hall, not to mention the must-have caterers and preferred limousines. Of course, Frederick would unquestionably assume the role of the bride's father, since her parents had passed on. Christine was not to worry about such mundane details when the bride had so many other details to consider, which would come in good time. The evening was for them to get to know each other, and they did.

Christine was thrilled that he had asked her to be his wife, and they would be very happy together. However the wedding would be in October, the thirteenth, or the elopement would be on the thirteenth. Inviting three or four hundred close friends was fine with her, despite not having any close friends and she had always thought simple was best. She would design her wedding dress, she would select the menu and she would oversee the entertainment. She didn't care whether the wedding was Catholic, Anglican or civil. She wasn't religious. She made excuse for her irreligious stance and she wouldn't be interviewed by a cleric who had no need to know anything about her as she would not be joining their congregation, or any other. Also, parenthood was no one's business but hers and Bret's.

She would walk down the aisle unescorted and would retain her name. Christine Gabrielle Benton would be the beautiful bride and wife of Bret Alexandre Wilmington who would marry her on her terms, which included moving away from his mother's home and becoming a man. He would also learn that Christine would be the mistress of their home, not merely his wife. She had no intention of marrying a man-boy who was comfortable living with his parents. Together they would find a home or condo in a suitable suburb as soon as he completed the exam that would give him the highly exalted and family-honoured M. Arch II. And the time had come to leave. She had stayed much too late, Frederick smelling of smoke when he shook her hand and Bret of liquor that wasn't expensive cognac. At least his father had that much sense, she thought.

The two men noticed an air of je ne sais quoi about the mother who somehow appeared distant and subdued, though Christine was pleasant and smiling as she sat on the leather ottoman in the elaborate vestibule to pull on her faux-fur-lined boots, then her faux-fur-lined coat.

All men were sluts, rich father and subservient son included, she thought, and Mother Bitch had found an excuse to be elsewhere when the wide doors opened and closed. She had met his parents. She had done what had been required and they had gotten to know each other for better or worse. Bret had brought his trophy home for close inspection, Mother Wilmington had done her absolute best to assert her position as the Wilmington matriarch and Christine cared about none of it. All she cared about was Bret, her husband-to-be.

# 121

MR. AND MRS. FREDERICK WILMINGTON, OF THE MONTREAL ARCHITECTURAL FIRM THE WILMINGTONS AND PENDLETON, ARE PROUD TO ANNOUNCE THE ENGAGEMENT OF THEIR SON, BRET ALEXANDRE WILMINGTON, TO MONTREAL BUSINESS WOMAN, MS. CHRISTINE GABRIELLE BENTON. A FORMAL ENGAGEMENT PARTY WILL BE HELD THIS VALENTINE WEEKEND AT THE FAMILY ESTATE IN THE LAURENTIANS. AN EARLY FALL WEDDING IS BEING PLANNED.

# 122

Valentine's wasn't as important an event in Mexico as in North America where most men were traditionally reminded and guided through the process of remembering what their women would like most. Latinos knew what their women liked: they liked Latinos.

Maria's Valentine e-mail to Ercilia and Pilar was loving and heartfelt and the phone call came within minutes of its receipt. Maria barely understood a word. They loved her and missed her and would soon be part of each other's lives. They were coming to Montreal to work and be with her. Señor El Rio had been talking with them and had told them the delay would not be very long, though Pilar and Ercilia made Maria promise she wouldn't say anything to him or la Señora H in the meantime. He wanted to surprise her and she had to swear.

Her Valentines could not have been better without Addison and she knew Addison was happy knowing she would never again be alone.

# 123

Christine had no one to invite to her engagement party, though she was a hit with the men who either owned summer homes or boats and who insisted she and Bret should visit as soon as possible and stay for the weekend. Whatever the wives had to say they said to Suzanne, not the bride-to-be, and a few younger women whom she believed had been carefully selected were each disappointed when Christine declined their offers to be her maid of honour. She saw no need to have a matron or maids. She wanted simplicity and all that remained to discuss after she rejected the idea of a bachelorette party at a well-known club with male dancers were her plans to start a family.

She thanked them profusely for everything. They were sweet for wanting to make her feel welcome, but she didn't find the thought of sweaty and exaggerated male genitalia swinging around her face, or anything else of hers, very exciting. Besides, her hectic agenda didn't allow for much personal time. As for a family, and what she planned to do with her future husband's genitalia, she had no immediate plans to disrupt her career or spoil her life and body with childbearing.

That particular piece of trivia travelled to Suzanne and her aging entourage as quickly as the summertime invitations, and when Suzanne asked if they might speak privately Christine replied that another time would be more appropriate, unless they were going to talk about children, in which case the topic was verboten.

She also met the famous Shane Pendleton, Bret's shadow, the one who would be his best man. She had wondered about him over the past five months. She had never met him at the office, surprised by his smaller stature even though he was the same height as Bret. Everything she heard about him had made her think he'd be more imposing. His manners were practiced, too affected for Christine who didn't have to wonder about what he was thinking, though she did wonder whether Bret would ever be so vulgar as to describe her nude body or tell him how she was in bed, once she let that happen. She was certain he would and Shane was disappointed Christine wouldn't be joining them in Myrtle Beach in April.

"I beg your pardon, Shane. Did you just imply that Bret intends to spend time in Myrtle Beach with you, and without me?"

"Hey, Chrissie, it's…"

"Christine, please, and it's what?"

"His last chance to spend some meaningful time with the guys." He shrugged, smiling. "It's not like we'll be chasing girls or anything like that. Strictly above board. He's crazy about you. I think he proved that when he signed up."

"When he what?"

"Your little contracts…when he signed up for a dry summer."

"That's vulgar, and so are the both of you. If he thinks he's going to Spring Break with you, he's very mistaken."

"It's not for Spring Break. We both need some quality guy time."

"You want to get laid and you know it. You screwed up big time. Being a gentleman isn't your strong point." She swivelled from her hips in both directions to search for Bret. "The bad news for you is," she paused, "he's not going. The good news…there'll be more for you and hopefully they'll all be over eighteen."

"These days, are you kidding," he chortled. "There's nothing squeaky clean at eighteen."

"Do you really think so, Shane?"

He caught himself, deeply regretting he'd thought to

introduce himself. "Present company excluded, of course, though you do have to admit it's pretty rare for a woman not to put out these days."

"When did you book the trip…when did he?"

He shrugged, feigning uncertainty, and she looked around once more for Bret.

"He won't like it, Christine."

"What he likes doesn't matter, and it doesn't have very much to do with you."

"I know him. He won't like being told what to do."

"He's been told what to do all his life by his mommy, and I suspect often enough by you. That's over, as of right now."

So was the conversation. She saw Bret coming towards them from the corner of her eye and left Shane without saying another word. When they came together she took Bret's arm, whispering not at all tenderly that they needed to talk. Then she went home alone.

# 124

Bret phoned her early the next morning, unrepentant, insisting nothing was wrong with him going with Shane for some R & R before his final exams. Instead he discovered the power of feminine resolve. He was not going to Myrtle Beach. Shane would go alone and he would stay home and study for the exams. She slammed receiver into the cradle at his first "but", then she spent the day not thinking anymore about it. When he called her that evening nothing had changed. He still wanted to vacation with his best friend and she still insisted he wouldn't, unless he wanted to explain to his parents why there would be no October wedding, and unless he wanted to explain to his father and Pendleton senior that she would immediately cease doing business with the firm.

She had no intention of playing second fiddle to a Spring Break whore when her fiancé, who supposedly loved her, should be thinking about his career and his life with her, which included house-hunting for the home they would share after the wedding. Also, Shane had suggested to Christine that Bret had invited her, and that she had refused the invitation to join them. Bret never had, and why not? If he had no plans to be unfaithful, why couldn't she go with them to a resort area known for wild parties, lewdness and young girls who liked to drink and didn't know when to stop? As far as she was concerned they had nothing further to discuss. He wasn't going, period, she fumed. He would either get over not going with Shane or get used to not being with her and if she had made a two-faced enemy in Shane Pendleton, too bad. She'd take care of him in her own time and the fact he'd be the best man made no difference.

# 125

Shane left on the10th and would be back on March 24<sup>th,</sup> claiming he needed warm weather and sunshine to revitalize him before the finals. Pendleton senior had disapproved of the timing, not believing his son would spend much of his time studying. Suzanne and Frederick Wilmington left the day after, delaying their annual month-long vacation onboard the Executive Decision by several days in order to prepare for the engagement party. When they arrived in Miami the Sea Ray was ready for cruising between the home port, the Keys, and the Bahamas.

Bret delved into his studies, reluctantly taking the month off from Christine and her project which was about on schedule, though he hadn't yet made up the time lost when she had decided to remodel rather than build. She had approved a maximum six-week delay, despite knowing construction probably wouldn't begin until after the wedding.

Christine needed every day of the six weeks to jump start her plans for the perfect wedding. She had a gown to design, a competent seamstress to find who wouldn't be intimidated by the unconventional, and the dress would not be stored away in a dark closet after the ceremony as so many brides would do. She would also design her ensembles for the reception and honeymoon and the next six months would barely be enough time for the fittings, let alone finding the perfect accessories to complement her creations, all of which she would do on her own, without Suzanne. She had no intention of being seen as some eighteenth century, male-dominated bimbo. She was a vital woman, sexual and sensual, and if Bret didn't know by now, he would then.

Suzanne would plan the menu, Christine conceded, the

church she cared nothing about, the guest list and the reception. Music was the one point of contention and for the bride-to-be and Bach was out of the question as much as Beethoven.

# 126

Maria and Michele Baroque were spending more time together as each day Addisons became more of a reality. She still spoke with Pilar and Ercilia every week, crying herself to sleep each night. She didn't want to think of a time of guilt and deep remorse when she would stop crying, when she hadn't yet started to heal.

Her time frame was specific, though Angelo had been very clear: there would be no drama, no vanity and no trace of any kind. She would create no agenda, no calendar, nor a girlish diary written in any form that might later be used as evidence. The police had a way of conveniently converting an otherwise innocent act into guilt, their solution to the burden of proof. She would leave no evidence, not even phone calls, and Phallicia Hunter would do what she was told implicitly. She agreed.

To Maria Phallicia was real, thus far existing solely in the darkness of night and within the infinity of Maria's bedroom mirror, when Phallica would bring her back to a dark and ominous reality. But what they had done to Addison was darker, more ominous, and she would not falter. Nor would she ever seek forgiveness for her transformation. She had gone beyond redemption, deciding not to burden herself with the guilt of deceiving so many, content her father and Marcus knew the truth: the real Maria. They also knew something Maria did not, something she wouldn't believe even if she were to hear the words. They knew the real Maria would once again be with them when all was said and done.

## 127

John Franklin spent the eleven weeks since Christmas dreaming of the day when he would see the dock crew affixing the Dauphin-styled letters P-e-r-f-e-c-t-E-s-c-a-p-e onto the transom and prow of the deep-emerald green and sparkling white San Juan. He had planned his perfect escape for years and would do nothing to jeopardize his dream. He had never been in better health and had given up drinking alone at home; finally understanding that drinking would never bring her back or absolve him. Perfect Retreat would always be their retreat, his and hers, and he would willingly die before ever giving it up.

The Hiding Out had gone to another port with new owners who hadn't wanted to change the registered name: a seafarer's rule, a superstition: the purchaser of a documented craft must never change the name of that craft, or he must be responsible for its horrible fate. Good luck to them, he thought. Anyone feeble-minded enough to think like that would certainly be a competent yachtsman as long he stayed tied to the dock, hired someone capable to maintain the engine room and stayed far away from him.

Franklin didn't intend to visit his island after his two-day visit to the office, nor did he intend to stay in Miami. He had no particular liking for the city beyond its convenience for shipping and its Latin flavour, even though his Spanish was far from fluent. The town was continuously congested with standstill traffic, endless lines of impatient restaurant goers and overly crowded beaches with shoulder-to-shoulder sunbathers who either hoped to see some topless Latin or European flavour, or were shocked when they did.

He flew into Miami on Tuesday evening and was expected in Montreal the following Monday, intending to charter a single-engine island hopper to cross the 300 kilometres to the less hectic Nassau, until the dealer offered him the use of a fully equipped twelve-metre sport cruiser demo for the weekend and he forgot Nassau to plot a course for Perfect Retreat. The offer was too good to refuse and he wasted no time manoeuvring away from the dock. Within moments he was cruising on a plane with bubbling white foam behind him and the clear horizon ahead.

The seas were calm, the brilliant noonday sun making the day stifling. The cruiser was fully provisioned and fuelled for the long weekend and Franklin had the ocean to himself when most yachtsmen and boaters were either arriving early at the marina for the weekend or still at the office thinking about being there.

# 128

Boaters familiar with the waters knew which of the private islands were accessible or friendly. Perfect Retreat was friendly, to a point. Beyond that point, several signs were clearly posted that were as friendly as they were dissuasive and visitors had never been recorded by the several motion-activated cameras. When his island came into view six o'clock was moments away, the sun was high in the sky and the boats beached in the centre of his half-kilometre of white sand shone like two bright beacons. He saw them up close through the boat's binoculars long before the couples had any idea he was coming in directly behind them at idle speed.

When they did see him, metres from shore, they were visibly disappointed at losing their privacy and serenity to another boater who had the same idea about a sunset picnic and dip. Killing the engines he saw disappointment growing across each of their faces, changing to frustration when they believed he was about to drop anchor so close to their boats. They began standing as he clicked the dial on the VHF radio to the loudhailer function, squeezing the microphone's release. He was making ready his lines for the dock, he explained, and they were welcome to spend the evening or night as guests of his island.

The night was idyllic. The sky was splattered with stars, the sea was calm and the night air was comfortably warm. He could see the Bimini tops of the boats the captains had secured to trees from the bows and anchors from the sterns. He heard the giggles of the women he couldn't see splashing and frolicking in the shallow black water breaking a silence as encompassing as the night was dark. He enjoyed hearing them and closed his eyes to dream of better times as sleep slowly took him over to make his dreams real.

# 129

As the sun came up Franklin stayed in the hammock with his eyes closed, listening to the quiet. Going back wouldn't be easy for him, but he had given his word and so many others depended on him.

The boaters left the island before noon, leaving two bottles of expensive French Bourgogne on the dock where he would find them. He waited until hearing the engines fade in the distance before going alone to bathe and linger in the precious solitude remaining. A low pressure system would move into the Miami area early Monday, bringing high seas and severe wind gusts he wanted to avoid. By mid-afternoon Sunday the quiet island was once again deserted and would remain that way for three months except for occasional beach seekers and weekly visits from the couple who did his gardening and housekeeping.

He would return in June for a longer stay, taking proud ownership of the Perfect Escape, but at the moment he was pushing the sport cruiser to its limit. Compared to the Bertram and the San Juan she handled like a sports car and he'd spent most of Friday's cruise getting used to her smaller size and easy manoeuvrability. The ride took thirty minutes longer than Friday's smooth water cruise. Headwinds increased steadily to twenty-knots changing the calm surface to metre-high swells by the time he reached port, the sun refracting brilliant bursts of coloured light from the tinted picture-window panes of deluxe condo towers and commercial high-rises lining the jagged Miami skyline.

Waiting as long as he dared, he throttled back effortlessly from 4000 rpms to a sluggish six-hundred, maintaining proper headway to cruise past the breakwater and into the narrow channel opening into the basin and a one-hour wait at the gas docks. Free-floating pleasure yachts barely moved in the calm waters, experienced captains demonstrating their skill by not rushing to the helm in a panic to move away from other crafts closing in. The Sea Rays had taken a while to close the wide gap between them, at least one cocktail, as each captain eyed the other with mutual respect as recognition of solid experience and the easy demeanour of confidence. Franklin didn't bother to notice the registry of the other mid-range yacht. He was going home the next day, and wasn't thinking they would become fast friends and go for dinner. He didn't care about people that way, even though he was friendly to most strangers. He enjoyed his time alone, when he could feel good about himself and feel completely free.

The other Sea Ray slowly creeping along his port side was unconcerned, identical in every way except for the coloured Bimini top extended to protect the captain and his passenger from the late-day sun. Mr. and Mrs. Snotty Boater, Franklin thought: the typical Miami boating couple. Who needed the bullshit? And at the moment he would have paid double to be aboard his sixteen-metre San Juan. Each openly evaluated the other from head to as low as they could see. Then they openly evaluated each other's boat and what followed was expected, each one relishing the stereotypical compliments which were the essence of boating decorum and protocol.

"Nice yacht," said the man.

It wasn't a yacht, idiot. The thing was a big boat. "Thanks, so is yours."

"Here for the gas? Noticed you have no name."

"The name's John. It's the boat that doesn't have a name. It's a dealer demo, a loaner for the weekend. This is my dealer's marina, not mine"

"Are you stepping up?"

He shook his first head, taking his time to answer. "No,

to a San Juan this summer, a forty-eight. Fifty-one LOA," he added."

The other man nodded in return, suitably impressed. "That's a serious outlay of cash."

Franklin shrugged. "We can't take it with us. Might as well spend it while we can. Never know when we wake up to the final day."

"A sound philosophy, obviously from a man who's lived his life without the dubious benefit of family."

Franklin nodded. "Very astute…and quite accurate."

"Where do you hail from?"

"Miami, though I spend most of my time in the Bahamas. My time's finally come; just starting to get used to the idea."

"Are we talking retirement?"

"I am."

"I envy you." The man nodded again, smiling at his wife who was still facing away from Franklin. "A few more years for us, I'm afraid. We still have a son in university. He's studying for a Masters."

"Smart kid if he's going for a Masters. What field?"

"Architectural design," he answered proudly. "He's getting married in the fall, though a bit soon for our liking. However, it's what he wants."

The dockhand signalled Wilmington in first. Then he signalled Franklin in behind him as soon as the area was free of the boat which was still in the process of venting possible fumes from the bilge, when Franklin noticed Executive Decision in bold letters across the transom. "Your accent is out-of-state. I take it you're from the Northeast."

"Montreal, actually. We're Frederick and Suzanne."

"I like the name of your yacht. Who's the executive?"

"I am, outside the home of course. The Wilmingtons and Pendleton, we're an architectural firm." Wilmington turned to see the gallons and dollars spinning upward on the metre and reached for his card, paying no attention to Franklin. "It's the corporate yacht, actually, for the partners and their guests, somewhat of a floating time-share."

"Nice perk."

"What were you in before retirement?"

"Import export."

"Any firm I know?"

"No. I would doubt it."

"We're here for two more weeks. If you're in the area drop by. Very likely we'll be at dock for the next few days. The current forecast is for unstable conditions through midweek."

"I might do that, if I can fit it into my schedule. I'm still busier than I would like."

"We do manage time here occasionally throughout the year, though usually the entire month of March. We had a bit of a late start this year, what with unexpected engagements and that sort of thing."

"Maybe I'll see you over the summer. Cruising the islands is always more fun and safer in numbers, particularly if you're rafting."

"We haven't rafted in years. We used to all the time." He paused, possibly remembering better times. "I suppose we all change more than we should, or before we realize the extent."

"I enjoyed talking with you. Good luck to your son and his bride."

Wilmington pursed his lips. "No good will come of it. Isn't that right mother? I'm afraid he's not ready for it. She's a nice enough girl, very forward, very imposing, and I'm afraid he's thinking with the wrong head if you understand my meaning. She is quite a looker and I can't say I blame him on a carnal level, but she doesn't understand social constraints, unabashedly shocking those around her, if you know what I mean. She simply won't fit in."

"She'll adapt."

"Just a matter of improper upbringing, I'm afraid. That sort of thing can always be traced to the parents."

Franklin leaned over the bow rail to take Wilmington's card before checking his watch and making an excuse to end the conversation. He wanted to dock and clean the boat before leaving early to beat the infamous 1A1 traffic. He was certain he would see them again. They might even do a rafting weekend.

By the time Wilmington thought to ask Franklin for a card in return, Franklin manoeuvred the Sea Ray away from the dock and into the crowded basin, reversing to starboard as the dockhand slowly released the braided line through a forward cleat. June would be out of the question and he would make certain his second-quarter business meeting wouldn't take too much of his time away from the Perfect Escape.

As Wilmington switched the VHF to the marina's channel 06, Franklin switched his off. He would remember the Executive Decision. He hadn't rafted with another couple in years, either, so why not with them the following March. The timing would be ideal. By then his home would be sold, the sale of the company complete, his financial affairs transferred to Miami and the Caymans and he would be ready for full retirement.

# 130

Christine hadn't seen Bret in over the six weeks, waiting one week longer until the first of May to break the news he couldn't believe, infuriated with himself for having no idea how to be furious with her. The design work was all but complete, with only a few minor details to work out, and he argued with her throughout the morning to dissuade her before going into his father's office for help.

Frederick was adamant that timing did not allow for changes to the design work and that taking advantage of her recent status as family to attempt coercion without increased fees was all the more inappropriate. She would have to pay penalties and any delay due to her changes would be her responsibility. She had to understand they had several other obligations, Bret added.

Christine was also adamant. The changes would be made or she would withhold payment. She had sold the building to a consortium that wanted to convert the property into an upscale condo. Her profit on the recent acquisition was several hundred thousand. So shut up. The project would once again be a new construction, on the South Shore, ideal because that was where she intended to make her home. Anyway, she maintained, very little of what Bret had done would be lost. He could easily use much of his original work and complete the project in under three months. Though she did agree he could wait one more month, until he graduated, and that's when she knew Wilmington senior would come over to her side.

# 131

Madeleine Harnais planned the ground breaking celebration to have the biggest impact for everyone who would be sharing the second most important event in Maria's young life. Pilar and Ercilia would be with her, sharing the excitement before returning to Mexico to await the final papers that would give them landed status.

A month earlier Michele Baroque had invited Maria to dinner to announce the completion of the first phase of her first major contract and to thank her client for giving her such a career-altering opportunity. She had handed Addisons over to the contractors and construction would begin on time. When Maria asked what date had been set Michele laughed, suggesting they discuss it over the special dessert she'd arranged.

A procession of waiters had encircled the table on cue, with all the pomp and ceremony Michele could have hoped for, the headwaiter bowing as he handed a surprised Maria the complete set of final drawings. The high-gloss rosewood tube was sealed at both ends with polished brass screw caps and a discreet brass plaque at the centre read: Addisons, May 03. Happy Birthday, Addison.

Pilar and Ercilia flew in the night before aboard the LCL. Jean-Émile had changed fundamentally, doing his absolute best to make amends for his past neglect towards Addison, with Madeleine Harnais' help, and the word "no" didn't exist where Maria was concerned. The property covered over 12000 square metres, a full three acres facing the scenic Lachine Canal midway along its thirteen kilometres. The canal was a designated and little known water parkway for pleasure craft, allowing boaters to circumvent the time-consuming and intimidating Saint-Lambert locks en route to the diminishing French flavour of expensive restaurants, forgotten history and the introverted joie-de-vivre of Le Vieux-Port.

The building would take up a small portion of the expansive property. The balance would be a fenced-in garden with waterfalls, a running brook, fish ponds, a full-service café-terrace, a seasonal outdoor pool and whirlpool, outdoor lounge furniture, tennis, badminton and basketball courts and full security. The project would take one year to complete.

Earlier Madeleine informed the contractors that the ladies had no intention of wearing workwear for the occasion; she wanted a perfectly smooth path cleared and carpeted in red so the ladies could wear appropriate footwear and they were not to tell Maria.

The crew didn't disappoint her. In fact they went one step farther, building and decorating a low platform for the attendees to stand on. The brass-plated shovel went into the ground at 10:00 AM, after Maria asked the chief forewoman how far she should throw the dirt and where. The woman answered just not as far as the buffet table the caterers had laid out.

The day was beautiful. Maria hadn't needed to ask for favours or money to fund the project, nor did she have any need to shake hands with those who would think more of photo ops with Maria Bardollini, the mob boss' daughter and, to that end, she hadn't invited the mayor or city councilman. The day was hers and the champagne came after all the hugs and the kisses that even the contractor and chief forewoman shared in.

Jean-Émile's face off with Madeleine came at the insistence of the young women and the macho bravado from women and men accustomed to hard work and hard play. He acquiesced with the most brotherly embrace any of them had ever seen and a kiss on the cheek which prompted the contractor to intercede and compensate with a tight hug and a charming kiss on her cheek to the cheers of everyone but Jean-Émile. Even the pilot and Jeff the chauffeur had been invited by Maria. Both had gladly accepted, much to the surprise of Jean-Émile who discovered speaking with the men was rather easy and unexpectedly enjoyable.

Pilar and Ercilia exchanged telling nods during the toast. They understood the Spanish, most of the English and very little of the French. Señor El Rio was an impressive man and they had decided months earlier that they liked him. He was a special man, Pilar whispered to the other three girls so Jean-Émile couldn't hear, but impossibly blind. And, she added, Madeleine was no better.

The massive shovels came at noon along with truckloads of materials, when all but the four young women and Madeleine had gone. They took their glasses and champagne bottles across the street to the canal, commandeering a solitary picnic table after promising Jean-Émile to stay away from the construction site. They would have ample opportunity to visit the site, though nothing would seem worthwhile for weeks, he insisted, and in no way were they to go on-site while celebrating. Madeleine rightly interpreted the instruction as an order and nodded. The limo would return to pick them up as soon as he was dropped off at the office. No one was to drive, he admonished, including Madeleine who didn't have a car.

They spent the next few hours watching fully loaded trucks arriving and empty trucks leaving, waiting to see the huge shovels begin to making piles of dirt and rock as Pilar was being Pilar. Michele was French and spoke English. Her Spanish was nonexistent which didn't stop Pilar from trying to explain in her newly adopted languages that Spanish was the language of life, laugher and love. The French might be sexy, to the French, but no way could they dance like Latinos, and the English were, she paused to fill her glass, not to decide on the proper wording; well, they were English. Then she sipped her champagne.

They all burst out laughing, except Pilar. Even Madeleine held her stomach as she reminded Pilar that Maria was lots of things, but certainly not English, giving Michele an insight she hadn't been privy to previously. Maria had eventually told her about Addison because she wanted Michele to have a sense of the emotion and love that would be integral to Addisons, not to make a statement. Maria's lifestyle hadn't mattered to Michele then and certainly didn't matter to her by the edge of the canal where they were simply women laughing, giggling and drinking champagne. Michele had come to think of Maria as a good friend and stood quietly to toast Addison with a few simple words that brought tears to their eyes. The four other women stood, raising their glasses, each one whispering the different nicknames they had given Addison and suddenly Maria, fraught with emotion, felt compelled to tell them she would never forget Addie. No one had ever doubted she would, crowding around her to hug and comfort her. What Maria Bardollini didn't know was that within a few short months a woman called Christine Gabrielle Benton would bring into her life the one other person she would come to love as deeply as Addison for the rest of her life.

The men watched them until the LCL limo pulled up in front of the women. Maria hadn't noticed until then, but she would have known them anywhere. She broke into a wide smile, waving unabashedly at her father and Marcus on the opposite bank of the canal. Then all the ladies waved, not knowing at whom. The men bowed discreetly before leaving and when they were gone Maria proudly told her friends who they had seen. Madeleine Harnais fanned herself, secretly thrilled she had just seen real-life gangsters.

# 132

Bret hadn't had time to work on the modifications and study, as well as design a home. What he thought would be house-hunting had become property-hunting. Christine was adamant. She wanted a home built to her specifications and Bret was able to convince his father to assign a junior designer to work with her.

By the end of May the drawings were approved with a completion date of September 30. Work was set to begin on an elegant carriage-styled home and landscaping which wouldn't be within his means for several years and the firm had co-signed the million dollar loan because Christine's assets were locked into her business centre. Everything in the house would be brand new. She wanted nothing from the Wilmingtons' home in hers, or from hers and his father and Pendleton agreed on the basis that Bret complete his Masters with above average grades.

## 133

Maria's Father's Day weekend was taken up with her two fathers and a cousin who acted more like her brother, though bringing Angelo and Jean-Émile being together would never be appropriate. Angelo was content knowing Larivière would always care for by when he could no longer do so and the day was coming closer. Although he was spending less time away from his home, wanting to avoid unnecessary attention, he did attend the ground breaking ceremony as he had promised and was a proud father when she saw him and waved. He had wanted to tell Marcus what Michele had recited to the women in her toast to Addison, but he couldn't without disclosing an asset inherent to Angie Bardollini that made him the cunning and elusive crime boss he was.

He had perfected the skill thirty years earlier to ensure his longevity in the criminal world. Angie Bardollini could read lips fluently in three languages and more men than he could ever remember had died because they hadn't known to keep their mouths shut. He'd taken over the family businesses from his father and grandfather, and for years he'd been tormented by not having a son to take over from him, though he had recently come to terms with the end of his line and himself. Marcus would take over, the one man Angelo trusted.

He was the one person privy to Maria and Phallicia Hunter and had sworn a solemn oath to Angelo on his life never to betray her. He would never be seen with Phallicia Hunter, excepting the four men, he would never refer to her as Phallicia and he would restrict his meetings with her to the appointed times and places. Most important: Phallicia Hunter would not kill anyone. The honour of the Bardollini family had been slighted and the obligation was theirs as

Bardollini men, not Maria's. The sequence of executions had been decided, though when would depend greatly on the fourth man's thought processes as he would very soon become aware of the other three executions and be consumed with the fear that was so important to Maria.

She wanted them to die horribly, to pay for the cruelty they inflicted on an innocent girl; she wanted them to know the fear of death, particularly the fourth man. The contingency strategy was strictly a precaution to ensure success, albeit easier and quicker for each of the four and without the fear built into the primary plan formulated, and in the interim they would input much more data into the four encrypted files.

Angelo let Marcus select the best men for the job of getting into the homes and cars of Rivers and Williams, not wanting distance to become problematic. Pendleton and Wilmington could wait. To that end, Marcus would supervise the outcome of each break-in from a safe distance with explicit instructions from Angelo to carry out the contingency plan at the first sign of interference or trouble.

# 134

John Franklin arrived in Miami very early on the Saturday for the launching of his San Juan. He regretted planning meetings for the Monday and Tuesday, though the rest of the time would be his aboard the Perfect Escape trying to forget his return to Montreal on July 02 for yet another meeting.

IES was no longer his company. The Newark office had always been independent over the years and he hadn't seen the need to micromanage them in over a year. Conversely, Miami had always been affected by a different set of complications and they continued asking for his guidance in matters that secretly made him wish them well. The sale of EIS to the participating management group and salaried employees who were now legally the masters of their collective fate had concluded to everyone's satisfaction. The senior management group were learning to do without his regular input, yet they still relied on him to make Miami more self-reliant, unaware that his June trip might be his last opportunity to do so.

He did remind them that his agreement to assist with the transition would terminate between June 30 and September 30 at his discretion and no one paid particular attention when he left the offices at the end of business on Tuesday. Perhaps they were eager to get home, perhaps assuming they would see him at least once or twice more before the end of September, though he knew differently as he walked along the wharf to his gleaming new yacht.

# 135

The Perfect Escape could not have been more perfect, worth every penny of the two million US dollars. Knowing how proud he would be of her had been a year-long tease and finally knowing how good she would feel and handle was well worth the wait. Her sleek seventeen-metre LOA would get him to the island in four hours, propelled at optimum cruising speed by twin 825 diesels.

He had five full days to enjoy the envy of others as he put the yacht through its paces, incommunicado from the world of business. The following Monday evening would be his last meeting with the Montreal office, he had discontinued his corporate cell phone service and all that remained was for him to slowly adapt to the life he had worked so hard towards.

She would have approved of the Perfect Escape. She'd been gone five years and not a day passed that he didn't think of her. He had enjoyed the company of other women during that time, but never completely. He deeply believed she was still with him, by his side every day. She had told him many times that if something were to happen to her, she would expect him to remarry and not live like a monk. He had always wanted to be angry with her for talking that way, but never could be, and when she was finally taken from him he met her half way and eventually hired an attractive housekeeper.

The home they had shared for so many years would be put up for sale in the fall and he wondered if he'd be ready when the time came. He had no doubt the property would sell quickly through a private broker, in keeping with his private lifestyle. The area was privileged, secluded and peaceful, and none of the residents would enjoy Sunday drivers and the curious parading around otherwise tranquil roads. The sale would not take long, and what would follow was not so much a question as when or how. He would have much to do. He would sell the Audi AB and buy another in Miami, the housekeeper and landscaping staff would be dismissed with generous severances and references, and the final bank transfers would be made to Switzerland and the Caymans.

He felt younger every day, and although no one would argue that life hadn't always been kind to him, life was about to get much better. The first step would be returning to Montreal in five days, though his immediate concern was finding a bottle opener and some SPF.

# 136

Maria, Pilar and Ercilia hadn't stopped since the girls stepped from the jet on July 01st, their first Canada Day which had been absolutely beautiful, though Pilar had insisted the pilot return her to Mexico immediately after he told her Montreal was experiencing a freak snowstorm.

Ercilia liked the pilot, as men go, and hadn't needed an excess of feminine wiles to persuade him to let her occupy the co-pilot's seat. As much as she liked girls, so did he, and she was particularly gorgeous, not taking long to show that her mischievousness was limitless and equally contagious. When he said he couldn't turn around because he'd passed something called the point of no return, Pilar pulled down the sun shade and promised herself out loud in her version of English that she would take the first plane back home, forgetting the threat completely when Ercilia yelled over the intercom for her to look out the portside porthole. She did, waving frantically, blurring her face from Maria, Jean-Émile, Madeleine and Jeff in the process. Then she gave Ercilia and the pilot a rapid piece of her Spanish mind for their childish humour as the door converted to steps and she hurried through, the ones on the ground wondering at the shared giggles and shrugging shoulders behind her.

"Childs," she blurted, "they are childs. No I have reason, Mr. River?"

"Pilar, if it will in any way assist you with the linguistic challenges which lay ahead, perhaps I might suggest that you call me Jean-Émile. Any name but Mr. River, I beg of you young lady."

She tried and the result was equally amusing, Madeleine giving him one of those looks he chose to ignore. He let Pilar hug him before she went to the others, then he waited for his other hug before opening his palms in a silent question to his pilot who answered his boss with a discreet headshake and his waving hands.

Whatever, he thought. If Jean-Émile had learned anything over the past fifteen months, he'd learned that everything had changed for the better and he enjoyed not knowing everything, as long as his devoted Mme. Harnais did. What would he do without her, he wondered? And in a blink Labour Day had come and they hadn't seen him for the better part of two months. They all spoke to him from time to time, and to Madeleine who was the unofficial go-between when he was unavailable. Though the girls had come to realize the two were often unavailable at the same time and they made a pact to get to the bottom of it all.

Pilar and Ercilia were busy attaining accreditation as physiotherapists by March, learning languages and wondering how, with all the expenses, they would be able to pay for the equipment they had begun to order. They hadn't shopped for clothes in months, mostly because there hadn't been time, though they insisted on paying room and board to Maria and now they would have to work at part time jobs to make up the extra. What they both agreed was where they would not go for the money.

Maria was unwavering. The answer was no. Business was business. She was shocked by what the girls were required to spend for language courses and accreditations and would not accept either one losing sight of what was most important: Addisons, and the precious little time they would have to share in the coming months. She would loan them the money, with favourable terms, end of discussion. They would not work anywhere but Addisons and never at part-time jobs serving doughnuts to-ne'er-do-well salesmen and lazy cops. That was the deal.

They were not be distracted by trivial matters like money and she scolded them for even thinking she wouldn't help. She closed the door behind her, not feigning her disappointment. Addisons was six months away from completion with so much left to do. Of course she would have loaned them the money. What were they thinking? But Maria wasn't bothered by the money. She was annoyed by the thought of not having them with her. The next six months would be difficult. She would be gone much of the time and wouldn't be able to tell them why or where without lying to them. She had already, and would again. Business was business, and that business was far from finished. She also knew a kind and loving God wouldn't help anyone who got in her way. She had gone from being a young girl on the inside to an old woman who thought more of death than life and she wanted so badly to regain her youth and be happy again.

# 137

Christine's life had been a whirlwind since the return of her future in-laws from Florida, when she explained to Suzanne that even one more phone call, no matter how short, would cause her to have a brain tumour. That had been a big mistake. Suzanne insisted on having her home phone number, refusing to hang up until Christine saw reason. Her home number was a business number, unlisted to any who didn't have a business card. Her cell was for future friends, not a future mother-in-law whose day finished after her husband left for work and her day went to hell from there with Frederick calling, wanting to know why she had upset Suzanne. Then Bret called wanting to know what she had said to his mother, and to his father; even Shane called to invite her to dinner to discuss the situation. Her one question to Bret when she called him back was: how would they be able to make love on her wedding night when Shane owned his balls, and what was his fucking friend doing calling to take her to dinner on a number she hadn't given him? Then the line went dead and stayed dead for two days.

The custom-designed wedding gown had been fitted, approved, paid for, and was hanging somewhere safe along with her honeymoon wardrobe of lingerie, sleepwear and swimwear she designed without the interference of Mother Bitch. And then came dinner with the Wilmingtons on the fifteenth, intended to make the past week go away. They had acted horribly towards her, very unbecoming of the entire family, and wanted to apologize. They were all overly tense due to the mounting pressure of the coming event, as Christine must realize. They toasted the new house that would be ready in three weeks, one week behind schedule, their son's graduation, the minister, the church and the guests. They toasted everyone but her.

During the course of the evening the Wilmingtons became light-headed, inebriated, or drunk where Christine came from, and she made it very clear to Bret that she was quickly getting pissed herself, pissed enough to call off the wedding and kill Mother Bitch where she sat. She knew what love was, certainly the bitch didn't, and she wondered about Bret's interpretation of love and romance. The wedding was four weeks away and she had serious doubts.

Her big day was almost upon her and she had no one to share it with. She was alone and she wondered at the happiness most brides display on the biggest day of their lives. Or was it a live performance for the benefit of those who had paid for their meals, made easy after only one rehearsal? Either way, real or fake, the reality was hers, not his or theirs.

# 138

Maria was invited to every pillow fight in the guest room since Pilar's and Ercilia's arrival. She refused to speak Spanish with them and both girls were becoming increasingly fluent in both languages, Pilar leaning toward English and Ercilia gravitating towards French. Maria had been right to invite the girls to join her. They would be everything they had promised her. She was proud of them and told them so the day she left for a three-week European trip to drum up clientele for the spa boasting specially designed vacation packages.

Ercilia gave her the tightest hug, insisting that Maria call them each night to let them know she was safe. She would, and they would see her on the twenty-first. They weren't to worry. She had poured them a deep bath in her private en-suite spa, she confessed mischievously, complete with candles and sparkling wine and she sneaked out when she heard the cork pop.

# 139

Marcus had given the men a narrow timeframe. They were the best B & E men in the business with no jail time between them and if they worried that Angelo had instructed Marcus to deal with any unforeseen situation, the concern didn't show. What mattered was getting the job done that Angelo Bardollini had personally ordered.

The break-ins went surprisingly well, particularly at Williams' place where they had all day to work in the house and much of that same night to work on the car. Conversely, Rivers' high-rise bachelor apartment caused concern because he often went home for lunch and at night his car was parked in an underground garage with cameras. The apartment was also very small, giving them less to work with, but they managed and very soon Angelo would be able to monitor every sound made by Rivers and Williams at home or in their cars.

# 140

The lap of luxury was renowned as a premium gentlemen's club where platinum or gold were the preferred currencies, cash was discouraged, and those who came to the door in polyester were turned away. The girls working at the club looked more like European Call Girls than Montreal strippers. Working at the best club in town meant being the best and they all did well. Most were university students, others were models and some were actually trained dancers who worked for Angelo between more traditional performances.

They were all young with perfect bodies that any client was free to ogle. Touching was allowed at twenty for three minutes and anything else that might happen in the private salons was added to the tab at two-fifty an hour per client. All the girls were required to dance on one of five platforms five times per shift, with or without tips, and when they weren't bending and sliding at eye-level they served drinks, encouraged high-end Cubans and danced at tables that would require the client to initial a chit.

Girl-on-girl entertainment was restricted to the salons or to those nights Angelo wasn't at the club, which was more frequent. He had implemented the house rule some years earlier and the girls knew why. It's what the clients enjoyed the most, even at forty for three minutes or five hundred for an hour in a salon. For the girls, doing doubles was an opportunity to make more money because most clients lost track of time and, what the hell, the chit had already been signed.

Frequent aficionados of the club knew most of the girls danced for each other, not for the clients, which was a moot point. Most of them came to work and left as couples and performing for men meant nothing to them because they attached no sexuality to their work, excluding occasions when sophisticated clients would come in with wives or girlfriends. Otherwise, men were seen as a constant and predictable source of income and working the salons wasn't mandatory, although the money was an excellent incentive. What was mandatory was that, once they were in the salon, the girls had full control. On rare occasions when a dispute between a client and dancer might arise, the girl was always right and the client was always wrong.

Two of the men were stylish dressers who gave the appearance of money and were very relaxed and urbane in the sophisticated setting, their thick cigars doing nothing to enhance the desired effect. Every eager-to-earn dancer suggested a private hour, separately or together, with two girls or one. All the girls ignored the two other men who were borderline acceptable, not as well-dressed and openly ogling the girls who were parading around naked or in panties.

Marcus saw them first, taking a moment to appreciate the irony. Then he took another moment to speak with the barman before walking between the men who were always at Angelo's office door. He didn't knock, and within seconds the high definition flat screen filled with one flushed face, then another, then Marcus switched cameras to zoom through a curtain of blue smoke to bring Bret Wilmington and Shane Pendleton into focus.

"How fucking strange is this?" was all Angelo said, staring into the screen.

"It doesn't get stranger."

"Whose card are they using?"

"Pendleton's"

"How much so far?"

"Six-fifty, and the night's young."

"They want a room for the four of them, each with a girl. That's another grand, minimum."

Marcus shrugged indifferently. "It wouldn't surprise me. You okay with that?"

"No. I am not okay with that. You tell the girls no fucking, absolutely no fucking unless they want to lose their jobs."

"That's not something we want getting around. Stuff like that spreads pretty fast. Could be easier to throw them out. Getting them drunk won't be hard."

"And they'd go somewhere else where we couldn't watch them." Angelo switched cameras and zoomed in. "Those two don't have enough money and they're worried about catching something, or being taped." Then he switched to the groom and best man.

"And you know that how?" asked Marcus.

"Just get out there and make sure they know the salons are booked for most of the night. Offer them a round and a dance on the house, after you find out it's his bachelor party...and tell the girls they'll get an extra hundred per hour for each salon. I want those rooms full."

"We should have taken care of business long before this. She'd have gotten over it."

"She doesn't get over anything. She's worse than her mother."

Marcus nodded. "I have to admit I'm anxious."

"Two months. These two fuckers are worried about cameras in a strip club and have no clue about their homes and cars." He paused, shaking his head with frustration, feeling a strong urge to order their deaths for that evening. "Get out there, before we both do something that's too easy."

When Marcus walked out Angelo opened a second screen, positioning both cameras to read the conversation between the four men after Marcus left them. The screens went black when they left the bar at closing, drunk and put off not being able to touch the bare buttocks, flat bellies and firm breasts teasingly brushing against them as the girls danced.

He would be seeing all four again in less than seven hours.

# 141

Angelo and Marcus stayed downtown, Marcus leaving the hotel by eight to meet the B & E men waiting for him across from the Pendleton residence as though they were meeting for a cup of coffee. They were at the Wilmington residence a week earlier, though Bret Wilmington's home had been the easiest to do as the central alarm system and designer locks were being installed.

Angelo knew Shane Pendleton would leave home at nine to meet with the groom, and his parents would leave for the church by noon. He left on time and the limo arrived for the parents precisely at noon. Shane Pendleton was the last. By 1:00 PM he no longer had secrets, Marcus was en route to meet with Angelo and the two B & E guys went to burglar-proof more new homes with expensive alarm systems and the best pick-proof locks.

# 142

Marcus raised the window, dropping the camera onto the front seat of the LX570. He knew he'd soon be taking over from Angie and as boss he'd be ordering executions, not carrying them out, and hoped that would still be months away. The four men were a family debt, a matter of honour and Marcus wanted three of them for himself. The driver was another matter. He'd been under virtual house arrest for the past several weeks, watched twenty-four-seven and the reason he hadn't been killed earlier was that Angelo needed him to leak specific information to the task force and feed John Gunn whatever tidbit of false information would pay the most.

There was absolutely no doubt he was the leak. Marcus grinned as the procession of white limos pulled away from the church. The driver would have his final, most critical meeting with John Gunn the following week, one which would delay the indictment by three or four months.

# 143

Task teams had been working on the indictment for over two years, and getting very close to putting Angie Bardollini away. They knew the case had to be air-tight, or he'd walk and they'd never get him back. Every fact or fiction was minutely analyzed and sorted into separate files. Screwing up would only take one murder he hadn't ordered or committed, a single money laundering scheme not of his doing, one protection victim who hadn't been a victim at all, or one raid on a bar where no video gambling had taken place.

More than a few people wanted him put away, and the cops knew many more would benefit from his being locked up. He was all that mattered, and if a few died in the process, collateral damage was secondary. He was key and they wanted him badly enough to bide their time. Though, they wouldn't wait much longer once news began leaking onto the streets.

Killings were expected. They knew Bardollini was receiving sporadic reports of their activities, which would later lead to a separate investigation, but, by and large, they didn't care about any but the best witnesses. Special security was in place to protect against those murders, however funds were always limited and the small part of the task force assigned to protect the best and most reliable witnesses couldn't be everywhere at once. Nor could they protect the driver from one of his own.

John Gunn was another matter. He was a key witness. He knew everyone who made up the fabric of Montreal's underworld, including Angie Bardollini, as he would often boast after his fourth or fifth bar scotch at the end of each twelve-hour work day which normally ended at 9:00 AM when he submitted his column to the editor.

Angelo hoped that killing John Gunn would delay the indictment by a few months. Killing the driver would extend the timeframe by another one or two and the silent order had been given by the simple gesture of throwing a section of newspaper onto a car seat. Gunn had become a drunk at a point in his life he hadn't been able to remember for years, and had remained one. Not long after the transformation, when being drunk most of the time no longer did much good, he began popping pills with a constant source to feed a constant need. He slept with whores for free because he knew cops who needed pills as badly as he did and he brokered for both parties.

Recently he'd been told to change his lifestyle by a doctor who wouldn't think to examine the aging drunk without the precaution of silicone gloves. Gunn's response was a snide laugh. Outwardly he wanted to show indifference to his fate, knowing full-well his destiny had been predetermined and how much he drank, smoked or fucked cheap whores without his own silicone protection didn't matter. He'd soon be dead and not from any of life's luxuries.

# 144

Helicopters were reserved for the likes of Angie Bardollini, as were the pseudo-commandos of the Special Tactical Squad. Gunn, as important as he was to the cause, was watched at the local precinct's shift commander's discretion. The task force could have had a photo studio set up in front of his east-end duplex apartment, yet when the driver walked up the outside steps they still wouldn't have stopped him. Moreno had become Gunn's major source of information and, through him, the cops'. The deal was simple: Moreno would speak to them through Gunn and they would tell Gunn when and what to publish for the gullible public.

They would pay Gunn and Gunn would pay Moreno. Everyone walked away happy, knowing eventually Gunn and Moreno would be found dead. He was fifty-nine, in a body closer to seventy-nine. His skin was yellowed with thick purple veins and his eyes were permanently streaked with red. He was small in stature, his hair was never combed, he was completely without tone and his yellowed nails were chewed to raw cuticles constantly outlined with fibre-thin lines of brown blood. He breathed through his mouth as though gasping his last breath, not a day went by that he didn't smell of sweat and he had spent the last half of his life without the benefit of a dentist.

Over the years he had become indifferent to his state of decay, so what did dying matter, as long as the end came fast. What mattered was crying. He didn't want to cry. As much as he knew what he was, he cared about crying. He didn't want to cry because he knew most men did when faced with death. Curiously, his death would be his one opportunity to find the man inside who had deserted him years ago.

The bell rang once, then twice, before Moreno's gloved fist struck the door. Gunn always began and ended his day the same way and he answered the door in a stupor, not thinking to ask who was on the other side: a moot point. The door was cheap and he was a cheap drunk. Moreno followed without looking behind. The rented car was still running and Marcus sat in the front seat. House rule: Never go to a kill in a company car.

"You've got big fucking balls coming here. You know the cops don't need more information. They've got enough shit to sort through and pretty soon Angie'll find out you've been fucking him up the back."

"Gunn, I don't have time to talk shit. Yeah, the cops don't need more info, but Bardollini still wants the source cut off."

"He knows?"

"No shit he knows, about you, not me."

Fetid yellow water dribbled from under the cuffs of Gunn's pants. "Now?"

"Yeah. We both knew he'd put you away one day. I just didn't think I'd be doing you. You want to turn around? It'll be easier." Moreno extracted the Magnum from under his coat. "It'll be fast. Do yourself a favour. It'll take less than a second."

Gunn was trembling involuntarily. He'd seen the results of enough sanctioned hits to know exactly what Moreno's gun would do to him. He tried swallowing what was left in his glass as he swung around as quickly as he could without stumbling; possibly thinking he had a chance of being found without excrement in his pants if he could die quickly. And if he realized he'd let the old-fashioned fall from his hand, he hadn't heard the sound of glass shattering on the floor. Neither did Moreno who'd been right about how quickly Gunn would die without cowardly tears. Not that the crime scene techies would know. The reporter had inadvertently slumped forward, the first shot impacting at the base of his skull, blowing away the back half of his head and jerking his feet from the floor. The requisite second served the purpose of tradition and blowing what was left of Gunn's tattered face off the floor.

# 145

Moreno casually walked away after the kill, feeling nothing, knowing the low-income or immigrant neighbours would be blind, deaf or mute later that morning. They would never get involved, damned if they did, damned if they didn't, living in a high crime area most of them would never leave. To most of them the mob was the law and the police were the mob, most agreeing that organized crime was no threat to good people, rich or poor. They all had more to fear from street punks, muggers and racist cops: permanently in the wrong place at the wrong time and speaking with the cops just made things worse.

At one time the driver had been one of Angelo's most trusted men until, for reasons Angelo cared nothing about, the moment he made the decision to become an informant and believe he could survive. To the task force he was a treasure trove of information, material made available to Moreno in various ways which made the acquisition appear inadvertent, by virtue of meetings, phone conversations, or assignments, which would soon put an end to the Bardollini family.

Angelo Bardollini's career was being dissected and classified in order of importance. What they didn't realize, what Moreno wouldn't be telling them, was that Angelo was becoming less active and less visible. Even Marcus Difiore, the cousin Moreno didn't know would soon take over as the new crime boss, was seldom where they thought he would be.

The information was unidirectional in the minds of the task force, too arrogant or driven to believe one of their own might be indebted for favours once asked, leaving Angelo with reliable input as months became weeks that dwindle into days before the task force would raid his club and other business interests as they attempted to penetrate his home to arrest him. The time frame had changed, as he had told Maria it might. The stakes were too high to gamble on the time left to him. He hoped he would have several more weeks, and that killing Moreno would give him the extra time he needed, the one certainty being Murphy's Law and imagining the outcome accomplished nothing beyond false hope.

Moreno stepped onto the sidewalk, walking the half-block to the car as though leaving home for a nine-to-five office job and not wanting to miss the last rush-hour bus. He didn't slow at seeing Marcus leaning against the trunk with his coat open and his arms extended downward in a wide V to his gloved hands gripping the dull black 10mm Glock. Asking why was pointless. He knew why. Marcus wasn't in the night air dispelling digestive gases or checking the taillights to avoid being pulled over by the cops. The one true answer was in his face, in his eyes. Moreno had worn the same expression when Gunn opened the door to him and he knew Marcus was well-acquainted with body and facial language. He'd been sanctioned, with nowhere to run or hide, not from Angie. The most he could hope for was a day, a half-day, before they found him, and he would have to kill Marcus first.

He focused on his beige raincoat as he came to a stop, as though he hadn't seen the gun in Marcus' relaxed hand. "We'll stop off at a dumpster so I can dump the coat. The old guy had a lot of shit in his head."

Marcus shook his head. "No need, Moreno, not this time."

"Why not? What's different about this one? You know the rule: no evidence."

"He knows, Moreno. Give me your gun, unless this is where it ends."

"No...not here, and I have to do myself. You know I

have to do myself."

Marcus nodded. "Sure. Now give me your gun and get in the fucking car. You're driving, and do not fuck me up."

The confrontation had taken a few seconds, a few seconds more for the car to disappear off the street. Marcus left one round from the Magnum, hurling the others from the backseat window while the untraceable Glock rested in his lap. The driver maintained the legal limit, turning when told and staying silent, knowing Marcus would save him the trouble of blowing his own head from his shoulders. He wasn't nervous. He was calm, waiting for instructions. Then, too soon for Moreno, they pulled to the curb a short walk from Marcus' Navigator.

"Here's how it plays out, Moreno," Marcus began, breaking the silence. "You get the gun, one round, and one chance. I get out of the car, stand behind you, and you have the count of three after I close the door. My shot comes on my count of four and if you haven't done your thing, the second comes on five. Ready?"

"One thing, Marcus: tell him I'm sorry. They had me tighter than a whore's hand on my dick. I had no choice. I was in shit to my neck, big time. Tell him I'm sorry. We'll see each other in hell."

Marcus opened his door, the gun's muzzle at the side of Moreno's headrest. "He won't be joining you anytime soon, Moreno... by the count of three." He fired, sparing Moreno an eternity of seconds. Expectation was the worst, Moreno's last thought exploding across the entire inside of the rental vehicle. The door slammed, the second shot shattering the driver's side window, blowing off what little was left of his head.

## 146
## October 21

Christine felt nothing like Cinderella or Sleeping Beauty after the kiss when Bret opened the door of her home for the first time since the final inspection with the contractor. She was instantly livid, and not because she had to walk across the threshold into the foyer. The entire house reeked of week-old vomit, some of which was visibly caked on the heated bathroom floor. Dirty dishes were strewn across the kitchen counter, liquor bottles were everywhere and a set of her new sheets lay rumpled on her new sofa. What infuriated her most was Bret having invited Chad and Thurston to stay in her new home from the Thursday until their early departure the evening of the wedding.

She felt as though she'd vomit herself, hating the thought of going to work the next day to meet with several potential clients. Walking into his filth she had found her breaking point. Without warning the plate closest to her trembling hands flew across the room faster than he could react and it missed his expressionless face by mere centimetres before exploding noisily into dozens of wild projectiles against the wall behind him.

What he had done was an inexcusable violation of her home and during the previous week he hadn't once thought to explain what he had done. She stormed from the house in a silent rage to spend the evening at the condo which was still hers alone, where all her clothes still hung and where she could be away from him for as long as she chose.

She lay back gently, letting the steaming water cascade over her shoulders as she parted her legs to let the heat surge inward. She looked at her vagina as one hand hovered over her hip and the other floated, coming to rest over the delicate folds. She studied herself for several minutes, mesmerized, until she arched and the scented bath water washed over her body with refreshing coolness. She was beautiful, vital, a sensual young woman who had spontaneous urges and needs. She had no doubt about her sexuality. Even though her urges had waned over recent months, she believed sex without feeling or romance was something paid for or rape. Otherwise, what was the point when climax didn't require a partner? She was still a virgin bride, partly her doing, mostly his fault, and she fell asleep not thinking of him or the honeymoon he had ruined. She was content to be a Wilmington.

# 147

When Christine awoke the morning after her wedding, she'd forgotten crying herself to sleep. She didn't turn over. She didn't need to see him. She could smell the expensive liquor and Cuban cigars which had become cheap booze and stale smoke as he slept. She had heard how some men abruptly change when they feel they have control over their women, asserting their maleness as though retaliating against over-bearing mothers who would do anything to prevent their precious boys from leaving the nest. She wondered whether Bret suffered from the delusion, or Mother Bitch. If so, good luck to either one. She was stronger than both of them.

She had never been in bed with a man and was uneasy when he had come into the room, reeling. She had stripped for him the day before on a whim, not meaning to, blaming her tease on the champagne. She had never felt a penis inside her and the thought of him spewing himself into her, smelling of liquor and sweat, had made her nauseous at the time, remembering her relief when she dared to touch him and he hadn't stirred.

She was his wife and eventually he would try to take from her what she was afraid to give, though she wondered how such a little thing could hurt her. Such was the big day she would remember, along with the odours accompanying a concert of noises she'd never heard him make and the dark bruise on one of her breasts. And the honeymoon wasn't any more memorable. They had spent a week together and had barely made the airport on time, despite her being dressed and packed an hour before he was even awake.

He lay in bed with the red puffiness of indulgence spread across a face that had darkened during sleep with a course shadow, his hair matted with sweat that hadn't dried. She wasn't prepared to see anything else. She wrote a note on hotel stationary, telling him she'd gone for breakfast, the sharp sound of the spring-loaded dead bolt sliding into the doorframe as she stepped from the room waking him. When he finally did join her at the table, he barely managed to pop pills and drink coffee.

Christine caught the glances several women who she believed had probably seen the happy couple the day before and she wanted desperately to get away from what they were thinking. She was embarrassed. They could see he was refusing to talk with her, appearing angry when she asked him what was so important that he spent her wedding night getting drunk with his friends. She had wanted an all-inclusive honeymoon in Mexico where young couples could be young and sexy without stereotypical North Americans gawking. But he'd thought of dozens of reasons why they shouldn't go to Mexico and she hadn't argued. They could go to Jamaica, an island she wanted to see, though Jamaica was out of the question because of inflated costs; especially after all they had spent, not to mention Mother's opinion of all-inclusive clubs and the type of person attracted by what those places offered.

He convinced her Miami was a practical alternative, where they could spend the entire week aboard the Executive Decision. The Bahamas and Cuba were only a few hours away and crossing over in groups for safety was a common event. Nor would she have to worry about not understanding a foreign language because Cubans were acclimated to speaking English. She didn't argue. Neither did she agree or thank Wilmington senior for the corporate-expense offer.

She did what she was accustomed to doing. She did what she wanted to do and when they arrived in Miami he quickly discovered they'd be staying in the fashionable Art

Deco district, in a luxury hotel with fresh linen every day and room service. They would spend days on the beach or at sidewalk cafés, evenings in fine restaurants and dance bars. She would not sleep onboard someone else's boat, even if they called the thing a yacht, and certainly not in any bed or berth his mother slept in. Neither would she cruise offshore in a boat he had no idea how to navigate, although one evening onboard would be nice for a glass of wine, the moon and romantic dancing.

# 148

She witnessed a different side of him clearly revealed during the honeymoon. He had an eye for young ladies, especially topless and b ackless young ladies, and she reminded him on several occasions that sunglasses didn't make him invisible. The first morning, Christine wore a plain one-piece that was décolleté and high-rise on the hip and when she suggested buying a thong bikini and going topless at the end of the beach, he refused, insisting he'd be the only man seeing her nude. He acted no differently in restaurants, particularly Latino restaurants where he openly stared at waitresses and patrons dressed much more seductively than most Americans.

Her wardrobe for the week was sexy, eye-catching, admiring glances from the Latinos telling her she was as desirable as any Latina in the district. For the evening on the boat she wore a bright yellow bra-top halter with a yellow-on-white gypsy-styled miniskirt with splashes of black and a tulle hem that was the focus of anyone at the marina who saw her stroll to the rocking Executive Decision with her black leather slide sandals swinging in her hand.

He held a bottle of champagne in one hand, not that he hadn't consumed enough from his private stock of scotch at the hotel, and not that the boat wasn't fully provisioned. And as she stepped over the narrow gap of water from the dock to the platform he took the opportunity to see whether she had chosen bikini, thong or sheer. When he joined her she took the bottle, inverted it in her hand, and told him without the slightest humour that if he ever once even thought of lifting her skirt in public again he'd be sorry for the longest time. She was his wife, not some vacation whore, and if she hadn't broken the bottle she had certainly managed to break the mood.

He stayed onboard for as long as he thought he should without making her any more furious, eventually making an excuse about going up to the chandlery to buy something as a thank-you to his father for the use of the boat. She sipped her wine, watching him walk away. When he disappeared from sight she went into the cabin where she stayed for as long as he was gone. When he returned she told him that she needed to use the ladies' room because she didn't trust the head onboard and in the time she was gone he downed three more scotches and dancing was out of the question.

That was their second to last night, an unromantic evening that would leave each of them with a different perspective of the last day. She spent most of Saturday strolling South Beach, feeling envious of girls in bikinis much skimpier than hers, Bret would barely remember laying on the beach in a stupor, converting each difficult word into an indiscernible groan. He had spent their honeymoon drunk, either thinking nothing of what he'd done or too embarrassed to admit he had acted immaturely.

All she could manage to say en route to the airport the next day was that she couldn't imagine how he would have acted if he had gone with Shane to Myrtle Beach.

They were new to each other, and would need time to adapt to one another, which didn't excuse him for ruining her honeymoon by constantly being drunk and acting like a jerk. He would change. He was a husband, not a college buddy, and the sooner he understood difference the sooner she'd begin acting like a real wife.

# 149

Christine stayed at her apartment for most of the week, not impressed he tried to call her every night on the only number she had ever given him. Late Friday afternoon she did answer the phone, not because Bret was calling, because he wasn't. The hospital had called to advise that her husband had been admitted to emergency with very severe trauma to both legs, his left arm and his face, as an apparent victim of a carjacking. He'd been found face-up and unconscious on a sidewalk not far from their home by a motorist on his way to the airport at around 4:00 AM.

His knees were severely injured and one arm was broken, as were his nose, jaw and several teeth. He had lacerations to the back of his head, probably caused by his head striking whatever was behind him when he was being beaten. The second call came from the police. His BMW had been stolen along with his wallet, his money clip, his watch and identification. For that reason they and the hospital staff had necessarily waited several hours after surgery for his first fleeting moments of consciousness to determine his identity and contact information.

He was found alone, his excessive blood-alcohol level was a matter of record, which would probably lead to DUI charges by the police who first responded to the anonymous Samaritan's call. No witnesses to the accident were expected to come forth and they weren't certain the car wasn't already in some east-end hack shop in a hundred different pieces.

Christine phoned Shane at the office to ask one question and, when he admitted they had gone to The Lap of Luxury, she hung up. She could imagine the rest and wouldn't believe anything further he had to say. She'd been married less than two weeks and her husband had shamelessly gone to a strip bar. Then she called Frederick to tell him what happened, that she would meet him and Suzanne at the hospital.

The attending physician had spoken candidly on the phone. Bret was lucky to be alive. The attack was brutal and she stood at the closed door peering through the glass panel for several seconds, wondering what she would say to him, and what she wouldn't, as she watched the ever dramatic bitch stroking and cooing over her pup.

He had spent most of the morning in the OR and would require full hospital care for three, and possibly as much as four weeks. Once released he would require several more weeks of home rest and eventually some degree of physiotherapy before regaining mobility which they couldn't guarantee would be as complete as before the attack. The couple was to expect some degree of permanent impairment, they warned. More importantly, he had survived without any internal injuries.

# 150

What Christine felt was strange to her. She felt no connection with him, no bond between husband and wife, as though the man wasn't her husband at all and she remained silent as Suzanne continued on centre stage.

She informed them matter-of-factly that she would begin making necessary arrangements for twenty-four hour private nursing to take over sometime near the end of November and that he would have the best care possible at home, knowing full-well Suzanne would hear none of it. If Christine had been a proper wife to him in the first place this never would have happened, Suzanne retorted. She had acted despicably walking out on her husband after only one week, to go God knows where and to do God knows what. Had she been a proper wife to him he wouldn't have resorted to being in such a horrible place with Shane.

Christine ignored her and went to the closet, throwing Bret's pants onto the bed and challenging his mother to smell them above the knee before asking her if she had any recent memory of the pungent scent, as a proper wife.

She had no reason to stay. Bret was barely conscious. His jaw was wired shut and for the second time in a week he had managed to seriously upset her agenda. Once he was conscious enough to make a decision, if he ever had been, and if he was willing to spend the next several weeks at their home, she wouldn't argue. The incident couldn't have happened at worse time for her business, she added caustically, and perhaps mommy could also manage to wean her little boy off his bottle.

In the interim Christine would return to her condo. She would delay her upcoming trip until Bret was transferred to the Wilmington residence after which she would visit him as often as was feasible, and Bret would deal with the matter of driving under the influence. She had no intention of being questioned about her drunken husband who didn't know when to push a naked, wet whore from his lap. And since Suzanne was so concerned about everything being done to perfection, and since she had her whole day to do it, she could be responsible for calling his bank and insurance company, not to mention the health insurance and motor vehicle bureau. She would come again that evening, when Bret might do more than mumble and groan incoherently, which, she added, would remind her of the last day on South Beach were it not for the mummy-like plaster and bandages.

# 151

The night before Bret had no trouble convincing Shane to join him at The Lap of Luxury. Shane's reaction to hearing about his friend's forced abstinence during the honeymoon was to laugh and offer to service Christine the way she needed. After all, what were friends for, and when Bret laughed with him, Marcus continued listening from kilometres away as he called Angelo.

All the girls in at The Lap remembered the good clients, as well as the bad, and Marcus had not needed to tell them again. Salon privileges would not be available to the men who were expected to arrive around eight, and this time Angelo wouldn't be paying bonuses. When they arrived they were escorted to the same table minutes after the hour and stayed at the club until well past 2:00 AM enjoying twelve girl-on-girl dances, several cognacs and a cigar each.

Everyone in the club was aware of ways to touch the dancers that the girls normally didn't mind, particularly with familiar clients who were good tippers: A nose could inadvertently brush against a breast or a nipple; a hand might accidentally come into easy contact with thighs or buttocks. For very good clients the girls might occasionally sit on a lap at the very moment the client chose to straighten his pant leg, nothing else. Any client who wanted to touch that paid two-fifty up front.

Shane tried as much as he could with each girl; Bret preferred raising his knee as each girl straddled him with open thighs, each one refusing an invitation to a late dinner and drinks. The word had spread that something was going on. One of them had been in Angelo's office earlier and saw Marcus sitting at the desk monitoring the flat screens with close-up views of the men.

They were drunk when they left. A regular bar would

have cut them off before midnight, asked for the car keys and sent them home in a taxi. Strip bars had a different set of values which the girls capitalized on the more the clients drank, and the four hundred dollars each didn't seem excessive to them as they swallowed their last cognacs and Bret Wilmington signed the receipt.

Most girls believed the men wouldn't be coming back.

# 152

The next morning, Shane wouldn't recall his easy, meandering drive home. Bret crossed the Pont Champlain, notorious as much for impromptu police roadblocks as for its deteriorating condition. He made his way to the South Shore without being stopped, feeling invincible. He had twenty kilometres left when Shane was moments away from crawling into bed. He could manage route 132, however at 2:30, and with only one other car in sight, he'd either be driving too slowly, too quickly, or in the wrong lane for any cop car parked on the shoulder with the lights off.

He opted to stay on the less-used and surveillance-free service road which would take him most of the way home without having to worry about being pulled over. The drive would take longer because of the countless red lights the city had never programmed to flash during low-traffic hours, but he'd be safe from the cops, certain the guy behind him was thinking the same thing. When he slowed to a stop at yet another interminable red light, he tried focusing on the illuminated hands and dots of his watch. Doing so at that exact moment likely saved his life as the crowbar smashed through the window and into his raised forearm.

They pulled him out from the car so quickly and expertly that he had had no time to react or realize his left forearm was shattered before the impact of the huge gloved fist stunned him into bewilderment, producing an immediate anaesthetizing effect he didn't know to be thankful for. The first blow mulched the bone and cartilage that had been his nose. The second broke his jaw, and the third turned his top row of perfect teeth into jagged shards. They were close to him, one pressing a hand hard against his chest, pinning him to the car and he wondered why neither one had a face.

They knew he would pass out from the sudden and cumulative pain, and not scream out in agony as the precise impacts of the crowbar smashed apart his kneecaps. What happened after would always be conjecture, but they took his money, his wallet, his watch and his car before leaving him at the curbside in time for the green light.

# 153

Maria had stayed away one week longer than she had originally planned, though she managed to speak with the girls every day, particularly on Thanksgiving when she called them at Jean-Émile's where they were being treated to a bizarre mixture of Quebecoise and Latin dishes. The vacation packages were a success and Addisons' international client list had begun growing beyond her wildest expectations she told them excitedly.

She loved them all. She had surprises for each of them. She would see them very soon and they weren't to worry when they saw how she had changed because she'd been working very hard. The strain was beginning to show, but the most difficult part, the waiting, would soon be over. Only Jean-Émile understood the imperceptible change in Maria's voice and he wondered later that night what her surprise for him would be, praying silently she hadn't been speaking of her complete loss of innocence. He had come to love the girls as much as he hated himself.

He had memorized each new private number, which he was expected to use when even suspecting Maria's well-being was threatened. But was anyone thinking of her innocence? Addison's innocence had been violently taken from her and those same men would soon be responsible for Maria's loss of innocence, which was no less vile.

He wasn't nervous. He was wealthy beyond words, had survived two heart attacks and wasn't one to care what people thought of him. They were fathers, sharing one precious daughter. He dialled the ten-digit number, astonished by the calmness of the voice answering immediately with a simple: "Do we have a problem?"

"No. I don't believe so, not at this particular moment. However that does not preclude difficulties of a social or psychological nature at a later date. I believe now is the appropriate time for concern."

"There will be no difficulty of any kind. I've implemented measures to protect the part of her we're equally concerned about. She'll be normal again very soon, she'll become a successful businesswoman and she'll get on with life. She won't be involved beyond what she needs to find the closure she believes she can't do without, though she does appear to have a creative nature which I'm very glad she's never thought to use against me."

"When might I expect word of the first appointment…and the last?"

"Mid-December through mid-April."

The line went dead without formality, leaving Jean-Émile to shiver and struggle to think about his Christmas plans for the girls without considering they might have plans of their own.

# 154

By the time Maria returned at the end of October, the Moreno and Gunn killings were old news and the space allotted by the press for the Bardollini indictment was virtually non-existent. Apparently no one wanted to take over where John Gunn had left off.

Her first night at home Pilar and Ercilia were shocked by how exhausted Maria looked without the age-old artifice of make-up. After endless hugs and kisses the second order of business was her favourite CD, her favourite wine, candles, and her favourite scented oil in deep steaming water.

Pilar tried to pull Ercilia from the private spa, to no avail. So she went for the wine and extra glasses as Ercilia slipped her feet into the bath and they talked incessantly until the water cooled and Maria reached for a towel, stepping out onto the cool tiles. They insisted she wouldn't sleep alone and she didn't, the three awaking the next morning like tousled and innocent waifs, fleecy orphans huddled in a row, each one rubbing the sleep from her eyes and sitting to stretch in different directions before jumping from the bed and racing for first place.

Michele Baroque come to the condo Sunday afternoon, anxious and excited to report she had been to the site every day during Maria's absence, and the project was ahead of schedule. Addisons would open on time, on May 03, Addison's birthday, and each member of the mostly female crew was working hard to make the deadline. She was even more excited when Maria told her about the growing number of clients and the universal reaction to the portfolio Michele had put together to help Maria promote the spa. She stayed for pizza and wine, talked some girl-talk with them and left by 4:00. When she had gone Maria dropped into her MX-5 and drove to a downtown hotel before jumping into a taxi that would take her north.

# 155

She had become comfortable with her duplicity and Marcus had much to do with the adjustment, as well as what and who Phallicia Hunter had become. At times she felt as though she was on the verge of becoming a comic book heroine, most times well aware she'd be participating in the deaths of four men, undecided as to whether she was anxious for the deaths or for the deaths to be over. What she did know was that she was ready.

Their deaths wouldn't be murder. They would suffer the ultimate retribution she owed to Addison as much as she wanted satisfaction for herself. The first one would come soon, she already knew who he was and she'd be ready for the call. Marcus would be in place to decide the appropriate timing for the kill, and Phallicia would then be given twenty-four hours' notice to arrive on site. That was the deal. She was the newcomer, not them. Father or no father, she would follow his rules or the four would simply be killed. And she would not be late for any reason. Being late was not an option, or all four would be executed at once.

Marcus had specific orders: If Phallicia Hunter did not arrive on time he would take care of each man the usual way, with no bullshit from female amateurs. She was onboard or she wasn't, and they were about to find out. Maria arrived at her father's home for dinner as an early fall darkness was setting in and the gates opened once the entire area had been scanned. The door was unlocked and she walked in to see her father and Marcus leaning from the same sofa, filling their mouths from the same bowl of chips.

"A typical family Sunday afternoon."

Neither man stood. Instead they signalled her over and proffered chip-loaded cheeks for a kiss.

"Go get a glass and join us," Angelo said. She did,

sitting across from them with a fine Chianti in her glass. "You look like shit."

"I know. I've been busy."

"How was Europe?"

"Europe was great, really good. We're booked through most of the summer with week-long and weekend packages. It's going to work, papa, and Michele told me today we're ahead of schedule."

"And?" Her puzzled expression wasn't real enough. "Don't play stupid with me, Maria. I asked you a question. Answer me."

"Everything went according to plan, and I'm fine, papa." She turned to Marcus. "Markie, tell him I'm fine."

"I don't know who you are, and he's right. You look terrible. I don't like what's happening to my little sis."

"I'm not your sis and stop treating me like a fucking baby." she snapped, instantly regretting her words.

He shrugged, dipping his free hand into the bowl.

"Let's stop the bullshit. Marcus is right. And you do look like shit."

"That's bullshit. So let's cut to the chase." She gulped her wine. "Was Wilmington supposed to be killed last Thursday? If so, I'll be better off doing this whole thing myself. You promised, papa. You promised me."

"Promised what? I didn't promise you shit." Angelo dropped a handful of chips into the bowl and leaned forward.

"You promised I'd be there for each one…that's what."

"Wilmington won't be the first one, that's what I promised, and the thing on Thursday was purely coincidental," Angelo lied. "What would we gain by putting a piece of shit in the hospital? And have no doubt about it, girl. If I wanted him dead, he'd be fucking dead."

"So, what happened was an accident? He was in the wrong place at the wrong time?"

They both said: "Absolutely."

"It's been over eighteen months, papa. It's time."

Angelo nodded his agreement, lacing his fingers, searching his daughter's eyes for the least doubt. "Phallicia Hunter will arrive in Vancouver on Thursday, December 13<sup>th</sup>, early. Her return flight will be the following Monday."

Her face beamed and she let out an involuntary shriek. "It's Rivers, papa? He's the first?"

"He thinks he's leaving for a ski week at Whistler, alone, on the fifteenth."

"What do you mean, he thinks?"

They both ignored the question and Marcus took over from his uncle. "That'll leave pretty near three weeks before he'll be expected at the office, figuring Christmas and New Year's."

"So…?"

"So, if Phallicia Hunter fucks up for any reason, Marcus won't. The ski trip won't happen." Angelo poured more wine into his tumbler. "Understand this for the umpteenth time: Phallicia Hunter goes, you stay. Everything about you stays. Do you understand that? Absolutely nothing of yours goes with her, not one fucking thing. When you're done, everything, and I mean everything, will be packed and tossed. And Marcus will tell you again when I can't."

"I do understand, papa, a separate set of clothes for that one time and two suitcases so Markie can use one to get rid of all my clothes and my shoes. No evidence, right?" She turned to Marcus who was filling his mouth with more chips." I won't disappoint you, Markie." He shrugged, ignoring her. "All of a sudden, I don't know what to feel."

"Just don't get brain-fucked over this or I'll have a lot of explaining to do to a certain interested party who seems to care what all this will do to you, if something isn't happening already."

She hesitated. "You've been talking with Jean-Émile,

papa?"

"Who I talk with isn't your business. And don't ask questions you know I won't answer."

Maria ignored her father, sipping her wine. His tone hadn't been harsh. "Thank you, papa. Markie, thank you. Thanks for wanting to help me stay who I am, and nothing's happening to me. Tell Jean-Émile I'm fine, that I'll always be fine." She put rested her glass "Now Markie…what can your little sister make you for dinner?"

# 156

Marcus left the table holding both ends of his open belt, making sure his zipper was up, and poured his last glass of wine before walking home. Angelo wasn't much better and nothing was left of the roast beef. Neither was anything left of the evening and both men insisted that she stay the night and leave after breakfast. They wanted her to get some rest, and the next morning father and daughter sat together with no talk of business, although when he asked how her Mexican friends were doing he got the unedited version which included their Christmas plans.

# 157

Christine moved back into the house and brought with her all her clothing and jewellery, though she would keep her condo until the current lease expired. The attack on Bret was inopportune and she blamed his male stupidity for what happened, which she was making increasingly clear to everyone. Delaying her next trip until the hospital released him into homecare was too ridiculous to consider, especially since his mother would certainly continue fussing over him.

She decided to leave as originally planned; pleased he was alone in the hospital room when she arrived to tell him. She cared in no way what his mother thought about her, or anything else for that matter, she simply didn't need the hassle of a free show for the other patients and staff. She had selected her outfit for him, though she had to admit she would have enjoyed seeing the old cow's reaction.

Her light beige stiletto suede boots with tassels were meant for show, not winter, her emerald-coloured suede micro-mini skirt meant to display as much leg has she had to show. The turquoise iridescent faux-wrap silk top fit loosely in a wide V, leaving no question as to the quality of her embroidered silk-on-satin turquoise push-up bra revealing as much of her breasts as she wanted, and she wanted. She had gone out without stockings, pushing the season, but she had gorgeous legs and his seeing her side-vented turquoise tap pants was the bigger issue.

The bandages were still on, covering all but his bruised and split lips and his eyes, as though he belonged in a comical B-rate horror film and how she looked would either cure him or kill him. Certainly her chic fashion would have killed his mother. She stood by the head of the bed that smelled of bleach and wondered if he realized he'd been propped up. She leaned over him, exploring for some sign of life through his ragged, cotton peep holes. She saw none and blew through them with a single burst of air.

"We'll have to start over when you're well again, Bret." She whispered, as the red eyes blinked open and blinked again, trying to wash away the dryness. "You know, you would have been better off if I had hit you with the plate. At least I might have missed your arm and your legs with the second one."

Another set of blinks.

"I've decided I will leave town on business for a couple of weeks, as planned, and should be back in time to help with setting you up with Frederick and your mommy. I'd touch you, Bret, but where? Your other arm's a veritable pin cushion. My God, anyone might believe you're a genuine mummy. Does that hurt very much? Do you need something? Should I call a nurse?"

She removed her coat, slowly, throwing it over the railing before pulling herself onto the lower half of the bed so he could see her as clearly as possibly. She intended for her skirt to ride past the very tops of her legs to her hips, and even if she hadn't, pushing it down would be awkward. Then she leaned against her coat, releasing the flimsy silk belt holding her top together.

Her skin was perfectly smooth, glistening with the scented moisture from her bath, her bra accentuating the fullness and curvature of her breasts.

"Do you like my bra and panties, Bret? I wore them especially for you. Can you see them?" She leaned forward, arching her back so he could see the detail on her bra and the way her skin glowed. He couldn't smell her, and probably wouldn't for quite some time. "I'll wait until you're better to bring you a little something, Bret. I'll bring you something from out of town. The doctor says by then you should be able to talk, at least a little, at least enough to tell me why you let some smelly twenty-dollar slut sit on your legs when, if you hadn't been such a fool, you could have been in your new home and in your new wife who, by the way, is still a virgin…if I need to remind you."

She didn't need to part her legs for him to see her panties. They were completely uncovered. She did anyway, pulling at the silky turquoise to show her soft lips and let him see how divinely pink and moist they were. The head moved a little, though she had no idea what it was trying to say.

"I don't understand, Bret. Are you disappointed because I had to use a little gloss instead of a man to make me wet. Or does that mean you're sorry, that you'd like this, right here, right now?"

Another set of rapid blinks.

"Does that mean we can start over and put all this behind us?" More blinks, and either a nod or a twitch. "Good, I'll take that as a yes, and these are the rules: No more sucking up to mommy, no more excessive drinking, no more outings with your buddy Shane, no more dancers and we'll take another honeymoon when you're able to be a man and before you begin working on my business complex." She paused. "And that's something else we'll have to talk about when you're better. As of now I won't be paying monthly fees until you reopen the file. Oh, and I did give some thought to giving the project over to another firm since you and Shane are the only ones in the company with fresh ideas and you won't be active again until January at the earliest. And, forget your pig-friend."

The blinking was rapid, the red-streaked eyes glaring whiter, his free hand waving to and fro, the thin intravenous tube keeping him hydrated with fluids resisting the erratic movement. She ignored the plea.

"Don't worry about your daddy, changing firms was a passing thought, and don't get too accustomed to being coddled by mommy, Bret. I expect you at the house by the end of January and I suppose you realize you've screwed Christmas for us as well." She stopped talking, crossing one boot over the other, rubbing an open hand slowly along one smooth leg, then the other. "So I'll be spending my usual time in the country, at the spa, if I haven't waited too long to reserve. I can't see myself spending Christmas and New Years with your parents." She chortled. "I'd rather trade places with you."

His hand moved again, this time more slowly.

"I suppose you're right." Christine couldn't resist laughing. "Maybe she should trade places with you. That would be a better idea. By the way, your driver's permit's suspended for six months, which isn't a big deal. The problem is only I drive the Cayman, so I guess we'll be taking taxis for a while until you can bend your legs again." She slid from the bed, bunching the short skirt and her panties at her hips, pausing a moment while facing away from him before adjusting both and depriving him of all but the memory. "Do you realize you never told me you love me during the honeymoon, Bret? Why do you suppose? Anyway, what's done is done and I have to speak with the doctor for a few minutes so he and the staff understand I'm not your mother and she's not your wife. You should try to rest. Did you see how drop-dead gorgeous the guy is, and single? I'll say goodnight when I come for my coat, if you're awake. And why are these hospitals always so damned cold?" She put a hand ever so gently on his leg, barely touching the top sheet. "I read somewhere that true lovemaking is in the mind, and sex is merely a function of our genitalia." She belted her blouse after pressing a hand against where she was certain the throbbing must be adding to his discomfort. "My God, Bret, I'll have a nurse come and take care of that, you poor man. You must really be anxious for the honeymoon."

When she came into the room some time later she saw a white and bandaged semblance of a man, not certain whether he saw her or not. She threw the tapered suede coat over her shoulders, sliding in both arms, then she pulled at the faux-fur Cossack hat she'd been wearing and tugged on her matching fur-trimmed gloves, all the while staring at him.

"It's not over, Bret. It begins again when you're better able to cope with me."

# 158

The timing wasn't right, common sense and practicality aside. She wouldn't be ready for several weeks, yet she hadn't been able to get the young woman out of her mind. There was no doubt she was beautiful, which was a plus. She'd be perfect for what Christine had in mind, but not with everything else going on and she hated herself for even contemplating what she would do next.

Two weeks somewhere was a good idea, though not the spa. And why shouldn't she? Escaping would do more for her than running the Porsche into the red zone along the meandering A-10 leading her through the dark quiet of l'Estrie and into the Cantons de l'Est. And what would she do except turn around, and what would she have proven? As fast as she drove, the dilemma remained in the car with her. If she had learned anything in life, she'd learned cynicism and maybe Selena wouldn't be interested. So why should she worry about someone she didn't know, or get herself killed. She skidded to a halt on the shoulder, did a U-turn, went to her condo instead of the house, got very drunk and told herself she didn't give a shit.

# 159

That was then. The next morning, repenting on bended knee and wide-eyed regret into the white ceramic bowl, she thought differently, unable to block out the resonance of her retching or the unpleasant gastric smell. She even thought of God once or twice, stopping short of asking for the forgiveness she knew she didn't deserve. She needed forgiveness more from the ladies' room attendant for what she'd been thinking as a result of her pent-up anger. And she hoped Bret's penis had snapped in half at some point after she'd gone as he thought of how her virgin folds glistened when she pulled her panties away from what she had made particularly perfect for him.

He didn't matter, she did. All men could go to hell, she thought, swallowing the bitter pills with orange juice. Take away their little penises and what were they? They were all useless androids genetically engineered to burp and fart at will. To hell with all of them, especially the arrogant shithead who answered the hotel phone.

Christine slowly began feeling human again at 12:00, human enough to hate and forgive herself. By 1:00 she showered and made herself reasonably presentable, which to most others meant to-die-for. By 1:30 she left to go shopping at one of the city's finest stores for women. One-stop shopping for those with a sense of the best and if any one deserved, she did.

She arrived home by 4:00 and by 6:00 she was luxuriating with a single glass of wine in a warm bath. She redid her make-up to complement her outfit and by 7:00 she left for an exquisite supper, feeling as good about herself as she could expect: a probable side effect of the wine. When the white-gloved waiter came to her with a pitcher of water, she refused. Water wouldn't be part of her menu. She ordered a bottle of the most expensive Bordeaux and a premium vodka, hoping she wouldn't finish the Bordeaux on her own, and driving wasn't an issue because she had come by taxi. The issue was her hangover and she swore never again.

She ordered the entrée, not the main course or dessert. She ordered for two, telling the waiter she wasn't entirely certain whether she'd be joined and that he might want to wait until she returned from the ladies' room before serving. Then she took care of the vodka with three hurried sips as the wine arrived moments later, leaving the man with no idea how to react when she covered her crystal glass with her hand. However he was a sommelier in a very exclusive hotel restaurant and, as she stood, he pulled away her chair and watched as she took the bottle of wine, two glasses and walked away from the table.

At first Selena thought nothing of the crazy rich lady, until the woman put the bottle and glasses on the counter and called her by name, speaking to her in a language she hadn't heard at work in weeks.

"Selena, I promised you we would see each other again. I couldn't wait, although I know the timing isn't quite right."

Selena stood, frozen, dumbfounded. She saw so many women each day and they were all rude to her, or ignored her. Why would this one come to her, saying she couldn't wait, and then: "¡Ay! señora la novia, es usted, ¿no?"

"Sí, Selena, es así." Christine replied. "How have you been since I last saw you?"

"It is so nice to see you again, señora. I remember you. I remember how beautiful you were and how you talked to me like we were friends."

"I talked with you, Selena. Don't ever forget the difference. I talked with you, not to you, and I haven't forgotten you. I have thought about you often since we first met."

"But, why, señora? ¿Por qué? I am nothing to you."

Christine poured wine into the crystal goblets. "We don't yet know that, Selena. More importantly, I'm willing to take a chance on you, if you're willing to take a bigger chance on me." She handed Selena a glass. "I believe you will be perfect for my business, if what you said to me is true, that you were trained as an administrator."

"No comprendo, señora, de ninguna manera." Selena looked at the glass as though she'd never seen wine.

"I know, and it's bizarre that we're speaking of your future in a public bathroom. The truth is, the last time, when I left you here, I waited for a long time outside the door, Selena. I knew I would see you again. I just didn't know when until today, and I'm certain I wasn't wrong to come back."

"For what reason? I do not understand what you are saying, señora."

"Do you remember when I cried? Do you remember how you held me, how you told me all would be well, that I was being a nervous bride, and how you helped me with my garter?"

"Sí, claro. I do. I also cried after you left because you were so beautiful and I was certain you would never come back the way that you said, that you were being kind to me."

"You were wrong, Selena. I was not being kind to you. You were being kind to me." She paused, sipping her wine. "Here's the thing: I'm a very demanding woman, I need help, and I want you to work with me as my Executive Assistant, starting this very moment." Christine raised her glass again, feeling better than she had in a month.

"¿Cómo? Eso no es posible, señora…"

"Christine, o Cristina, Selena. Pero nunca señora, ¿comprendes?"

And Selena wasn't certain that she did understand. Cristina was so beautiful, even though she seemed more tired than a bride should be, Selena thought. What could she possibly have to offer such a woman?

For Christine the proposal was simple and not complicated at all. What did Selena have to lose? She was being offered a full-time position as her private Executive Assistant, she explained. All she required was for Selena de la Vega to sign the employment contract before receiving her first cheque, a very tangible ten thousand dollars that would be a two-month advance on her salary. Otherwise the cheque would be cancelled.

"Did I forget to mention, Selena," Christine said in French, "that dinner is waiting for us?"

Selena's wine spilled over onto the floor, splashing up on both women. She was barely able to put the glass on the counter before exploding into tears and, this time, Christine was the one to hug Selena until the crying stopped and she felt Selena's arms tighten around her.

"Muchísimas gracias, señora. Merci."

"No more señora, Selena. Now do you think you can sign this thing so we can eat something? You have no idea how hungry I am. I haven't been myself lately, though suddenly I do feel much better." She filled Selena's glass. "A toast...to us."

"Cristina, no puedo." Selena examined herself, shaking her head. "No tengo nada que ponerme para el restaurante. No es posible. Mi jefe, y toda la gente allí..."

"We have a lot to talk about, Selena, and you don't work here anymore. You work with me, so don't worry about your boss and those ladies in the restaurant aren't going to recognize you."

She put the oversized bag she had brought in with her into Selena's hand, pushing the young Venezuelan gently toward one of the private stalls before Selena could react.

Then she leaned against the counter, sipping her wine, elated by string of happy Spanish exclamations before leaving Selena to her contortions. She advised the curious waiter to serve the first course for two, and that a second bottle of wine would be required with fresh glasses.

She had thought of everything from the barrette and make-up to her purse and shoes, including lingerie and a slim silver bracelet watch. Christine paused from shock when she walked back into the ladies' room, stumbling. She'd been right: no one in the restaurant or management would recognize her. Selena was stunningly beautiful, despite the fresh mascara beginning to run, and Christine found herself staring as the excited and blurring Latina eyes implored her silently for help to put on her lip gloss.

The sleeveless cashmere turtle neck dress came to a hand above her knees, clinging to every curve and centimetre of her body without a single ripple. The low-heeled pumps completed the classic look. Selena had freed her hair from its tight knot, which was as thick and lustrous as Christine's when she was home alone, which Christine would later discover she preferred wearing untied. Not then, and she asked Cristina to help her once more with the barrette a little off to the side.

What Selena thought was the final touch was the ivory white ruffled placket cardigan that matched the dress and the deep-blue leather Carolina Herrera purse to match her shoes. Not so, neither was the cheque Christine slipped into her purse before walking out arm in arm like trendy sisters and leaving the bag filled with a neatly folded black and white uniform and thick-heeled black shoes. Her underwear and stockings had gone in the garbage with a half-full bottle of wine and empty change purse.

No one did recognize her, though they all stopped to gaze at the two women walking into the dining room with natural and enviable poise, the hotel staff included.

# 160

Selena hadn't eaten such an elaborate meal in over a year and even though Christine expected as much, she was all the same surprised at how graceful, well-spoken and conversant Selena was. The evening was for girl-talk, not business, and the next day would a girls' day with no work for Christine, no toilets for Selena, and by the end of the evening they were laughing and acting as though they had known each other for years. Though when the time came to leave Christine made very clear to Selena what would and would not happen. She would not go back to her one-room apartment on The Main, le boulevard Saint-Laurent: the worst roach-infested and crime ravaged collection of low-rent housing and strip bars in the city, not to mention the hookers, pimps, bad cops and drug addicts. She would spend the night at the condo, no buts, and the next day they would return to the hotel to officially leave her job and then to her apartment to cancel her lease and remove her personal effects. After lunch, they could do whatever Selena wanted, or nothing. Everything else would come in due time.

Selena took Cristina's hand from across the table, squeezing as she told Christine she would never come back to the hotel if she wasn't living a cruel dream.

"You're not in a cruel dream. I'm real, Selena. This is true, and I am real. Selena you must have the greatest confidence in me. Very soon you will once again be the woman you deserve to be. First, we must work very hard." She paused, squeezing Selena's other hand. "And we can succeed."

Selena nodded, smiling, saying she would be a few moments. Christine shook her head so wildly she heard a warbling sound from within. She had no intention of missing the show. If Selena was going to resign to the hotel manager who had noticed her several times during the evening without seeing her, Christine would witness the event. Better yet, he would come to them.

They both giggled, waiting for the waiter to bring the check before asking to speak with the manager, who at first thought he was the victim of a joke. No joke. Selena pulled the familiar elasticized key band from her designer purse and stood to clear out her locker while Christine paid with cash and went to the coat check, letting him know by her expression that not thinking to help either woman with her chair was an inexcusable discourtesy.

Christine was standing with ticket stubs in her hand when Selena returned holding her clutch without wondering what the man must be thinking. She had discarded everything. She would not leave the hotel covered in an ugly forty-dollar winter coat and everything else had fit into her purse. She would suffer the chill, and besides, a taxi was always stationed under the heated awning at the hotel entrance and after everything that had happened to her in so few hours, she could not be any more numbed by the cold.

Christine put her purse on the counter, taking a moment to put on her coat and hat as Selena scanned the lobby. She was probably thinking good riddance, Christine thought, not wanting to rush the young woman's private moment, though she finally cleared her throat, wanting to break Selena's daze.

When Selena finally turned, she saw the most luxurious and coziest cashmere ensemble of cape, scarf, gloves and hat she had ever seen.

# 161

Selena had no idea to what extent her life had changed that October evening, the last day of October and the last day of a desperate life she had determined would not go on forever. She was living the first day of a new life she had dreamt of each night, the life she deserved, a life she could not even imagine as she drove along Montreal streets she had never seen. She was awestruck by the buildings she had never seen up close and the people who were all as well-dressed as she and Cristina, probably many of the same people whose loose change she had so often counted at the end of each long day.

Nor did she notice how her hand had gravitated towards Cristina's, or how hard she'd been squeezing until Cristina fumbled in her purse with her free hand and leaned over to wipe Selena's eyes. She had nothing to take with her into Cristina's home, nothing to offer her new friend and she glanced at the lady beside her who was looking straight ahead, not caring that her hand was being held so tightly. She was too elated to understand everything about to happen to her, including what she would be doing for Cristina, choking on the only simple words she could think to say: "Gracias, Cristina."

Then she spent the few remaining moments peering from her window until the doorman bowed to Cristina as she climbed out, after she discreetly making certain Selena would stay in the car until he had opened her side of the taxi for her. And the high-speed ride to the eighteenth floor was as exciting as the taxi ride, for a different reason. She was about to see how Cristina lived with her husband.

"No, Selena. This is my retreat, my refuge and my office, at least for a while. Now it is your home, and your office, until we can find you a more suitable home and the complex is completed. You can stay here as long as you want until then. I told my husband I would continue working here until the lease expires," she paused, "and as a place to be alone. Now, I no longer need it to be alone."

"This will always be your refuge, Cristina, and your office. We will work together and I will make you proud of me."

"I already am. This is our floor, and this is your key. Open your door."

# 162

Every square metre of the luxury two-bedroom condo exuded the successful, modern woman with a designer décor in muted tones balanced to produce calm and relaxation. The several murals on the walls were inoffensive soft abstracts or shadowed images of the female nude. The bedroom and living room furniture was Scandinavian, covered in soft colours and fabrics, the kitchen opened onto the dining room, the bathroom was cream-coloured marble with colour-keyed ceramic fixtures and Christine had converted the second bedroom into a fully functional office where not even a paperclip was out of place. She had central security, an intercom connected to the plasma screen and phone in the living room, an outdoor balcony which was completely inaccessible and a spectacular night-time view of the city.

After Christine walked Selena around her new home she poured some wine and poured a bath as Selena continued walking around in a daze until Christine called her name. She followed the sound of rushing water to the bathroom lighted with candles around a steaming bath scented with oils and filled with a mountain of fluffy clouds.

The fleecy-soft pyjamas and socks on the ledge were brand new. The music was easy-listening Latin and a thick fleecy robe hung from a stainless steel wall hook that she saw as Christine closed the door behind her, waving a finger and admonishing Selena not to fall asleep in the tub, which would be very hard to explain to the authorities. She was to take as long as she wanted. She was at home, and Selena soon came out wrapped from head to toe in fleece, the towel on her head fashioned into a tight turban. She hadn't wanted to use the hairdryer that wasn't hers, and Christine slipped into Spanish as she finished tucking sheets into the futon she would sleep on, reminding Selena she was at home. She could use whatever she wanted, which included a good night's sleep.

Selena didn't want to sleep. Why would she want to wake up from yet another dream to find herself on the same crowded bus, in the same horrible clothes, spending her day either listening to washroom noises or trying to speak French to herself into a mirror? She hadn't completely understood what Cristina had said to her, watching Cristina prepare the futon while dressed in pyjamas and socks, assuming her saviour had called her husband while she'd been in the bath. She hoped she wasn't living a beautiful dream that would become another terrible awakening. She hoped.

When she finished Christine took Selena into her bedroom where she pulled off the turban, sat her at the vanity and spent the next half-hour drying, combing and stroking her hair. When she finished, she was amazed at the fullness and lustrousness of Selena's hair, even more surprised when Selena plopped her in front of the mirror and began pulling apart her tight French braid and combing out her twisted hair. She had nothing else to offer and would not disappoint her angel. She would make her proud, starting the very next day.

Christine could imagine why Selena cried as her hair was being combed and stroked, whereas Selena had no idea at all why Cristina was fighting so hard not to cry. When she finished they both stared into the larger free-standing wardrobe mirror, openly shocked. They could truly have been sisters, in flannel pyjamas and socks and they ran from the room laughing to curl up on the futon and talk. Christine listened to her story, spellbound.

Cristina was easy to talk with. So much time had gone by since she had spoken with anyone. Selena was twenty-two, her birthday was the day before Christmas and she had no family. She was a Spanish citizen and had moved to Venezuela with her father and mother when she was a little girl, for his work that he couldn't find at home. They were killed in a car accident a few years earlier, and she decided to come to Canada to get away from what was worse than working in a public toilet.

Before they married he'd been handsome and gallant, and for a while after they married she thought nothing could go wrong. Life was good. They weren't rich, and never would be, which didn't matter as long as they loved each other. Then he lost his job at the plant and the only work he could find at the beginning was menial. He began drinking to where even menial work was impossible for him to find and he began beating her. The first time was when the savings ran out, then he began taking her paycheque from her to buy liquor before groceries or before paying the rent and he would hit her if she said anything about it. Normally he'd just smack her face, or shove her, then he grew worse and began pushing her against walls and into furniture, using his fist where the bruises wouldn't show when she went to her job at the plant where they had once worked together.

The last time was the previous year's Christmas morning. He hadn't bought her a birthday gift and she knew not to expect anything for Christmas, though she had bought him a very little gift so that he would have something to open, something to make him happy, and the bruising had taken months to fade. Coming to Canada was easy. The difficult part was living from day to day, though she never complained, not even to herself, because she knew an angel would soon come to her and one day she would be happy again. And her angel did come to her.

"You're my angel, Cristina. I knew you would come to me."

"Selena, what you see isn't the face of an angel. Does he

know where you are?"

"No, I changed my passport and used my maiden name. He has no idea." She sipped the wine she hadn't touched. "I hope he doesn't."

"It doesn't matter whether he does or not, Selena." The crinkled brow asked the question. "It does not matter, believe me. You're safe here, and you will be safe anywhere you go. He won't find you. All men are cowards, Selena, when their final moment comes, particularly those who attack defenceless women. You're safe here, believe what I say."

Selena put her glass down and wrapped her arms tightly around Cristina's neck, enjoying the warmth of her angel's warm hands pressing into her back until she was eased away and led by the hand into her bedroom where she was tucked in under the luxurious duvet. Eight hours had passed since Christine first walked into the hotel and the agenda for the coming day would have to necessarily begin a little later than originally planned. The day had been long and she felt good for having gone through with her plan for Selena, but she was tired. She pulled the blanket up over her shoulders and fell into a deep sleep.

Selena lay awake, too excited to sleep. She wanted to talk about her job, talk with her angel, Cristina, and hear about Cristina's husband. Finally having a friend to speak with and be a girl with was so exciting and wonderful. She knew exactly what she would do as soon as Cristina said they could leave. She would buy a wardrobe and something nice for Cristina, then they would go for lunch and she would listen to everything all over again.

She didn't want to see her old apartment, though she would, after she went to the bank so she could pay the old, rude man in cash for what was left of the two-year lease she had signed. Then she realized she had no clean underwear for the morning, or stockings, so she climbed from her bed and tiptoed into the bathroom to wash out the silk panties and nylons Cristina had bought her.

The apartment was warm, and she was warm. Putting on the robe just made her feel good. The panorama had changed and the Montreal skyline was dark with vague silhouettes of buildings illuminated by a clear sky. She went to the futon and knelt beside Cristina whose breathing was barely audible. She looked peaceful and beautiful with her hands pressed together under her cheek, Selena thought, and so tired. Then she leaned closer, seeing the sparkle of tiny droplets that hadn't dried in the corners of Cristina's eyes, feeling her heart constrict from the deep sadness emanating from her angel.

She wondered where Cristina was as she lay there, and with whom. She hadn't spoken of her husband and Selena wondered if all men were as bad as the one she had fled. She laid her head on the futon beside the pillow, gently placing a warm hand over Cristina's arm, trying not to move, feeling the warm wetness of another teardrop trickle onto her hand, not understanding any of Cristina's whispered words.

# 163

Selena didn't tell Cristina she had cried in her sleep, or that she had spoken so softly in French that Selena hadn't understood a word of what she had said, or to whom. When she woke she saw Selena kneeling beside her, with wide eyes, and she asked groggily how long her Executive Assistant had been staring at her. The answer was: a little while, and Selena leaned over and kissed her boss' cheek. She wanted to talk. She wanted to tell Cristina over and over again the night before hadn't been a dream, unless she was sleeping in and that as her Executive Assistant she had organized their first day together. And when Cristina asked exactly when she had done all this, the answer was: all night, as she lay awake in bed.

At eight o'clock Christine had no chance of rolling over and covering her head with the pillow. Selena had made her sit up and listen to the plans, not realizing they were having their first business meeting in pyjamas and socks. She stopped when Christine put her hand over Selena's mouth, pushing her backwards onto the futon, asking if she would always talk as much and telling her she had to pee. So could the Executive Assistant please assist with a coffee?

The coffee was ready when Christine came back, showered, and into a barrage of questions: Did she take sugar? No. Did she take milk? Yes. Did she like her toast dark or light? Light. Did she always wear flannel pyjamas? Never, unless she was sick. She preferred silk and satin, and she would the next time she was invited to stay over. Did she eat lunch? Of course, she did. Did she have a favourite restaurant? Yes. Could they go shopping together, first, before they were boss and assistant? No. They would go as friends and they would always go shopping as friends. She didn't believe in the boss thing. Could they go to the bank first so she could pay the dirty old man for the next year? Say what!

The tone of the conversation changed in a split second, Christine metamorphosing from friend to businesswoman, not realizing Selena was taken aback, afraid Cristina would think such a stupid woman could never work for her. There was no way the old fart in an area infamous for one-hour sluts and drive-up BJs would get a single dime and she told Selena in a firm voice to get ready. They were going out, and not to the bank. Breakfast could wait and, she admonished, Selena did not need to wash out her undies. What lady wouldn't buy two of any style?

The mission was one small adjustment to Selena's agenda, and far from a pleasant intrusion into the day of the man who had insisted that Selena sign a two-year lease for the sparsely furnished and dank flat decorated with paper posters on the wall and perfumed with smells from the Greek and Chinese restaurants under the apartment. He wanted to settle for three, then two, then one month, after all he had done for her, and then Christine leaned into his foul breath so that Selena would not hear. A minute later he produced the original lease, cancelled, as Selena went about gathering her school books, one small jewellery box, and a photo album of her parents.

As they drove away she asked Cristina how the man had agreed so quickly, a sly grin crossing Christine's lips in response and Girls' Day was on.

# 164

By the end of November Selena had unquestionably earned the first half of the ten grand, proving to Cristina she could do the job. Her winter wardrobe was complete, she loved working with her boss who travelled with her for two of the four weeks, seeing the country for the first time in one year, and she loved how Cristina never removed the pink gold friendship ring that was her first purchase with her newfound affluence.

When Christine told her that she'd be gone for another week without her, she listened intently and took notes, and when Christine returned everything had been done, including many new clients. She was becoming more valuable than a polished and precisely cut gem. The more they worked together the more Christine realized how impossible the task of continuing her demanding schedule would be without help and Selena filled the void. She had embraced the concept and parameters of the business as though fulfilling her own dream and, by the end of the month, Christine had shown her appreciation by adding Marketing Manager to Selena's responsibilities, though the salary increase would have to wait a little while longer.

They knew virtually everything about each other, to the extent each one wanted to confess her life. Selena heard about the club, the beating, Bret's convalescence at the Wilmingtons and how Cristina was so disgusted with him she had decided to spend a month away from him. Selena had quietly reached across the restaurant table to hold her hand, remembering how her friend had cried the first night.

Selena Consuelo de Vega would spend about four months, starting in January, interviewing potential employees of the highest calibre and when she wasn't doing that she would develop promotional programmes. They would meet weekly at the condo when their schedules allowed, on evenings convenient to Selena, until the complex was ready to occupy.

Selena would be alone for most of December and Christine would be free to focus on herself and the husband she had ignored for the better part of a month. She had never intended to book two weeks at the spa, though wouldn't tell him differently. She needed time alone at home to rest, not that she was accustomed to making excuses.

# 165

The hospital stay lasted four weeks and three days due to a clerical error requiring them to extend his stay by another weekend before Bret was transferred to the Wilmingtons, an ordeal no one enjoyed, especially Bret who believed wincing and groaning with every movement would make him feel better. Suzanne winced in concert with him as Frederick issued instructions to the ambulance technicians to be more careful, Christine looking on secretly grateful Suzanne was interceding, unwittingly giving her at least two months grace before he would be at home to begin his therapy.

His bandages had been removed midway through his stay in the hospital and the wire from his jaw a few days before his release. He was gaunt from a starvation diet of intravenous and straw-fed fluids, his sunken eyes had a ghoulish black-blue tinge against his skin that was whiter than she would have thought possible. His arm would be in a cast until the end of December, his legs until the end of January, and rehabilitation would depend on how well his knees would mend over the next couple of months. The short-term would not be pleasant. The inflicted damage was much worse than originally believed. The doctors couldn't imagine what type of person could do such a horrific thing to another human being, though the police could. The question was: Why?

Bret had been unable to speak with them and Christine was constantly unavailable to them, reminding Suzanne several times by phone she would never speak to them about his drunken outing. Though she hadn't known the police file remained active and the detectives in charge of the case required of the hospital that they be advised of Bret's release date and condition.

The last Monday of November they arrived at the Wilmingtons an hour after Bret had been set up in his room, as Christine was preparing to leave. They didn't stay long. Bret didn't remember where he and Shane went the night of the beating, saying they'd been bar hopping and went their separate ways later in the evening. Shane had given them the same information weeks earlier.

All Christine said was that she was disgusted with both of them and if he'd been at home the carjacking would not have happened. As far as she was concerned the case was closed. With absolutely no information to proceed with the detectives agreed with her. The case was closed and she told him not to expect her to visit every day. Instead she would call frequently for progress reports and visit when she could, neither parent showing disappointment when hearing the daughter-in-law would not join them over Christmas and New Year's. There could never be two Mrs. Wilmingtons under the same roof for longer than a rushed meal.

# 166

Pilar would not hear of Christmas without Maria, especially this Christmas, and she ranted on in Spanish for most of the day. They hadn't seen her for over a month, even if the spa was the reason. She wanted Maria in Mexico with Ercilia, Madeleine and Señor El Rio. They had spent weeks planning his surprise. Madeleine promised Señor El Rio would be with them, but wouldn't tell him until the last minute because he was planning a special Christmas for them at the farm.

Pilar's parents and Ercilia's were so thankful to Jean-Émile for reuniting them with the girls they had gotten together to plan a Christmas for all of them in Mexico. They wanted to see their daughters and their daughters' special friends, especially Maria, or cariño, the same cariño who wanted to stay home and sleep while they were all having a special Christmas which they would all swear an oath not to tell her about.

Pilar had advised Madeleine the three girls would travel a week earlier and return a week later to get better fares, but that she and Señor El Rio could come in the private jet at their leisure. Madeleine had thought the idea was wonderful. However everyone would arrive together. The old fool had nothing else to spend his money on and if he thought for a moment the girls had deprived him of any opportunity to be a grumpy step-father he would be deeply hurt. So they were flying together in the corporate jet, everyone except cariño who wanted to stay home and sleep and disappoint Señor El Rio who would miss her very much and be hurt.

Maria was adamant. She would not go for Christmas. However she would try very hard to join them for New Years. The feeble commitment wasn't good enough until Maria walked to the phone, called the airline, booked her flights for December thirtieth and January second, and promised Jean-Émile would not be hurt. He would understand her need to stay home and she walked out leaving Ercilia between a rock and a hard place, dealing with their first argument as Maria sat in the car staring at her phone for long moments before she dialled. Pilar answered in English. Maria was sorry and she adored Pilar. Pilar was sorrier and she adored Maria more. One little argument wasn't so bad for two lesbians, they agreed, neither one feeling any better when the line went dead after the sound of sad kisses.

Jean-Émile would understand, Maria told her, though Pilar would not for many years to come.

# 167

Maria went home that evening and all was well. Ercilia possessed an effusive energy which disallowed poutiness and soon Pilar and Maria were laughing and hugging. New Year's would be acceptable and she promised to call them. Not to say Señor El Rio wouldn't be disappointed, because Pilar always had the last word.

She spent the week working at home as Pilar and Ercilia were at school during the day to earn accreditation as physiotherapists and at night for the languages they were beginning to master. They'd been working very hard over the past several months. They deserved to spend time with their families and Maria knew they felt as much pressure as she did to succeed. Addisons was important to all of them and when they spoke about the spa they each knew they were speaking about the girl each of them missed so much.

She was instructed to stay away from her father's home. She knew the schedule and would either be on-site or not. She was one of three people who knew Chad Rivers had less than a week to enjoy what was left of his miserable life and Phallicia Hunter became increasingly confident during the first three days of the week. She could do it, and she would. What she wondered about was whether Addison's Maria would be protected by a blonde wig and blue contact lenses, or had that Maria changed imperceptibly over the past twenty months to where she was one with Phallicia, inseparable. Or did it matter? What did matter was that each one would pay for what they did to Addison. Each one would die knowing the fear she knew as they splayed her legs like a cheap whore on the table and didn't stop hurting her.

Each day Phallicia came out and each night she went away, then came the thirteenth. She had expected the phone to ring. It didn't. Marcus was in Vancouver and she was not to contact him unless she was in danger. Angelo told her during their last evening that he loved her, Marcus told her by spending the rest of the evening pretending to rub the huge hand that had smacked her bum.

# 168

The direct flight lifted off sixty minutes late due to a slow-moving squall and the mandatory wintertime de-icing process. The flight would arrive in Vancouver at 11:40 AM local time. Phallicia Hunter had come to life and was sitting in Executive Class, lost in calm reverie, thinking of everyone and everything, of no one and nothing. She didn't know what to think. The passengers around her were reading, typing, sleeping and drinking too early in the day because they could and not one of them had the slightest inclination she would be a remorseless witness to a coward's death in three days. Rivers wouldn't die on the Saturday. He'd die on the Sunday exactly as planned, after whimpering in front of her and begging for his life when she'd laugh at him the way he must have laughed when he was violating and killing the most important person in her life.

She tried sleeping, but couldn't. She ordered her first drink instead, drinking it neat. The second helped her a bit more and the third brought on the desired effect, not thinking she would wake up feeling confused and not because of the screeching sound of rubber on concrete. The jet landed in Vancouver an hour late. She landed in her dreams of the past twenty months and was the last one to disembark. Her bags were on the floor of the Jetway, florescent tags pinching together the thin canvas handles and no one was at the gate to greet her.

She checked into the Hilton for her four-day stay and spent the rest of the day taking a tour. She ate dinner at the hotel, waiting in her room the next day for the disposable cell to ring. When the phone did ring at 4:00 PM the flip top was open in her palm and she listened intently, saying not a single word before the line went dead.

The familiar voice sounded foreign to her. His instructions were concise and specific. She was to arrive at Rivers' apartment at precisely 10:00 AM the next morning. She would wear a hat, she would not look up at any time after leaving the cab, she would wear silicone gloves under her regular gloves and she would phone him once before ringing #802 as a confirmation he wouldn't be opening the door to anyone else.

The rainy weather was a welcome aid, her wide-brimmed vinyl hat more appropriate than the soaked cotton hoods and newspapers everyone else was wearing. Her vinyl jacket felt horrible, but they told her to dress the way everyone else did in the neighbourhood. The area wasn't poor, although far from silk, satin and fur and no one paid attention to her shapeless sweater, her no-name jeans or the vinyl shoes that pinched her toes and made her feet sweat. She was there to kill Rivers, not stand out and be noticed. He wouldn't care if she were naked, she was told. He would be killed and they would leave. Understood?

# 169

The taxi came to a stop in front of the aging ten-story brown-brick building moments before 10:00 and she forced herself not to think about the hours ahead because Phallicia didn't care and Maria wasn't there. The weather had worsened since she flagged the taxi a few blocks from the hotel and possible hail was in the forecast. So she wouldn't spoil his weekend completely.

She did as instructed, snapping her phone closed as she rang the buzzer with her head lowered. She took the empty elevator to the eighth floor and went to the open door of apartment 802 where he was sitting with his hands between the thick padding of his purple après-ski outfit, saying nothing. Marcus hadn't removed his coat and was slouched on the one other chair in the single room, holding a very big gun. She knew not to use his name, though she had never seen him with a gun in his hands and her first thought was not to do anything that would harm Markie. She had wondered for the past twenty months how this moment would play out and seeing Rivers sitting meekly told her she wouldn't be disappointed.

"Good morning, Chad. I can call you Chad, can't I? I feel as though I know everything about you. And, you know what? I do." He said nothing. "My name's Phallicia Hunter. I've waited a long time and I've come a long way to kill you, Chad. Very apropos don't you think? Hunter explains how I've hunted you for close to two years, the way you stalked her. Phallicia explains the phallus, the man, the thing I've come to kill: you." She spoke to Marcus who was more interested in his gun. "Have you guys been here long? Have you spoken with each other?"

"Six hours. No," Marcus answered.

"We're talking now, Chad, for the next twenty-four

hours. Do you want to know why?"

"This is about her, isn't it? The girl in Mexico…Addison?"

"Very good, you remember her name, kudos. Do you remember anything else about her, apart from fucking her?"

"I knew you were coming." He looked at Marcus. "Not you. You weren't the one, but I knew someone was coming, the man in the church, the way he watched me and Thurston without blinking. He made me afraid, and I told them. I told them why he was there and they didn't believe me. I knew you were coming, that you knew who we were and what we did. Actually, I'm happy it's over. I'm surprised you waited this long."

Phallicia walked toward Marcus, sitting on the arm of his chair. "You'll care, Chad. By tomorrow you'll care. You're not dying today. You're dying tomorrow, in the morning. In the meantime we'll get you ready and talk about what's going to happen, which is, in short, payback for robbing me of life."

Then she ignored him and stepped onto the balcony to see the dull grey vista of rooftops and wet city streets, stepping in disappointed and leaving the patio doors open. The plan required revision. More than likely people would be standing on the balconies of the two top floors at some point before dark, even in December, and his body would be clearly visible. Marcus wasn't surprised when she asked him in Italian. He was pleased she was thinking rationally. He didn't care one way or the other and went to the thermostat, adjusting the dial from AUTO to OFF while Phallicia went to stand in front of Rivers.

"Get out of the chair, Chad, and strip."

His hands were still between his knees where the man with the gun had told him to put them. "What?"

"Stand up and take off your clothes…everything." He had no doubt she was serious, staying as he was to rationalize what she had said, not intending to upset or disobey her. "Strip, Chad, right now, right here. When Addison was found the next morning she was stripped naked, wide open for everyone to see, and dead. So strip or I'll cut off your balls with a fucking carving knife and shove them into your fucking mouth after I get my friend here to strip you."

She sat in his chair to watch the show, telling him when he was moving too slowly. When he finished she told him to put away all his clothes and unpack the suitcase by the door. When he finished she told him to stand in the middle of the room and not talk until spoken to, which was eight hours later when she finished listening to the relentless tapping on the window pane. She seemed distant, expressionless, and Marcus began thinking that what was coming wasn't good. She quickly glanced his way, then at the window stained with water droplets. Still, she could see the hundreds of tiny white projectiles bouncing off the glass and went to the door to step out.

When she came in she leaned against the doorframe. "It's dark. The balcony's covered with white. No one's coming out in this weather." She paused, speaking to Marcus, looking at Rivers. "They left her out in a storm to die. All night they left her out in the cold with no one to help her. Now no one's out there to help him."

The grim man stroked the suppressor attached to his weapon pensively. He stood and went to the doors, holstering the gun, telling her to get a belt and washcloth. Then he went to Rivers who closed his eyes, terrified, feeling his mouth stuffed with the soapy rag and his hands tied behind his back before his body jerked from the floor by his neck and danced along the floor to the outside. He grunted once, dropped onto the balcony face-up. An hour later he was dragged inside by his feet, after his visitors packed away a pizza carton, an empty bottle of wine and the thermostat once again went to OFF.

His body was shaking. His hair and skin were coated, his eyes were glazed, his ears were white and his lips were blue. When she yanked the cloth from his mouth, she was surprised to hear he had to go, being that guys could pull it out anywhere, and she went with him after freeing his wrists from the belt.

She sat on the edge of the tub to watch, asking if he was going to take forever. When he finally did begin urinating she stifled a shriek as his pent-up volume first dribbled out, down his leg, around the rim of the bowl and onto the floor before becoming a sporadic spurt and once again a dribble. She told him that's why girls sit and asked if he wasn't supposed to shake it, or something. He said nothing, barely controlling his trembling.

She told him to wash his hands, and his legs. The girls were right, she thought. Then he stood in the middle of the room and she went to her vinyl purse before going to him with an open hand as her friend moved in beside her.

"Take them, Chad, all six." He stared into the open hand, every bone in his body aching and trembling from the damp cold. "What? Never had a roofie, Chad? Never been fucked with your body loaded with this shit? How many did you give her, Chad? Five...six? We think six, with tequila of course."

He saw the man gesturing with the gun. "I wasn't the one who killed her. I wanted to take her to my room, to a hallway or something. I didn't because the others told me she was okay, that she'd wake up and leave when she was ready."

"She wasn't okay. She was dead. Take them, Chad, all of them, with the tequila or, I swear, he'll bash in every one of your fucking teeth with that thing before I force feed you."

"I'm sorry for everything. I only wanted to meet her, to

spend some time with her. I was never very good at meeting women and she was so beautiful."

"She was beautiful, Chad, inside and out. She was beautiful and fun and radiant and she was my entire life," Phallicia paused, forgetting him to think of Addison, "and for all those reasons I'm killing you, starting with these."

"You were one of the girls on the boat, and in the bar. You had red hair."

"Yes."

"You were together?"

"Yes. So take your medicine like a good little rapist-killer." He put one tab in his mouth and she pushed in the neck of the bottle, tilting it so quickly that he coughed out a wide splash along with a broken tooth and the drug. "Pick it up and swallow these with it. And don't stand up." She threw the five others at him and passed the bottle to Marcus before walking to her purse. "What did you do with her panties, Chad? When she was found like some stray dog her panties were missing. What did you do with them?"

"Bret took them. It's his thing, he calls them his trophies."

"Trophies…like some kind of contest? He thinks women's panties are fucking trophies?"

"I'm just saying. It wasn't me. I wanted to spend time with her, to talk with her. Why would I kill her?"

"Talk with her? And what did you say to her when you were fucking her to death, Chad, that you loved her? Did you tell her you loved her when you were pushing this little thing into her? Drink that fucking tequila, right now. And don't be shy. There's more."

"And then what?"

"And then this, Chad." She took a pharmaceutical bottle from its carton, pushing the carton into a pocket. "You sodomized her. She had blood there, and I'm going to sodomize you. Men found her. Did you know that? They covered her and the hotel manager told me later they prayed for her because they all had daughters and they wanted me to understand not all men are bad." She unscrewed the cap, replacing it with the conical tip. "When they find you, they'll see blood too, and a whole lot more. Now, get on all fours and open wide."

He stayed on his knees, frozen. "I never did that, never. I would never have done such a horrible thing to her."

"Three of you did, not even with condoms. Did it feel tight, Chad? Did you like it?"

"I didn't, never. They did it, the others, probably when I went for more beer."

"You went for more beer? You thought you'd chug a few while she was lying there naked, before you fucked her again?" He shook his head. "Listen up, Chad. This little barrel is plastic. The one he's holding is steel, very big, and has a thingy on the end for keeping our evening quiet...I suppose depending what he does with it. Your choice, and put this in your mouth. We can't have the neighbours thinking you're having fun." The dishcloth went into his mouth and he leaned forward, forgetting the cold and the aching. "You're forgetting the open wide part, Chad. Put your head to the floor and spread the cheeks."

Marcus holstered his weapon and kneeled, grabbing a handful of hair with one hand and Rivers' neck with the other as Phallicia took her time inverting the bottle and judging the best distance before guiding the narrow shaft in a swift arc with close to perfect accuracy. His head was pinned to the floor, his eyes bulging and the sound emanating from his stuffed mouth was an ungodly, guttural scream as she squeezed the liquid contents into him.

"Two more on the way, Chad. Three's a good number, don't you think? We have to make sure this stuff works on you before we leave in the morning."

He couldn't move, thinking the bones in his face were

**405**

imploding. He was crying, choking on the wet rag, his legs jerking involuntarily as he did his best to keep them spread wide apart for her as she considered her next best angle of attack. This time her aim was pleasingly imperfect as the bleeding walls of his anus guided the tip inward where it stayed until the bottle emptied and he crumpled.

She let him stay by the door where the parquetry was as cold as the balcony and went for the tequila. Rivers looked up at the man, pleadingly. Marcus answered with a silent shrug, pulling back Rivers' head to pour in several more gulps that were another step towards the eternal damnation he was beginning to think of as eternal peace.

Phallicia stepped to the side, watching him bleeding from between his buttocks and mouth as she unscrewed the third cap and Marcus went to flush the tooth in the toilet. Rivers was ridiculous lying on the floor, his shrivelled penis peeking out from behind a mass of hair that resembled a dirty scouring pad. He was white, his nipples were hard from the cold and his stomach was heaving, not his chest. He had no idea what the time was, though he saw the darkness outside. He felt better than he should, he thought. He wasn't hungry, yet his stomach was gurgling and making loud noises.

He didn't have very many problems in life, not now, and he had gotten used to being naked in front of them. She had stopped laughing at the way it was because of the cold and was hardly paying him any attention. His job was okay, his single debt was a school loan and he had no girlfriend. Perhaps one day he would, if they weren't serious about killing him. They were watching television with their coats on, so they weren't leaving and he didn't know whether that was good or bad. Then he whimpered. She was coming towards him with the bottle, telling him to position himself, and the man was coming with her. That was the worst part and he convulsed, choking and coughing.

"I've been wondering, Chad. How can you fuck someone with that thing? I've never been with a man, neither had Addison, so I'm kind of curious how the process works. Think you can show me." He lay staring at pant legs and shoes. "She was a virgin, Chad. You must have noticed that much. We're you the first, or were Williams or Pendleton, or maybe the Wilmington guy, the panty guy? " She pulled him up. "Drink up, Chad. Your party's not over. You still have seven hours and we have to help the hypothermia along. So you'll have to move for us." She waited a moment. "You'll have to get yourself into the bathroom. Take your time. You can crawl if you feel better on the floor."

He took ten minutes crossing the room, collapsing with every attempt at lifting himself to his knees. The most difficult part was crawling over the side of the tub, and when she told him to stop for the final penetration. The easiest part was falling in face-up before Phallicia yanked the shower curtain around him, pulled the shower lever and turned the green-dotted knob as she told him what goes around, comes around.

Marcus explained how everything would be over by 10:00, making certain she understood what to do as soon as she arrived at her hotel before meeting again with him precisely at noon. She could rest later, or see a movie, whatever she wanted or needed after she met him at noon with the travel bag filled with everything she was wearing, including both pairs of gloves.

They searched Rivers' cell for specific numbers, deleting them, and his computer for any connection to The Wilmingtons and Pendleton such as copies of his résumé, letters of reference, e-mails, or digital images of past vacations that might include certain young women on a boat or around a pool, and his three friends. Then they went through his wallet and personal papers for anything obvious.

The choreography of Rivers' death produced the desired results by nine-thirty, when the gurgling noises slowed to a stop and several bursts of loud air filled the shallow channel between his legs with liquefied feces.

The shower was turned off, the heat remained off and the patio doors remained open. The stench of his feces would soon combine with the decay of his body and the cold of winter and go unnoticed until his planned return to work when a tequila bottle, three enemas covered with his prints and an empty bottle of Rohypnol would be found with no one to attest to his particular tastes.

When they left, Marcus used his own key to lock the door. He had done as instructed and would report that she hadn't killed Rivers. Not long after Phallicia met him with the bag, per his instructions, and wouldn't see him again. She left alone en route to Montreal the next day at 11:10, feeling refreshed after a good night's sleep and a fine meal in her room with Addison.

# 170

Jean-Émile was in his office Tuesday by eight, as he was every morning when he was in town. Madeleine went in with his first coffee by 8:05. Were the girls ready for a week at the farm, he wanted to know and had Madeleine finalized the surprise planned for them? Yes, she replied. However, and regrettably, the girls hadn't expected the invitation and had made other plans. They wouldn't be available to join him as expected, and Madeleine hadn't seen the colour drain from his face as quickly in over a year.

No. They weren't staying with Mr. Bardollini. How could they, she answered, with everything she had read in the papers? They were going home to Mexico to spend Christmas with their parents. They had been ready to book ridiculously expensive flights, until, Madeleine confessed, she insisted they fly travel on the LCL instead, and the lost colour flooded over his face as quickly as it had gone, reminding her that he owned the damned plane, not her.

She ignored him and went on with a condescending smirk. The four of them would travel together. Pilar, Ercilia, her, and he was welcome to join them because the girls' parents were anxious to receive him, though she had no idea why they would want an obnoxious old man in their homes. However, she did know he could hope for no better way to give them their surprise.

When Jean-Émile enquired as to why she had not included Maria, she told him as she reached to answer the phone. A gentleman was at the reception, insisting he personally deliver a package which Monsieur Larivière was expecting, something about a December instalment. Madeleine hadn't begun replacing the receiver before Jean-Émile rushed from his office, instructing her to leave him for the rest of the morning. The delivery man was familiar, he soon discovered, and better attired than many executives. They first met a few days before Christmas, though this time there was no pleasantry, no underlying good wishes. Nothing was said. The surprisingly small package changed hands and the man left. No words could have been more explicit than his telling smirk.

In the privacy of his quiet office the wrapping paper fell from the edge of his desk and he stared at the tiny velvet box until his fingers stopped shaking. Pulling it closer, grasping it in both hands, the black velvet felt rich to his touch and he wouldn't have been surprised to find a diamond ring inside. But he knew differently, expecting he would more likely see a finger or an eye. He had hoped for a note, something to tell him, though what he saw when he eased open the lid told him everything he needed to know. The felt lining was bright white, and resting on the bottom was a single red jellybean.

He would be taking no calls for the rest of the day and Madeleine wasn't to disturb him for any reason. What he feared the most, what he hoped for the most, had begun. Which one or where didn't matter. It had finally begun after so many months of wondering and he put the souvenir on his mantel, knowing three more would soon complete the set. Then he took the gold-embossed King James Version he hadn't touched for almost two years from the same ledge. He blew a light coating of dust from the top of the filigreed pages, held the open scriptures to his chest and prayed for her innocence.

# 171

Maria would never know about that box or the three others soon to follow. Neither did she know Jean-Émile was aware of the timeframe. She was told, however, never to discuss the fates of the four men with him under any condition.

She went home and straight to bed on the Monday, explaining to the girls the flight had been one of her worst and she needed to rest. In truth, she didn't want to be with them. She needed her space, to come to terms with what she had done. She had killed a man, which she didn't regret for a moment. Yet she needed to confront herself and not pretend reality was fiction.

Chad Rivers was dead, killed according to plan, though not with the fear which accompanies the expectation of one's own death, because of the drugs, which wouldn't be the same for the others. Though Rivers would be found lying naked in his own filth that had come through a ruptured rectum and she accepted that as due compensation.

# 172

The limo drove up for the girls at 10:00 AM on the Thursday so they would arrive in Mexico well before dark and begin enjoying Christmas with their parents a few days early. Jean-Émile had insisted Madeleine contact the families to confirm the girls' invitation and acquire a few more details so they might be properly prepared guests and not appear as though they were taking advantage of their hospitality. She had already, and told him so.

Maria stayed in the doorway waving to them, saying she would see them soon and how much she loved them, when unexpectedly the front passenger door opened and Jean-Émile stepped out forgoing the usual protocol. He brushed his coat for no reason, not looking at Maria, and reached into the limo. He was a smart-looking man, Maria thought, a gentleman, and she knew many of her neighbours were peeking from their windows. They always did when the limo drove up to her condo. Even on snooty Nun's Island personal chauffeurs were curiosities, as were the neighbours who stepped into them.

He had no intention of subjecting himself to needless female chatter when even the slightest possibility of escape presented itself, he told her at the door, and had earlier advised the pilot that he would be the co-pilot for the flight, or at least be occupying said seat, "and I will be sending the jet for you, child. I don't want you flying at that time of year by yourself."

"I have my tickets, dad. I'll be fine."

"Don't be argumentative. I will send the jet for you and the pilot will call to advise what time the driver will arrive for you. And we'll all fly home together, the way we should, not to mention you're the only one who doesn't carry on so. I need you nearby for particularly selfish reasons."

"I need you, too. You are my other papa, after all, and I have to say just as much trouble as the other one."

"Indeed." He cleared his throat. "I have a gift for you, Maria, a special gift which you may open now if you wish."

She pulled him into the living room. "I have one for you, too. I should wait until Mexico, but now I can't. You go first...for the dad who has everything."

Johnnie Walker Blue was his favourite and would have been sufficient. The craftsmanship of the crystal set of twin monogrammed old-fashioned glasses and matching decanter was beyond words. He opened the original packaging as though mesmerized by unknown beauty or the rarest gem. Then he twisted the top free and poured a full shot into one of the glasses, smiling as he selfishly replaced the cap and moved the bottle away from her with a wide, satisfied smile. He then put his gift to her in front of Maria, while enjoying the balance and aromas of his scotch.

"For the daughter who will soon have almost everything." He took a sip to steel himself from what was a mere breath away. "It's one of the most special gifts I could think to give such a lovely young lady. Although I must confess that I first bought it for another young lady as a birthday gift, two years ago. I had intended for Addison to be all the lovelier on her twenty-fifth birthday, since which I've always wondered whether she would have thrown the damn thing at me."

Maria had never seen a diamond necklace as beautiful. He had made the selection himself, he added. He didn't require Madame Harnais' assistance for everything in life, despite what anyone thought, and he had a remarkable Christmas gift for all the girls which would not be opened until they were together. He was not prepared to give her any clues and quickly changed the subject. She was all the lovelier in diamonds, he told her as he helped her with the clasp, and she answered that the only thing Addison would have thrown at him would have been her arms around his neck, and she showed him exactly how.

As much as he wanted to stay with her, he had to go, and asked if he might have a moment longer to compose himself and not give the women any more to chatter about. First, however, he did have a secret she might want to hear if she promised to tell absolutely no one. Then he sat, watching her jump up and down, firmly reminding her of her promise. He let her hug him one last time, knowing she liked that type of thing, shooing her away and watching her race up the stairs yelling to him that she had to see herself in her beautiful new necklace.

He took a few moments, once more brushing his coat, taking the number of deep breaths he thought adequate, not aware Maria had kissed a trail of red across both sides of his face.

# 173

She needed someone to speak with, and her father was the one person who would understand. She didn't want to talk about Chad Rivers. She needed to talk about guilt. As much as she had always loved her father, she had only recently come to understand him, as she had recently come to understand Marcus. She knew guilt could never figure into their make-up. They were what and who they were, but above all they were her family and they would be alone at Christmas because of her. That was her dilemma as she stared at the phone.

Angelo listened, understanding, and running out of ways to tell her so. Yes, he loved her. Yes, her cousin loved her. And whether she visited with them on Christmas Eve, Christmas Day, or the day after made no difference. Christmas had come, for Christ sake, not the end of the frigging world and the time had come he scolded her. If she felt the timing was right, then it was about frigging time. And Marcus wouldn't care one way or the other what day she came as long as she came and he could loosen his belt. The meal would taste fantastic whenever she came to cook for them and what made her think they couldn't survive a few days without her.

When she finally allowed him to hang up Angelo looked over to Marcus with open hands and rolling his eyes. "Worse than her mother ever was. Be here on Boxing Day and whatever you do, do not frigging eat first."

# 174

Christine spoke with Bret on several occasions. He was gaining weight, walking on crutches, though he wouldn't be home with her until the end of January at the earliest. Mother was a great help to him and he had explained Christine's decision to halt fee payments to the firm, once Frederick had asked him about the account discrepancy. He had forgotten to tell his father, but he did remember how sexy she was that night in the hospital and couldn't wait until she could torment him again.

He'd be a good husband. He had gone to The Lap because of Shane and would never go again. He hadn't done anything, he swore. He had a few drinks, maybe a few too many, and he was paying a heavy price for his mistakes. He'd never disappoint her again. She had to believe him, he implored, and she could hear the sigh of relief when she told him she did. She wished him Merry Christmas and Happy New Year. She would try to visit him between her trip to the spa and her first business trip which was planned for early January and, in the spirit of a true Wilmington, he hung up without saying he loved her or needed her.

Christine began Christmas Eve day by cleaning the house. He wouldn't be home for another month and she wondered how everything would work out with him. What she did know was Mother Bitch wasn't moving in unless she was moving out, like that would ever happen, and she didn't hear the distinctive ring of the cell phone she had tossed onto the sofa after vacuuming under the cushions. And not until mid-afternoon did she notice the red flashing dot.

"Cristina, hi y hola. This is your very most favourite English-speaking Executive Administrator and Marketing lady. Today is the twenty-four of diciembre and I want to call to say we have no talked so much and that I wish you a good Christmas and also to hope you a best New Year and to tell to you that you are my angel. Good-bye and love to my angel."

Crap, and double crap, of all the people to forget. What the hell was happening to her? She had intended to call Selena later in the day and had completely forgotten her birthday. She glanced at her watch before returning Selena's call. She had three hours to get dressed and get downtown to do some shopping on the worst day of the year. She had always enjoyed Christmas, not this year. This year was a bitch and she hated everything from coloured lights to decorations to cheery carols to herself.

She hoped Selena wouldn't answer the phone, and she didn't. "Selena, this is Christine. Happy Birthday, girl! I'm sorry I waited so long to call you and that I missed yours this afternoon. I'm coming by your place in a few hours. If you're busy I'll leave you a little gift and get out of your way. See you soon."

And she had no idea what little gift.

# 175

"Hi."

"You don't say hi. You say, who is it? Or yes as a question, Selena."

"Who is it?"

Christine rolled her eyes at the doorman. "It's me, silly, Christine. Now buzz me up."

The buzzer let her in and as she turned the corner on Selena's floor all she could see was hair, legs and arms flying along the hallway at an illegal speed before wrapping around her and Christine wondered if all her employees would be as wild.

She was wearing a snug-fitting wool T-neck halter mini-dress that clung to her and accentuated every smooth curve, the mini becoming micro-mini before the two women collided. She wasn't wearing nylons; her feet were bare with bright red toenails. She was breathtaking.

When she asked where Cristina's bags were, Selena shook her head at the answer and said no importa, disregarding the strange look her friend was giving her. So what? She wouldn't be alone on her birthday and tomorrow was Christmas. What else could she ask for? She was going to have the best birthday ever and if Cristina thought for a moment Selena was going to let her be anywhere else, well, she hoped not. The little Christmas tree was cute: one metre-high and decorated with miniature pink and white balls and lights. On the top was a miniature angel and around the base were a few dozen gifts and envelopes and Christine asked whose presents they could possibly be.

They were Selena's. She had no friends or family and she loved opening gifts. The big bird was another matter, which was much too big for her to eat by herself. She would start cooking very early in the morning and hoped she wouldn't wake Cristina.

"I wasn't expecting to stay over, Selena. I have so much to do. I simply wanted to give you a little something for your birthday and Christmas."

"I understand you are a busy woman with a family, but you will stay very late and take a taxi, no? Please."

"Yes," she agreed, "as late as I can, and I hate taxis as much as I hate cell phones."

Selena shrugged, walking into the kitchen to pour them each a glass of wine. When she came back she curled onto the sofa beside Cristina, seeming very excited.

"I am the owner, Cristina."

"You're the what?"

"Yes, I am the owner of my apartment. I did buy my apartment this week, with the bank." She sprang from the sofa and ran to her tree, reaching for an envelope. "This is my first Christmas regalo to you, my angel. El señor did agree giving me some of your money if I did buy this place before this year is finished. I insisted that no. He was not good enough." She handed Cristina the envelope. "I did get all your money for you."

"You own this place?"

"Yes, I do."

"I'm proud of you, and thank you." She waved the envelope and Selena sat on her knees, staring at Cristina and saying nothing. "Now what, did you buy a car at the same time?"

"I want my regalo. You said to me that you did buy me a regalo for my birthday."

"Selena," she said seriously, taking the other's hand, "my problem is…I have two gifts for you and I can't decide which one is for your birthday and which is for Christmas."

Selena had no problem deciding. "The smallest one, give me the smallest one and put the other under our tree, with yours, which is the green and silver one."

"Selena I won't be able to stay. I'm sorry. But I promise we'll see each other before I leave the country."

"Otra vez Europa?"

"Sí, otra vez," and she reached for the smallest package in the bag.

Selena took it from her gently, pulling at the ribbons, opening the folds one by one, staring at the long, flat mahogany box.

"The box won't open itself, Selena. Happy birthday, girl," and she leaned over to kiss Selena on the cheek before most of the air in the room was sucked into her Latin lungs.

"Ay, ¿qué es? Cristina."

"A locking bracelet and the necklace is also a key. The bracelet is for you; the necklace is for me. Once I lock the bracelet on your wrist you have to ask me to unlock it, something I can only do if I'm wearing the necklace and I don't think I ever will. I don't ever want you to leave me. The company needs you, and I need you."

Selena took both delicate pieces from the box. She opened the bracelet with the eighteen karat key, closing the band onto a puzzled Cristina's wrist before putting the necklace around her own neck and repeating Cristina's last words. "Never I want to leave you. I do need you also."

# 176

She couldn't stay, she insisted. She hadn't brought a change of clothes and Selena jumped from the sofa and ran back to the tree to retrieve gifts she had wrapped for herself. Cristina did have something to wear and she would stay the night. The only question was: Would they open their Christmas presents right away or wait for morning. They agreed: right away, as soon as they got comfy and comfy meant silk and satin. Then they began tearing at Selena's elaborate bows, once Cristina introduced her to eggnog and its special ingredient which Selena decided early on she liked very much.

They set up the futon for Christine while they could and when they were done Selena climbed into the middle and snuggled into her friend's lap. No man would ever beat her again, never. She was free and would stay free. She told Cristina how much she adored her angel as she wriggled her little finger into the bracelet that was hers, an angel who would always be special. Christine did believe she would always be Selena's angel. She also knew heaven was very far from her thoughts and that Selena would think very differently about brandy in the morning.

"I did kiss you."

"Pardon?"

"I kissed you the first morning, Cristina. I also lied to you." Selena said, slipping into Spanish.

"I know you kissed me. You kissed me on the cheek and made me feel so good that I was able to make you happy. We're friends, Selena, and you would never lie to me. Why would you say such a silly thing?"

"I told you I was in bed all night, when I was not. I was beside you all night. I was thinking how sad you are and how beautiful. I was unhappy because I couldn't do anything to make you better. So I kissed your lips. You were crying in your sleep, Cristina, and all I could do to make you feel better was to kiss you." She reacted to Christine's hand on her back, snuggling more into her lap. "It felt nice, Cristina. I was surprised and it didn't hurt like the other times. I kissed you again. That is all. Lo juro. I wanted to comfort you, but I was the one who felt better and I stayed with you until you opened your eyes."

Selena started to cry, not wanting to lose her friend. Christine looked at the girl curled into her lap and began crying with her. "Selena, we're girls, right? We can do silly things whenever we want. We never have to worry or feel bad. We're girls."

"Y amigas, Cristina."

"Yes. We'll always be friends."

She stroked Selena's hair until her breathing told Christine she had drifted into a dreamy sleep. No one would ever hurt Selena again. There was so much she wanted to tell her new friend, Christmas simply wasn't the time. Her husband was no better than Selena's. He had lied to her about the night at the club. The smell of women was all over his clothes and the violent beating wasn't a simple carjacking at all. He'd been targeted and with a smirk she imagined Shane lying in bed alongside his mummified friend.

As sleep overtook her she drifted from a world of haunting darkness where dreams were never real, where angels could never belong, into a world where only angels could belong, where dreams were everlasting, where she wanted to stay forever, and one day she would.

She kept her eyes closed for several long moments, not wanting her dreams to fade, wanting to luxuriate in the warmth and touch of her bare skin. Then she was afraid to open her eyes, to see the truth, to see Selena whom she knew was watching her. She hadn't moved during the night, though Selena had, with one hand still locked with gold into Christine's whose other hand had been gently kneading at the juncture of Selena's soft inner thighs and maroon-coloured silk.

Christine's eyes were still closed when she felt the warmth of Selena's palm against her cheek. "Do not cry, Cristina. You make me so sad to see you this unhappy. You are my friend."

"Yes, we are friends, Selena." She opened her eyes, shocked and afraid to move her hand, afraid not to. "I'm sorry. I didn't mean to do this. I was dreaming. I'm sorry."

Selena put a hand over Christine's. "Your face was happy Cristina, then you became sad and you started crying before you thought you should feel sorry. Why?"

"I didn't mean to. I was in another place, another time, a time that was so happy. How long have you been awake?"

She pressed her hand onto Cristina's. "Since you woke me, or do you want me to lie? I am not nervous, Cristina. How can I be when I feel the way I do?"

"And how is that?"

"Free, Cristina. For the first time in so long, I feel free. And, now, you do not." She unlocked her hand to run her fingers through Cristina's hair. "This is your home, Cristina, when you need to escape, when you need to feel free."

She wanted to pull Cristina into her and kiss her the way she had weeks earlier, a little part of her still curious. She seemed so vulnerable, yet Selena resisted the temptation. Instead, she wiped away Cristina's lingering tears and locked herself onto her friend's wrist. They fell into silence, neither one with anything to say to make the moment better or worse. Christine's heart was racing, pounding, as she wondered how the rest of the day would be.

Selena hadn't moved her head that was still in Cristina's lap, knowing she had lied once more to her friend. She was very nervous, for her friend, and the rest of the day would be absolutely perfect. The big, ugly bird could wait.

# 177

The limo arrived on time, Maria was ready, and the jet was standing by. By the time the wheels touched down in Mexico City's Juarez International her backed-up paperwork was complete and she could relax for a few days. She had never seen Pilar and Ercilia so excited and their parents welcomed Maria at the airport as though she were the greatest lady in Mexico. She looked exceptional, and exceptionally happy, even though she spent only two days with her father and Marcus who once again insisted she stay over to rest, even though the transparent motive was another home-cooked meal.

Madeleine was beautiful. The girls hadn't let her be for the better part of the week and the transformation was incredible to Maria, not to mention to the lady herself. Jean-Émile was distant, greeting her as though she wasn't one of the four most important persons in his life, admonishing her for the impropriety of her actions. Then he allowed her to peck him on the cheek, making a show of wiping the gloss onto his monogrammed handkerchief. Did she tell anyone, he wanted to know? No, she did not, she insisted. Was she very certain? Yes, she was. Why, then, had Madeleine changed so much since their arrival, acting suspiciously peculiar and very unlike the Madeleine he'd known for so many years. Was he making a mistake? No. How did she know? She knew, and so did he.

Those few days before December 31, La Nochevieja, Jean-Émile was a nervous wreck and found every reason to distance himself from Madeleine. Maria did not say anything to Madeleine, though she never promised that Madeleine wouldn't be the most beautiful woman at the celebration. Her dark hair was highlighted with blonde strands; he had never seen so much of her cleavage and didn't know how to react to the admiration of all the men, young and old. Her blouse was peasant, he could have done without the ribbons in her hair and her skirt was perhaps a little too short and billowy, to which he supposed he could acclimate himself. And if he was ever to discover his little waif of a girl had revealed his secret, he would make very certain she walked every kilometre back to Montreal and he would be right behind her to make certain she did. And he told her so as he let Maria adjust his tie.

Maria giggled and squeezed him, playing with the already perfect tie and adjusting his lapels before leading him into the two-family setting he had very quickly become accustomed to. The warm ambiance wasn't enough. He needed Maria by his side and wasn't releasing his grip on the little hand that was steadier than his. None of them thought of him as a multi-millionaire or a worldly business executive. He was Juan, the father of Adisita, and their homes were his homes. He stayed in one, Madeleine in the other for the sake of available space and propriety, nonetheless they were family and he stood gazing helplessly at Maria as Pilar's oldest brother pulled away Juan's perfect tie and the youngest good-naturedly loosened the top few top buttons of Juan's shirt.

The two fathers toasted their families and friends, they all drank champagne and kissed each other at midnight, and when he thought the moment appropriate Juan stepped into the centre of the room at the same time as Madeleine's three girls crowded around her. He and Madeleine had enjoyed their gracious company immensely over the past week, he began. He thanked their hosts for their friendship and hospitality, regretting deeply they would never meet his daughter who, in great part, was responsible for all of them being together. Addison's would open on May 03, and he would not think of detracting from the girls' happiest hour. For that reason he would delay the inauguration of the

Addison Foundation until July 30, from which day forward the Larivière family estate would be remodelled with the help of Michele Baroque to become a safe haven in perpetuity for abused women of all ages. Maria, Pilar and Ercilia would sit on the three-woman board of directors.

Maria burst into tears, pulled into a tight circle by Pilar and Ercilia to comfort her as Jean-Émile did his best to remain stoic, thinking he might be wiser to briefly leave the room. No one followed. When he returned, Madeleine was in the centre of the girls with her arms wrapped around all three, proud of Jean-Émile and wondering at the old fool's expression.

# 178

"Maria, you were the epicentre of my daughter's universe, and she was yours, and for that reason the Foundation must be managed by you and her best friends." He cleared his throat. "Addison was a special girl, sometimes too special, whom I shall miss for the rest of my life. And I have no idea where I'm going with this other than to say that I have, over the past several months, come to understand that we cannot walk through this life without help...or love, I suppose." Maria gripped Madeleine's hand. "Madeleine Harnais, I would appreciate very much if you were to marry me." He paused, hoping for a glimpse of any little part of Madeleine not covered by the girls. "It's not as though you don't act the part already."

"Give her the ring." Maria said sternly, wiping her eyes. "You can't say anything like that to a lady without giving her a ring."

Jean-Émile opened the little box towards a very flustered Madeleine amidst whistles and gasps. Maria had told him what to do, and he obstinately agreed. He knelt in front of her, holding his breath as he slid the two-karat bauble onto her finger and suddenly he didn't exist. The evening instantly became Madeleine's. All eyes were on her, and the room fell quiet as Jean-Émile hoped he hadn't provoked his third heart attack. She flushed deep crimson, wiping her eyes with her free hand, staring at the perfect stone. Of course she would marry him, she replied. Who else would want to care for him? And the mood became even more celebratory. The women ooohed over the ring and the men slapped his back, dragging him into the kitchen where they could drink more, and Maria went to the phone.

They next morning the men awoke feeling as they expected to feel on the first day of the year, the women had been up for hours planning a special engagement feast, and Madeleine was still very flustered. She hadn't slept. She never thought in her wildest dreams the old fool would ever. They never so much as held hands, and now what, repeatedly telling the girls to behave themselves as they spent the morning role-playing the soon-to-be newlyweds before Jean-Émile suggested she join him for a walk in the plaza before the meal.

Jean-Émile had one more toast to make to his bride-to-be and the families. They were all invited to join him, Madeleine and the girls at his farm for the inauguration of the Foundation. They would have the distinction of being the last family guests invited and Madeleine agreed with him. There could be no better time or place for the wedding.

# 179

Suzanne Wilmington reluctantly released her son into his wife's care at the end of January, arguing he should stay longer because his wife thought more of her business trips than she did of him. Christine viewed the situation differently. Despite the discomfort Bret was hobbling around well enough on crutches, his was in the final stage of reconstructive bridgework, and if he could manage that he could manage living in his own home. She had hired a live-in therapist to help speed his recovery, which he needed a lot more than an overbearing and suffocating mother.

Christine would adjust her schedule to spend as much time as possible with him throughout February and fully expected W & P to deliver her complete client file to their home so he could begin working and not waste more of her time. The orthopaedic contraption he'd be sleeping on would be in the living room along with the rest of the therapeutic equipment, the therapist would occupy the guest room for as long as she was needed, and Christine would come and go.

# 180

Most times Maria understood when she was talking with her father and when she was talking with Angie Bardollini. This time she was speaking with her father, explaining what she had decided to do and when. When the time came to speak with his other persona, the tone changed.

Certainly before the end of March, he answered, though the end of February wouldn't be unrealistic. Having said that, he impressed upon her that she was not to believe anything she would read or hear about him in the coming weeks. The press were notorious for printing half-truths and elaborating on any innuendo that would increase circulation numbers.

He would keep his promise to her, though when the time came for her instructions to come directly from Marcus, she would follow them implicitly. Marcus would soon be the head of the family. A family summit to that affect was slated for mid-February, which wasn't the reason he asked her to come by. Phallicia Hunter would arrive in Toronto before noon on Thursday, January 31. She would return on the Sunday. She would check into a hotel, not the Hilton this time, and would wait in her room for the call. Angelo passed her the unused disposable phone, reminding her that the same rules applied. She would wear new clothes, top to bottom, she would wear two sets of gloves and she would later give absolutely everything to Marcus for disposal.

# 181

The call came at noon on Friday, a few hours before Thurston Williams would say goodbye to his wife for the last time, watching as she cleared airport security en route to a weekend seminar in Chicago. He left once the departure of her flight was confirmed and Phallicia Hunter walked into his home with a pizza, sandwiches, a bottle of red wine and gifts for her host.

They took a taxi from the mall, climbing out several blocks from the address, appearing as nondescript as many other couples the driver would forget by the end of his shift. Neither one removed their coat when they entered, though Phallicia did pull a thick towel from her bag to wipe away the snow they tracked in on their boots.

At 6:00 PM, inside the house was pitch black until a wide beam of light shot through the living room window moments before they heard the car door slam and the front door to the modest house was kicked open to let in the cold. They knew he was coming, that he'd be late. They had heard every profane word of his monologue on his way home in bumper-to-bumper traffic. The tirade continued as he barged through the door without turning on the lights, cursing as he threw off his coat and kicked off his boots. He should have been home earlier, and would have been had the snow not worsened. Though for Marcus and Phallicia the heavy snowfall was a godsend. Their deep footprints leading to the front door completely disappeared under a fresh five-centimetre carpet of white which was one less hindrance for Marcus to consider. Then a light did go on, and another, before Thurston Williams walked into the kitchen and flipped that light switch, jumping back.

"Good evening, Thurston. I hope we didn't startle you."

Marcus remained quiet, signalling Williams to the

centre of the floor, holding his palm out when Williams had stepped in far enough.

"Home invasion? Is that what this is?"

"Yes, Thurston, it's a home invasion. That's why I know your name." She waited a moment, enjoying his shock. "No, it's not a home invasion. It's your execution, which won't happen until this time tomorrow. So let's go to the basement where we can be comfortable and I'll tell you how this will all play out. By the way, have you spoken to your friend Chad lately?"

"This is a joke, right"

"It's no joke, Thurston. Chad knows we weren't joking. He's dead." She knew what he was thinking. "Yeah, he's dead, so there's really no point in talking about him. You must remember the man in the church, Thurston. You and Chad were right, he was watching you, and now we're here to watch you. Get your ass into the basement."

"Watch me do what?"

"Watch you die. Go."

The basement was windowless, damp, musty and quiet, decorated with a single chair, dozens of half-filled cardboard boxes, paint cans, a worktable and aging tools the previous owner left behind. A single bare bulb and wiring hung from the unfinished ceiling, an assortment of household utensils was stacked in a corner and sports equipment leaned in between the two-by-four studs of unfinished walls.

"I learned a lot from Chad, Thurston." He didn't respond, too fixated on the gun in Marcus' hand. "I learned that I have to explain everything to you right away, before the drugs take affect and you think you're enjoying yourself instead of dying. But first I need you to strip. Take off all your clothes, everything, right now."

"I'm not stripping for you or anyone."

"Yes, you will. You pulled her clothes off before you

raped and killed her. So you will strip, right now." Marcus moved in quickly. He gripped Williams' throat in a huge hand, forcing him backward and smashing his head into a support beam without saying a word. "Strip, Thurston. He doesn't care about your little thingy. Neither do I, though I do want to see what you fucked her with."

His suit came off first, then the tie and the shirt. The pants came next, then his socks before she hurled the hammer viciously onto one of his feet, causing him to leap into the air screaming, falling over as he tried to grab the wounded appendage.

"Stay on the floor and pull off the underwear or I'll do your other foot. Then you're going to lie on your back while I explain what happens next." He did. "Is that what you did it with? Is that what you raped my girlfriend with before you killed her?"

"I didn't kill anyone, and if you're talking about the girl in Mexico, she was asking for it. She got what she wanted, big time. That doesn't mean we killed her."

"You raped her, you sodomized her, and you killed her like she was piece of meat. She was twenty-five, asshole."

"Yeah, and old enough to know what she wanted."

"Here's what we do. First I'll show you some photos of your friend Chad, taken after he died. Then I'll tell you how your wife will find you." He lay silently on the floor, watching Phallicia go to her bag for the photo album. When she told him to sit up and look at them, he did so without comment, awkwardly leaning on a forearm. "I've made some refinements, but this is essentially what she'll find: you lying naked and dead in a cold tub of your own shit." She closed the album. "She might also see the blood and broken glass, which is the refinement thanks to Chad. Though we'll have to wait and see, I suppose. I can explain in a bit more detail after you put your feet in with the sump pump. Go on, while I turn off the heat."

"You're serious? You're going to kill me?"

"Oh, yeah, we're serious."

"Then fuck you, and fuck your friend."

Marcus' boot struck Williams' bare side once, lifting him from the floor.

"The more you cooperate the longer you'll live and the less you'll realize you're dying. Try fighting, which is pointless, and your death will come more quickly, though not too quickly, and you will realize. I promise you. So, it's your decision."

He obeyed, standing awkwardly, until another instruction to lower himself onto all fours and crawl to the pump. He lifted the floor-level lid from the shallow well, staring into the black, cold water as his feet disappeared. "I can't."

"No gun, Thurston, not unless you fuck up, but it'll be your balls we blow off first, not the head, not the bleed-like-a-pig groin. No. The balls, one at a time. So don't fuck up." She pulled over the chair and sat. "First off, you've eaten your last meal and you've had your last drink of whatever you like to drink. In thirteen or fourteen hours you're going to wash down six roofies with some tequila, and right after that I'm going to sodomize you before the roofies take effect."

Williams couldn't stop his teeth from chattering and his feet began burning from the frigid water, more frightened by Marcus who was watching him with no expression. "Why not kill me and get it over with? I'm not his type."

"It's not what you think, Thurston. He's not into men." Phallicia pulled three glass capillary tubes and a screwdriver from her bag, smiling contentedly at his reaction. "Good, you understand. That's good. They're going in one after the other, Thurston. They're pretty fragile, so you can expect a little discomfort and they're only coming out one way after you drink a special cocktail I've

435

brought for you." She showed him the three bottles of high-strength laxatives, "Yummy shit, so to speak."

"This is crazy," he spurted. "We were just having a bit of fun with her and things went wrong, but she was alive when we left her. She was."

"You left her outside in the rain, wide open for the men who found her to see. You made her bleed in the back, her vagina looked like raw meat, and that's what they'll see when they find you: bloodied raw meat, humiliated, sodomized and very dead."

"I wasn't the one. Rivers was. He wanted to do her. He had it real bad for her. He followed her everywhere for a week and finally Wilmington was the one who made it happen on the last night because he wanted the redhead who was with her. He wanted to do her worse than Rivers wanted the blonde. Rivers was a loser. Wilmington's the killer. Without him she'd still be alive."

His body jerked unexpectedly with a spasm.

"I was the redhead, Thurston. My name's Phallicia Hunter. Do you know her name, the girl you raped?"

"No."

"Her name was Addison. We were lovers. Did you know that?"

"We thought you might have been dykes, but…"

The hammer struck his knee with a crack and right then she knew he'd be much better than Chad. He could yell as much as he wanted. Absolutely no one would hear. She went to Marcus and whispered in his ear before returning to Williams.

"I was asking my friend here if I can tell you who I really am. He's agreed, with the provisos that I whisper and that he puts a bullet in your head when we're done tomorrow. Curious?"

"No."

She laughed. "I didn't think so, but it's not like you

won't be dead by the time we leave. Sure?"

He jerked. "Yeah, I'm sure."

"I'll tell you anyway. Hunter is my travel name," she whispered leaning into his ear, "my real name is Maria Bardollini and the man in the church was my father, crime boss Angelo Bardollini and you've been tracked virtually from the time you left Mexico. Talk about deep shit. Now, by this time tomorrow you won't have a head. So sorry, Thurston, I just really wanted to tell you. You chose the wrong girl to fuck, but I have to know. Would I have been on the table beside her if I hadn't gone to my room?"

He didn't answer, unless uncontrolled sobbing and muscle spasms lasting through the night as Williams alternated between footbaths and lying on a cold, damp floor was an answer. Marcus and Phallicia finished their dinner of wine and pizza before ordering him to stand, not surprised when he couldn't.

"Get up, Thurston. Crawl if you have to, but don't fuck with me. We're going upstairs. It's time for your special spa treatment."

He was naked, still conscious, and terrified. He had no feeling in his feet which would most certainly require amputation had he not only hours to live. He crawled on his knees from the basement to the second story, crying on each of the twenty-eight steps that he didn't want to die. He was sorry. He'd do anything to bring her friend back if he could. They only wanted a little fun with her. Everyone was there for the same reason, even the girls. So what was the harm? They didn't mean to leave her. Wilmington was the one who said she was alright and she was Rivers' thing, not his. Rivers should have taken care of her.

"Thing...fun...you murdered my girlfriend for fun." She swung the shaft of the screwdriver into his side, evoking a yelp and collapsing his body onto the upper landing "Who took her panties?" She raised her arm when he didn't

437

answer, waving the shaft. "Who took her panties?"

"Wilmington, I suppose. I don't know. The other girls never seemed to mind, sort of like something to remember them by."

"Or a trophy?"

"I didn't say that."

"Chad said that. Did she cry? Tell me…did she cry?"

"She tried to, once, but Wilmington stopped her. He thought she was going to scream. After that she stayed quiet."

"Was she alive when you left her?"

"Yes. She must have been? We did her again just before leaving."

She kicked him hard, asking Marcus for help who dragged Williams into the bathroom by a single arm, dropped him and kicked the side of his face. Phallicia brought out the tequila and a pair of scissors she found.

"If you drink more than enough to swallow the six pills, I'll cut off your dick, if I can find it."

She put the pills into his cupped hand, waiting, and when she was ready she pushed the bottle into his mouth and tilted his head in a single motion. He swallowed once, coughing, and she let him drink a little more. The time was 8:00 AM and Williams' heart was pounding.

"You have ten hours, Thurston, maybe. Anyway, a lot more time than you gave Addison, which should be comforting to you. Especially with what's up next, so to speak: glass tubes up your ass. Did you tell Addison? Did you tell her you were going to do her that way? Isn't that your expression, do her? Lean over the tub asshole." He couldn't. Instead he crumpled onto the floor, sobbing. "I said lean over the tub, Williams." She kicked him. "Did you ever once think how your dick felt to her, inside her, terrifying her," she kicked him again, more violently, "doing your fucking guy shit, fucking one more beautiful

438

and innocent girl?"

Marcus was a casual observer, understanding how she felt and why. He never before attached emotion to executions, yet he literally felt Phallicia's intense hatred, happy he was with her both to prevent potentially dangerous mistakes and to witness her wrath.

She smacked the side of Williams' head with the screwdriver to get his attention. She wanted him to see her lubricating the first glass tube at the end of the half-metre-long screwdriver. When she stood he was quivering and crying. As she inserted the tube slowly and easily into his rectum she asked if it felt good. He said no and she told him not to move. Moments later the contoured edge disappeared and she twisted until his legs jerked spastically out from under him, blood beginning to trickle down his legs. Then she took her time lubricating and inserting the second tube before reaching into the tub for the screwdriver that had rolled off his back.

She poured the three laxatives into the bathroom glass as she explained what he should expect, watching him crumple into a foetal position and whimper.

"In one end or the other, Thurston, your choice, though, from my perspective, this end seems to be getting a little crowded. So drink up and, a word of caution…don't spill a drop. This is how you die, Thurston, but not when. Ten more hours, then we're out of your life, and so are you. So sit up for round two. In a few minutes you can lay anyway you want, after you drink up. The stuff's horrible tasting shit, but swallow in one shot or those small balls come off. And let's not forget you left her lying in the rain."

He took the glass in hands he couldn't control, twisting his head to the side, unaware she had chortled in a way that wasn't humorous, in a way Marcus wanted to forget. The sound he made when she smashed the second tube was a ghoulish retch, nothing exiting his mouth as his legs flailed outward and his head crashed against the tub's porcelain bottom. She let him relax, ignoring his sobbing, taking her time to break the third tube and lubricate the jagged half before the urgent and final thrust. His face contorted with agony, his body convulsing when Marcus took him by one twitching arm to jerk him onto his back.

All the lights and thermostats in the house were off and the rear windows open, including the bathroom. Phallicia turned the shower to a fine mist. Then she accounted for each of her accoutrements and the broken end of the third capillary tube. Marcus verified each piece.

Thurston Williams died slightly ahead of schedule, his death as horrible as she had wanted. His wife would see that he died cravenly, his open eyes stained red with tears, his mouth twisted with the fright of his final moments, the agony of his last twenty-four hours etched into face. She would see the discoloured body of the man she married lying in a mélange of his foul body fluids and staring out from under the same thin layer of ice that had begun coating the walls of his temporary tomb. She would be spared the bullet wound, Marcus decided, though he had gone in one last time with the tradition in mind. Her husband was dead enough and they left with photographs which would serve to dramatize the immediate future of whoever was next.

# 182

Phallicia boarded the plane at 2:00 PM on Sunday and Maria was at home having dinner with the girls by six, first soaking in her personal spa with the lights dimmed and a single fluted glass of champagne. She whispered the toast, crying when she realized she hadn't.

The following morning the same man arrived at the Larivière offices moments after Jean-Émile who turned at hearing his name as he was passing through the second set of glass doors. He could have been an executive judging by his dress, though he wasn't. The tone of his voice was commanding, addressing Jean-Émile directly, not the receptionist as he held out the small package. Neither man had reason to speak and walked away from one another with nothing beyond the niceties of the business world.

The wrapping was thrown into the mahogany waste paper receptacle and the black velvet box was placed in the centre of his desk at the moment Madeleine walked through her private doorway with his coffee. He asked her to give him a moment longer. His coffee could wait. He needed time to himself. He would call her when she could come in. In the meantime she was to hold all calls. They had slowly become lovers over the past few weeks, sharing intimate evenings, however during the day he was the boss and she closed the door.

The second of four instalments had been delivered. Two men had paid for a despicable crime, killed in less than two months and he wondered whether the remaining two were aware of the first and second reprisals. He hoped so and pulled the box closer, curious as to whether he would see one or two red jellybeans. He saw one, and stared at the crescent confectionary for the longest time before putting the box on the mantle beside the first and taking up the bible. He had always thought of himself as a religious man, a believer in the existence of heaven and hell as much as he had always believed in truth, justice, and the system.

He tugged at the purple silk ribbon and clutched the open filigreed pages to his chest. Had the system failed him, or had he failed the system by not being truthful. He knew who the men were. He could easily have gone to the system against the wishes of a young woman whose sense of vengeance was so profound. So why hadn't he? And why had he made a pact with the devil to be an accomplice, to seek retribution and not state-defined justice. He hadn't feared death during his first encounter with Angelo in the limo. So what had compelled him to go to Mexico, obsessed with compiling such precise information that more than a year and a half later would serve a darker parallel system that knew the justice of passion?

What correlation existed between truth and real justice, he mused, and who was to say? In law, justice was a dispassionate interpretation based on the existence of proof and negotiation. Law was devoid of passion. The agony and fear Addison endured during the final moments of her young life would be reduced in the courtroom to hyperbole and debate that would result in first-time reduced sentences for all four. Addison deserved more. She deserved the same passion which had always been part of her in life, and who was the real devil, after all, he asked aloud?

One would have thought Jean-Émile was praying, though he wasn't. He was explaining in a whisper that the devil was no one he knew and Maria Bardollini deserved one day to be together once again with Addison in a place of eternal peace and happiness. Though, he prayed, not for a very long time.

# 183

Christine travelled out of town more often throughout February than she had planned, honestly shocked when she returned home on the twenty-ninth to see him standing without help. Though four months after the beating the pain was still very real when not controlled with painkillers. He could only stand for short intervals and she retained the therapist for one more month.

The therapist had told the Wilmingtons in Christine's absence that the notion of taking their son with them to Florida for the month was ludicrous, unless they wanted him never to walk properly again. That encounter was unpleasant enough, but when Shane Pendleton came over wanting to convince him to spend a two-week March getaway in Myrtle Beach, she phoned Christine.

She asked whether he had forgotten they would be going somewhere in April for a second attempt at a honeymoon and, if he so much as joked about going to Myrtle with Pendleton, the only place she'd be going with him was divorce court. His last night with Shane had overshadowed the last four months, and she was done with his so-called friend. How did he expect to get around on a confined boat and floating docks when he could barely stand for moments at a time and had to sleep in an orthopaedic contraption still cluttering the living room?

Bret thought how easily he could hate her. His parents did, and at the moment he felt his anger surging. He couldn't dress or undress himself. He needed help to sit where most men preferred sitting alone, and pulling his zipper in either direction while balancing himself on crutches was a frequent struggle. The absolute worst was his daily bath. Climbing into the tub and onto the cold bench to ease off his underwear took forever, before

Hildegard the Ugly came to fill the tub with water that was never deep enough to cover his parts.

Getting out from the tub was no better. Yes, he would wait for that second honeymoon. He had no choice. Getting out of bed was difficult enough, let alone doing her the way he dreamt of every night. He would wait. Then she'd get the best first fucking ever.

# 184

Marcus called a few days before the end of February. She was to meet him at the Delta. He hadn't treated his little sister to lunch and drinks in a long time and after lunch they would go for a drive. When she asked where, he simply said: wherever.

Being with him was like old times. He joked, he teased her about some nice young guy he could set her up with, he told her how beautiful she was, and how she must never change. Who and what she was were too important to him, or he'd put her over his knee and enjoy every moment. He was a pig, a male slut, like every other man. No, he wasn't, he retorted. He was Italian and enjoyed the feel of a big, round rump in his hands. Everyone in the restaurant gaped at them as the pretty young woman stood to punch the dapper young man on an arm that was as thick as she was round.

Marcus put a finger to his lips when she asked where they were going, and, when she realized, she asked what he was up to. As they pulled up to the construction site, Marcus paid no attention to the taxi parked across the street. Moments later the passenger stepped briskly from the cab and hurried straight to the main doors of Addisons, knowing the doors were open and the crews had gone home for the day. The cabbie was paid to wait and when Maria saw her father she ran to him with open arms. Then she ran to Marcus.

"I thought I'd visit while men are still allowed in here."

"Papa, you'll always be allowed in here, until we open."

"Meme, I want to see everything you've done. Then we'll talk. I brought wine, if that's okay." Not waiting for an answer, he passed the bottle and glasses to Marcus. "Give me a good show, Meme. I've got high expectations."

She didn't disappoint him. He loved what he saw, so did Marcus. She described each room, each studio, how the spa would look when finished and what purpose each area would serve. He stood in awe, showing honest amazement. The mega project would have been daunting for anyone, but for a girl of twenty-four nothing less than what he expected. He gave her a long, slim box telling her to contain her curiosity for the time being.

"Maria, I love you as much as your mother loved you. You know that, don't you?"

"Yes, papa."

"Meme, we all pay a price for who we are and for what we do: the price we pay for the life we choose to live. Understand?"

"No, papa."

"Listen to me. You are not to believe whatever you may read or hear in the coming days. Do you remember when I told you about the press and innuendo?"

"Yes, papa, I do."

"Do you remember when I told you not to believe front page sensationalism?"

"Yes, papa, I do" and she began one tear at a time to cry.

"Meme the time has come. Your cousin Marcus is now the head of the family and he's sworn on his life that he will always take care of you. You'll never be alone."

"What about you, papa?"

"All I ask is that you do not believe anything you read. I'm honoured you have allowed me into your world and you will never know how proud I am. We will see each other again, Meme, in another life, and I long for the moment when we don't have to see each other behind steel shutters, vibrating windows and cameras. The day will come, I swear to you."

Angelo turned to Marcus, suggesting he should find the men's room. Then he asked Maria if there was a men's room. Instead she suggested her private office where he might enjoy his glass of wine while perusing the latest in spa fashion magazines.

"I don't understand, papa. How close are we talking?"

"As close as right now, Meme, this very moment. This is goodbye. This is when I leave you," Angelo paused, "but not when I stop loving you or thinking of you. You'll always be my little girl. Don't forget that, but now you must let me talk and you must listen. My oath to you and Addison will not be broken, if you do two things for me. First, you must listen to Marcus and do as he instructs without question throughout the coming month. He'll protect you with his life."

"Yes, papa, and I would do the same for both of you." She knew he believed her.

"I know, Meme. If I didn't before, I do now and you must listen to me as never before."

He went through the monologue once, the second time she repeated each word he had spoken and Marcus was never to know. Did she understand? She did, and he picked her up with such passion and regret that he thought he had hurt her. Marcus would see her home safely. Addisons would be a great success, and she was not to forget a single word he said.

She listened quietly as he told her everything while saying nothing. He was Angelo Bardollini and when he said listen, one listened, irrespective of family privilege. He was the biggest man in the world to her, the most dangerous, the warmest and the loveliest. He was her papa and she would die first.

After he left she opened her gift, a gold pendent much like the one she had placed around Addison's neck. Inside were miniature sepia photographs of Angelo and Carmella Bardollini.

# 185

MOB BOSS ANGIE BARDOLLINI THOUHGT TO
HAVE FLED
POLICE MYSTIFIED TO DISCOVER BOSS'
FORTIFIED MANSION EMPTY
INDICTMENT ON HOLD AS BARDOLLINI SOUGHT
ON WORLD-WIDE WARRANT

Maria went on to read all three reports that her father had gone missing and the ownership of her father's mansion had been transferred to Marcus Difiore, a known relative of the notorious mob boss. The secure home was found completely devoid of furnishings, the interior exhaustively sanitized for the new owner who claimed not to have seen Angie Bardollini for weeks, and the police were baffled.

Maria spent her day smiling. Her papa had succeeded and the night was one of the few in nearly two years she didn't cry in her sleep. The next morning she woke feeling happier than she had in weeks, until she walked into the kitchen to find a pale Pilar with a dictionary in her hands.

# 186

CHARRED REMAINS THOUGHT TO BE MISSING
CRIME BOSS
INVESTIGATORS SEARCH FOR DNA EVIDENCE:
RESULTS DOUBTFUL
BARDOLLINI DEATH WISH, FACT OR FICTION:
POLICE WONDER

Jean-Émile was the first to call her, before Madeleine
brought in his coffee, upset both times that the line was
busy and he instructed Madeleine that her strictest priority
was to locate Maria.

Maria's first call told her there was no longer any way
of speaking with him, her second was to Marcus who didn't
answer and then she didn't know who to call, even though
she should have. Instead she threw down the cell phone, not
realizing she had set the vibration mode.

Pilar and Ercilia stayed with her. Maria needed them
more than they needed verbs and tenses and when Pilar
noticed the red flashing light she hurried to Maria who
listened and pressed redial. She could say no more than
hello before listening to a well-deserved scolding from
Madeleine. Pilar and Ercilia were equally culpable, she
criticized, and the three girls were to be at home that
evening. She and Jean-Émile would arrive precisely at 5:00
PM. He was upset with them and would require the rest of
the day to calm his nerves, though she wasn't to worry. Nor
was she to attach any validity to whatever she may have
read.

It was the first time all five had been in Maria's home
together. Jean-Émile breathed in deeply as he closed the
door behind him, insisting the visit would be brief and to
the point. They hadn't come for dinner, despite the hour.

He was there to speak with Maria in private, not to spend the evening with three unthinking urchins who were content to chatter with him about trivial matters, but when matters of importance were at hand he was summarily disregarded.

Pilar went to speak before Madeleine could stop her and was answered by a pointed finger and Jean-Émile's stern reminder that private meant private, a tête-à-tête between two individuals, not five. He did say private, did he not?

Pilar understood most of the French words, though both girls understood completely when Madeleine took their arms and led them into the living room. Maria had no idea what to expect, but she did know he was right and led him into her office where he spent a few moments reviewing the three headlines spread neatly across the small conference table.

"May I take your coat?"

"No, you may not. Thank you. As previously indicated, we will not stay any longer than necessary."

"Yes sir."

When they were both seated Maria felt as though she'd been called to the principal's, not her own. She knew he hadn't come for supper. He was the type to call two weeks ahead to say he would understand entirely if she had something of greater consequence or interest to do. She should have called him. She understood he was angry.

He reached into his coat pocket. "Your father told me once, what seems so long ago, that he and I would never see one another again, and at the time I thought the suggestion to be quite marvellous. Though none of us really understands what the future holds." He paused, seeing the newspapers. "This is all very tragic." He chortled, grinning, shaking his head, leaving Maria not knowing what to say or do, not certain she wasn't about to smack his face and order him from her home. "Did he ever tell you about our first meeting?"

"No, never."

"Words such as exhilarating and adrenalin rush fail to compose adequate imagery, to say the very least. Our rendezvous was very dramatic and very memorable, the stuff of television and Chicago in the thirties with guns in the dark of night and threats of...well, whatever. Extremely exciting, I must say. I will never forget your father...Meme." Her shocked expression brought a smile to his face he could not conceal and he took her trembling hand. "Yes, he told me I could call you by his special name for you. I feel very honoured."

"When could he have told you, if you never saw him?"

"That is not what I said, child. What I said was: he once said we never would. We were together in my office today, Meme, though he asked me not to say at precisely what hour. I can say, however, that he arrived after those press releases."

"Then he's alive?"

Jean-Émile ignored the question. "He left this envelope for you."

"He's alive?"

"My God, child, do I speak your plain language so terribly? Have you no idea of tenses?" He handed her the envelope. "I am, of course, privy to its contents. He was adamant that I burden myself with the responsibility of becoming your surrogate father, whereas my current thinking is that I would be better off had he shot me that first day. Very possibly I'll shoot myself and have done with it."

She leaned into his arm. "I'm sorry, Jean-Émile. Please forgive me."

"There is nothing to forgive. He also wanted you to know the original father would always be nearby for you. He said you would soon understand. There is no doubt in my mind that he risked his life to meet with me today,

Meme."

"Where is he?"

"We will never know, or, better said, I will never know." He patted her knee. "I believe, in this particular instance, not knowing is preferable." She tore at the seal, understanding. "It is a receipt for all the equipment Pilar and Ercilia have selected for their studio, and more, paid for in full by your father."

"Why would he do that?"

"Need you ask, silly girl? He wants you to know he listens when you talk and this is his way of thanking the girls for always being with you when he could not. Your offer to them was very generous, Maria. However, your father knows a good deal about honour and pride. He wants the girls to know he wishes them well and that he's grateful to them. This way they shall never be indebted to you"

"Will I see him again?"

"You know the answer, Maria. He told you himself, not very long ago." He patted her knee once more, standing to remove his coat. He threw it over where he'd been sitting. "Now, did I detect the aroma of a delicious lasagna upon our arrival, or must I tolerate one more evening alone with that horribly frustrating woman?"

"My best lasagna yet and plenty of it. Plus I poured your favourite Johnnie Walker."

"Somewhat presumptuous of you, young lady, although I might possibly have brought a bottle of Bordeaux. I shall have to call the car to verify." He extended his hand, helping her stand. "I suppose now I must make some semblance of an apology to Pilar, or I won't be left alone to enjoy my meal in peace without no importa this and no importa that. May I rely on your arm to get me through yet another gauntlet of unquestionably likeminded women?"

She pursed her lips into a smirk and shook her head unsympathetically as she pulled her hand away and gave him a gentle push forward. "Madeleine is teaching you well, dad, and no one said anything about leaving you alone."

# 187

He had been the head of the family for thirty years, since his father's untimely death, and now he could never again go home. The car was a small loss, the man inside an even smaller loss, or what was left of him.

Angelo would miss his home, the memories of watching his wife raising Meme and all the good times they once shared as a family. The bad times had only come with the death of his wife and he was thankful they had come to an end, thinking of the evening he laid eyes on Addison Larivière without whom Maria might never have come back to him.

Marcus was the head of the family and those under him had sworn an oath of fealty. The contents of his home were already in the more secure mansion made ready for him with fresh paint and professional cleaning and delivery of his special-order vehicle was expected within days. Angelo lamented he would never see Marcus again, though not seeing him had always been part of the plan. Marcus knew he wasn't dead and that's all he needed to know. After their final handshake and embrace as uncle and nephew, he simply waited until Marcus disappeared from sight before walking away from his own death.

Two AM Sunday morning was a perfect time. The task force had no money for weekend overtime and the municipal incinerators wouldn't cease operations for the weekly refractory and burner inspection until eight. The neighbourhood lights were out by the time the fully loaded eighteen-wheeler reversed into the main dumping area of the incinerators and the hydraulic lift let gravity take over as a privileged few witnessed everything he owned being converted to cinders.

By six his worldly goods were completely destroyed and

Marcus would never discover the mechanism Angelo had permanently deactivated and concealed behind paint and plaster. The wall panel in his office would never again slide open to reveal a steel door and thirty-year-old passageway which he also disabled from the other side. Angelo would stay where he was for five days, resisting the temptation to do anything sentimental or unthinking that would challenge or threaten his freedom.

He had disposed of his jewellery over the past several weeks in rivers and lakes off limits to swimmers, his paperwork shredded and destroyed in what, from an aerial perspective, would have appeared as daily barbeques. He was dead, and would stay dead for five days without running the risk of being recognized by some twenty-dollar hooker, drug dealer or family member with issues.

## 188

Christine and Selena didn't see much of each other over January and February due to conflicting schedules and workloads. The meetings they did have were focused on business and the subject of an invitation never came up. She hadn't stayed over at the condo since Christmas. There was no need, or there had been no invitation, and not until early March did Selena think that way.

She had spoken often with Cristina on business matters by phone, never thinking to invite her. She knew Cristina's home life was deteriorating and that was part of the reason she travelled as frequently as she did. Her husband wasn't a caballero. He wasn't being any kind of man to her, and what bride wanted to know her husband had gone to a strip club a week after her wedding? She picked up the phone and dialled.

"Cristina, hola, soy Selena, tu amiga, y estoy esperándote para cenar conmigo esta fin de semana, si es posible para ti y si quieres. Te amo y siempre pienso en ti, tú lo sabes, amiga. Otra vez, soy Selena."

When Christine heard the message she giggled, Selena always made her giggle as though she hadn't a care in the world. She returned the call right away, confirming dinner, asking whether she could come by early, about 10:00 AM. They could do some girl stuff, like shopping.

When she arrived the first thing she did was return her condo key to Selena who refused the gesture, telling her friend she must keep one key as long as she wore the other around her neck. Christine pulled the gold chain and key from under her silk blouse and put the door key away, thankful for a second home.

# 189

Sunday, March 09, Selena awoke to a clean kitchen, a mild throbbing sensation in her temples and new spring outfits strewn across her living room floor. When they came home the night before, they cooked the evening meal together while enjoying a few glasses of wine. They were like young girls, giggly teenagers, amigas who wouldn't see each other for a month and Selena spent the next day finalizing her preparations for her three-week promotional trip to Spain.
*

Christine woke the next morning with the same sensation at her temples, her clothes stuffed into a bag instead of being strewn across a living room floor. What was strewn across the living room when she arrived home was Bret, asleep in his bed, and she had gone straight to what was still her bedroom.

The subsequent conversation didn't go well. His tone was accusatory, not that she cared. Until he demonstrated the slightest manliness she would treat him as though he wasn't one, she scowled. She had come home well before midnight. She had a girlfriend and they had gone shopping, nothing more. She might even have brought the woman home had she not expected to see him spread eagle in the living room. She had also made plans for the vacation, the real honeymoon in April, and if he still wanted to be married by then the time would never be better for him to shut his mouth.
*

Maria's big day was a short eight weeks away, working hard with Michele to that end as well as taking her mind off the next two phone calls she knew to expect at any time. Pi and Ercilia were into the final six weeks of studying. They would be accredited therapists by mid-April and the

language courses were showing exemplary results. Madeleine was getting giddier by the day and Jean-Émile wondered what horrible crime he might have committed in a previous life to deserve all of it.
*

John Franklin scanned the backyard of his expansive home from what was now someone else's office. His D-Day had arrived, the day he would walk away with few laments and spend the rest of his life on Perfect Retreat and aboard the Perfect Escape. The house was sold in a private transaction by an agent who excelled far beyond the anticipated selling price and what the new owners didn't want as part of the agreement he gave to the mission. He returned the Audi A8 to the dealer with four months owing to honour the long-term lease and all that remained was to pack his clothes.

The agent had suggested to Franklin that he have a few rooms freshly painted to enhance the value of his property. He did the work in the dining room and great room himself, mostly to pass the time. Lastly, he worked on his office. The view looked out over the back half of the property, which would be a selling feature, though the interior had to be brighter, less stuffy, and more spacious. He ripped out the private bathroom and walk-in closet, revamping the space entirely with new drywall and a few coats of paint. The desired result was a sun-filled solarium which the new owners would never suspect was more than a simple home office to John Franklin.

The few changes had sold the house, along with the view he'd soon forget. The taxi arrived at nine, checking his watch when the doorbell rang. By nine that evening he'd be enjoying his first cocktail on Perfect Retreat.
*

That morning Shane stopped by the house at a time he was certain the she-wolf wouldn't be there, intent on convincing Bret to join him for a week in Myrtle Beach, rationalizing that if the therapist was going to hang around for only two more weeks he should be able to spend those weeks at the beach. Bret could use the time away to think, Shane argued, to rethink his life, hopefully realize he'd made a crotch-driven mistake and have the marriage annulled on grounds of mental cruelty and forced abstinence before it was too late. In short, get rid of the arrogant bitch.

"You haven't done her once yet, and you've been with her for five frigging months. You haven't even touched it, let alone use it."

"You're talking about my wife, Shane. Come on."

"Come on, shit. If she wasn't pissing you off you wouldn't have told me, like the time you were half-dead in the hospital and she flashed her pussy from the other end of the bed. Tell that to a judge and see how long she'd be around wanting to cash in."

"I love her, and she loves me. And cash in on what? I'm a pauper compared to her, so you're wrong, and we're doing another honeymoon in April. That's why I have to get this goddamn therapy over with. It's hard being a man when I can't even hold myself up on my knees."

"She has knees too." Shane glanced at Bret's midsection, smirking. "Does it get up by itself since the attack?"

"Yeah, so what."

"Then she has no reason not to fuck you. She's playing you."

"The therapist's always around."

"So what? Since when have you been afraid of company? Could be they'd both learn something." He checked his watch. "Don't think about it. Do it. One week at most, then we come back. I have the old man's four-door. You could sleep your way there. One week, for Christ sake. She'll probably be gone somewhere anyway and it'll probably be your last chance to get something different. Remember what you missed out on last year."

"I can't, Shane. I can't."

Shane shook his head. "Then I'm gone. It'll be an all-nighter if I want to get there by noon, before all the good stuff's taken. Anything I can get you before I leave, maybe a beer?"

"I'm good, thanks. Call me." Bret grinned. "If I can't go, the least you can do is let me listen."

"I'll go one better. I'll bring you a souvenir and tell you all about her."

"Wouldn't be the same if I'm not there to take the prize myself."

"Then come with me. One week."

Bret shook his head as Shane turned to leave, stopping short. "Seriously, Bret, you've got to get rid of her. She's no good and nothing's going to change any time soon. She's using this therapy stuff as an excuse not to get laid, and there's a whole lot more out there."

Bret chortled. "You haven't seen her naked, I have. It's very nice, the way we like it."

"Close your eyes and they're all the same. You wouldn't buy a Lamborghini and not drive it, unless you're a shit driver."

"Go get fucked."

"The smartest thing you've said since I got here. Just get rid of her."

Shane first dropped off his father's car in the city, transferring his luggage to his BMW convertible which would better suit his needs. He would be in Myrtle Beach by noon on Monday, the same time John Franklin would be strolling the path to his private beach without a care in the world.
*

The first day of Franklin's new life was essentially insignificant to him, what he always called North American insurance-company-freedom-fifty-five bullshit. Of greater importance was the day before: the last day of his previous life. He was walking towards the good times he had let slip away all those years while working at solving other people's problems, resolving issues and striving to save enough money after taxes to pay cash for the Perfect Escape.

The tenth had come and gone, as would the rest of the week, during which time he had sworn to do nothing. So far he was being true to his word, which didn't include cruising on the Perfect Escape, anchored offshore with an extended scope so he could spend the entire day watching her resist gentle waves that soon after lapped along his private shore.

# 190

The call came on her third disposable phone Tuesday morning while the girls were at school. Phallicia was expected in Myrtle Beach by dinnertime Wednesday, the twelfth, to attend a one-day seminar of her choice and she should plan to depart early Friday. US Customs and Immigration would probably not be interested in what seminar, though she should be prepared for the question and she was not to stay at the Sunrise Hotel & Lounge or the Tidal Reef.

She booked business class. The flight schedule would take her first through Philly, then Charlotte, and would make the sixty-hour excursion gruelling. The first flight would leave Montreal at 6:30 AM. The third would arrive in Myrtle Beach from Charlotte at 3:14. If all went well she'd arrive at the hotel by 5:00 PM, Wednesday. The return portion would begin with a 7:20 AM flight and tight connections, getting her into Montreal by 3:00 PM and home in time for dinner on Friday, leaving Phallicia Hunter a thirty-six hour window to kill Shane Pendleton with somewhat more creativity than two bullets to the back of his head.

# 191

She packed her two-day wardrobe that night and put aside the clothes she would wear for the trip once she could do so without interruption. The two skirts were the shortest she could find, her blouses were the most décolleté, her panties were the whitest for a reason and her shoes were stilettos. There would be no bras or nylons to detract him or discourage him. She wanted him to see her, and he would. She hadn't worn a bikini in months and the ones she packed would be the smallest on the beach. The notebook and seminar reading materials were pure subterfuge, so was the SPF 30.

The flight came in early, surprising none but the frequent flyers onboard, and Phallicia arrived at her hotel at four-thirty. By eight she was in the Sunrise Hotel & Lounge in a black silk flared skirt that was so short she could barely breathe without showing what little she wore underneath. The double-layered crossover mesh top plunged in a deep V to her bare midriff, making a clear statement that anyone without sufficient funds should stay away.

The man diagonally across from her had just brought the wine glass away from his mouth as she swayed in and had barely enough time to bring up his napkin to prevent the wine from blowing out. She was gorgeous, sexy in the extreme, and if she thought she'd get away without a supreme scolding she was seriously wrong, cousin or not. She had no reason at all to dress that way. She was already alluring without exposing everything she owned, which did nothing to stop him from continuing to watch her as the waiter seated her at the table she requested. He couldn't imagine what her father would say. Thank God he wasn't there.

Pendleton came down his first couple of nights near

seven, sitting near the main entrance and both nights went to his room with different girls he'd met in the lounge after seeing them come in alone to the restaurant. He ate early and partied late, kicking them out by four or five. When this one dropped her napkin, she leaned to one side to retrieve it and Marcus' eyes immediately focused on Pendleton's, knowing exactly what the dead man was seeing and thinking.

# 192

Pendleton couldn't believe what he was seeing. She was leaning far enough over to show him the barest ass he'd ever seen outside of bed or the beach and when she straightened she adjusted her skirt so that he caught a glimpse of white from the front. He finished his meal and ordered another beer to keep the table, hoping she had intentionally shown her panties to come on to him and that she'd do it again. She didn't. She finished her salad and signalled the waiter to ask him something that caused the man to look at his watch. Then she looked at hers.

The waiter brought her the check as she finished her wine. She paid cash, standing when he left, swinging out one leg at a time and Pendleton had no doubt she'd be his Wednesday campaign. She walked out passing in front of his table, ignoring him completely, stopping at a pillar for support as she leaned forward to adjust a strap on one of her shoes. He wanted her, and he was going to have her exactly that way: in stilettos, leaning forward. He snapped his fingers for the waiter, scrawling in the air to show he wanted the check, catching a final glance of her as the elevator doors closed.

The waiter answered that she had wanted to know what time the restaurant opened for breakfast and the best time to get a good spot at the beach, which was 9:00 at the latest. Pendleton went straight to the lounge, pacing his drinking until midnight, hoping she would come through the doors. When she didn't, he left to drink alone in his room, not noticing the big man who walked out after him.

# 193

The restaurant served breakfast from six-thirty to accommodate business travellers. Pendleton was there fifteen minutes later and by eight-thirty he was shaking from the effects of caffeine and had read all the personal ads at least twice for SWMs, SWFs, GWFs GWMs, BWCs and couples where the woman was bi and the man was a casual spectator. He wondered why only white people fucked around, noting the contact codes of one couple and one SWF he would call first.

Phallicia's skirt was pale beige, as short as the one she'd worn the night before, and tighter, showing everything including the detail on the front of her panties. When she passed him the single detail was the inside seam. Her muslin top was loose fitting with strategic front pockets, the buttons were undone to show the swell of her breasts and her sandals were dressy ankle wraps.

The waiter from the night before was at her table instantly, pulling out her chair. Moments later he set down a coffee pot and filled the two cups. Pendleton's first thought was that he had left the lounge too early, but she was ordering and not waiting for anyone. Interrupting a woman while she was eating wasn't good pick-up procedure, especially if someone was joining her, and he waited to see whether she would do something like she had during dinner, or glance at him the way she did from the elevator.

She was talking with the waiter who would only do her in his dreams. She was early twenties, he was late forties, bald, and not by choice. She was asking for the check, anxious, looking at her watch. She was going to the beach, and when she left she made eye contact without breaking her stride. He was certain he'd have his hands all over her ass before dinner and followed her out, maintaining a discreet distance and facing away as she turned in the elevator.

As soon as the elevator stopped at eleven he hurried to press the up button before anyone got in his way. He was on the second, which gave him the extra few seconds he needed. She'd be at least ten minutes, all he needed was five; unaware Phallicia had already changed into her bikini in the stairwell before once again stepping into the elevator and out into the lobby where every head craned to watch her strolling through to the beach.

Marcus was planted on a towel he borrowed from the pool, joining the many fixated passers-by. She was virtually naked and he couldn't help but stare, his face awash with deep purple heat when she turned to face him with a slight tilt as she ran an open hand over a very smooth, very bare ass. When he saw her coming towards him his mouth went bone dry, until she stopped and giggled.

He had to get himself a woman, she scolded. He'd been missing out for far too long. Shit, there wasn't the slightest bump or lump on her, not even the slightest crease at the bottom of her butt. He grimaced, she blew him a kiss. He'd spend a long time erasing the image of her from the same mind he was losing because he'd never see her in a sweater again without thinking about her perfectly shaped breasts as skimpily covered as everything else she was showing the world.

He remembered the times her father had turned her upside down as a child to slap her bottom, pretending he was angry, and how she would giggle. He shook his head, hard, dispelling the up-dated version. She was in big trouble. The last time he'd seen a bikini that small was on one of the dancers at The Lap and this was no way the same. She was on a public beach and if shithead even thought of touching her, his head would be instant history.

# 194

She wouldn't be the only girl wearing a skimpy bikini, merely the skimpiest. The combination of side strings disappearing between her buttocks, a tiny front triangle covering the very minimum and smaller triangles covering her breasts obviated any need to go topless, unless other girls were.

From Pendleton's vantage she might have been completely nude. He would have stared longer, but he was too close. He didn't want to screw up twice. Standing to one side of her, he scanned the beach. When he chanced a second glimpse she was poised on one knee coating her legs with sun cream, switching sides and smoothing what was left over her buttocks before sitting to do her front and face. That's when she noticed him.

"Hi. You're the guy from the restaurant."

"Yeah, seems we're pretty much the first ones out."

"Yeah, I could have stayed in bed a while longer, but I wanted first choice. I'm Phallicia."

"Shane."

"If you're not meeting someone, this is as good a place as any."

"You don't mind? I thought I saw the waiter pour two cups of coffee at your table, not that I was watching." He hesitated for affect. "Actually, my first lie of the day. I was watching you."

"Thank you. The double cup thing keeps the cheap pickup lines to a minimum."

"So you're alone?"

"Yeah, for a few days of sun, a few drinks and a few dances. I come here every year to even my tan."

He took the cue. "Seems pretty even to me."

She like that, flipping over as he spread out his towel.

"New York is so not the place to get a tan."

"Are you from there?"

"Originally from California. Ever been to Venice Beach."

"No."

"You should go sometime. Closest thing we Americans have to Eden. And you?"

"Montreal."

"You're French?"

"No, but I speak enough to get by. I'm an architect. Actually, I'm a senior partner with the firm."

Asshole. "Wow. That sounds way more interesting than my job."

"Which is?"

"I'm a sex therapist, a good one, but it's boring. Know what I mean? And believe me, it's not what you think. That's why I come here every year, or to Miami, for a little excitement where no one knows me."

"Life's too short not to have a little fun."

"Aren't you a little old for Spring Break?" She laughed, turning over, letting her knees separate enough to distract any male. "I'm sorry. I didn't mean you're old."

"I don't know much about Spring Break. I didn't even think about it." He paused long enough. "I'd really like to hear more about your job, which might be boring to you but sounds interesting to me."

She noticed the time, blowing a thin stream of air from between her lips. "It's only nine- thirty. My start time's eleven."

"It's eleven in Newfoundland."

"Where?"

"Newfoundland," he began to explain. "Never mind, it's far enough eastward to be 11:00 and far enough northward to still have snow."

"Sounds terrible. Ever been there?"

"No. It's the end of the world...and super boring."

Then how would you know, asshole? "We're better off here." She reached for her purse, searching for a twenty. "You're sure it's eleven there?"

"Yes."

"Get me a Corona. I'll go for the next one."

When he left she went into her purse again, as Marcus was trying his hardest not to get turned on. When Pendleton returned she was sitting facing the ocean and held up both hands to take the frosted plastic mugs from him.

"I'll hold them while you get ready. You won't get a burn on wearing those clothes." She put both mugs between her legs, waiting until he pulled the tee shirt over his head to pass him the lotion. "This stuff is phenomenal. A little bit lasts all day and doesn't wash off with sweat or sea water."

The beers emptied quickly, the empty mugs still frosted as Phallicia reached forward for her purse, wriggling onto her knees to line up a very small piece of thin material at the bottom of a perfect belly directly with his face.

"I'll go, Phallicia. Don't bother. Besides, you paid for the last one."

"Well, aren't you such a gentleman? Thank you, Shane. That's so not like American guys." She squatted in front of him, handing him the money that she wasn't surprised he accepted.

"I won't be long."

"I know," you filthy pig, "then I'll tell you about my job and you can tell me about yours."

When Pendleton came back she was lying on her front with her straps undone. He spoke about his job for too long, which might have been more credible if she hadn't known him or if he'd been eighty-five. Neither applied and he only stopped talking when she tied her strings and pulled on her cover-up, hoping he might see something more.

She insisted she would go for the third set of beers,

thinking she had to escape his self-infatuated babble. Walking away she winked at a frowning Marcus, holding out the fingers of both hands, then a single forefinger letting him know to start packing up. She had drunk very little of her first and second beers, spilling each one by her side, and Pendleton would neither notice nor care that she would do the same with her third. His third would be his last on the beach. The tequila would come out in his room when she wouldn't need to worry about revealing what women find fascinating about penises, despite the fact she didn't know, or what men didn't know about vaginas, which was everything.

"No, not clinical, not in the sense that I can prescribe medication. I'm strictly a creative director with knowledge of anatomical functionality."

"Which means?"

"I understand the correlation between the vagina and heart as well as the penis and brain, and I'm able to coach couples about the relative importance of each organ."

"Mostly old folk I guess."

"Wrong. Middle-aged. The oldies and the younger ones don't care, for different reasons, and that's unfortunate because pushing in and out for three or four minutes is so not what it's all about. Anyway, that's what most people do and by the time they hit thirty it's too late for them to admit they've been doing it wrong. So they start cheating, paying, or forgetting about it."

"Then they go to you?"

"Some do. Normally the women come first for a few sessions before the men. They always have the same reaction. They all think I'm going to make them undress and do it in front of me while I'm naked in high-heeled boots and holding a whip."

"What does happen?"

"I show them how to communicate, how to touch."

471

"That's it? No one's ever…?"

"Yeah, it's happened a few times, though I've never undressed with them. I'm strictly a creative director."

"It must be hard."

She laughed. "That's the whole idea."

Pendleton returned the laugh. "Not what I meant. I meant for a guy to do his wife, who's probably nowhere near as drop-dead gorgeous as you, and not want to touch you."

"I didn't say they don't touch, and thank you. Sometimes I let them touch, if I feel touching will help them turn on, or sometimes I sit away from them. Men love seeing under women's dresses, so do women. Did you know that? I could be with you all day in this thing and tonight you'd still want to see under my dress. I guarantee."

"I'm not like that, but who could blame me if I did?"

She ignored the remark. "Hey, Shane, it's eleven o'clock. I need to get out of the sun and eat something. Want to join me for lunch?"

"Sounds good. Where?"

"Give me ten minutes to change. I'll stop off at the second floor and wait for you. I won't be long. My room's so small and the worst view ever."

"I've got a great view, besides you. Why don't you knock on 218 instead of waiting in the corridor?" He crossed his heart. "I'll be a perfect gentleman." He pointed up. "Hey, I've got a better idea. Why not order in room service? I mean, could the view be better?"

She nodded. "Let's do it, what the hell."

Pendleton was on his feet. "Give me a head start so I can make sure housekeeping's been in. Say, fifteen minutes."

"Ten. I'm starved."

# 195

He was on the balcony when she walked through the door he left ajar. When she came through the patio doors he was facing her with a half-finished beer, pointing to the one he opened for her.

"I thought you might have changed your mind."

"I decided to have a shower to get the grime off."

"French dips and house wine should be here in a few minutes. That okay with you?"

"I could eat a horse." She took up the beer. "The view's to die for."

"You're dressed as though you want to ride one. What's with the gloves? I was sort of hoping you'd be wearing what you had on this morning, or last night."

She hummed a wow, giving him hope, pressing her palms against the top of her cowgirl hat. "Not twice in the same week, but…" She undid another button on her denim shirt that was tucked into her boot jeans. "That better?"

"Much."

"The skirt I have for tonight is a cute little flirt skirt with matching boyshort panties."

"What's that?"

She could have smacked him. "You don't know, seriously? You keep this up and I might have to take you on as a client." She tapped the neck of her bottle against his. "Drink up, big boy. The day is so not over and get the door while I use the little girl's room."

When the bus boy went she came out. Pendleton was opening the wine. "I hope you don't get any sauce on your blouse."

"I'd take it off, if I was wearing a bra. Not much difference between a bra and a bikini top. Naked is something else."

"Like what you had on at the beach," he tried.

"Good point. Let's finish our beers first and see what happens. Anyway, I want to show you something."

"What?"

"First let me put on the "No Moleste", since the food's here." She went to the door and put the sign on the outside handle before letting it ease closed. "This is so cool, Shane. You're going to love what I show you after I close the patio. I think I might have overdone this morning with my thong and now the heat's bothering me. Did you like seeing me in it?"

"No kidding."

"The little triangles don't cover very much, sort of like being legally naked. The last time I wore anything that small was in Mexico, which seems like forever ago." She put the photo albums on the ottoman beside him. "Do you like dirty pictures, Shane?"

He grinned from ear to ear. "I'd like to take some."

"I bet." She paused. "Go ahead, take a peek," she prompted, and before he was able to process the images she said, "The first two are Chad, the second two are Thurston." He was stunned into silence. "Chad gave me his version, so did Thurston, and, as you can see, talking didn't help them much. However, you'd be surprised how much more they wanted to talk near the end. So here's the deal, big boy: you're going to die sometime between midnight and 4:00 AM. That's when I have to leave. You sodomized my girlfriend, asshole. By the way, do you remember her, Addison, the blonde girl you and your friends fucked all night in Mexico until she died? Her name was Addison, she was turning twenty-five, she was a virgin, she was my lover and you killed her for a fast fuck." The door opened slowly as Marcus stepped in. Shane Pendleton was mute, glued to the four images. "Anyway, you sodomized her and I'm going to do you the same way, with these, and it'll hurt like a son of a bitch." She took three capillary tubes and a new screwdriver from her bag. "But before that you're going to have a triple laxative cocktail. By the way, no more food or drink, except all the tequila you want. Wasn't that your favourite drink in Mexico?" No answer came. "Here's the good part. You're going to kill yourself," she paused, "with this. And, oh, if you don't, I will"

"This can't be fucking real."

"Good choice of words and, yeah, it is real. You should have listened to Rivers and Williams. They knew the day of your buddy's wedding, which is somewhat of a moot point." She continued working. "I've learned you'll go through stages. You'll cry, beg, and whimper. You'll blame the others. You'll say what you did was just Spring Break fun. You'll urinate involuntarily, and, oh yes…take off your clothes and don't pretend you don't want to. You've been waiting to fuck me since last night, big boy. Come on. Let's see exactly how big a man you really are." He didn't move. "My friend is here to make sure you do what I say. See the gun? I make more noise when I pee. So take off your clothes."

When Pendleton was naked she passed him six tabs, the bottle of tequila, ordering him to drink one mouthful. "You can have more later, Shane. In fact, you're going to finish the whole bottle. How are the roofies doing? Feel them yet? Six, that's what you gave her, and I'm sort of curious how many you put in my beers, the ones did didn't drink." She tossed the bottle onto the bed, passing him a glass filled with the three purgatives. "Swallow every drop," she told him. "I'm assuming this'll make it seven. You know better than me, but certainly not the first time you've mixed your drinks."

"I never drugged anyone. She was drunk. We all were."

"Six: the magic number, what you gave Addison. By the way, I'm the redhead who was with her…if you're wondering. I hear your friend wanted to do me as badly as Chad wanted my girlfriend. Would you have killed me, too?" She put the three vials in the bag along with the two beer bottles and Marcus did a preliminary search for anything and everything, including Pendleton's digital Canon and spare memory cards. "Shane, when they find you sometime tomorrow, or the day after, you'll be lying in your shit mixed with blood, glass and urine. You may throw up, and if you do that's okay because you'll be dead. Oh, and if you cry, everyone will know. The eyes stay red. This has been a real learning experience for me and I couldn't have done it without you four guys."

"We all had too much to drink, her included, and she didn't mind coming with us. She didn't."

"Shane, Shane, Shane. That's beginning to sound a little like begging, and a little premature." She paused. "She was a frigging lesbian for Christ sake." She paused again, not realizing how closely Marcus was watching her. "Chad was the first one to stick his little dick inside her, ever. Who was the second?"

He answered when he saw the man standing with a gun in his hand. "Me or Thurston, I don't remember."

"How many times, total? And be careful, I know the truth."

"Seven...maybe eight."

"You fucked her eight times?"

"Yeah, I suppose."

She was silent, remembering the day after. "I have photographs of her and the reason I'm not showing them to you is that I don't want you to see her naked. Do you have any idea what you did to her bum?"

"I didn't do her that way, the others did."

"Yes, you did. Chad was the one who stood by and watched as the three of you flipped over the love of his life."

"Listen, my father has a lot of money, and I'm a partner in the firm. This doesn't have to happen."

"You're not a partner. You're a junior like Wilmington. He's next and, yes, this does have to happen. And we will have to rush you along because we're on sort of a tight schedule, though I would prefer more time with you. Chad and Thurston both had twenty-four hours. I feel as though I'm cheating you with nineteen," she noted the time, "actually sixteen now. We have to leave at four, sorry. The good news is, you'll be dead and won't miss us."

"They'll tie us in. They'll catch you."

"No, they won't. Like I told Thurston, you guys chose the wrong girl to fuck, meaning me. Phallicia Hunter isn't my real name, more of a travel convenience, sort of like an upgrade."

"So who are you?"

"I'm a girl who has a friend with a big gun, so you can assume I'm not the girl next door. Now, go lie on the bed, on your stomach, so he and I can eat our lunch. I want you to spread eagle. I'll be over to see you in a moment and you might want to have some more tequila."

After a lunch of French dip and wine, Marcus put the plates, glasses and flatware in his bag. Then he went to Pendleton's bag for a pair of socks he immediately stuffed into the trembling man's mouth as Phallicia instructed Pendleton regarding the proper position he should assume for an easier insertion. It was his choice. One way or the other the tube was going in. He would feel a sharp piercing sensation, she explained, warning him to maintain his position for the second tube, and the third.

The whimpering began, becoming muffled groans as Marcus wrapped Pendleton's head face down into a pillow. He was crying, unable to free his head as much as he strained. At first he felt a cold, tickling sensation, though as the tube went deeper and Phallicia got the rhythm right it felt warm. She inserted the screwdriver, gave Marcus a second's warning, tapped the end and asked Pendleton how he was doing. Had she gone deep enough, was the tube thick enough for him? She hadn't understood a word. One, two, three, and Marcus pressed the head deeper into the pillow.

The second tube would feel different, she explained, because the tissue was terribly perforated in several places and the tube might not go in as smoothly, not even with the water soluble lubricant. He might feel a little discomfort, but she had to complete the procedure before the laxatives began working and his ass became a fountain. Was he ready? One, two, and Marcus thought he'd snapped Pendleton's neck. Blood was trickling from his lacerated anus to his open legs, Phallicia stepping away to prepare the third. She broke off the contoured end, lubricated the remaining length, inserted the screwdriver and completed the insertion with one fluid motion.

The sun disappeared by six o'clock and by eight heavy clouds rolled in at the same time as Pendleton was having trouble retaining his gases, weak from loss of blood. Phallicia stepped onto the balcony with her hat pulled down, returning moments later, grinning and asking Marcus if they could put Pendleton outside for the rest of his time instead of the bathtub. He gave her an unequivocal no. She would have to settle for the bathtub, although he did agree the rain would have befitted the moment.

Pendleton had gone through a few stages, offering to double a payoff of an unknown amount, offering to call his father. He wet the bed when urine suddenly spurted from his shrunken and upward pointing penis, which did nothing for Marcus who had just taken another mouthful of French dip. He cried, he begged for everything from his life to being allowed to sit on the toilet because he was going soil himself, to a glass of water, and each time he asked for water she gave him tequila.

She suggested he'd be better off trying to hold it in as long as possible because shitting broken glass was going to be a real eye opener. By eight he was ready for the tub, a light spray, and the socks stayed in. She didn't think he needed help, he was a big boy. Though he did need help when he got to the tub and Marcus lifted him over the edge with one swift movement.

"Bret Wilmington is next Shane, if he matters to you at a moment like this. And if you're curious about the time, it's ten. Chad died exactly this way, on schedule. Of course, we were able to play a little bit with the weather, the way you left her, in the rain. Thurston, same thing, except he died covered in ice. The problem is we're in South Carolina. Do you understand the issue, Shane? Do you?" She gave him more tequila. "You have somewhere between zero and six hours, then we have to go. So, here's what I think we should do. You take the straight edge, it's a new one, and either cut your throat or your wrists. I can't, I'm not allowed, but if you don't my friend will. He says the wrists are easier, but the results take longer. He says for the throat you really do have to focus, but, like I said, the thing's new."

She dropped the razor onto his chest and walked out. The laxatives worked completely for one full hour between eleven and twelve and Marcus went in during each session to make sure Pendleton hadn't removed or spit out the socks, commenting once that they were probably preventing him from chewing off his own tongue. The patio doors were opened well before twelve and they took turns standing in the light rain to get away from the stench.

When Marcus went in at 1:00 AM he saw a thin line across one of Pendleton's wrists. The slice wasn't deep enough and the hand holding the blade was twitching. At one-thirty Pendleton was still alive, convulsing from the combined effects of his day and the fine spray of cold water.

Marcus leaned forward to see the eyes. He put two fingers to the left side of his neck and simply said "internal and external jugular", then he snapped his fingers.

Pendleton was beyond thinking when he brought the blade to his neck, not realizing he'd left a jagged trail of red along his chest. He needed all his strength and concentration to properly place the blade, acknowledging the man's help when he pointed and held out his palms to indicate all was ready.

By 2:00 AM Marcus had photographed the scene and the duo walked out together, leaving behind the razor. It didn't matter that the time would show on the hotel computer and he reminded her to keep her head lowered.

She would meet him at five with her bag containing absolutely everything she had worn that day, and when she returned home she would remove everything worn for the trip and get rid of it, including the twenty-dollar watch.

# 196

John Franklin might have stayed in Miami a few days longer, had he not been anxious to keep a promise he'd made to himself. Thursday, as the sun was rising, he cast off from the dock and set the Perfect Escape on a heading that would put him in Elbow Cay on Abaco by nine for breakfast and supplies. The breakfast started with a complimentary mimosa, ending with a promise to the owner that he'd be a regular, the groceries would last three weeks and his fourth hour was on the house with the five hundred litres.

The marina was half-full, not yet populated with weekenders from Palm Beach and four hours was all the time needed before plotting a course along the turquoise coast to find a sandbar or private cove, or not. If he didn't, the following week wasn't far off. Everyone zoomed in occasionally and he was no exception. Boaters who claimed never to have used high-powered binoculars to see what neighbouring ladies were or weren't wearing were either liars or eunuchs. When he came up to the Sea Ray he put them aside. Suzanne Wilmington was definitely not someone he wanted to see romping gaily in the buff. He hadn't thought to call them on the VHF either. There was no point in a public greeting and he didn't have their cell phone number.

The Executive Decision was beached with one anchor off the bow and one off the stern, Frederick was enjoying an early start to his day and his wife was working at completing a natural make-over of her winter white. He and the couple weren't yet on good enough terms for him to interrupt their privacy and he continued due south along the coast, dropping his anchor well out of sight where he opened his cooler and jumped in for his morning bath.

Life didn't get any better, but nothing would bring her back to him and he was a one-woman man. She was still with him each night, and would be during his long lazy days when she would be as close as his vivid memories of her.

The evening was idyllic. The sinking sun casting a golden hue across calm seas earlier in the day surrendered to a star-filled sky, a single moonbeam carpeting the ocean in silver and he'd be back at Perfect Retreat for a late dinner within two hours of hoisting the anchor. Any craft approaching from the north would see the sleek San Juan as red and white specks of light, from the south, green and white. Inside the cabin the muted blue of the GPS screen showed a westward heading he would alter to a compass course of north-north-west, the red screen of the radar unit showed no other vessel in the vicinity.

The captain and crew of the Executive Decision were still at their playful day-harbour, deciding against the security of a marina. He didn't give them another thought, nor would he ever think of the shock wave he was leaving in the turbulent white fjords of his wake, or the horror and confusion twenty-four hundred kilometres away.

# 197

Shane Pendleton wasn't discovered until mid-morning Saturday. The Sunrise Hotel had a twenty-four hour privacy policy, particularly during Spring Break, irrespective of any request for privacy hanging on the door. By noon the entire floor was cordoned off and Pendleton's shame was complete.

The Wilmingtons were found late Friday when another craft beached not too far from them, extending the courtesy of calling the Executive Decision to ask if they might beach close enough to have safety in numbers, yet privacy. When they still didn't respond and weren't seen by the time most boaters would be enjoying cocktails a call went out on channel sixteen and soon after a Bahamian Police patrol boat arrived. Within an hour of the horrific discovery the Coast Guard arrived, Bahamian papers headlining the brutal killings on Saturday, the Myrtle Beach papers on Sunday and in Montreal the vague details were front page news by 6:00 AM Monday.

-----

Montreal Businessman and Wife Not Believed Killed By Modern Day Pirates
Bizarre Coincidence As Junior Partner Found Dead In Apparent Drug Related Macabre Suicide

-----

Frederick J. Wilmington of The Wilmingtons and Pendleton and his wife were found shot to death aboard their yacht in the Bahamas Friday evening by other boaters, each with double gunshot wounds to the head, hours before Shane Pendleton, a junior partner with the same firm, was found dead in a Myrtle Beach hotel where he had been vacationing.

Bahamian authorities believe robbery was not the

motive as they downplay piracy in an effort to reassure visitors to the popular boating community, though island police and Coast Guard officers admit they have no leads as they continue to question local boaters and residents.

Myrtle Beach Police are continuing to investigate what they considered the masochistic suicide of Shane Pendleton, while refusing to release details on the community's first murder of the year as they exchange information with mystified Bahamian police.

Family members whose presence was requested in order to confirm the identity of the victims have assisted in both investigations and are expected to meet with Montreal authorities Tuesday, March 18. No press conference has yet been announced.

# 198

Christine arrived home for dinner on Friday in an unusually good mood, with a bottle of wine and tickets for two full weeks in Savannah. Best of all, the therapist told her a week earlier that her services would not be required beyond the end of the week when the bed was scheduled to be removed. Bret was completely capable of walking. With minor exercises performed each day there was no reason they couldn't vacation for a few weeks as long as he didn't exert himself.

The evening was the first without confrontation in weeks or months and they watched television until Bret fell asleep on the bed from the effects of his first taste of wine since the attack. At midnight Christine was awake to answer the phone, curious to hear why they would be calling at such an hour. The last time was to tell her of Bret's beating. This time was no better. Her flesh turned cold, the moisture in her mouth evaporating instantly. When Tremblay asked if he could come by she said yes and went to her husband.

"Bret, wake up. Wake up, Bret." The wine had relaxed him and she took her time to wake him without unnerving him.

When he opened his eyes he was smiling and simply said: "What?"

"Bret, the police called. They're coming over."

He dragged himself upright. "At this hour? Have they found out something?"

"Bret, your parents are dead. They were murdered on the boat."

"What? Are you kidding me? They're dead?"

She shook her head, beginning to cry as the reality set in. "They've been shot."

"My God. When?"

"Sometime today, they're not sure. They're coming to talk with us. They want us to fly to the Bahamas as soon as possible."

The detectives were the same two who handled Bret's case file in October and Bret could think of no reason why anyone would kill his parents in such a horrible way, convinced his beating was an unrelated and random act. When the detectives left they were no further ahead. Bret called Shane's father, while Christine did her ticketing on-line for first class tickets to Fort Lauderdale with a connecting flight to Freeport City. Whatever else they had to do would wait until they arrived by mid-afternoon Saturday, including the return flight.

Horrified, Broderick insisted he should go with the young couple to identify the bodies. Christine should book three seats and Bret wasn't to worry, Broderick would call his son in Myrtle Beach immediately. Bret refused politely, telling Broderick to expect the police at his home later in the morning. He and Christine would be fine and he reiterated what he had told the detectives about the absurdity of his beating being related to the killings and the older man agreed the idea was indeed preposterous.

# 199

The American Airline two-stop flight via Dallas got them into Fort Lauderdale at 3:16 and they were promptly met at the gate by officials to facilitate the connecting flight. An urgent message was waiting for them. Broderick Pendleton had called regarding a matter of utmost urgency. They were to call him at the earliest possible moment.

Bret kept his cell phone to his ear as he collapsed to the ground, too disoriented to balance on his cane, crashing his elbow into the carpeted floor before anyone could prevent his fall. Christine grabbed the phone as airline personnel helped Bret to his feet. Shane Pendleton was found dead, Broderick told her. His throat had been cut and that's all the police would tell him. There were no flights out until the next morning, delaying his arrival in Myrtle Beach until mid-afternoon, and Montreal detectives were asking more questions. He asked Christine rhetorically what was going on and when he hung up she asked her unstable and white-faced husband the same question, which he hadn't answered by the time the private island hopper landed them on Abaco late Saturday afternoon.

Frederick and Suzanne Wilmington of Montreal were identified and the black polypropylene bags were zippered and tagged. Autopsies would not be required. The cause of her death was one gunshot to the forehead and a second to her occipital bone. Frederick killed by a shot that took out his left eye along with the zygomatic and sphenoid bones, the entire left side of his head. Both died quickly, murdered by someone who was good with a gun and not a pirate who would have simply thrown them overboard before taking the boat. However no one was willing to consider the killings a professional hit.

The police and Coast Guard would not question Bret

and Christine until Sunday morning, after which there would be paperwork to complete before returning the bodies to Montreal where they would be processed by the system. Beyond that, only one person would ever know the truth and he was very unlikely to tell anyone about his day. There was absolutely no evidence.

# 200

Coming alongside to beach the San Juan had taken a few minutes. He hadn't intended to stay for dinner, he explained, expressing sincere pleasure at seeing them as he climbed the transom ladder uninvited. They had seen him coming and he hadn't missed a syllable of what Wilmington whispered to his wife as he stood from the aft lounge to greet him.

"We would have been much better prepared, had you called on the radio. I'm afraid you've caught us without much to offer."

"I won't be staying long. I was in the area and wanted to say hello and good-bye." He pulled the gun from the back of his belt.

"If this is your idea of a joke, it's in very poor taste."

"No joke, Wilmington."

"What's this all about? Are we being kidnapped?"

"No. You're being executed," he paused, "as a belated wedding gift to your son and his bride. Unfortunately for your son, he won't live long enough to enjoy the proceeds."

"What are you talking about?" Wilmington's mouth was dry, gagging on the words.

"Your son's a criminal. He killed a girl nearly two years ago in Mexico, after he and his buddies took turns raping her."

Their shock was real. "No, he didn't. I know my son. He wouldn't do such a vile thing. He's a Wilmington."

"You don't know shit. Rivers and Williams are already dead. Pendleton will be today or tomorrow and your son will join him inside of a month."

"I don't believe you."

"What you believe doesn't matter. You'll be seeing all of them in less than a minute, except your son."

"Shane is hours from here. What you're suggesting is

impossible."

"Turn around. We're done."

"Why kill us?" Frederick's tone changed, hugging his speechless wife mostly to support himself and help stop his limbs from trembling. "If what you say is true, and I don't believe you for an instant, my son committed the crime, not us."

"To use your words: he's a Wilmington, like father, like son. Turn around. I'll do her first, then you. It'll be fast with no pain." He stared deep into Wilmington's eyes. "Turn around. It'll be easier for both of you. You'll be dead before she hits the floor."

"Go fuck yourself."

He sneered. "No, fuck you." Suzanne jerked out of his arms, a single dark hole indicating the exact centre of her forehead. "Like I said, fuck you." The architect lunged forward a second too late, slammed against the closed door of the companionway. The impact of the blast burst the soft egg-shaped ball leaving a hollow black hole in a mask of distorted skin that paled with disbelief against a backdrop of splattered, abstract red. Within the two minutes he had promised, the couple were alone in the dark.

# 201

Bret hadn't eaten for most of the day and after hearing about Pendleton he refused to eat. His mother appeared surreal with the hole in the exact centre of her head, though his father wasn't as horrible as he'd been told to expect. Everyone agreed they had died instantaneously, before hitting the ground, as though talking about actors in a movie and not his parents.

The police were sympathetic, but needed to know about Shane Pendleton and would send a car for him early the following morning, by which time they would have exchanged preliminary reports with the Myrtle Beach police and Bret would still be over the legal limit.

"Drinking won't help, Bret. Talk to me. Please tell me what's going on."

"Shut up, Chrissie. Please shut the fuck up. You don't understand."

"I want to understand, but you're not making things easy." He poured three fingers of coarse house scotch, shaking his head and pacing on legs throbbing from exertion and the humidity. "What have you done, Bret? Tell me. I have a right to know if you're in trouble." She paused. "Are you gambling, or doing drugs?"

He drained his drink instead of answering when he saw how frantic she was. "I'm fucked. I am truly fucked."

"Why? What have you done?"

"Nothing, Chrissie. Nothing I can tell the cops about, because of the way things would look."

"Is Shane involved?"

"Yes."

"Then tell me…for better or worse. Remember?"

"I thought you stopped loving me."

"If I hadn't been strong for us your mother would have

taken over. You know she was obsessed with control and the fact she's no longer here doesn't change the hold she had on you. I needed you to be free of her."

"You still love me?"

"As I've said, you'll be the first, but you must be honest with me, and with the police."

"What happened isn't easy to explain. It'll sound worse than it was."

"You're scaring me, Bret."

He managed to pour another drink and not spill any before sitting across from her, extending both legs.

"Two years ago we had a little fun with a girl in Mexico."

"Who…and what do you mean a little fun? Like what, exactly?"

"Me, Shane, Thurston and Chad," he paused, she waited. The moment was too precious. "We had her at the beach where no one could see. The whole thing was innocent, Chrissie. We were all a little drunk and wanted to have some fun. She wanted to play as much as we did and when we finished we had another beer before leaving. She wanted us to stay and party so we left her alone to get dressed, thinking she was okay, but she didn't get up and somehow she died." He buried his face into his open hands, letting his tears filter through. "The police said she died from hyperthermia. She would have been okay if she had gone with Chad like she said she would. None of us thought for a second she'd die."

"And you think her boyfriend or husband is coming after you?"

"That's not possible. No one saw us. No one knew, and now, for no reason, we're totally fucked."

"You have to tell the police."

"And say what, that my best friend's dead because we had some fun with some girl who didn't know when the party was over?"

"Did you rape her?"

"No, we did not rape her. I swear she wanted the four of us like she had some sort of a fantasy. Chrissie, she even suggested where to go. The beach was her idea. You know how things happen during Spring Break after a few drinks. Everything would have been fine if she'd gone with Chad, like he wanted. I doubt she'd even remember our names. It's not like I cheated on you, Chrissie."

"You have to tell the police, so they can protect you. I'll stand by you, Bret, but you have to tell them so they can warn Chad and Thurston."

The expression on his face revealed sheer terror. He hadn't thought of either one since the phone call and checked his watch. "I haven't spoken to them since the wedding."

"Call them."

"The dead girl is the reason they left Montreal, why they didn't hang around after the wedding?" He swallowed, grimacing as the scotch burned his throat. "Chad said he saw some guy at the church who was staring straight at them. He said he was certain the guy knew what we did, that he came to let us know. We didn't take him seriously."

"Phone them, right now, or I will." She stood, going to his jacket for his phone. "Right now, Bret. I'm not spending my entire night wondering whether your friends are dead."

Seconds past 10:00 PM Pacific Time, he heard the recording. Rivers' number was no longer in service and moments after 1:00 AM in Toronto a woman's voice answered Williams' number with a harsh. "What?"

"I'm sorry to intrude at such a late hour. My name is Bret Wilmington. I'm calling to speak with Thurston Williams."

"Who's this again?"

"Bret Wilmington. We attended school together. It's

very important."

"He's dead. He was murdered a month ago."

"My God! Where?"

"Here, upstairs in the bathroom. And you're calling…why?"

"I was a friend," he stammered. "Thank you. I'm sorry." He pressed END and struggled to his feet for a refill. "They're both dead. I'm the last one."

# 202

Bret maintained he had no idea who would want his parents dead, whether the killings were a professional hit or not, and Shane Pendleton had not a single problem in the world. The last thing he would have done is commit suicide, especially that way, drugs or no drugs. No one can drink enough tequila or swallow enough roofies to cut his throat. Besides, he never owned a straight edge. Bret was frustrated with the questioning. Yes, Shane was a heavy drinker, though no more than anyone else on vacation. He wasn't a saint and he certainly wasn't gay. He would never have done that to himself or anyone else. Where was all this going, he wanted to know? Shane Pendleton never hurt a fly, and Bret Wilmington walked out sweating, waiting for Christine to join him an hour later.

The papers were signed and his parents' bodies would be transported to Montreal by the end of the week when Canadian authorities would take over. An unmarked island car drove them to the hotel and from the hotel to the airport, Christine remaining silent throughout, knowing the investigation wasn't over. Eventually her husband would have to confess to the police about the incident in Mexico and she wondered how that would affect her future plans. She imagined him lying on a table in an orange jump suit, a needle stuck in his arm, as the police car pulled into the No Parking at departures and the driver jumped out.

"Bret, I'm curious. I have a question."

"Why I didn't tell them," which wasn't a question.

"No. I'm curious how four men can do that to one woman in such a short time and derive any pleasure, especially with the other three watching. Is that a turn-on, letting other guys watch?"

He sighed, clambering out, walking away from her,

leaving her to tell the cop she could manage the bags herself. He was on death row, walking his last mile with not much farther to go, unless. The others hadn't known. He did, which gave him an advantage. Of course, he'd be leaving Christine far behind. But if not having her meant surviving, he could do without her. He knew they would never be. He saw the unmistakable loathing in her eyes and sometime soon he'd find another Christine somewhere. He was certain she would never be the wife he wanted. Worse: now she would be in his way.

# 203

Monday morning a pale Jean-Émile was late coming to the office, after instructing Jeff to circle the block several times. He knew someone would be at the reception waiting for him to arrive, with yet another black box. The box itself didn't bother him. What did bother him was the number of jellybeans he expected to see and prayed he would see only one as he folded the early morning newspaper and told Jeff to let him out.

The same man was standing by the main doors and casually extended a hand gloved in fine leather. "I believe you were expecting the third of four instalments. Good day."

Marcus turned and walked out.

Jean-Émile walked to the receptionist. "Call Madame Harnais. Tell her I mustn't be disturbed by anyone." And he didn't have time to remove his coat or put the wrapped box on his desk before his cell hummed. "Yes?"

"Dad, it's Maria."

"Why are you calling so early in the day? Is something amiss, child?"

"Yes, and I want you to know I wasn't involved. I promise you. I know nothing about what happened."

"I know."

"You believe me?"

"I do without question, child, unequivocally." He wanted to ask what he knew he could not. "Are you well, Maria?"

"I'm very well, dad," she lied.

"Then I suppose you're expecting an invitation to disrupt my quiet and eat more of my food with your chatty friends?"

"Yes, very soon. I love you." Then the line went quiet.

"Yes, of course, and I feel quite the same way. Goodbye now."

He pressed end and threw his coat over one of the three deep leather seats beside him, reaching for the box as he sat on the edge of his desk. When unwrapped the box was identical, a perfect set of three. When opened, a single red jellybean rested on white velvet. His expression was sombre. He now knew the name of the fourth man.

He placed the box on the mantle, reaching for the bible, whispering a simple thank you with closed eyes, asking forgiveness in her name. She was an angel doing what he was too afraid to do and he should pay the final atonement for the sin of their collective vengeance, although he didn't pray for the Wilmingtons and didn't bother wondering why.

# 204

Christine didn't have to pretend that she was haggard. She hadn't slept for three days. She had dealt with the police in two countries and had only spoken with Selena for a few moments between her flights on Saturday and Monday while Bret drank himself very close to being refused boarding privileges before she cut him off.

Monday night the red light was flashing. She had forgotten to call the men who were coming for the bed, which worked out for the better because Bret made it no farther after pulling a cognac bottle from the liquor cabinet and pouring half a glass. He ignored her, lost in thought as he twisted and wriggled his way onto his rented bed. Christine poured a cognac for herself and went into her room to call Selena without, forgetting him. She thought she knew what was going through his mind. She didn't. Midnight: seventy-two hours past Friday and she wanted so badly to pack a suitcase and spend a few days working with her friend or, better yet, enjoy a few days not working.

Selena was a joy to speak with and be with and would never be welcome in Christine's home. Cristina was more than a friend and employer to her and she knew Cristina's husband was a bad man. She wasn't letting the best person in her life spend the evening by herself, even if they couldn't be together. She asked Cristina to wait while she poured a glass of wine, then she went for her cell phone to put 9-1-1 on speed dial. They spoke until the sun came up, mixing business with girl-talk, and when the time came to end the call Selena insisted she would call every half hour until the police arrived, and if she didn't answer the police would arrive much earlier.

The police came at nine on the dot, as Selena was calling for the sixth time, hanging up when certain Cristina would meet her for lunch at her condo. Christine argued she hadn't slept for four days and Selena countered that lunch would be anytime she woke up, that she would be sleep at the condo and this time she was the boss. So deal with it, chica.

Christine took a deep breath before opening the door to her home to detectives Tremblay and Larose, the Smith and Jones of la Francophonie and extremely courteous, until they saw Bret lying in bed.

"Do you wish to be excused from this part of the interview, Madame Wilmington? We can speak with you later, perhaps separately, when the issues are less sensitive." Tremblay understood her anxiety. "It's not a question of dividing and conquering anyone, madame. My concern is one of the content becoming somewhat base."

"Thank you, Detective, I'll be fine. I'm not as fragile as I seem. Please understand. We haven't slept for quite a few days."

"Entendu, madame."

"Shall we begin, Monsieur Wilmington?" Tremblay suggested, curtly.

"I have nothing to add to the reports I'm sure you've received from the Bahamas."

"And Myrtle Beach, as the story grows more interesting."

"The two are unrelated."

"From this point we will be recording our conversation… any objection?"

"Am I a suspect?"

"No. You're a victim. The questions are: Who else, and when? We will forego the questions of your previous testimony about gambling. In spite of which, we do have related questions."

"Such as?"

"Such as, why didn't you tell us you were at The Lap of

Luxury the night of your attack?"

"I wasn't." He hesitated, seeming to think back. "Maybe I was, I don't remember. They're all the same after a few drinks. We went to a few places."

"Did you pay cash in those places?"

"No. I expensed it. My father's idea."

"Then you went nowhere after you left. You were at The Lap, monsieur."

"And you know that how?"

"This has become a murder investigation. We don't need permission to investigate suspects or witnesses, and you're a witness. We did a credit card check on you and Pendleton. We've established you were at the club most of the night." Tremblay turned to Christine. "Madame?"

"Go ahead, Detective."

"You had a charge you could easily have rounded off to eight hundred which is pretty steep for two young guys grabbing a few brews, Monsieur Wilmington."

"That's all we had, a few brews."

Larose cut in. "Let's cut the crap. You're not the only one who hasn't slept. You either did a helluva lot of lapping or you did a couple of girls in a private room. The owner of the club is Angelo Bardollini. Do you read the papers, Wilmington? Do you know who he is?"

"No."

The cops exchanged smirks. "You don't know? You don't read the newspapers, a smart guy like you? Well, he's a very dangerous man, extremely unforgiving, and we believe you pissed him off."

Tremblay took over. "Monsieur, what was it you and your friend did to piss him off?"

"Nothing."

"Yes. Wilmington, you're moments away from crapping in your pants. So why don't you tell us the truth? If you weren't having a little too much fun with a few of his girls, what did you do? You did something bad."

"Listen to me, detectives. I don't know. I have absolutely no idea what you're talking about."

"You're lying. Listen, that wasn't your first time at the club." Tremblay unfolded a copy of a credit card receipt. "October 10, last year, a receipt for two grand signed for by Shane Pendleton. Two grand. An office party, Monsieur Wilmington?"

Christine cut in, livid. "No...the eve of my wedding...you bastard."

Larose continued. "Who else was there, Wilmington? Two grand is too much for two guys to blow alone, even for big spenders like you and Pendleton."

"We were alone, no one else."

"That's bullshit." argued Larose. "At two hundred a pop per lady, add in a few drinks, that's four hours each in a private, or eighty laps. That's a pretty wet leg for anyone, Wilmington, even with girl-girl action. "

Christine cut in. "Pardon me, Detective? Girl-girl?"

Tremblay gave his partner a look that didn't mean much. "My apologies, madame, I am not accustomed to more refined women. It's an entertainment preferred by some men. Somewhat more than the usual fantasy, I suppose."

"You mean women dancing naked together for men?" Tremblay nodded. "You paid to watch naked girls the night before we were getting married. You son of a bitch."

"No. What they're saying didn't happen, Chrissie. We had a couple of drinks and left. What Shane put on his card, I have no idea. In fact, they probably screwed him on the bill."

"Did you take one or more of the girls to a room outside the bar?"

"No, of course not."

Tremblay turned to Christine. "Madame, a moment alone with your husband. Please. We won't be long. It's rather sensitive."

Glaring at Bret as though he was the purest filth, she left.

Larose continued. "Mr. Wilmington we have photographs of how your friend died, of how it's likely to go for you. Are you ready?" He explained each of the photos as he flipped each glossy one at a time. "He may have died by his own hand, but not as a result of suicide, Wilmington. He was murdered and it doesn't matter a shit that he might have cut his own throat because he was dead anyway. They stuffed his ass with three glass tubes and smashed them with something, probably a screwdriver or a steel rod. Before that they force fed him an overdose of laxatives so he would blow his shit, guts and glass into the tub. But, to give the devil his due, they did give him six tabs of roofies and a full seven-fifty of tequila, the cheap shit with the worm. See, the worm's gone. Maybe that's what made him puke all over himself, or maybe the smell of his shit." He thumbed the last few pages for Bret who sat paralyzed. "See the eyes, they're red. Your friend cried like baby for his life before he pulled the blade across his own throat. See the blade? It's a drugstore brand, one hundred percent ordinary, sharp as shit, a useless forensic souvenir and they left nothing behind besides the socks in his mouth. The cops there have never seen such a clean site, even for a hotel. Check this." Larose pointed to the centre of another photo. "He pissed himself in the bed."

"Wilmington," Tremblay cut in. "You and Pendleton have made someone very angry and, if it's not Bardollini, we'd like to know who."

"Wilmington, this isn't a mob kill. They wouldn't take the time. This is payback, so what the fuck happened with you and Pendleton?"

"Nothing happened, nothing. It's all too crazy."

"So, did you get your parents killed, or are they getting

503

you killed? Old man Pendleton's about ready to jump out a window. Is he next?"

"No. I don't know."

"That's unfortunate, for you, because when we leave here it's officially out of our jurisdiction. There's nothing we can do. The one link we have to any of this is your beating in October, but we have no motive, no suspect, nothing, because you have nothing to say."

"Is the file closed?"

"The lid is on the box so to speak, out of sight out of mind. Isn't that the expression? We won't be wasting our time with an investigation until you decide you know something." Tremblay went in the direction Christine had walked. "Madame Wilmington, would you please join us."

She was red-faced, her eyes were streaked and she was shaking. "I heard everything, Detective. Can we have protection? We'll pay whatever price."

"No, madame, I'm afraid you cannot, and hiring private security will do no good. The question isn't one of cost. They will wait for a good time, the perfect time. These people, they don't make mistakes. The ones you hear about, they're expendable. Don't be deceived by the news. The only one of the five Ws these people don't care about is when. They can be very patient. Believe me when I say they have not forgotten him." He looked over to Bret. "Until your husband is honest with us and tells us what he's hiding, or why he's afraid, our hands are tied. He's not a very good liar, nor is he a suspect. So we can do nothing for either of you. If he changes his mind, call me. If you need us, Mrs. Wilmington, call me."

"Am I in danger?"

"I truly hope not, madame. However neither should your mother-in-law have been and she's dead." He turned his attention to Bret. "We have those photos as well, Mr. Willington. Would they help you remember?"

"I've seen my parents. Thank you."

"Your wife, I believe, has not. Has she seen how your mother is with a hole in her forehead and the other half of her head missing? Or your father with an eye blown out the side of his head which isn't missing?"

Christine sobbed, sinking to the couch. "Bret, tell them. Tell them."

The cops looked at Bret with a practiced coolness. "Tell us what?"

"She knows I have nothing to say. You've succeeded in making her think I'm hiding something, when I'm not, that I was spending the night before our wedding with whores." He gulped a mouthful of cognac. "Are we done?"

Larose leaned over so Christine wouldn't hear. Tremblay stood, indifferent. "We're done, Wilmington. Wishing you good luck would be a waste of words. You're royally fucked and the countdown starts now. You'll need as much luck as you can scrape from your gutter floor. That's where you'll have to go to hide and, then, they'll find you. This guy Bardollini is everywhere."

While Larose was talking Tremblay gave Christine a card and said "at any time, madame. Je vous en prie." Not long after they were gone Christine put on her coat and boots by the door, explaining to Bret that she'd be gone for most of the day.

"Where to this time?"

"I'm going to see Broderick Pendleton, after that I'll be working at Selena's. Don't wait up for me. Fall asleep whenever you've had enough to drink."

He managed a snide laugh. "Not another meeting with your favourite toilet maid."

She ignored the barb, walking to his bed as though ready to give him a goodbye kiss. Instead, she took up one of his aluminum walking canes and swung with enough force against the foot of the steel bed frame to bend the stick completely in half. Then, in a fluid movement she picked up the second one which had fallen to the floor, raised her arms high over his knees and asked him to repeat himself.

# 205

Her visit to Broderick Pendleton's home was uneasy at best. He was tired and beleaguered. The police had no new information, nor could he contribute anything which would assist in the investigation. He wanted to be left alone. His son's body would arrive on Thursday. The funeral would be on Saturday and he asked if she knew the names of his friends. She didn't, though she and Bret would certainly attend.

Why did she think the killings happened, Broderick questioned? She answered as non-judgmentally as she could that Shane and Bret had done something in their past that they were being called to account for, something bad enough for someone to believe torture and murder were appropriate. But what of Suzanne and Frederick, what of them, he mumbled to himself? When what he actually meant was, was he in danger? She had no way of knowing, she answered, wondering without any sadness at his lack of concern for her.

# 206

She knew Selena would be angry if she buzzed the apartment. She did anyway, not waiting to hear the greeting. The doorman knew her. The apartment door was open, Selena standing in a lavender off-the-shoulder terry sweater and matching low-rise drawstrings, wearing the guilty expression she had practiced.

"You bitch!" said Christine, walking through, dropping her case and purse on the floor. "How could you?"

"I am the boss for this afternoon. I wanted a little time with you. We have not talked together like girls since a very long time. I will work harder tomorrow."

"I don't mean that, silly. I'm talking about how beautiful you are. How dare you when I feel like crap?" Selena's brow furrowed. "Mierda, Selena, mierda. And didn't your mamá ever tell you to wear panties in case of an accident?" Cristina added.

"I am wearing my panties, see." She tugged at the narrow mauve band. "Now you have to stay with me longer today to teach me more bad words, Cristina." She squeezed her friend into a comical and limp hourglass shape. "And I do not like the way that I am seeing you. Come, I am taking care of you. En primero, you are taking a bath, después, you are sleeping forever until you open your eyes. Then we will eat my best cooking ever."

"I can't bathe and put on the same clothes. Yuck."

"Yuck is a dirty word?"

"No, not dirty, but, yeah, it means dirty."

"We still have your silk things for sleeping and I have new panties for you, in case of an accident." She beamed. "So go to your bath like a good employee, girl."

"That's what I call you. You can't call me the same thing."

"Today, yes. I can and I do. Go, girl."

The wine glass was filled halfway with red, the few lighted candles and bath oils were pear-scented, a large fleecy towel lay on the ledge, the music was soothing Latin instrumental and the blinds were drawn to block out the light. When Christine heard the door close behind her she looked at the bath hoping she wouldn't drown, or that she would. She undressed as quickly as she could, rationalizing she'd rather drown in an inviting bath than collapse on the tiled floor.

Thirty minutes later, a few moments to Christine, Selena knocked on the door. She laid silk tap pants and a camisole beside the towel and hung the longer silk robe on a wall hook, telling Cristina her bed was ready and she was expected to be asleep very soon, or else. Or else what? And Selena wasn't sure.

"I can't Selena," Christine argued. "That's your bed."

"Not today. Today my bed is your bed because I am to cook me and you a very excellent dinner."

"Lunch, Selena. You meant to say lunch."

Selena pushed her into the bed and pulled the covers up to her shoulders. "I know so well what I was saying. Dinner. You are staying with me for dinner because you will sleep until the night." She leaned over, kissing Cristina on the cheek before leaving the room with instructions for Cristina not to get out of bed unless she had to pee. Selena paused as she was closing the door. "¿Cómo? Cristina."

"Nada, chica. Decía gracias." Christine lied, and sleep took her over before the door closed.

When it opened again she hadn't heard, though when she twisted between the sheets to stretch, languishing in the release of pent-up tension, she saw the blackest eyes she could imagine staring at her from under a mass of cascading midnight black curls. She could feel and smell the sweetness of Selena's breath, feeling her own heart rush as quickly as her mind. Selena had dimmed the lighting to the minimum setting so she wouldn't wake Cristina with a start and spent the last hour lying by her friend, stroking her shoulders and hair, thinking she wasn't yuck.

"You are not yuck."

"Thanks to you. What's the time?"

"The time is for dinner."

"No, really, what's the time, Selena?"

"Eleven-thirty. You did sleep for almost twelve hours."

Christine tried to absorb the timeframe, pushing herself onto one elbow. "I have to go, Selena. Really, I have to go."

"No, Cristina. Still I am the boss and I do not want you to go. I want you to eat and I want you to talk with me. I did read all the stories in the papers. I will help you as you did help me."

"You're sweet Selena, but you can't help me."

"Yes, I can, if you stay here. Here you are safe. We both are. It is what you told to me." Selena let her hand glide over Cristina's cheek. "You will stay, for you, and for me, because I did work too hard for our dinner and I do not want that you go."

"I'll call him."

"No, Cristina, you must not. Believe in me, I know. You must not."

Christine forced a smile as Selena still stroked her face, watching as she drifted away to another place. "How long have you been watching me?"

"One hour."

"You need a life, girl, and I'm starved," she swept Selena's hair from her face. "I said I'm starved, hungry. Tengo hambre, chica. ¿Comprendes?" The faint smile began slowly to grow. "And I hope breakfast is just as good."

She barely felt Selena's lips brush against hers in a kiss that wasn't a kiss. They ate a scrumptious dinner on the living room floor watching ancient late-night movies, talking girl-talk and when the time came for Selena to be the tired one she fell onto the laid-out futon and drifted into a theatre of dreams. When morning came Christine jumped out of Selena's bed and ran through to the living room to pretend she'd been there all night. She wanted to see Selena open her eyes so she could giggle and tell her friend she'd spent the entire night snoring like a man and insulting Cristina.

"No, Cristina, nunca." She rubbed he eyes. "Nunca would I say such a terrible thing about you. Te amo. Lo sabes."

"It's true, Selena. You sounded like a man who smokes too much and you said terrible things about me. You said I was fat and ugly, that I smelled like a dog in the rain."

"¡Ay, no!"

Selena was on her knees, on the verge of tears.

"I asked you two questions, and you said yes. Do you remember?" The quizzical expression wasn't the answer she wanted. "Anyway, you said yes."

"To what did I say yes, Cristina?" She wrapped her arms around her friend, pulling her in close. "Never would I say these bad things about you."

"You said I could wear your new blue sweater, that you would make me the best coffee ever, and we could spend the day together No work." Christine squeezed back. "But I must leave by six." Selena shrieked with joy and pulled away to jump from the futon and run to the kitchen to start the coffee she hadn't smelled brewing, but Christine pulled her back, not letting go of her hands. "We'll learn about each other in time, Selena. In the meantime know that I am so happy we met and that we like each other."

"I like my home. I love my friend."

At that Christine became serious. "I'll be gone for the next month, Selena, after which I expect the business will be fully functional. I could never have done as much without you. So I want you to do something for yourself. I want you to go anywhere you want while I'm gone, to relax and be with other people. I've treated you so badly for the past five months and I've taken too much of your time."

Selena slouched with her legs crossed. "You tell me I am a man in bed and that I said so many bad things about you and that was maybe funny. Now you tell me to find another friend and that is not too funny. You are my friend."

"I always will be, Selena. You know I love you. I didn't mean for you to replace me."

"Cristina, I do love you so much. I always did love you, and when you did come for me that day I did think God was laughing at me for being bad, that you could not be true. I did believe that I could never be happy again, like I am with you, but I was not the bad one. He was the bad one."

"Selena…"

"I sit here every night I do not travel and I think of that night."

"What night?"

Selena's voice was as tender "La Navidad. Do you remember?"

Christine had pushed, when she should have pulled. What she was thinking couldn't happen, yet she was about to lose someone she cared for deeply and she couldn't let that happen either.

"Yes, Selena, I remember."

The words were a whisper barely heard, yet all she could manage to say as she raised her cupped hands to Selena's cheeks and their foreheads came together with a flood of warm tears dampening the space between.

# 207

Christine felt years younger returning home later that evening in Selena's designer jeans and blue angora sweater, after a day of relaxing in the hot tub and sauna at the condo. She hadn't lost a friend and Selena would not be taking any time off. She was too busy. They would talk on the phone at least once every day and if Selena thought for a moment Cristina was in trouble she'd call the detective whose number she had copied from the card.

Bret was asleep in his living room bed and the entire room smelled of liquor. He hadn't eaten in the thirty hours she'd been gone, nor did he listen to the message confirming his parents' arrival on Friday. No autopsy would be performed, which she took to mean she was free to take care of the details while he drank. She had heard nothing further from the police and was adamant that nothing would spoil her day. She called Selena to confirm she was safe before pouring a small glass of wine, putting a chair firmly against the bedroom doorknob and going to bed. The next morning Bret began early, sitting up with one finger of cognac left in his glass when she walked in.

"I'm leaving for the day," she told him matter-of-factly. "Shane's funeral is on Saturday. I told Broderick we'd attend. Your parents will be flown in on Friday and their funeral will take place on Sunday. I'll make the arrangement this morning, as you seem a little under the weather, and I'll stop by your office to advise whoever's interested in attending. If you think of anyone else, note the name if you can." She paused. "Whatever you do, don't talk with anyone. You've already made a mess of your reputation and the last thing we need is for anyone to know you're a whoring drunk." She paused, seeing his canes. "One more thing: if you ever again say anything like what you said yesterday about Selena, I'll bash in your fucking head." He listened inattentively, not trying to keep up with her until she jerked the bed. "By the time I get back I want you cleaned-up, dressed, and with some idea of what we're going to do about all this. I believe Larose was very right. You are fucked, and if you're not dressed, or if this bed isn't out of here by the time I get back, you won't know how much."

"Whatever." He stared at her as he swallowed what was left in his glass. Then he refilled it.

"Good start, big man. How big were you when you saw those pictures yesterday? A couple more things before I go: First, you can forget sleeping with me until hell freezes over. You disgust me. If you even think of touching me you'll need those canes the rest of your life. Second, don't forget what I said about Selena. I was absolutely serious."

She walked out, saying nothing more. Her first stop was at the funeral home. Her second was the offices of W & P where she spoke with senior secretaries about who to notify. Then she went into Bret's private office where she stayed for the rest of the day with the door closed, calling Frederick's personal assistant to order lunch. Then she called the firm's chief legal advisor.

When she arrived home Bret was on the couch. The bed was gone. He was dressed, shaved, he had eaten lunch and a vial of pain relievers was uncapped beside him. He was sorry, he told her repeatedly. He was sorry, she agreed. She would always think of him as a sorry man. The funeral would be at two o'clock Sunday, his secretaries would call those who should be called and his Chief Attorney had prepared a Power of Attorney for her that he, Bret, would sign. The pre-nup and the living wills were one thing, but if she'd be making decisions which would normally require joint input the least he could do is give her the ability.

Christine went to the door to let in the corporate

attorney. The well wishes and condolences were a formality, as was the living will. The document was signed by both parties, witnessed by him, and he left. Bret would have to appear sober for three days, though whether he did or not didn't concern her. If she had to explain his absence on Saturday she would, and everyone would pretend to understand. The same held true for Sunday. If he wanted to attend his parents' funeral smelling of booze and acting the town drunk, that was his decision. Oh yes, one other thing: The house was being sold. The agent would meet with them the following day.

She had expected a completely different reaction: anger, or refusal and a slew of questions. What she got was a single nod of agreement before he poured another cognac.

## 208

Michele assured Maria of completion by April 25<sup>th</sup>, ten days ahead of schedule: thirty-six days and counting. They had surpassed the anticipated number of clients, a competent staff was eager to begin working and whatever detail remained would be done by female contractors. The men had gone elsewhere with thousand-dollar cash bonuses which Maria gave them personally.

Pilar and Ercilia had one week left in their language courses and Friday they would receive certificates identifying them as fully accredited physiotherapists. Unfortunately, the day would go unnoticed. No importa. Maria would be busy working out last minute concerns with Michele, Jean-Émile and Madeleine had tickets for the theatre, though they did promise to get together soon, conveying their congratulations all the same, and the girls would order in pizza.

Pilar was on one phone with her parents, Ercilia on the other with hers, each one telling the other to answer the door. Ercilia put down her phone first and opened the door to Jeff after verifying the monitor of the surveillance system Maria's father had insisted upon immediately following their reconciliation. The rain was torrential and she pulled him in, telling him to take off his coat and hat as she would an older brother, surprised to see he wasn't wearing his usual cap and underneath his coat was a fine woollen suit. He was elegant and holding two long boxes wrapped in cellophane which prompted an excited Ercilia to yell for Pi who ran to the door in a flurry, still holding her phone.

Monsieur Larivière was sending his felicitations, Jeff explained, and was very sorry not to be with them to celebrate a wonderful success. However, he hoped they would enjoy the pizza. Jeff inhaled deeply, smiling mischievously. He loved pizza. Pizza was his favourite food, although he would understand if they were busy. Perhaps he would stop off and pick one up for himself before going home. Pilar rattled off in Spanish, punching him and taking her flowers. Ercilia followed through with a punch to his stomach, taking hers.

To Jeff the attacks were like being hit with feathers, conceding that he did have some time to spare. They slammed the door behind him and dragged him into the living room. The matter was settled. He was staying for pizza. They took his coat, pushed him onto the sofa and told him they would order right away. Then each girl hurried to say goodbye to her parents.

Jeff chuckled at the attention, reaching into a pocket for two little boxes when they reappeared with beaming faces. He and his wife wanted to acknowledge the girls' achievements. Pilar and Ercilia were speechless, which Jeff was certain no one would believe, until they saw the gold signet bracelets. He hadn't been kissed so much since high school and they insisted they call his wife to thank her, disappointed when she didn't answer.

"I'm sorry, Pilar. I should have remembered. She was invited to a party."

Pilar shrugged her shoulders. No importa. She would call the next day. The bracelets were gorgeous and they kissed him again before running into the kitchen for another wineglass. When they hurried in, each admiring the other's bracelet, Jeff thought to mention that he had an idea. He could phone Maria, suddenly remembering his wife was actually with Maria at the same party and, now that he thought of it, so were Mademoiselle Madeleine, Monsieur Larivière and Michele Baroque. He crossed his arms, putting an index finger to his temple. Actually, if he wasn't mistaken, so were the pilot and his wife.

The girls were shocked, chattering together in Spanish,

waving their arms when Jeff's cell phone beeped once. "Ladies, ladies, excuse me. Monsieur Larivière is calling. He wishes to know how much longer they must wait for you to join them at your graduation party." He paused, not covering the phone. "Should I tell him we're otherwise engaged for the evening, with our pizza?" He put the phone to his ear, holding up a finger to ask for quiet. "Maria suggests your black dress would be appropriate, Pilar, and Ercilia, your green." He watched them fly up the stairs. "Sir, I believe we should be at the restaurant within the hour."

# 209

Saturday morning Pilar and Ercilia woke beside each other, squeezed sleep from blurry eyes and hugged. Then Ercilia jumped from the bed to see all the gifts from their friends at the party. Jean-Émile had laughed hysterically as Jeff walked into the revolving rooftop lounge, red-faced with lip gloss.

The first thing Pilar had done was to give everyone a scolding which half of them didn't understand while Ercilia ran around the table giving each of them a tight hug, except Jeff's wife. She got as much lip gloss on her face as her husband, though the celebration wasn't over and Maria came through the door the following morning with three curative mimosas, a fruit bowl, her best crêpes and three Latin-strength coffees for a fine breakfast in bed until Pilar confessed she had something to say.

The time the girls had shared together over the past several months was precious to each of them, she began. They enjoyed every moment together, however the time was right for them to move out. As long as they remained in her home she would forget the most important thing in her life: herself, Maria. They would practically be neighbours. They were staying on the island and would never be far away. Nor would they be leaving for another month. But Maria was a beautiful and vibrant young woman and they wouldn't allow themselves to stand in her way.

"¿Comprendes, chica?" Pilar asked, taking her hand. "Tell us you understand."

"I do understand." She embraced them both in a tight squeeze, pinching Ercilia's cheeks and rubbing their noses together. "Now I suppose I have to plan another party. Thanks a lot."

# 210

St. Anthony's was half-full. As junior partner Shane Pendleton had few business contacts, as a human being he had fewer friends. He wasn't important, and those who attended his funeral did so for the sake of his grief-stricken father who sat quietly with Christine and Bret Wilmington at the edge of the front pew looking at the closed coffin.

The funeral director had politely discouraged a viewing, advising Broderick to resist the temptation of seeing his son for the last time. Broderick had done his share of drinking to get through the week. He rationalized the Wilmingtons and his son were separate and unrelated events, a coincidence, irrespective of police speculation. He knew his partner intimately and not the slightest possibility existed that Frederick was involved in anything unlawful.

The murder was a case of mistaken identity, or a random killing, being in the wrong place at the wrong time. He was certain the Wilmington tragedy was in no way a settling of accounts, though not so certain of his son who'd been a heavy drinker throughout his school years and openly spoke of women as convenient vessels to where many women at the office had threatened action if he continued his derisive comments. None of them had come to say a final farewell. For them his death was no real loss to the world. He had gambled his way through university, he lived beyond his means and any other W & P employee would have been dismissed for abusing expenses the way Shane had. And young Wilmington was no better.

Broderick couldn't answer when asked by the detectives whether the two might somehow be indebted to the mob, and his son's reputation didn't figure into his frustration. Shane didn't have one, at least not a good one. He knew everything about The Lap of Luxury; that Bret was with

Shane the evening of Bret's beating. So why was his son not attacked? Tremblay and Larose had no answer. He declined when the minister asked him to speak a few words about his son during the ceremony, as did Bret. So did Christine, saying that everyone present already knew who and what Shane Pendleton was.

Broderick attended his son's cremation matter-of-factly, standing disconsolate and disconnected between Bret, and Christine. Within forty-five minutes the orange-white flames roaring from six burners at 980° C converted Shane to dark grey cinders and desiccated bones which the operator would later pulverize to fill the brass urn Broderick would refuse with instructions to bury it nowhere near his wife. Then he turned to Bret without emotion and passed him a bundle which he retrieved from the trunk of his car. He faced Christine to thank her and left without speaking another word.

# 211

The Sunday funeral was filled to capacity. Broderick sat in the front pew on the left side of the church with other W & P executives. Bret sat in the right-side front pew with Christine. Most attendees spoke trite words of condolence to them, though no one offered to speak from the pulpit about the Wilmington's lives, including Bret who was suffering the after-effects of what had been a full bottle of cognac the previous night. Nor had Broderick anything to say and Christine hadn't changed her opinion of Mother Bitch simply because she was dead.

There was no question of a viewing or visitation. The bodies came in on the Friday to spend a few hours at the coroner's office for official processing and transference to the funeral home whose director didn't bother phoning Christine. She knew the bodies and limousines would be ready for transport to the church by noon on Sunday. One limo and a hearse would make up the procession and the church service would be expedient. Bret, Christine and Broderick would be alone to witness the couple's interment on the side of the city's Mount Royal and no one would attend the placing of the stone some weeks later.

Christine spent Sunday evening packing for three nights out of town. She would return late Thursday and Bret spent the entire evening drinking quietly, pleased she was leaving and saying nothing to set her off. He'd adapted to her frequent travels, though he had seldom been alone. Prior to the wedding he'd spent most of her out-of-town evenings with Shane and after the wedding with the therapist. This time he was happy she was going. She wouldn't be around to bitch about his drinking, he thought, and that would give him the time he needed.

That he would spend the night on the couch was a given.

What he didn't know was that Christine once again wedged a chair under the doorknob and wasn't sleeping longer than moments at a time. When she left the house early Monday morning he was unconscious and would be for hours.

# 212

Maria's cell phone flashed silently Tuesday morning at 9:00AM. Bret Wilmington had left his home three hours earlier. He was taking a flight from Burlington, Vermont to Miami where he wouldn't be staying on the Executive Decision. On Thursday he would fly from Miami to Atlanta and Denver, stay three nights, and fly to Chicago on Sunday where he'd stay three nights before continuing on to New York. He would arrive on Wednesday, April 02 and stay four nights to wait for his one-way excursion flight to Heathrow on Sunday, April 06.

The flights and hotels had been booked through an agent on the Monday, where he later went to settle the account with cash. He had taken one suitcase and called no one but the travel agent before leaving to drive across the border. He'd be staying at the Central Park Plaza during his New York lay over and had requested a room on the executive Concierge floor as he had with the other hotels. Marcus thought England would be the best venue for the meeting. She disagreed without saying so. Marcus was the pro; she was the amateur, though this time Marcus wouldn't be involved.

She had memorized the number, given to her with strict instructions never to call unless she felt threatened, and this was a threat. She knew he wouldn't answer, that she wasn't to speak his name or anyone else's, that she should simply leave a succinct a message and wait. She dialled the number, repeating Marcus' message to the letter, repeating the New York dates, and pressed end. Then she destroyed the disposable unit she knew to use once.

# 213

Tuesday, the twenty-fifth, Phallicia Hunter booked her First Class return flights from Montreal to New York for Tuesday, April 01. She would return on Thursday, the third, and Bret Wilmington would die at some point in-between. On Friday the twenty-eighth she went shopping for a phone and a wardrobe appropriate for someone staying on the Concierge floor of Central Park Plaza.

# 214

When Christine returned home on Thursday he wasn't there, nor was he when she woke the next morning and she called Broderick to know if he had spoken with Bret. He hadn't. He had no idea where Bret might be and was stunned into telling the truth when she asked him what had been in the bundle he had given her husband at Shane's funeral.

When she heard eighty thousand US dollars in hundreds and fifties against his shares in the firm, Christine called Tremblay to ask what she could do to find and protect her husband. The answer was: nothing. No warrant would be issued, nor protective custody offered. Her husband had refused to help them when they might possibly have done something to help him. In short, Bret Wilmington was on his own until he came forth voluntarily with information that would assist the investigation. She told him about the money. He answered that she should be prepared for the worst. If he had decided to run he'd find out soon enough that running was pointless. Tremblay was also convinced she was safe. The people interested in her husband didn't kill without a reason. If she had done nothing wrong, she was safe.

When she returned home late that evening she poured a glass of wine, called Selena, left a message that they would speak over the weekend and went to bed with the door open as her husband sat with a bottle of cognac in a Denver hotel room. Saturday she spent the day making the house perfect for prospective buyers and cross-shredded her entire W & P file that had been delivered to the house for Bret to complete. Then she went to the Wilmington residence to sign documents on behalf of Bret that would put the home on the market and left with anything she considered personal, including computers, cell phones and personal financial portfolios so she'd be ready the moment the banks released the funds. By midnight she was familiar with every detail of the couple's financial standing. With an estimated four million for the insured home, his insurance policy as senior partner, hers as spouse of a senior partner, corporate shares, an equal amount in retirement funds and one million more in liquid assets, Bret had walked away from twenty-two million dollars.

The boat and cars were company-owned, and if he wasn't back by the time the house was sold she would hold a marathon first-come give away of all the contents of the elegant home. She put the basis of that implication out of her mind, though she couldn't resist smiling at the thought of Suzanne turning in her grave at the thought of rich and poor neighbours flooding through her home and leaving with whatever most suited their taste or greed.

Sunday at noon the third couple visiting her home made an offer she refused. They would have until Friday noon to consider the counter offer, but nothing under one-point-two would be acceptable. On the Monday she examined Bret's portfolio which she hadn't previously been privy to, bewildered by someone so privileged working so effortlessly at self-destruction. The quarter-million in stocks and bonds he'd inherited at twenty-one from his paternal grandmother had doubled in value, he was insured for one million as a junior partner, he had fifty thousand in shares and had cleared out eight thousand from his account on Monday, which he probably used to pay for travel expenses. He had a job that gave him one hundred a year, a car and expenses, private club privileges, four weeks off each year and his first year-end bonus came to twenty-five thousand of those shares.

At twenty-seven his net worth wasn't far from twenty-three million, running from a lucrative career to hide with a bottle in his hands and grovel in a dark hotel room, convincing himself no one was the wiser. They were, and ten times his worth would do nothing to help him once they found him. Christine knew he would never come home, that she would never go to Savannah. What she didn't know was how she'd react when answering the inevitable phone call.

# 215

The April 01st drive from JFK to the Plaza was a frenzied obstacle course and exuberant discord of daily life in the Big Apple. Finger waving pedestrians who were a mix of the best and worst dressed anywhere weaved between quadruple-parked cars and illegally parked delivery vans, showing contempt for the horns and sirens blaring around them. Cops on the beat ignored the hectic cacophony, going about making their quotas and street corner food vendors mechanically greeted customers who stood eagerly in endless lines for their midday intake of glucose, sodium phosphate and tasteless sauerkraut stuffed in a steaming bun.

She was the only one whose door was opened by a taxi driver at the airport, which likely had nothing to do with good manners and everything to do with her. Striding through arrivals the outside melee of porters, taxis and limos, she left a trail of happy gazes. Her herringbone shorts were very short, accentuated with five-centimetre alligator pumps and the length of nylon covering her bare legs in-between, a black high-neck jersey with oversized buttons, a tweed cap with leather visor and long blonde hair tied into a simple pony tail. And she tipped him well because he drove the most direct route and didn't speak after asking her destination.

The hotel doorman enjoyed the part of his day which included helping her out from the cab, and the young women who checked her in thought her outfit was to die for. The time was one-thirty. She had precisely twenty-two hours and her phone wouldn't ring until the next morning, if at all, though she had to believe it would.

She requested a room situated far from the elevator and a spare electronic key, declining the turndown service and complimentary massage extended exclusively to Concierge guests as the bellman happily escorted her to her room. Suite 1800 was at the far end of the north wing, the farthest room from the elevators and private Concierge Lounge where a full range of hors- d'oeuvres and beverages were offered between 2:00 and 11:00 PM, he explained.

He swept apart the drapes, explaining the view of the park, delaying his departure by mentioning that Concierge guests enjoyed privileged key-access to the floor and the option of relaxed in-room service or being served a lighter menu in the private lounge. Most guests arrived between five and six due to traffic congestion or happy hours, he went on, though they were expecting fewer than normal guests, half of whom were women, and if he could do anything to make her experience a more memorable one, his name was Henry. He left ten dollars richer and she could do nothing more until morning. She was incommunicado from both ends, hoping no unforeseen change or impediment to the agenda had taken place. She was isolated and could only presume where everyone else was.

At three o'clock she went to the lounge, poured a glass of 1999 Bordeaux and returned to her room where she stayed for a room-service dinner. For breakfast the following morning she went to the main dining room as early as she could, wearing a denim skirt, an off-the-shoulder raglan sweater, mid-calf cowhide boots and a denim baseball cap. Her phone hadn't buzzed or flashed all morning and staying in her room would put her on edge as the hours passed.

She went to the park to sit quietly and be with Addison, thinking of their time together and the past two years without her. She tried dispelling the selfishness of the pain she felt which could never compare with Addison's pain and she swore silently that the last one would die a miserable death within the next eighteen hours. She knew

Addison felt the new pain which was troubling her, as much as she knew Maria still loved her and cried for her each night. The young man beside her who had thought to try his luck stood and walked away, scared off by the flood of tears and multiple languages he mistook for garbled rambling.

By eleven she was in the lobby, anxiously waiting. He arrived at precisely 11:30, as promised, proceeding to do exactly what he said he would do had they met in Savannah. He went to the white courtesy phone, took the receiver in one hand as he put the other discreetly over the chromed cradle to prevent an open line, scanning the lobby for her.

She would have known him anywhere the way he stood, the way he strode amongst other men who waddled or slouched along. Even with the fedora and trench coat she recognized her father. He was there. He'd come for her and she couldn't stop her lips from trembling until he stared straight at her and made a swift, short arc with an extended finger, scolding her as sternly as though he had screamed the words.

They went for lunch, sitting at separate tables, which was hard for Phallicia who struggled to ignore him. He had no such temptation. She left the dining room at 12:15, he left at 1:00, and when the elevator doors opened he walked through and said nothing for eighteen floors. The concierge wouldn't be on the floor for another half-hour and every hour after that to note special requests, restock the bar or replenish the hors-d'oeuvres.

Once in the room she hugged him. "I love you."

"What do you mean by saying that I'm here, that I came for you?"

"I never said that."

"You did, in the lobby." He hugged her again. "How do you think I always understood what you and your mother were saying even when you were in another room?" He chortled. "Never mind, I love you and would never disappoint you. It's enough that I wasn't there for her."

"I know you love me."

"You also know the rules."

"She nodded. "Yes."

"You're beautiful, perhaps a bit too sexy with that sweater and bra strap thing, but beautiful nevertheless."

"Wait until I change for the evening. I'm going to be so hot. You'll really be angry with me." She hugged him again. "I can't believe how you've changed. You look young enough to be my boyfriend." She giggled. "Is there something you're not telling me…a woman?"

"No. Retirement."

"It was still hard for me to read the headlines. I cried all day even after our friend told me I should have faith in you and that you met with him."

"Didn't I tell you myself not to believe what you would read?"

"Yes."

"Enough said."

"My other friends were so happy you thought of them that way, and so sad they'll never be able to thank you. They're pretty mushy about things like that." She frowned. "They cried for you. Then they prayed for you."

"Their prayers were heard. Just don't tell them I'm in a better place."

# 216

She hadn't been wrong. He was angry; not that being angry did any good. She had changed for the evening into high-heeled stilettos and a clinging silk shirtdress that was mid-thigh and unbuttoned from the waist to the hem with only the first few buttoned above the waist. When he started to argue she explained why. Wilmington was a pig. He hadn't had any for at least six months and was likely to spend his nights in his room drinking in the dark unless he had a reason not to. Then she demonstrated for her father who about passed out when she stuck the hem of her dress in the bathroom door and pretended to walk away, separating the dress to show the full length of her legs covered with stay-ups and the front of her panties.

Angelo went to the lobby at 3:00 PM, needing to occupy his mind. Wilmington was expected between three-thirty and four. He would call her on the cell as soon as Wilmington got to the desk and would hang-up once the elevator doors closed so he could tell her how many had gone in. Bret Wilmington arrived at 3:50. Five minutes later he walked through the elevator doors with the bellman. Angelo wished her luck. Any other time he would have rolled on the floor laughing at her gasp when she heard about Henry, the pimple-faced and infatuated eighteen-year-old bellman.

"Damn it! Goddamn it. Lousy dress."

Henry was the first out of the elevator and immediately peered in the direction of the desperate voice, thrown into a state of flux between the cerebral and visual information he was receiving. His guest exited seconds later, stumbling against his cane, and both men walked cautiously toward the woman in front of 1800 who was half out of the dress she'd caught in the door as she was leaving her room to visit the lounge.

"Ma'am?"

She twisted abruptly. "Henry, I'm sorry. I hate embarrassing you like this. I ripped my dress when I got caught in the door and dropped my key out of reach." She pointed to the floor, tugging at the back of her dress to cover her half-bare buttocks while succeeding in exposing the front of her legs and her panties. She was clearly mortified. "Gentlemen, I'm truly sorry. I was unbuttoning the rest of my dress so I could get to the key when you caught me."

"You have no reason to be sorry, miss. Henry, the lady's key."

The boy reached for the card, passing it to Phallicia who allowed them both a good look as she slid the card into the lock. "Henry, stay here a moment and hold the door, please." She ran into the room for her purse with her dress held together by two buttons. They had already seen most of her anyway, so why not. She gave him a twenty. "Henry, I know you're a gentleman, right?"

"Yes, ma'am, I am. Thank you."

"Now I certainly do need a drink in the lounge. Thank you, Henry. Sir, I'm sorry you had to see me this way."

She backed into room, allowing him to see most of her one last time before closing the door. She put her dress in the bag, pulled out a short A-line skirt, an off-white silk blouse, a lace bra which she intended him to see along with nicely accentuated breasts she would moisturize and scent, and went to the empty lounge for a glass of the same Bordeaux she enjoyed the previous day. As she sat her skirt rose nicely, showing the detail at the tops of her stockings that would shock or excite anyone joining her, tugging at her blouse until she was satisfied that her breasts and bra would not fail to entice.

At 4:30 she heard shuffling feet at the double doors and

prayed another woman wasn't coming in who would be inclined to talk with another single woman. Single men seldom spoke with other men and usually approached attractive women when in the company of other men or sufficiently fortified with liquor. Neither was the case, raising her upper leg higher and towards her in a rubbing motion, revealing bare flesh between the top her nylons and the sofa cushion, giving the impression to any who might see her that nothing else was between her and the cushion.

"I see you've changed."

She glanced up, blushing. "I'm so sorry, not to mention a little embarrassed. It's not every day a lady gets caught half-naked in a hotel corridor."

"Unfortunately your distress was my pleasure." He paused. "I think anything else I say might sound like a pick-up line."

"I'm sure you have a few."

"I'm out of practice, I'm afraid. I had a car accident last year. I'm only now beginning to walk more or less properly."

"I'm so sorry." She pointed a finger at the cane. "So I suppose your walking stick is temporary?"

"Yes. A few more weeks, I hope. I really don't need the thing. It's more of a crutch than anything. No pun intended."

"I'm Phallicia Hunter."

"Bret Wilmington." He paused. "Phallicia, what an extraordinary name. Listen, I'd feel odd sitting somewhere else after all we've been through together. May I join you?"

"Please," she patted the cushion beside her. "I was about to go for another wine, can I get you something?" She read his mind like a cheap novel. "Thanks for the thought. Sit. I was going anyway."

He sat after she stood, letting her skirt take charge of itself. When she returned she sat beside him and crossed the opposite leg, showing enough to achieve constant distraction. Their glasses clinked together and their evening began. He was in New York en route to the Chicago and Detroit, he told her, to investigate industrial opportunities for his firm. She was a language teacher at a junior college in Jacksonville, Florida. She wasn't Spanish-speaking, though she did speak the language most often and the influence was obvious. She spoke a little French. He didn't, never having had the opportunity to learn, and by seven o'clock she learned every lie she could imagine about him, including that one. He was single, his parents were globe-trotting, though he had moved from the family home at the age of nineteen seeking independence, he enjoyed the occasional drink and he never did drugs. Neither had he ever travelled outside the US, he had never had anyone to travel with, as much as he wanted to.

Could she invite him for dinner, she wanted to know, which was the least she could do after what she had put him through earlier? Dinner was a great idea, he agreed, countering that she was the most beautiful sight he'd seen in months and her unfortunate cause for embarrassment was his great delight. She was beautiful. Dinner would be his treat for being fortunate enough to see such beauty and she conceded. She would need ten or fifteen minutes to do girl things and would call him when she was ready, and perhaps even suggest an after dinner drink in the Concierge lounge. She smiled. She was starting to like New York. She never thought people there were so easy to talk with, asshole. He went the opposite way at the elevator after telling her "1850."

She had fifteen minutes and by the time Angelo arrived at her room ten remained. She stepped aside to let him prepare. He had already eaten dinner, now she would.

Wilmington could not have chosen a better hotel or room for his death. The rooms were situated in opposite wings of the courtyard and the camera at the elevator wouldn't identify with any certainty anyone travelling from one wing to the next. The instructions were simple: After Angelo left the room she would go to the main dining room for a light dinner dressed as she was, wearing wide, tinted glasses. She would then go to her room and change into jeans, a denim shirt, and silicone gloves under more fashionable kid leather. She would need her glasses and one of her hats for the brief walk under the cameras and would join him in 1850 until the time came for her to go.

He said goodbye to her once more, telling her that he loved her, that they would see each other again. She disappeared into his arms as he squeezed her and held her close for as long as he could. He wasn't about to share his precious moments with Wilmington and, when released her, she pulled him closer to whisper in his ear. "Just tell me one thing, papa."

"If you call me that once more I'll turn you upside down and spank your little bum, which I have no doubt is as bare as the last time, and don't think I won't. My business has never been yours and my retirement hasn't changed that. Call him." And he walked out.

When door number 1850 opened the man in the hall apologized to the occupant, leaning to one side as though verifying the number. Then he shrugged, slamming a brass-covered fist into Wilmington's face before closing the door behind him. At 7:40 PM Wilmington was sprawled on the floor halfway across the room.

"Don't get up." Wilmington tried. "I said don't get up. Stay on the floor and get over in the corner. I'll tell you when to move."

"Who are you?"

"You know who I am, so shut the fuck up."

"You're him, the mob guy."

"You're him," Angelo mimicked in a reasonably

satisfactory whimper, "the mob guy." Then he brought his foot up against Wilmington's face. "Be quiet. Sit in the corner with your knees in the air and be quiet. Whatever you do, don't piss yourself. I hate when guys piss themselves."

Angelo yanked at the bedcovers that hadn't been turned down and put his case on the white sheets before retrieving and twisting each tool in his hands in front of Wilmington as he laid them out in a single row. He admitted to a certain morbid curiosity about the rest of the evening, having told Phallicia very clearly that he wouldn't participate in the glass tube segment of her plan. Marcus had told him about the second-generation glass tubes and half-metre long screwdriver that had come after Rivers, as though the photographs hadn't been graphic enough. She understood. She was becoming undeniably deft at her technique and he doubted she would need his help. At precisely 8:30 she knocked at the door.

"Hi there, Bret. Sorry I had to leave you guys alone for so long. I was having dinner and the service was a little slow." She laughed. "There I go again, apologizing to you."

"Who are you?"

"I'm Phallicia Hunter. I'm the one who killed Rivers, Williams Pendleton, and I don't have much time. Sit in the chair and take off all your clothes. Then drink some tequila. It's the cheap stuff and tastes like shit, but a whole lot better than what comes after. So try to savour it. Strip."

"No." Angelo lifted the phone from the desk and crashed the receiver into the side of Wilmington's head. "The lady said strip, so strip."

Wilmington did, causing Angelo to comment that real men never take their pants off first. Pants were always the last to go and when Wilmington was naked she told him to stand in the middle of the king-size bed with his legs apart and his hands locked over his head.

"Bret, we have to improvise and I apologize, again, though first let me tell you why you're here and bring you up-to-date. And, really, what were you thinking with all those flights to nowhere...and England of all places." She opened a bottle of wine. "Mexico, April 22nd. Ring a bell?" She poured two glasses, giving one to Angelo. "Yeah, you know. The girl you raped and killed was my girlfriend. Actually, she was my best friend and lover, though you must have known that. What was the word you guys used, dyke? Anyway, just so you know, I'm the redhead who was with her, the one you wanted to fuck. And, surprise, surprise, after two years you finally got to see my panties. I hear you have a collection. Is that an olfactory thing, Bret, or tactile." She smiled up at him as she worked. "Bret, do you like wearing women's dirty panties?" She waited what she thought was long enough for an answer and slammed the screwdriver across his knee that was closest to her. The impact threw him from the bed. "Answer me, asshole. What did you do with her panties?"

"They're in a file drawer in my office."

"Which one?"

"Doesn't matter. It's a secure office."

She stood over him with the screwdriver raised over his head as Angelo sat on the small sofa to watch the show, amazed. Hell hath no fury. No shit, he thought.

"Which one?"

"The red one, in the bottom drawer and it's locked."

"Locks don't matter, so were your house and car. How do you think we knew about your trips, or when Shane would be in Myrtle, or when Thurston's wife would be away from home? By the way, I've got some great pictures for you as soon as we're finished with this part of your evening."

"Why so long?"

"That's an interesting question. I wanted you to

539

anticipate your death and be afraid. We could have killed you within days of finding you, which would have meant your dying without fear and depriving me of a great deal of pleasure." She paused, seemingly puzzled. "It's sort of like a car accident, Bret: As it's happening no one ever thinks they're going to die. They're subliminally too busy trying to find another moment in time, another space. But if they knew in advance they would die in a car accident, and when, well, then they'd be like you are right now... shitting themselves. So sit. You have about six hours and if you're interested we're not shooting you. Imagine, six long months after your knees got a little banged up and it's finally your turn." She took a sip of wine. "I also needed time to formulate exactly how I wanted you to feel. Right now you're naked in front of a lesbian and a man who thinks you're a fairy, which is sort of ironic in one way. So let's get started. Get over here on your knees with your hands behind your back. I want you to see these pictures properly. By the way, Bret, we'll understand if you pee yourself. Shane did, and Thurston, who was on a cold, damp basement floor and not very impressive. Get on your knees." She reached for the album and began with Chad. "He was the first because he was the farthest and took a full twenty-four hours. Not quite what I had hoped for but we've come a long way since then and you're the beneficiary of those improvements. Chad just sort of died all crunched up in his shower stall as you can see. Now check out Thurston who was pretty much like Chad, though he died with frozen feet, a totally ripped out rectum, hyperthermia, excessive alcohol intake and bad weather. He looks like the frigging ice man, don't you think? Do you like that word, Bret? Did you use it a lot when you were fucking my unconscious girlfriend to death?" She brought the screwdriver across his face and took another sip of wine. "This is Shane. Hard to tell, I have to admit, but believe me that is good old Shane. Again, we had more time to share with him, not that you won't get the attention you deserve. He was a variation on a theme because we got to talking about old times. You know, gang banging innocent young girls and all that fun party shit. He peed right in the middle of the bed, Bret. He squirted like a baby." She pointed at the photos. "This is puke, a tonne of it, and if you're thinking it's the tequila you're wrong. More like him. You'll see what I mean. Now take some more." She passed him the bottle. "Did you enjoy pouring this cheap shit down her throat before you did her in front of three other guys, which must mean you got it up in front of them? Did it happen on its own, or did you have to work at it? You know, that thing you guys do? The question's pretty simple, Bret. Think you can do that for me now? Would you believe I've only seen a hard-on in pictures?" She prodded his groin with the screwdriver. "I really can't believe this tiny little thing could grow big enough to kill someone."

"Fuck you."

Angelo's foot slammed into Wilmington's back and into his head when his torso rebounded from the mattress. His eyes conveyed to Phallicia what he was thinking. Seeing Bret Wilmington trying to get it up was something he could do without.

"It wasn't the tequila, Bret. Drink up. The smell of his shit mixed with his guts made him puke. He tried so hard to hold everything in and, when he couldn't, well, his face says it all. The best thing about Shane, he cut his own throat. That's how badly he wanted to die. Like you. You're going to have a quadruple laxative orally, three for Addison, one for me, and that's a good thing. Chad's wasn't so lucky and I have to admit my aim wasn't very good. I pretty well gave him a hole he didn't need. Then you'll have some more tequila and I'll insert these three capillary tubes into your ass and break them one at a time. The third one goes in broken. Did you enjoy doing her in the bum, Bret? Did she feel good for you as you were ripping out her insides?" She closed the album and threw it into the open bag. "Did you ever think of doing your wife's ass, Bret? I've seen her often. She's a doll. Think she'd like me after being with a pig like you?" She emptied the four vials of laxative into a glass and put it aside. "I have no roofies for you tonight, Bret, not like the others. Do you think that might have been a mistake? Do you think I inadvertently made their deaths better for them? Did roofies make it better for Addison as you were all fucking her eight times? I don't know. I'm asking. I've never taken them. Not using them on you was a major decision for me, I admit, but we're time poor. I have an early flight to Montreal for an appointment and you know what rush hour's like. So drink up."

She suggested he swallow the laxative first, not caring either way. She let him take his time reaching for the tequila, which he did when he saw Angelo stand with an obvious purpose, though his hands were trembling too much to take the glass from Phallicia and he didn't resist when Angelo jerked back his head and drained the purgatives into his throat. When he finished sputtering she gave him a pen and told him to write as she dictated: Advise Broderick Pendleton, of the Montreal firm The Wilmingtons and Pendleton, that they have no interest in him. He had no involvement in what has caused his son's death, or mine. Bret Wilmington.

"You haven't started crying yet, Bret, which is okay. You will. In the meantime go stand in the tub. Put the water on the coldest setting, at a drizzle, and don't move from the water or I'll put one of these tubes down your throat after I smash the one I put up your ass."

Angelo checked his watch, told her to relax with an in-room movie, filled his glass with wine and followed Wilmington into the bathroom with a handful of hardware, a one-millimetre diametre wire and the chair from the desk. Twenty minutes later he had firmly secured a hook into a crossbeam in the ceiling and three metres of wire rope hung from it.

When Wilmington began whining, splattering out incoherent words from under the narrow waterfall, Angelo stuffed his mouth with a facecloth and reprimanded him with a punch to the side of the head. Before leaving he explained graphically to Wilmington that a single strand would later be wrapped around his neck to produce a result between a hanging and a decapitation.

If his head were to droop when the time came and he somehow managed not to fall from the chair, he would simply hang. However, falling from the chair would be another matter, twisting and jerking spasmodically like a rag doll. The wire would constrict instantly and within an hour or so would slice through to his vertebrae, which wouldn't support him very long at all, perhaps another hour. At which point his head might fall off, or not, staying attached to the wire like a grotesque light bulb. He assumed. He wasn't sure. Most times he simply used a gun which was so much easier.

Angelo glanced at the dark yellow dribble mixing with the shower water at Wilmington's feet. He grinned, thinking he should be honest with the naked and trembling man. Either way would be horrific. Even though he'd be dead within seconds of falling from the chair, those seconds would seem eternal. He'd be unable to speed the process and the longer he waited the more gruesome his death would be, though Angelo did promise the chair would not be kicked out from under him. That was the stuff of B-rate westerns. Wilmington, the big man, would be the master of his few remaining moments, bearing in mind that how well he held his liquor and how slippery the effects of his laxative cocktail would make the seat of the chair would make all the difference.

At 11:00 PM Phallicia called him out from the tub, telling him to lie in a foetal position without moving. He could have as much tequila as he wanted first, in fact she insisted. She'd be leaving in four hours and the bottle would be finished, one way or another. The first tube went in easily, though even Angelo winced when Wilmington's eyes bulged at the same time as the dull sound of breaking glass emanated from somewhere within him. The second insertion was predictable for Phallicia who knew the lubricant was superfluous, not so for Wilmington whose nose sprayed blood from the strain and whose ears rang from the impact of Angelo's blood-stained glove against his ear.

She sat beside him. "The worst isn't over, Bret. The rest of the tequila should help a little, I suppose, and you have less than half left so pace yourself. Do you feel good knowing it's coming to an end? I have to leave the hotel by four to catch my plane, which means I'll leave you at three. After that it's not my issue. I only asked for one promise, Bret: that you go straight to hell. And you will. This man hasn't told me exactly how, and he won't let me in the bathroom, but I believe him and don't forget I get to see the photos. You won't."

"Please," he implored.

"Ah, yes, the requisite begging. Did she beg you, Bret? Did Addison beg you not to kill her?" She gave him more tequila from the bottle. "Crying feels good, Bret, doesn't it? Did Addison cry for you to stop, mother fucker? Did she beg for you to leave her alone?" She broke her wine glass against the side of his head. "Tell me, Bret, how long did she cry before she died? I know she cried, I read the report, and I know she was dead before you stopped, you necrophiliac son of a bitch." She reached for the third tube, snapped off the rounded lip, and inserted the screwdriver.

"Put your ass in the air for this one." When he didn't she removed the broken tube and struck his ribcage violently with the screwdriver. Angelo exerted incredible pressure against his head, covering Wilmington's mouth and Phallicia pushed apart his buttocks. "The tube went in with a single thrust, without the benefit of lubrication. "That was the worst part. The rest is easy. All you have to do is die." She pulled him from the bed so violently even Angelo was taken aback. "Get in the shower."

At 2:00 AM Thursday Wilmington stood shakily on the chair between full-length bathroom mirrors, his legs streaked with deep red veins of trickling blood. Angelo allowed Phallicia one quick approval before closing the door to complete his work borne of her idea. She was satisfied, and she knew where to pick up a copy of the New York Times in Montreal. When he came out they did one cursory check and a second which was more complete. Everything, including the smallest shard of glass was in the bag, and he made sure he'd be the one leaving with the photo album. No photos would be taken. The album had served its purpose and was now a liability.

Moments before she left at 3:00 AM she listened to the muffled hysteria from the bathroom which was soon complemented by the telling stench. She handed her father a small package and asked him to show Wilmington the contents before he died. She left the hotel at three-forty five wearing a simple dress and long coat against the cold morning air. She'd be home in less than five hours.

Angelo kept his promise right away, holding the contents of the package to Wilmington's face. Phallicia was making her point more explicitly than any words she might have spoken. Bret Wilmington stared at the miniature and faceless couple, at first not understanding. When he did, his eyes bulged with horror and disbelief.

Angelo sneered vindictively, relishing the moment as he

lowered the tiny bride and groom and kicked away the chair.

# 217

By 9:00AM Thursday Phallicia Hunter ceased to exist. Her first stop was the Airport Hilton in Montreal by taxi where she had left her car and a small overnight bag. The second stop was the ladies' washroom where one woman went in and another woman came out.

Each of her new outfits was disposed of separately in mission boxes, including the one she wore home. She discarded her costume jewellery and blonde wig in public trash receptacles, and meticulously snipped her photo IDs and credit cards into tiny pieces before flushing them as she changed. She left her suitcase in the hotel parking lot without a name tag or flight stickers and Maria arrived home exhausted. She curled onto the sofa, tucked a cushion under her head, and slept till noon when she woke to have a fast shower, a fast lunch and leave for the rest of the day.

# 218

Friday morning Christine woke moments before eight and nothing had changed, except she was living in someone else's house, alone again, and she lay in bed until her cell phone buzzed and rattled on the bedside table. Selena was asking if she was alright and if her girlfriend could have lunch or supper with her at the condo. Neither was possible. She had one late morning real-estate meeting followed by another in the afternoon. The previous day, after finalizing the sale of her home, her agent told her of two prospective buyers bidding on the Wilmington home and she was certain four million would become four-point-something before the end of business Friday.

She asked Selena for a rain cheque, redeemable very soon. Selena said no, laughing softly, thinking she knew what Cristina had said. She hung up after saying goodbye and wishing her good luck with the sale. That's all she said and Christine sat for an hour staring into space and muttering to herself as several kilometres away in a downtown office building a well-dressed man pushed through the main doors of the Larivière Corporation to deliver the fourth and final instalment.

Marcus simply said "the debt is paid in full," and walked out leaving Jean-Émile to think he would never want to see himself on the wrong side of those people, or their families. Then he realized he was part of their family and this time he didn't hesitate. The single red jellybean in a black velvet box was placed with the other three before he stared at his bible which remained unopened on the mantle. The drama was finally over after so many months and he called Madeleine to come in. She had seen him cry privately on one previous occasion and when he tried to explain that he couldn't tell her why she cradled his head as she stroked his hair.

She had never told him of the dark man she had seen by the canal, as he had never mentioned the same man, who was supposedly dead, coming to his office late one night. She did then, sharing his grief, gazing at the fourth of four black boxes she would never open.

He would take time to compose himself, she told him. They would have a healthy dose of cognac and they would call Maria who had been through a hell they had been spared and could not begin to contemplate. Maria needed them more than ever and they wouldn't disappoint her.

The message was clear and controlled, as she would have expected. He would tolerate no excuse. Maria would phone either one of them at the earliest possible moment or suffer dire consequences. The limo would be dispatched immediately to meet her. Madeleine needed to know she was safe and sound, out of harm's way, and he would have no peace with her until she had such assurances. Did she understand him, Jean-Émile asked sternly? He would accept no excuse for not seeing her without delay.

# 219

The Wilmington home went to the morning couple for four-point-three million and the broker wanted to celebrate, but Christine didn't. She was beyond making excuses. She needed time alone, not expecting that when she drove her Cayman into the driveway she would see Detective Tremblay sitting on the front steps writing a note on the back of a business card. Seeing the lack of expression on his face Christine crossed her arms against the steering wheel, let her head fall forward, and cried real tears. When she straightened into the contoured seat he was standing by her door, and as she climbed out she noticed how he turned his head once noticing the length of her dress. Nothing was said until they were inside.

"He's dead."

"Yes, Madame Wilmington."

"Where is he?"

"He's currently in New York. They found him this morning. He'd been dead for thirty hours, more or less."

"How?"

"Honestly, it wasn't very pleasant. The truth is," he paused, "you have no real need to know."

"I'll see him when he comes back. I'll have to identify him."

"No, madame. The formality will be waived out of consideration for you."

"My God, what happened?"

"He was killed, madame," he sighed deeply, "very thoroughly."

"Please sit, Detective. Would you like something to drink?"

"No, madame, merci. Your husband's death is, of course, of interest to the NYPD, but they agreed to transfer the file to us once they heard of the Pendleton murder. They also found a note indicating that Pendleton senior has no cause to worry for his well-being. They have no interest in him. He is aware of the note."

"When will he be sent back?"

"Tomorrow morning. The crime scene investigation was very brief. Once again, they left nothing behind. These people wanted him dead and were very competent. Whatever your husband and Pendleton did to them was unforgivable in the extreme."

"After Shane's death he knew the beating in October wasn't a random attack. You were right, Detective."

She hesitated, not needing to explain.

"He was found alone, madame. He was seen taking an apéro with a female guest earlier in the evening, nothing more."

"What's next? What happens now, Detective?"

"Nothing on our part, madame. We have no evidence, no link, nothing, including witnesses. The ones who did this were very good. The case, I regret to tell you, will remain closed. The funeral home you select will process the paperwork for you. Is there anyone you would like me to call?"

"No, thank you. Shane was his best friend. Anyone else can be contacted by the office."

"Will you be alright? I can stay a while to talk if you wish. No police stuff, just talk."

He was a nice man. "Detective Tremblay, thank you. I'll be fine. I'm so happy you came to see me instead of your partner. Your bedside manner is much better, but what I need most is a few hours of sleep."

"It's my experience that a little brandy won't hurt. However too much won't help at all. My sympathies, madame."

"Thank you, monsieur, for coming in person and not

phoning."

He bowed, definitely old school, she thought, closing the door behind him.

# 220

Maria promised Jean-Émile she was fine, but she needed time alone or she wouldn't be fine. Nothing was wrong, she insisted. She was the same Maria they had always known and she loved them dearly, but they had to believe she knew what was best for her. She wouldn't do anything stupid, and besides, what was all the fuss about because she hadn't called them in a few days?

He told her not to be cheeky, that such behaviour was not becoming of her. In fact, she was being rather rude and disrespectful and he passed the phone to Madeleine who spoke with her for as long as she needed to get a commitment for dinner at home with Pilar and Ercilia for the following Saturday. And, no, the old fool wasn't angry with her. He was simply being himself.

# 221

"Selena, hola, soy Cristina. I'm sorry if I sounded curt with you this morning. Curt means rude and I would never be rude with you. I was tired, the same way you are because of me, and I promise this won't last much longer." She took a deep breath. "My husband was killed yesterday in New York and I'm afraid I'll be busy for a while, which doesn't mean I'm not thinking about you and that you shouldn't call me if you have a problem. The police came by this afternoon to tell me. They were expecting something serious to happen." She gulped. "I see by your agenda that you're leaving early tomorrow for a week. Don't do that anymore. Don't you know weekends are the best time for girlfriends? Don't let anything happen to you, or I'll be very angry and, by the way, change your message to the plural. No one should know a pretty girl is living alone. It's too dangerous."

When she closed her phone the dial pad was as wet as her hand and she thought she'd lose her mind. She fell on the sofa with her cognac still in her hand, startled by the doorbell and Selena's insistent voice. She was staying the night, whether her boss wanted her company or not, and she would leave for the airport in the morning, if she wanted to. If not, Cristina would pay the penalty for a changed flight, or she would, and Christine had no idea how much time passed before Selena let her go.

Christine had a hot bath, two small snifters of warm cognac and Selena put her to bed, waiting until she was asleep before changing into one of Cristina's silk slips and sliding in beside her to spend the night combing her fingers through Cristina's hair, humming Spanish lullabies. The next morning when Christine awoke to hear the shower running, Bret was alive, and she was suddenly terrified until she saw her silk slip at the foot of the bed, trying to think as she threw the covers from the bed and hurried to the bathroom, quickly remembering Selena had come over, the same Selena showering and facing into the clear stall so few steps away.

Christine was mesmerized watching the girl's arms moving rhythmically and sensually around her body, thick black hair clinging to her back, a steady stream of steaming water flowing over her contours, trickling away from her elbows and apex of her legs. Christine stood spellbound, half wanting to run, half wanting to strip away her clothes. Then silence jarred her into real time and she ran to her bed. Several minutes later Selena came in wearing panties, a bra and holding two coffees.

"Thank you. You're precious."

"You are in bad troubles with me. I came only to use your make-up table."

"Vanity."

"Sí, sí. Lo sé. I know also rain cheque, which is a very stupid word."

"You're cheeky this morning."

"It is not good to speak English to me when I want to be mad with you."

"Angry."

"Mad."

"Can you imagine guys doing this: one wearing in a slip, the other in a spectacular bra and thong…or something like that?"

Selena ignored her while she blow-dried her hair, pretending not to hear. Then she turned. "Yuck, dos hombres. This is yuck, no?"

"Very yuck, girl. Thank you."

"I slept beside you, under the drapas." She chortled. "I am the company slut, no, sleeping with the boss."

"I know, I felt you, and I heard you singing to me before

I fell asleep. Where did you learn that word, slut? That's horrible. "

"I am sorry, Cristina, for your husband. That is why I am mad and angry with you. Friends must be with friends when the time is bad."

Christine went into Spanish. "He was a very bad man, Selena. I was expecting this to happen, as were the police. I'm fine." She sipped her coffee. "Great coffee. You're going out of town for a week and I hope you understood my message. This is the last trip on the weekend and we will talk when you come back. I have something important to tell you, something I'm not ready to discuss right now, but I'll be busy on Saturday night. So deal with it, chica. We'll have Sunday together, and Monday if we don't buy enough on Sunday."

"I do not want to leave you this way."

"And my coffee is finished. It's okay to sleep with the boss, but not to get her another coffee."

Selena went to the bed for Cristina's mug. She was hard not to stare at and Christine half hoped she'd be dressed when she came back, half hoping she wouldn't be.

"How do you keep your ass so great, bitch?" she yelled after her friend.

"I am Latina, cariño. My ass takes care of itself…bitch."

Christine hesitated. "Did you just call me darling?"

## 222

Bret Wilmington's funeral was on Thursday, April 10th. Christine called Broderick to speak with him for a few moments, to excuse him from attending. He was relieved to hear they were both safe from harm, he told her, though not surprised everyone had distanced themselves from another W & P-related funeral. She told him again that Bret and Shane had done something shameful and were called upon to atone for their actions, which had nothing to do with what she thought of him. He was a good man, he had suffered enough and Bret's funeral was a mere formality before his cremation. She saw no need for both of them to attend.

By Friday the Wilmington home was cleared of its belongings to the next in an endless line, one item per person, and any memory of Suzanne went with the last stick of furniture. Tremblay was aware of the take-all-for-nothing-sale and fairly certain when Christine would pull into her driveway.

"Did you do well on the sale, madame?"

She forced a sincerely weary smile. "I broke even. Do you have more news about my husband's death?"

"I have very interesting information about Wilmington and a few other people, madame. May we speak inside?"

"Yes, Detective, by all means."

This time he accepted the cognac she offered him. She poured one for herself, took a single sip and placed the snifter by her side, watching Tremblay contentedly inhale the aroma of his. "I'm retiring, madame. Next week is my last week on the job after thirty years."

"You've earned it, Detective. I wouldn't want your job for a day and I'm sure you didn't fight bridge traffic at this time of day to tell me that."

"May I call you Christine?"

"Yes, it's my name. Of course you may."

"Christine you're a beautiful girl. A young woman, I know, but a girl to me and a very pretty one." He took a long sip of cognac, grinning and waving a hand. "Please don't get the wrong idea. I'm much too old to even think of such miracles. I'm fifty-eight and I feel dead, Christine. I feel dead because twelve years ago my twenty-four-year-old daughter was raped and murdered, right here on the South Shore." He interrupted himself for another sip. "She was going home from her courses, not too far from here. She was the same age as another girl, Addison Larivière, who was on vacation with her friend, Maria Bardollini, when she was raped and killed in Mexico two years ago this very month. I never found the ones who killed my daughter, and I'm a cop. Imagine. There were at least two of them." He paused, staring into his glass. "Christine, after Pendleton was killed, and Wilmington's parents, and after we interviewed Wilmington, we knew he had very little time. Those men did something very bad, which was raping and killing Addison Larivière." His hand came up again. "Please, let me talk, though I would appreciate perhaps a little more of this fine cognac, if I may." When Christine returned, he continued. "I was unfortunate enough to see the photographs of Mademoiselle Larivière, a hardship I trust her father was spared. She was a very beautiful young lady, until she crossed paths with Wilmington, Pendleton and the two other guys on vacation with them: Chad Rivers and Thurston Williams, both dead. The four killing had several similarities, something normally done to make a point when the killers are good at what they do. Otherwise, such showmanship is very risky business." He ignored her attempt to ask a question. "There were tequila bottles, excessive traces of the same drug in their blood, except for Wilmington, and excessive quantities of a laxative ingested by three of the four. Rivers got to take his differently, hand delivered, if I may say so. The perpetrators were also very inventive: a shower, a snow storm of sorts and rather a bad shave. Of course, I won't describe what happened to Wilmington. These were calculated crimes of passion of the highest order, somewhat of a paradox rarely seen in police work." He took another long sip. "Mademoiselle Larivière came from a privileged family and Maria Bardollini, as you may know, is the daughter of Angelo Bardollini, the Montreal crime boss." He seemed pleased. "Can you imagine what kind of team they would be, Christine: big money, big crime, two angry parents? However, we do know Monsieur Larivière is as pure as snow." He swirled the snifter in his palms. "When we matched the four MOs by computer, and the names of the so-called victims, the rest was easy given Wilmington's beating and where he was that night: a girl's body shipped home from Mexico after she'd been raped, four men killed two years later with absolutely no evidence to follow up on, no witnesses, no one to point the finger at or arrest. Four men who were are known to have vacationed at the same place at the same time. And you know what, Christine?"

She shook her head. "No sir. What?"

"I'm happy. I have one week left and I'm happy I don't have to arrest anyone. The fact is I'm spending next week at a desk so I don't get killed next Friday at 4:59." She nodded, not knowing what to say. "There is one thing, however, another dead-end. The woman Wilmington had that drink with was Phallicia Hunter. She checked into the hotel the day before Wilmington arrived, and checked out the day of his murder. We also know she was in Myrtle Beach, Toronto and Vancouver at the same time as those murders. Whoever she is, she was in and out without a trace. Funny thing is, she doesn't exist. There is no Phallicia Hunter."

"How is that possible, Detective?"

"I suppose anything is possible when we want something badly enough, Christine, or know the right people. You can rest assured Wilmington's killers will never be found. They knew what they were doing and somehow managed to act in five different jurisdictions. Believe me when I say I grieve deeply for your loss and for what you have lived through as such a young woman. I know what it's like to lose the most important person in your life and I hope you can get on with yours. Remember what was happy in your past and enjoy the future." He took her hand in his without warning. "Of course, Maria Bardollini has never been a suspect, and never will be. She was in Montreal the whole time and we have absolutely no evidence to implicate her. Her father could be a suspect, I suppose, family honour even though we believe he's dead. So where does that get us?" He stood, making ready to leave. "We won't see each other again, Christine. I hope, when you get all this behind you, you will do well. I know you will. But don't rush. Don't be in a hurry. Enjoy what you have. Take some time for you, perhaps at a relaxing new spa. You deserve a rest if anyone does. I still miss my little girl every day after all this time. So I do know that Addisons will always be missed by those who loved her, how you will miss the one you once loved so much and lost. Good night… Christine."

He bowed slightly from the hip and walked out.

# 223

Saturday's dinner was the usual success, the conversation revolving around the spa's completion and how anxious everyone was for the grand opening, which was fine until they retired to the parlour and the conversation deteriorated to female chatter and Jean-Émile thought to seek refuge in his study.

"I shall bid you good evening, ladies. I suppose you might disturb me before you leave, if I'm not already asleep. And I would like you all at the farm next weekend. With your upcoming schedules I doubt we shall have very many more opportunities before the wedding and the ground-breaking for the Foundation, not that I find the thought of enjoying the pastoral quiet alone disagreeable."

"Dad, I can't. I'm sorry. I'll be busy."

His frown was real. "Then another time, child. The ambiance would not be the same without a complete set of nuisances. Ladies."

The three women looked at her quizzically. She had said clearly during dinner that she could finally begin to relax. Now she had nothing to say. However, Pilar did. She enjoyed being at the farm and wasn't pleased. "¿Chica, qué te pasa? You love going into the country."

"I can't this time. I'll be busy. I'm sorry."

"Child, what's the matter?" Madeleine asked "Are things not beginning to improve for you?"

"Yes, it's beginning."

"I understand that is so." Madeleine patted Maria's knee. "I'm not completely in the dark about certain issues. Suffice it to say I know what I know. Go to him. It's time for closure. Go."

Madeleine began serving coffee to Pilar and Ercilia without explaining. Maria got up and walked quickly to catch up with Jean-Émile as he was closing the door to his study, more than an hour elapsing before they came out. Maria's head was nestled under one of his arms, her face reddened and streaked with coloured tears. The three women in the parlour glared at him first as Madeleine hurried to take her away from him and sit on the couch beside her, wrapping her arms around Maria's shoulders as Pilar and Ercilia moved in.

"What have you done now, you old fool?"

Jean-Émile ignored the jibe. "Maria and I enjoyed a very interesting talk, much of which is privileged. However, Madeleine my dear, we are about to be burdened with yet another incorrigible daughter who shall likely be as troublesome as these three. I have no doubt whatsoever and, once again, if you ladies will excuse me, I shall retire to my private study for a pleasant digestive, the key word being private, to let the four of you wag your tongues about it all." He waited a moment before leaving, knowing full-well they wanted him gone. "Madeleine, please make the appropriate arrangements to meet this young lady as soon as possible. Perhaps now we can all go to the farm, if that is alright with the little devil beside you, and not too late for the young lady to consider joining us for the weekend." He turned and walked away. "Oh, God, to live in a world without women."

"You mean a world of old fools, I take it."

# 224

Christine decided she would never return to the house. She felt not the slightest attachment to it, or to the furnishings, which she had signed off to the buyers as part of the sale. She called Selena an hour earlier to ask if she could come over. She had so much to tell her, but she was so flustered Selena could barely make sense of what little she did say. She would be right over, soon, whenever, don't go anywhere, she said, and Selena soon became as flustered as Christine.

The car pulled up in front of the building at 11:00 PM and Selena felt a sense of relief that the doorman was with her in the lobby. When the man climbed from the limo and walked to the rear to open the door, he stood peering in, straight at her, smiling. She didn't like the feeling and couldn't see who climbed out because the doorman blocked her view as he went to welcome whoever was coming in. Then Cristina came running through doors towards her and Selena's eyes opened wider than Christine had ever seen them.

Christine was in no condition to drive. Her eyes were red with tears, her face was a mess of colours, her hair hung in loose thick curls and she had forgotten to wear her glasses. The two collided in a tangle of arms and Selena had no time to think or talk before Christine told her not to say a word until they were in the apartment. Selena was in shock, again. Since knowing Cristina her life had become a continuum of surprises, something that would never end, and she was in for the biggest. The elevator ride seemed to take forever for Christine, and for Selena not long enough to figure out what was wrong with her friend. When the apartment door closed behind them Christine dropped her purse and pulled Selena quietly into the living room where she stopped, her breathing slowly stabilizing.

"I can't go shopping with you tomorrow, Selena."

"That's alright. We will have more weekends."

"I didn't say I wouldn't be with you. I said we weren't going shopping. I don't think so."

"You are crazy tonight, chica." Selena smelled her breath. "Cognac, no?"

"Just a little. Two. You said once that you loved me. You told me that you think about me while you're sitting by yourself, that you think about Christmas."

"Yes, Cristina, I do."

"I love you, Selena."

"I love you also, girlfriend."

"That's not what I mean. I mean I love you."

Selena moved in to smell Cristina's breathe once again.

# 225

The next day the Porsche Cayman was parked in the visitor's parking, as Jean-Émile promised, though wouldn't be needed for the rest of the weekend. When the two girls woke their faces were living replicas of Mardi Gras street art and Selena spoke first, feeling shy, but not as shy as she was happy. They hadn't spent much time talking throughout the evening and into the night.

"Now I must have a little name for you."

"I thought you decided on cariño?" She kissed her darling. "You look funny."

"You are funnier."

"We have a lot to talk about and some of what I have to say might hurt. We're not shopping today because I want you to meet someone I've kept from you, and maybe you'll understand why I haven't been able to tell you how much I love you, but until then no questions and I'm going to cry like a baby. I'm scared because I don't know how to start. But I do know I love you," she placed a warm hand on Selena's bare hip, "and can I borrow some clothes?"

"Where are we going?"

"Not very far, and that's a question."

"Can I kiss you again?"

She turned over quickly, burying her face in her pillow to avoid Cristina's, a muffled scream coming after each smack. They would have three hours together before the phone would ring.

# 226

Selena walked past the limo towards the Cayman, slowing to a curious stop as Christine went to the driver, hugged him and disappeared inside. Then he was smiling at her, calling her by name and saying hello as he walked past her and stood waiting by the other side. Selena had never been chauffeured and felt strange as Jeff opened the door for her, staring silently at him as she came closer, walking around him and stepping in. When Jeff was seated behind the wheel he asked if they were comfortable and raised the smoked privacy screen, smiling into the rear-view mirror.

"He's laughing at me."

"No, he's not. He's smiling at your open mouth. I had the same reaction the first time. You'll get used to it." Selena saw the Cayman from her side window. "I'm returning it this week."

"Why, Cristina? We looked so good in it together."

"I know. So we'll buy you a new one next week. It's time you stopped taking taxis. You're going to bankrupt us."

"¡Ay, no!"

"¡Ay, yes! And I think you'd be sexy in a red one, I hope."

"You hope?"

She took Selena's hands. "Selena we'll be driving for an hour and I have lots to tell you, so I'm going to begin now."

"Yes, Cristina." She nestled into the plush seat, tucking one folded leg under the other. "I want to hear everything."

"My choices were to tell you everything, or tell you nothing. Not to tell you would have meant losing you. You will understand why when I'm finished." She felt the reassuring pressure of Selena's squeeze.

"I love you, cariño. Do not stop."

"A few days ago I sold the company. The new owners signed an agreement to purchase our goodwill and property. They wanted you as part of the deal, but I refused, and let me tell you why." She took a deep breath. "My real name is Maria Cristina Bardollini. My father is Angelo Bardollini, the man you have read about in the papers."

"Ay, Cristina." Selena broke free to wrap her arms around Maria. "Your papa is dead. I am so sorry for you." She eased back. "But why did you not tell me?"

"Let me finish. I don't think an hour will be long enough, but I'll try. The car we're riding in belongs to Jean-Émile Larivière. You'll love him. He pretends to be cranky, but he loves us. He's my second dad, and he's wonderful. He speaks fluent Spanish, so be careful. He'll pretend he doesn't understand a word. He was the father of Addison Larivière who was raped and murdered two years ago in Mexico by four men, when we should have been celebrating the rest of our lives together, a few days after we met Pilar and Ercilia who are waiting for us at the farm. So are Jean-Émile and Madeleine, but we won't see them right away. If you still want to go with me after I've finished. We were supposed to go next week, only they couldn't wait to meet you." Selena wiped Maria's eyes lightly with the palm of her hand and kissed her. "The first day I saw you Selena, when I was getting married, and I was crying, and I told you I was making a mistake," she sniffled, reaching for a tissue and not seeing Selena nod, "I was marrying one of the men who killed Addison, and the other three were with him at the wedding."

Selena stroke Maria's hair and wiped her eyes again, scarcely believing what she was hearing, and when Maria reached for the sealed photo album which Jeff had earlier placed on the rear seat her heart raced and her eyes opened wide. "Dios mio, Cristina."

"This is what they did to her, Selena." She thumbed

through the pages. "They put lots of drugs in her drink, they each raped her twice, and they poured tequila down her throat which probably choked her. Or she might have died when one of them forced his hand over her mouth so she couldn't scream. And they left her outside in the dark and the rain without any clothes while I was safe in my room asleep. That's why I cry every night, because I wasn't with her to help her. If I had stayed with her she never would have died." She inhaled deeply. "So I killed them, Selena, each one, and I'm not sorry. It's taken me a long time and I had lots of help from people you will never know about, though I swear I had nothing to do with his parents." She closed the album. "It's not too late for Jeff to take you home."

"Cristina, no. What do I care about four dead animals? Would I care if some crazy dog was shot by the person it did bite? No, and I do not care about them. I care about you." She looked at the privacy screen. "Who knows of this?"

"Jeff can't hear a word. Jean-Émile knows they're dead, though very little else, and no one knows I married one of them. None of them know Christine Benton who soon will not exist. She was created as a device to help me."

"The police?"

"They officially closed the case. They suspect someone called Phallicia Hunter was somehow involved, but they can't find her because, like Christine, she doesn't exist."

"You know this?"

"Yes, I do, because I was also Phallicia Hunter and all they know about Christine Benton is that she was married to a man who deserted her to run for his life. Christine won't exist either after next week."

Selena straightened her legs, remembering the past six months and stunned by the magnitude of what she was hearing. "Cristina, do you have your special key for my bracelet?"

"Yes, I do."

"Unlock my bracelet. I cannot wear it any longer." Maria did, slowly, not blaming Selena for what she must be thinking. "You must wear it, cariño, like you did the first day." She clamped bracelet onto Cristina's wrist. "This way Cristina will not disappear also." She held out her hand for the necklace and draped the key around her neck.

"Selena, nothing ever happened with him. The night of the wedding he was so drunk he fell asleep and he kept drinking during the honeymoon. The next week, when I was gone on business, he went to a club owned by my father and had an accident on the way home that no one can explain." She tried to smile. "My father was taking care of me. Then after the third man was killed, he began drinking more and one night I came close to breaking his knees a second time."

"Why?"

"He said something about you I didn't like."

"Jeff cannot hear this? You are sure?"

"No, and he doesn't speak Spanish."

"He can see us?"

"No."

"Then hold me very hard and let me squeeze you so tight." She put up her hand, holding a tissue. "But first I will squeeze your little nose and when we are finished holding each other you will have some water and tell me more, if you want." Selena kissed her. "Perhaps, cariño, you are not my only angel. Perhaps I have another, and her name is Addison, no?"

# 227

"I didn't want them dead, Selena. I wanted them completely destroyed and humiliated."

"I would die before telling anyone of this, Cristina."

"That was pretty much the bad news. The good news is your job description hasn't changed, maybe just a bit more fun. The name of the company we work for is Addisons and by the end of the year the Addison Foundation will open and the twenty-two million will be deposited into the Foundation's account."

"That is good, Cristina. But tell me about my real girlfriend. We will have more time for this story. I want to hear about Maria Cristina Bardollini, my Cristina, and I want to hear everything about Addison."

"I'm twenty-four, not twenty-eight. I have red hair, not cherry blonde and I don't wear glasses. My eyes are brown, not hazel, and I always wear my hair like you. I love silk and hate cotton. I hate cell phones and cell phone noises. I speak fluent Italian, I drive a yellow MX-5 which I am very hot in, and I own a condo on Nun's Island where Pi and Ercilia have stayed for almost a year. They're moving in a few weeks, not far away though, and you're going to love them very much. And they'll love you. I want you to move into my home, or we can find somewhere else to live, so you'll have to sell your condo because I rented it for Christine, not me. Sorry about that."

"Más despacio, chica." Selena giggled. "Slow down, and can you go back to the yellow MX?" Then she jumped.

"Maria, we're here. Please wait for me." Jeff chuckled. "My review is coming up. If you can't see them all staring from the windows, I can."

She patted Selena's knee. "Be nice to Jeff, Selena. He's really super. He fusses around me like a big brother."

The walk over to the grave was quiet and both women sat quietly for several minutes on the swing set Jean-Émile had installed to make Addison's visitors more comfortable, visitors like him who could spend long weekend hours reading and remembering.

"I do like Addison very much, Cristina."

"She would have liked you, also. She liked everybody." Maria giggled. "I think I might have been very jealous."

"I will never be jealous of Addison. I know you will love her forever. You must, and the more I know her the more I will love her." She had her hand resting over Maria's and felt the drop. "But, cariño, Addison wants your nights of crying to end. She does not blame you, no one does. I believe she is here with us now, and she is happy for both of us, and so proud of you. We will come here often to sit with her."

"Thank you. I will always love her, and I will always love you." Maria brought their hands to her cheek for a moment, taking a deep breath. "And now I'm going to introduce you to the crankiest man you'll ever meet. Come on. Your friends and family are waiting to meet you and don't let go of me."

"Is that him, the tall one?"

"Yes."

"¡Ay! Then do not let go of me."

## 228

He wasn't cranky at all. Madeleine had threatened to let the girls have free reign with him if he even thought of scaring Selena with his foolishness.

That evening, when conversation dwindled once again into chatter, he retired to his study after telling Selena he was delighted to finally have a girl in the house that showed no tendency towards pouting, whining or any other feminine frailty, like others he might mention. He would see them all in the morning, and Madeleine wasn't to forget about their outing the following weekend, which he would not attend.

# 229

By the following weekend Christine Gabrielle Benton was a multimillionaire who did not exist. Friday, after the final transfer of funds to a numbered Swiss account, which would later be transferred to the Addison Foundation, she disappeared leaving nothing behind. Her car was returned with monies owing paid in full. Her entire wardrobe was donated to the mission along with her jewellery and all documentation relating to her was destroyed, including W&P client-file information. She was free. She was once again Maria Bardollini. She was in love and for the first time since Addison was taken from her she was young and happy, and hadn't cried in days.

Jean-Émile's outing the weekend after the farm was a surprise shopping day for the girls, for the elegant gowns he expected they would wear to the special dinner they were preparing in his honour at Addisons. He would never be allowed in the spa after the official opening, but Maria wanted him to have a private tour, as she had done for her father, and invited him to Addisons to celebrate the eve of the day they had all waited for and worked so hard towards.

Addisons was a marvel. Whatever he had imagined paled in comparison he exclaimed and would truly be a little bit of heaven on earth for the women fortunate enough to share in it. Each of the girls excitedly explained their offices and studios in detail, and when they got to the Friendly Room he thought he might like to see the outside garden and rooftop. When they were done he asked for a moment alone with Maria.

"Madeleine is a little nervous about her first day at the spa tomorrow. She has been, I might say, giddy all week. I believe she's gratefully anticipating the safe companionship of Señora Rayo." He lifted her chin. "How much have I learned from such a young person? You have a big heart, Meme. There are so many who love you."

"She was so important to me when it happened, dad. She helped me survive and we've spoken many times over the past two years. She's helped me so much. I couldn't exclude her."

"And now you have Selena. She's very special." He took Maria's arm. "Enough of this unseemly prattle, let us look out over the canal," and he took a sip of his champagne. "We are all very proud of you, Meme, very proud indeed. You are a delight to anyone who knows you, precious beyond words, and if you breathe a word this sentimental discourse to anyone I am authorized to invert your person and paddle your bum...your bottom." Maria clasped her hand over her mouth, scanning the street below. "No, child, he is not with us, not physically. Though I can tell you he has a rather precise timepiece, of which I am rather envious, and his thoughts are of you as we speak, with his own glass of superb champagne." He guided her by the arm. "Perhaps we should stand more under the light, Meme."

He opened his hand, holding out a silver package until he had to proffer the gift ever so slightly, stepping away discreetly as she peeled away the foil wrapping. The handwritten note read: Congratulations, Meme. You did it. Your mother would be proud of you, as proud as we all are, and I'm anxious for the day when I'll meet your new friend Selena. We will see each other soon. Until then, Meme, I'll be as close as your bracelet. Love to both of you.

She went to speak.

"No, child. Not a word. I am not to know. He was very specific. He brought the gift to me the last time we met. He told me to wait for the appropriate moment and we agreed this night and time would be fitting. That is all I am privy to, and I must say that his doing so was a tremendous leap of faith on his part. We shall respect his wishes. Open your gift."

He stood by quietly, a faint smile crossing his lips as she opened the slender box. The titanium bracelet glittered under the light, the inscription appearing like dark etching: Innocence is youth, Meme. Stay young forever. Papa.

Jean-Émile remained stoic, watching a tearful Maria shaking her head.

"I believe it might be alright if I hear what is written on the outside, Meme. Though I might suggest that usually the inner inscription is of a more private nature."

She tilted the bracelet into the light, furrowing her brow. The inner inscription was simple, and specific: 26°19'54"N; 76°51'46"W.

"He wants me to stay young, innocent. How can I ever be innocent again?"

"How can you not? It is who you are. Addison would not have loved you otherwise, and Selena would not love you now." He held out his arm. "I believe they are both waiting for us, mademoiselle."

"They're in the lobby. Just don't start crying. We have to be strong for each other. I haven't seen her yet, either. Come on."

When they arrived in the lobby the young attendant replaced their fluted champagne glasses as two more of Maria's staff stood on either side of silk-covered life-size statue. Jean-Émile was front and centre with Madeline, Pilar and Ercilia on one side, Maria holding his hand and Selena's on the other. Only Selena spoke as the drape fell on cue as the other's gazed upward, awestruck.

"Cristina, como es bella tu Addison."

They squeezed their hands together. The artist had captured Addison's complete essence in the figurine, the same Addison living in each one of them in different ways. She would never come to life, Maria knew, but as long as Addison lived inside her they would be together.

Selena's arm came around Maria's waist as Jean-Émile put his around her shoulder and Madeleine pulled Pilar and Ercilia in close to her. She had family that loved her and they would come to love Selena whom she knew her father would meet one day soon, though for the time being she was content knowing he was safe and alive and thinking of her at that very moment. They raised their glasses in a salute and remained silent, each one in their private world until Jean-Émile broke the silence to make them aware his glass was quite dry, much to Madeleine's disapproval. When they were all refilled he stepped away and faced them.

"Ladies, if I may disrupt your thoughts, I have a few words that must be spoken. Firstly, I cannot remember when I was last in the company of such attractive and exquisitely dressed young women. You are visions to behold and I shall always remember you this way rather than the mischievous little devils I know you to be. Secondly, I reserve the honour as her father to toast my daughter Addison, and Addisons, which is all my daughters including my newest one, Selena, whom I dearly hope will not be excessively swayed by your conspiratorial ways. A toast, ladies, to Addison, to Addisons, yourselves, and Selena." Jean-Emile stepped to the side, took a sip he was thankful for, and continued. "Maria, whom we now also know as Cristina, could not have done this without all of you. I am proud of her. I am proud of you Pilar, and you Ercilia, and of Selena, for not abandoning her. However, we are missing one very special person who cannot be with us this evening to join in our celebration." He paused, raising his glass in a salute to Meme whose eyes were bright and glistening.
"To Angelo Bardollini."

# The 4<sup>th</sup> Man

# 230

I am Selena Consuelo de la Vega, and you already know me. I am sitting here watching them at the meadow, waiting for me, and playing like children. The day is so beautiful here in the country. Birds are singing, the sun is bright and the sky is so clear and blue.

Jean-Émile and Madeleine were always so kind to me, and to Pilar and Ercilia whom I came to love as sisters, but now they are gone and I see them only in my memories and in my dreams. What you may not remember is that, when I first saw Cristina in the ladies room of the hotel that very cold day in October so many years ago, she was so beautiful and elegant. I remember her dress and the way I placed her garter over her knee. I can still feel the weight of her foot upon my thigh, or at least I imagine that I do, and I remember the look we exchanged when we should have giggled the way young women do, but we did not.

I had not forgotten her when she left me to once again be the most stunning bride I had ever seen, and I cried for so many long hours that night thinking how happy she must have been, and how happy I was not. I thought I would never see her again, and that was why I cried, but she had been so kind to say we would and I thought she was so very nice. She was the kind of person everyone loved to be with, to hug and to kiss, and when Christine Gabrielle Benton ceased to be one beautiful and brilliant spring day long months after her wedding, Maria Cristina Bardollini began to live once again, though her healing took a very long time.

So do not judge her for what she did. Rather, judge the purity of the evil that caused her to do it, and the determination, courage and strength she summoned to see it through. If you cannot, then you must judge us all equally, for eventually we came to know the truth and we loved her all the more for what she had done.

Cristina died peacefully this morning, here at The Foundation. She's with Addie whom she spoke with throughout the night and whom she never forgot for a moment or a breath. She was eighty-two. Pi and Ercilia left us three years ago, within days of one another. For Cristina the loss was as though Addison had died all over again, and was no less painful for me. So now I am alone and long for that fleeting moment in time which I pray will come soon, a quiet journey which will bring us together as one. I know they are with me in all that I do. I see them in my dreams, and tonight I will see my angel with them, my cariño. I miss them terribly.

I have just spoken with a nice young man who will engrave my final gift to my best and life-long friend, a woman who was always so beautiful to me, and whose special love I have always shared with another whom I long to finally meet.

Maria Cristina Bardollini
**Where She Has To Be**
**Beside Her Addie**

# The 4<sup>th</sup> Man

## Other Mystery – Suspense - Thriller Novels

## By Doug Booth:

Split Verdict

The 4<sup>th</sup> Man

The Madam

Family Lies

Mother of Pearl

From Inside Her Bedroom

The Feast of Tombola

Deferred Prejudice

The Hunt for Gilligan Rose

The Fatal Diners' Club

Silent Conviction

A Christmas Killer, Comfort and Joy

Pariah In the Mirror

***

No One to Tell (Creative Non-fiction)

www.ingramcontent.com/pod-product-compliance
Lightning Source LLC
Chambersburg PA
CBHW030535020726
47494CB00005B/1382